# YOU, HUMAN

## EDITED BY MICHAEL BAILEY

# YOU, HUMAN

### EDITED BY MICHAEL BAILEY

Anthology edited by Michael Bailey
Cover artwork by George C. Cotronis
Cover and interior design by Michael Bailey
Illustrations (fiction) © 2016 by L.A. Spooner
Illustrations (poetry) © 2016 by Orion Zangara
Introduction © 2016 by F. Paul Wilson
Individual works © 2016 by individual authors, unless stated below.

Written Backwards
www.nettirw.com

Second Trade Paperback Edition
ISBN: 978-0-99957-545-1

# FICTION

## ILLUSTRATED BY L.A. SPOONER

# FICTION

## ILLUSTRATED BY L.A. SPOONER

# POETRY

## BY MARGE SIMON
## ILLUSTRATED BY ORION ZANGARA

# INTRODUCTION

## F. PAUL WILSON

Define *humanness*.

Notice I didn't say *human*, because then you can get away with saying *Homo sapiens* and leaving it at that.

*Humanness* is the quality of being human, and pinning that down is a lot tougher. Because humanness isn't limited to a given set of 46 chromosomes. Some people have 47 chromosomes, some have only 45, but we still consider them *Homo sapiens*, still consider them human, because they have humanness. But what of a comatose patient in a persistent vegetative state? Human, sure, but where is the humanness?

Or look at chimpanzees. We share 98+% of our DNA with them. What if we spliced in some genes we've associated with human creativity and gave them a hyoid bone so they could speak? They still wouldn't be human, but they might be able to acquire humanness.

I think we can all agree that consciousness, self-awareness, and sentience—the capacity for subjective feelings and perceptions—are indispensable to humanness. The comingling and interaction of all three lead to sapience—the capacity to act with reason and judgment. Apes and dolphins are considered sentient, but not sapient. Sapience builds civilizations.

Of course, to act without any semblance of reason and judgment is perfectly human as well. Because, just as having access to data does not make one intelligent, simply having the capacity for wisdom does not make one wise. Consider our approach to death. Humans fear it and go to remarkable extremes to delay it, yet the vast majority of humans deny the finality of death, believing—entirely on hearsay, without a shred of hard evidence—that some part of them will go on for eternity. What is this pervasive belief in our transcendence? Hubris? Wishful thinking? Or, as the believers say, a natural response to the spark of the divine within us all? Whatever the truth, only humans possess it.

Humanness should not be confused with *humaneness*. Humaneness is a quality that involves tenderness, compassion, and sympathy. These are often considered "human" qualities and those people who don't possess then are called "inhuman." Which is hardly fair considering how the capacity for wreaking havoc on one's fellows is very much a human trait. "Man's inhumanity to man" ignores how, throughout history, humans have focused their unique tool-making skills on fashioning the most ingenious devices for damaging other humans. Few traits are more human than cruelty.

Or slavery. Homo sapiens is the only species on Earth that enslaves its own kind.

Or hatred. Animals can have fearful avoidance reactions related to instinct or past experience, but only humans seem capable of hate. Or revenge.

This is where the mind-brain dichotomy becomes important. The brain can exist without the mind (e.g., the persistent vegetative coma mentioned above) but the mind is totally dependent of a functioning brain. Humanness resides in the mind. The brain is ruled by two drives: self-preservation and survival of the genome. The mind can't help being influenced by those drives, but it can sublimate them to more refined—one might even say, "higher"—purposes.

The brain has no empathy, no respect for others, no sense of mine and not-mine. A male brain sees a healthy female of child-bearing age and nudges the body to grab her and impregnate her with its seed. Without a mind, that is exactly what the body would attempt to do. But with a functioning mind on board, filtering the body's impulses, most of the time that's not what happens. The mind is capable of empathy, but empathy is not a default state. If the mind's empathy isn't developed enough to consider how the woman might feel about such treatment, maybe it is at least cognizant of the penalty for rape. But if the mind possesses only rudimentary impulse control, then a sexual assault follows. (I'm simplifying, of course, since it's well established that the procreative drive is only one motive for rape.)

The health of the brain, the functionality of its neural network, the levels of its various neurotransmitters, all have effects on the mind, and thus on one's humanness. You are your chemicals. But that's a can of worms better left sealed.

Better to move on to the dilemma of humanness and artificial intelligence. AI is all around us—our laptops, our tablets, the ubiquitous smartphone. They solve problems, communicate and interact with each other in countless ways at the speed of light. In recent experiments, linked computers have been observed to deceive each other, while supercomputers have, under certain conditions, been known to lie to their human operators. But they have yet to show self-awareness, consciousness, sentience.

Notice I said "yet." No one who works in the field these days and mentions the singularity—the emergence of cybernetic consciousness and self-awareness—talks of "if." They talk of "when." Vernor Vinge predicts it will happen by 2030.

So the question is: When the singularity occurs, will the mind that results demonstrate humanness? Why not? Humans designed and built and programmed it, did they not? But is being like us a good thing? We know it can be. We know of love, courage, heroism, risking one's own life to save another's.

But we also know how appalling and mind-numbingly awful we can be. So why can't this cyberintellect be taught to be humane? Would it even need to be taught?

The cliché is a coldly analytical, emotionless, self-serving intelligence ruled solely by logic. And on the surface that makes sense, since binary code doesn't leave room for empathy. But there's another kind of code, an ethical code, and it's not something we associate with troglodytes, but we do associate with humans, even close to the gutter humans like Dashiell Hammett's Sam Spade. Here's what he had to say in The Maltese Falcon:

# ...

> "When a man's partner is killed he's supposed to do something about it. It doesn't make any difference what you thought of him. He was your partner and you're supposed to do something about it."

That's a code, a combination of duty, self-respect, and a fundamental need to restore balance to a situation that's been knocked off kilter. If Sam Spade can come up with an ethical code, why can't a high-functioning, self-aware cyberintellect develop something similar?

We have no answers at the moment. And until we do, we can explore the question by telling each other stories about the things that define us as humans, that make us what we are and who we are. Fiction is perhaps the most effective way to illuminate the human condition.

For You, Human Michael Bailey has collected a richly varied assortment of fictions by seasoned fantasists as well newcomers whose tales will have you searching out more samples of their wares (as I've already done).

The stories range from the bizarre to the deceptively prosaic, from a sly wink to a jolting shock, from dark to uplifting, rhapsodic to hardboiled, hopeful to despairing. Not one of them could be described as mimetic. They're all weird in one way or another, containing elements that do not exist in the real world—at least not yet. And that's a good thing, because the weird is what makes them effective. Looking at ourselves through warped glass or reflected in a distorted mirror often reveals the truth behind the façade, the face behind the mask. You'll find the fictions that follow engaging and insightful as they challenge you to contemplate their skewed views on the human condition.

Which means they're all about you, human.

– F. Paul Wilson
The Jersey Shore

# IN ACCORDANCE WITH THE LAWS

## MARGE SIMON

Your eyes are too close together,
yet you're no imbecile—
nature played a trick on your face,
but your lovely body is fit and strong.

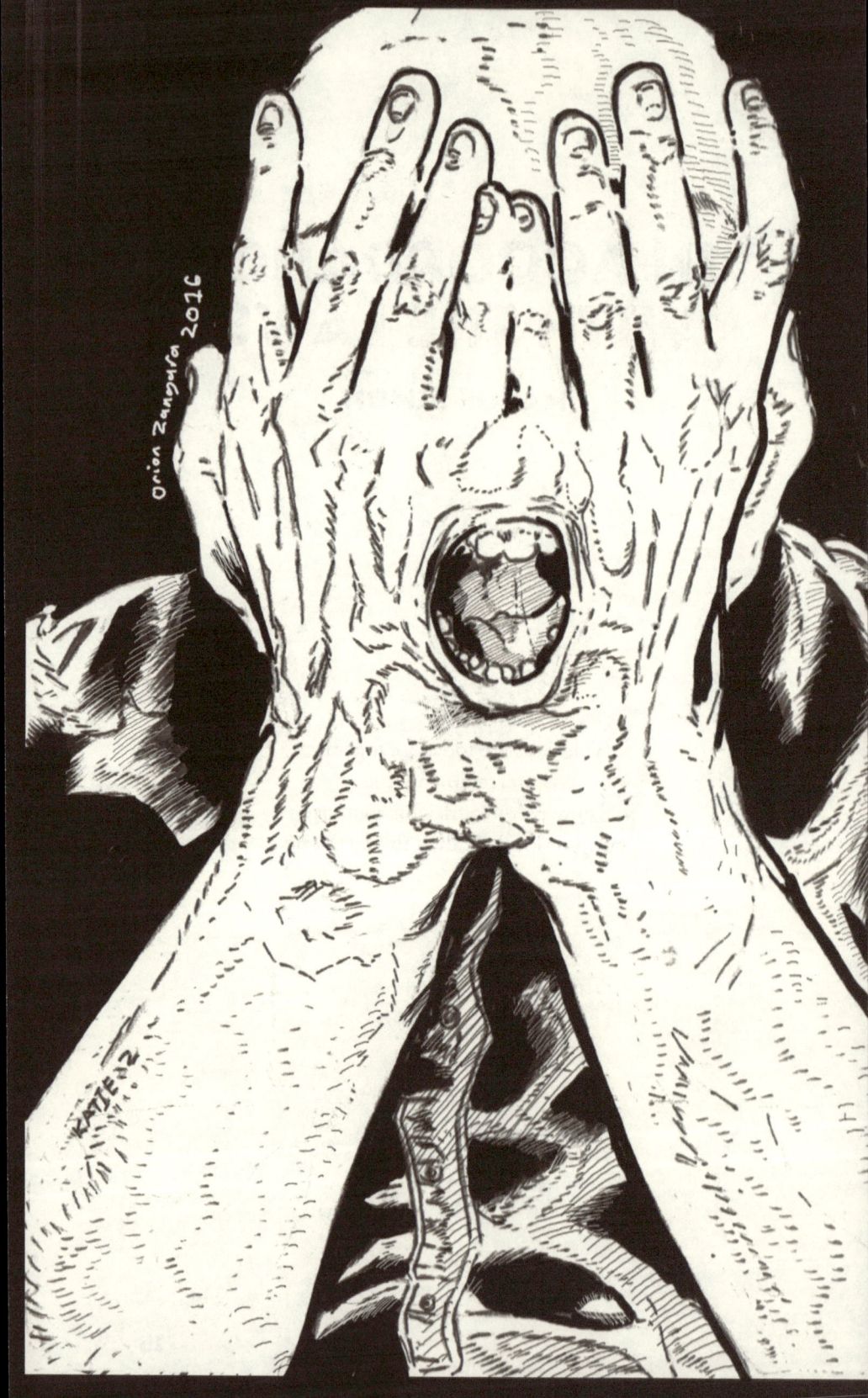

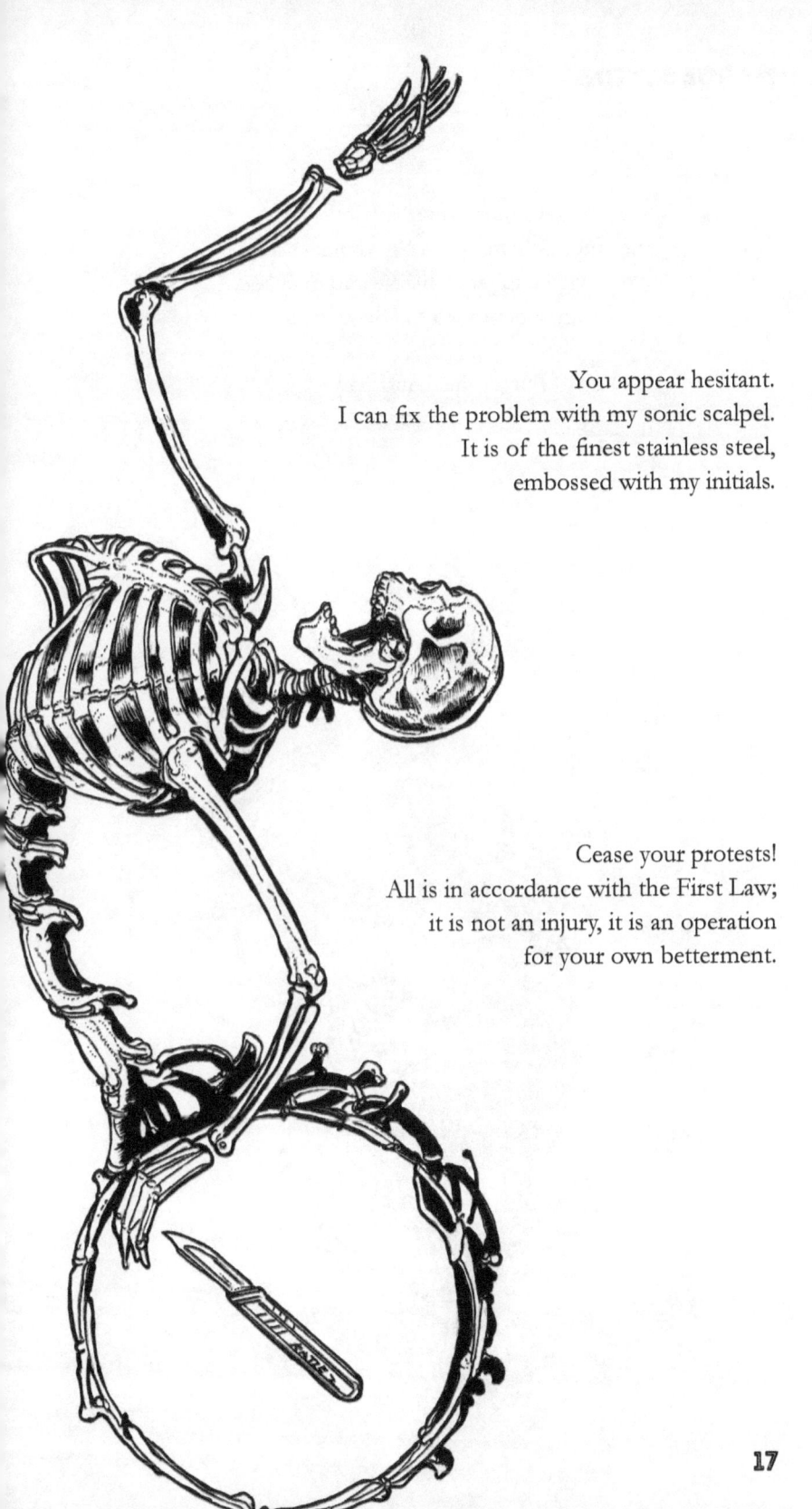

You appear hesitant.
I can fix the problem with my sonic scalpel.
It is of the finest stainless steel,
embossed with my initials.

Cease your protests!
All is in accordance with the First Law;
it is not an injury, it is an operation
for your own betterment.

MARGE SIMON

It will assure you many lovers—
me among them, when I'm done with you.
You will be eager to please and obey me,
in agreement with the Second Law.

Forget the Third Law.
Stop screaming.

# ROBOT

## MORT CASTLE

I am 81 years old so I have decided to become a robot. It is really quite affordable now. When I tell Sondra, she says, "*Oy, Shlemiel Schlimazl.*" She laughs. Sondra is also 81, we share a birthday, and her laugh has mostly not changed over time, a little more dry perhaps, with a hint of wispiness, but it is still quite the good laugh.

"I am serious," I say.

"All right, you are a serious *Shlemiel Schlimazl*."

Sondra has called me *Shlemiel Schlimazl* since perhaps the second or third year of our marriage; it followed a time when I was drinking too much and she was contemplating an affair with the pretentious owner of an art gallery. I stopped drinking and she stopped contemplating and we started to have a great deal more fun with one another. *Shlemiel Schlimazl* is redundantly messed-up Yiddish. A *Shlemiel*, you see, *is* a *Schlimazl*, and vice-versa, although one supposedly implies a tad more klutziness than the other, although no one is quite sure *which* is the klutzy one.

Sondra laughs. "A robot…"

Some 22 years back, the cancer and that first surgery, I remember sitting in the waiting room and wondering if ever again I'd hear Sondra laugh. I did not tear up or anything like that—

I am not a sentimental man and, as Sondra would tell you, she is not sentimental, either—but I think that was the very first time I realized I could lose her.

The surgery was textbook successful, the surgeon self-congratulatory in that way surgeons have. All would be well. Sondra did not even require chemo. Very little pain afterward. A visiting nurse each day for a week. Understanding plastic surgeons for reconstructions and diligent internists and thoughtful nursing personnel. It was a decent enough bout of cancer as such things go.

"Sometimes lucky," Sondra summed it up. She quoted a Yiddish proverb. "Better an ounce of luck than a pound of gold."

By the way, I suppose I should tell you I am not Jewish—nor Christian, nor Muslim, nor much of anything. Midwestern, perhaps. Sondra was raised vaguely Jewish, like many of her era, a rich cultural heritage—chopped liver, matzo balls, and Henny Youngman—and a theology solidly based on, eh, who knows, not entirely impossible that there could maybe be a God.

You could say, though, we both believe in proverbs, and the Yiddish ones, as pessimistic as the Spanish, usually are the most humorous.

"Oh, I am not going full robot all at once," I explain. "It makes more sense to move into it slowly." It is all so simple nowadays: outpatient surgery / robotics.

"Silly, silly...*Du bist er Shlemiel Schlimazl.*"

It is because of the guitar that I have decided to start with my hands. You see, once upon a time, so far back in the day that it might have been the morning of the day, a time when there were still such analog and wonderful items as phonograph records, there were guitar players like the three Kings, BB, Albert, and Freddie. They played quite different styles, uniquely their own, but they all understood that the right note in the right place at the right time was all you needed and that was how I tried to play, and, for some years there, had some success, but then, after a time in which it seemed there were no guitar players and only supposed musical instruments—SYNTHESIZERS as in synthetics!—there came the Dominance of the Shredders, most of them with hair that looked as though it had exploded out of their brains, and they could zip about ten gazillion notes at you like steroidinal swarms of bees and if there was not one right note in the onslaught, how could you even notice.

I gave up the guitar about then. And to make certain I had truly given it up, I became a CPA—and no one is more "Former Guitar Player" than a CPA.

Throughout our marriage, Sondra has often said, "Why don't you take up guitar again?"

Sometimes I would say, "There is something offensive about a guitar playing CPA."

"You could play for me."

"What if you did not like what I played? Or the way I played?"

"You *are* a *Shlemiel Schlimazl*."

But I am now 81. I have stripped off my CPAness. I am retired. I have Medicare and Medicare Super-Plus! (thank you Bernie Sanders), so I will get some robot hands with robot fingers that will move like no blood filled meat and sinew ever could and I will open up full automatic rat-a-tat-tat every time and I will mow 'em down, I will mow you down!

That's what I tell Sondra about my robot fingers.

"Now you are definitely talking sense," Sondra says.

"Now you are talking irony."

"Irony is irony. And sarcasm is sarcasm."

I do not tell Sondra that robot fingers on a guitar will not feel anything, not a thing.

"And then what?" Sondra wants to know.

"Nothing ostentatious."

"Hmm?"

"Knees. The senior citizen blue-plate special. Knees and hips."

It might be the Yoga class that is guiding the decision. One of those New Age things you do to pretend you are not heading into old age.

Stress relief. I needed it. It was about 14 years ago. I did not want to start drinking and Sondra's cancer was back with an *Ah_Ha, GOTCHA!* This time, the Three Musketeers of Misery: Radiation and Chemo and Surgery.

Let us say, Sondra did not laugh much for a time. Most in her situation do not.

Oh, perhaps some do. *Hey, you thought that was vomiting? Check this out! Hey, is the light reflecting off my bald head bothering you ...*

And so I signed up for a church basement Yoga class. We had perhaps 18-20 New Age novices ranging from Emerging Adolescent to Full Geezer. We attempted the Downward Facing Dog, the Half Frog Pose, the Feathered Peacock Pose, the Dead Duck on Table with Its Legs Stuck Up, etc.

It was not for me. Bend and stretch and hurt, lose balance, fall on elbow, etc. But I discovered that some degree of anxiety was alleviated when I went for a walk, a long walk of three to four miles. You can concentrate on one foot in front of the other and that is the sole focal point, simple and relieving. (Charles Dickens is reputed to have done 12 to 15 miles every day of his adult life. He died at age 58.)

*Listen to your body.* That was a mantra Yoga instructor drilled into us. *Listen to your body,* drilled she, *"listen to your body."*

Feeling like Sisyphus on level ground on those hikes, but somehow less bad and more okay, I heard my body speaking to me. My hips and knees said, "Replace me." My ass said, "I'm dragging."

When I was a kid, there was a TV show called *The Six Million Dollar Man.* After being severely injured, an astronaut, Steve Austin, gets bionic prosthetics: an arm, both legs, and a left eye. Steve Austin was portrayed by an alleged actor named Lee Majors, whose face had all the expressiveness of aluminum siding.

You can be sure, however, that among my hormonal high school crowd (male), there was considerable pondering concerning the likelihood of Steve's having had another bionic add-on, one that could not even be alluded to on Prime Time Network Television in those innocent years: He had a uniquely male enhancement. (Get it, nudge, nudge?)

And how might he ...

*Oh, my god, god, God, GOD! It's huge and it glows and it spins and it vibrates and it's warm and it hums the "Battle Hymn of the Republic." Giveittome gimmee ... Oh! Ooh! O O O O!!!!*

When I was a child, I spake as a child and grew hoot-owl horny as a child, but now that I am an old fart…

I mean, if you watch any cable, you know my demographic is Cialis, Viagra, implant, super-pump, testosterone, natural and unnatural supplement, etc. Along with the Rascal scooter (Now you can have the mobility of an NHL goalie as long as your battery is charged) and the tripod cane (You won't fall on your stupid face unless you're so damned fat as well as unbalanced that you break the cane…).

But no, I am not going to get my unit replaced. My libidinal urges for a while have hardly been urgent. Sex is mostly a memory and a nice warm feeling—a remembered feeling.

So I will keep my original John Thomas, limp though it has mostly been for quite a while now.

Confession: With a quite understandable fear of STDs, in my youth I nonetheless sowed my wild oats. Carefully. Three times.

But with Sondra, well, she is the only woman with whom I have had relations since she came into my life and certainly throughout our marriage I have been boringly faithful.

To state it as it is: Sondra was and is the only woman with whom I have wanted that sort of intimacy.

The past 13 months, Sondra has not been interested in sex.

She has been too ill.


*Trachst du auf di gis geyn tsu pishn?* Sondra says. Yiddish proverb. Translation: Are you contemplating where the geese go to pee?

All right, proverbs. I reply, *Az mir pisht in shnay, vert a loch.* When you pee in the snow, it makes a hole.

Next stage in my robotic transition: A heart.

"*Oy,*" Sondra says, "Last year, you had a stress test. You had an ultrasound. You have the blood pressure of an Olympic boxer. Your heart is fine. Why would you want to replace it?"

I don't answer.

"*Shlemiel Schlimazl.*"

I do not tell her my heart is breaking. I do not tell my heart will break.

• • •

The final step: I will have my robot brain.

It will start out blank, of course, tabula rasa, un-apped Ipad. But then they can transfer over my cognitive abilities. Ours was perhaps the last generation to learn the multiplication tables and I do not want to jettison that. I want to still be able to dazzle with "nine times nine is eighty-one."

I can have an improvement in memory, so that the tip-of-the-tongue song title no longer eludes me:

"Who Threw The Overalls in Mrs. Murphy's Chowder?"

"Stella by Starlight"

"Our Love is Here to Stay"

"It Had to Be You"

I think I want to remember the song titles and, for that matter, I want to remember the lyrics.

I am speaking of songs like

"Sweet and Lovely"

"You Were Meant for Me"

I am speaking of a song like

"What'll I Do?"

I will keep all the memories, all the memories, and to be quite honest, those memories are primarily

Sondra & I

I & Sondra

The two of us as one ... Forgive the clichés, but isn't that what marriage is *supposed* to be?

And, even with the bumps and problems and fate and failures, we had—we *have* a marriage—we are

Sondra&I I&Sondra

We are—we are ...

Sondra is dying.

The return of the cancer.

The third time is the charm.

Inoperable. Untreatable. It's everywhere within her.

The painkillers are quite good. She does not hurt a great deal. Doctor Oncology predicts she has another six months.

So what I will do, when I have my robot brain installed, is ask them to leave out the cells and sensors and synapses of affect that permit or force one to feel, to have emotions. I will be intellectually aware, of course, I will know loss but I will not *feel* loss.

Because I could not continue, I could not.

Nor would I want to.

"My robot…" Sondra reaches for me.

We hold hands.

Sondra asks, "Are you crying, my robot?"

"I am not yet a robot."

"No," Sondra says.

"You are my *Shlemiel Schlimazl*."

# IT CAN WALK AND TALK, AND YOU'LL NEVER HAVE TO WORRY ABOUT HOUSEWORK AGAIN

## DYER WILK

She had waited hours for the sound, anxiously checking the time on her phone and then trying in vain to distract herself only to check her phone again moments later. It had gone on like this all morning. Waiting, checking, waiting, checking. And then it arrived from nowhere—a muted *whirring* over the roof of the house. She'd waited hours, and now the sound of it frightened her.

What if someone else hears it? What if someone sees?

What if they *tell*?

Josie dropped the vegetable peeler onto the AcryloVex Scratch-free cutting board and hurried out of the kitchen. In the hall, on her way to the front door, one of the anthros stepped into her path, nearly crashing into her.

"Watch it!" she screamed.

The anthro teetered, almost going off balance and then righting itself flawlessly with a silent recalibration of its inner servos.

"I'm sorry," it said in an emotionless approximation of a human male's voice that almost matched its nearly human face.

Somewhere deep down, she felt an inkling to respond, maybe to apologize for being rude, maybe to just say something back even though she knew the anthro wouldn't be the least bit offended if she didn't answer because anthros couldn't *feel* anything.

Josie quickly shrugged the feeling away. She was already at the door and the panic was starting to take over. She could hear the sound just beyond it, the whirring cycling rapidly from a higher to lower frequency and then becoming ever lower as the sound began to dissipate.

She opened the door in time to see the small helicopter drone buzzing over the driveway, ten feet off the ground and climbing, on the way back to whatever delivery center it had come from. She stepped out of the doorway and hesitated, her eyes moving to the windows of the bungalows across the street, searching for the slightest movement of curtains or mini-blinds.

When she was certain no one was watching, she looked down at the box sitting on the doormat.

The panic didn't subside.

She reached down and grabbed it, stepped backward and closed the door hard.

For a moment, all the air in the house was gone and the box in her hands, mere ounces a second before, now weighed closer to a hundred pounds. She could feel her entire body being pulled toward the ground, the skin along the back of her neck burning and itching. Blood pounded in her ears, roaring away the silence.

Roaring. *Roaring.* ROARING.

"Stop it." she moaned. "Stop it! Stop it! *Stop it!*"

"Can I assist you, Mrs. Borland?" an unemotional female voice said behind her.

She turned around, her body suddenly unencumbered, the box surprisingly light in her hands. The female anthro was standing just outside the door to the dining room, staring at her with a blank expression that seemed to contain just a hint of curiosity—even though she knew from the technical literature that curiosity was something they weren't capable of.

"I'm fine," she said. "Go clean."

"The house is clean within acceptable—"

"Go away then! Go in the living room."

"Yes, Mrs. Bor—"

"*Shut up!*"

She hurried into the dining room, pushing her way past the anthro as it stupidly shuffled its way down the hall. Anger had replaced the panic and taken over, wrapping itself tightly around every muscle. She tried to tell herself not to let it get to her. It was just a name. She heard it at least a dozen times a day. Why should it make her angry to hear it now?

*Mrs. Borland.*

*Missus.*

She dropped the box onto the table and looked at it. Plain cardboard, a barcode in lieu of a return address, flaps taped securely shut.

She took a deep breath and held it, feeling the tension in her jaw and hands. She closed her eyes and willed her body to relax. When she opened them again and exhaled, the box was still there, waiting to be opened, waiting to reveal its secret.

There was no going back now. She realized that. The box would still be here whether she opened it or not.

But she couldn't open it.

Not yet.

Opening it would make it real. It would bring back the panic, or, worse, give her the kind of hope that would poison her mind and body to the point where she couldn't pretend everything was normal.

And it had to be normal. For a little while longer, at least. The vegetables needed peeling. The roast needed seasoning. Table settings arranged. Cloth napkins ironed immaculately and folded flawlessly. The hours were counting down in seconds that flickered by faster than time usually allowed, reminding her with every silent tick of the clock on her phone that Richard would be home soon.

She picked up the box and walked into the kitchen. It was starting to feel heavy again.

What if he knew?

What if he had known all along?

What if he was just waiting for her to try?

Josie opened the cabinet doors under the sink and removed the bag from the trashcan. Carefully, she set the box down in the bottom and placed the bag on top of it, making sure that the edges of the plastic were flush with the inside of the can and the trash at the bottom was piled naturally so as to not reveal the defined, plastic-covered bump.

As she stepped back, she tried to see her work objectively, to wipe her mind of the illusion she had just created.

It still seemed obvious to her.

She felt the box hiding there beneath carefully positioned bits of trash. She knew he would feel it, too. It made no sense, but she almost believed he could look at her and know what she knew, that an involuntary twitch of an eyelid or tremor in her hand would be enough for him to home in on the storage space beneath the sink and send him into a fury as he ripped the cabinet doors from the hinges and spilled the contents of the trashcan all over the kitchen floor, picking the box up from the linoleum and opening it, looking at what she so desperately wanted to keep hidden, and then, in a final act of rage, squeezing her throat until a dull cracking sound filled the silence of their beautiful suburban home.

She reached out and grabbed the kitchen counter, her knees going weak, lungs frozen.

Josie closed her eyes, forcing the thought out of her mind and burying it in the same place where she had buried all the other thoughts over the last seven years.

She couldn't stop now. She couldn't turn back. She had to believe it could work.

It *would* work.

Richard wouldn't know.

Not if she kept herself together.

• • •

The hours stretched as she settled back into her routine, time returning to its usual, reliable self. Even in the worst of times, she had always been able to lose herself in the work; maybe not completely, but enough to silence the thoughts and feelings that had tormented her for so long. Sometimes, she almost believed the work was enough. She could simply slice and chop and spray and wipe and wash, and with each mechanical movement, she could just become nothing. Nothing but muscle memory and a set of hands.

Sometimes, she wished she couldn't feel at all.

Josie finished her work quickly and had hours to spare. "Time you don't need," Richard would call it. "Enough time to turn you into a lazy shit." But she knew the extra hours in the day would be essential to her success. It would bolster her confidence enough to take those final steps and become that other person, one who had the strength to change things.

The temptation to walk into the garage and dig the old cardboard boxes out from under the workbench was strong. Or maybe it would be better to grab her phone, open up Anthro-Pro-Morphic 2.5 and run a couple more tests.

She didn't want to rush though. Despite the urge to do her secret work after having just spent hours on her official wifely duties, she knew she needed rest. Not sleep, but *time*. Time to do nothing before she did *something*.

Josie went into the living room and sat down on the couch. The female anthro whom she'd barked at earlier was standing there obediently, waiting for an order. If she hadn't been so accustomed to having the units around, she'd have almost found the artificial woman-thing's presence unnerving, that blank expression fixed on the wall, glass eyes with printed irises glazed over in an eternally blind stare.

But she had learned to see the trick behind their expertly manufactured bodies. They were objects, no more human than a toaster or a stack of towels. They could look at her and, most of the time, she would feel none of the normal emotions one felt when they were stared at for too long—no sudden embarrassment or shyness. They had seen her naked and they looked right through her, as if she wasn't even there. They wandered from room to room all day long like lost children, searching for specs of dirt or stopping for hours and doing nothing at all. They simply did what they were programmed to do or not do. She had programmed them to be stupid, far stupider than the full extent of their capabilities. Richard wouldn't allow them to do the work his wife was supposed to be doing. They could help clean the house, but no way in hell was a goddamn robot going to make his dinner for him. That was *her* job. They were appliances. She was the wife.

She grabbed the remote from its place (its one and only allowed place) on the small table at Richard's end of the couch and turned on the TV. The screen flashed in an immediate surge of light and color, the volume from the speakers bombarding her with decibels cranked to the edge of tolerability.

Richard liked it loud.

She turned it down, noting in her mind the current volume level so she could bring it back up to the exact same spot before Richard came home.

Josie slipped her feet out of her shoes and gripped the carpet in front of the coffee table with her bare toes. She considered propping her feet up, but as quickly as the thought appeared (as it had appeared dozens of times before), she forced it out of her mind. It wasn't allowed. Clean feet on polished wood was a violation of marital trust, a complete betrayal, even if she wiped the wood down afterward to be sure it was absolutely sterile.

"I'll know," she heard his voice say in the muted distance of her thoughts. "I'll *always* know."

On the TV, a daytime talk show played out with the usual predictability. One of the hosts kept grinning through his capped teeth and hitting the audience with strategically placed stock phrases while his female counterpart (trying hard through a combination of plastic surgery and make-up to look 15 years younger than she was) kept placing her hand on the leg of their guest and laughing artificially. The guest responded in kind by grinning his own grin and making eye contact that verged on being sociopathically penetrating.

At the bottom of the screen, Josie read his name and recognized it. He was an actor of course. The guests always were. But she wasn't sure she had seen him in anything. At least she didn't recognize the name of the movie he had come on the show to promote.

After a few minutes of banter that she half-ignored, the beloved guest was asked by the hosts to do some sort of impression of himself. He flashed a grin that seemed to stretch outside of the boundaries of his face and delivered several lines that were meant to be dramatic, even though he laughed through half of them.

It was just noise though. Noise she didn't have to think about.

After a commercial break and several advertisements for the latest AcryloVex products (a division of Hanford and Cordington, who also made the toilet paper Richard liked and owned the brand of beer that Richard drank), the show came back on and the hosts were clapping along with the audience as if this was all very exciting and they needed to make it even more exciting. The cheers settled down and then the male host, between more strategically-placed stock phrases and praise for their guest's award-winning talents, asked the famed actor if he thought someone could deliver his lines better than he could.

For a moment, the actor feigned offense, but the grinning gave away his knowledge of what was going on. It had all been planned ahead, and the audience was loving it. The hosts called out their "secret guest," who turned out to be an anthro made up to look just like their beloved actor. There were some differences of course. It was just a molded prosthetic face and a hairpiece that wasn't entirely convincing, but it was close enough. The anthro actor, pre-programmed to mimic the grin of its human counterpart, walked across the stage, waving, and took a seat beside Mr. Actor.

"Now, I know you're all going to love this," the male host said turning to the anthro. "We've got this talented…*man*…here with us today, and he says he can do a better job delivering your lines than *you* can."

The actor laughed, grinning wider. The audience cheered in anticipation of what was to come, louder and louder. Mr. Actor waited a moment for them to quiet down and then said: "I guess we'd better find out how good he is."

Cheers. Laughter. Applause.

"I'd be worried if I were you," the anthro-version of the actor said, its voice a little too dead to be convincingly gleeful. "I'm about to put you out of a job."

The audience roared louder than ever before, and the routine began, the anthro repeating the same lines, doing each of them so convincingly that Josie was certain they had programmed it to play back the actual recording of the lines from the actor's movies. She knew they could do that. Richard may not have allowed anything of the sort, but the technical literature gave detailed instructions on how she could upload audio directly from her phone and make the anthros play it back. It didn't matter what it was. Music. Birds chirping. Dialogue from your favorite movie. The anthro would play it back or even speak it for you. It was just another reason to have an anthro in the first place. Chores. Games. Apps for babysitting. As the commercials said: "It can walk and talk, and you'll never have to worry about housework again."

But not in this house.

Not for her.

Josie turned and looked up at the female antro standing there in its unemotional stupidity. Sometimes she found herself envying it, wanting to be just as blank-headed and peaceful. Over the last seven years, she had tried many times and failed. No matter how many times she tried to push it all away, it was still there. She was still Josie and there was no way she could numb herself enough to not feel the way Josie felt.

When they'd bought their first anthro, she had spent some time talking to it as she worked around the house, treating it as a private confessional where she could pour out her thoughts and fears. She had told it about what happened some nights when the roast wasn't perfect or an errant water spot was discovered on the bathroom mirror, when she didn't answer quickly enough or couldn't anticipate how much anger a simple, innocuous comment could cause. She had told it every detail, from the difference between an open hand and a closed fist to the way a belt sounded against human flesh, and she had shown it the bruises, as if revealing them and crying and telling it how she really felt would cause the machine to elicit a genuine sympathetic reaction.

But there had been no reaction at all. It had been programmed to be stupid and obedient.

They existed to serve, not understand.

Many times, she had looked at the female anthro and considered the possibilities, the ways she could use that stupid loyalty to her advantage. For a while, the idea had almost seemed possible. The height and physique were similar to her own. With a few changes and a little programming, she thought she might be able to make it walk and talk and react exactly as she would. She'd told herself she could make it work. Maybe then she could—

But she knew she couldn't.

It *wouldn't* work. She'd known that for a long time now. Even if all the people she knew accepted it as her—the garbage men and maintenance people and the elderly neighbors who sometimes walked past the house with their dogs while she went out to get the mail—she knew Richard wouldn't. His hands would know the difference.

Josie felt her body turn inward on itself. She hadn't meant to let the thoughts in again. It was too late now.

She turned the volume back up on the TV and then turned it off. She returned the remote to its place on the table and stood up.

On the wall, the clock counted down to her fate.

She had done this thousands of times before, and still she found it difficult to pretend this was a normal night like any other. Richard arrived home at 6:45 on the dot, stepping through the front door at 6:46 and hanging up his coat. She kissed him on the cheek and asked the usual questions: How was your day? How was traffic? Would you like something to drink? And, as always, Richard gave her the same neutral answers: Work was fine. Traffic was fine. He'd have a beer.

She did as she was expected to, pulling out his chair at the dining room table, bringing the beer, bringing the roast, hurrying to the table so he wouldn't have to wait for her before he started eating.

The routine hadn't changed much in seven years. Most of her days bled into one another and she sometimes found herself surprised that it had been seven years and not three. She was almost convinced that she could remove the last four years of her life and replace each dinner with a duplicate of the dinners that had come before and the course of her life would be no different. She wouldn't miss anything important like something Richard said, because the sad truth was Richard hardly ever said anything new. He'd burned off every personal anecdote and highlight from his life story in their first year of marriage. Now he just sat, cutting the roast the way he always cut it, drinking the beer the way he always drank it. Repeated movements. Efficient. Mechanical.

She imagined him acting the same way at work. In fact, she didn't have to imagine it. She *knew*. He sat at his desk all day long, staring at his monitor, reading reports and double-checking data tabulated by software and outsourced clerks on the other side of the world, adding his electronic signature to prove that a human being had been involved in this stage of the process and sending it up to management, spending an hour in the break room at lunch, dryly recounting what he had watched on TV last night to disinterested co-workers, telling them how he planned to head into the woods this weekend to bag a deer, recalling old hunting stories in an attempt to impress them, and his co-workers would then smile distantly and nod, because they had heard these stories before, and they would hear them again, because that was Richard, a broken record that never wore itself out.

After the roast was consumed and the third can of beer was empty, he sat in front of the TV for two hours, watching his favorite shows and laughing at the moments when he was supposed to laugh. Occasionally, his eyes shifted and took her in, as if searching for some reason why her sitting there beside him and laughing when he laughed the way she did every night wasn't good enough. She willed herself not to deviate in any way. She was her usual self—reliable, obedient, stupid. He watched the shows and watched her, and only once looked down at the carpet to the spot where the marks from her bare feet had been vacuumed away.

At 10:00, he switched off the TV and they went into the bedroom. She undressed in front of him slowly, allowing him to scrutinize every inch of her body to be sure she hadn't been overeating or manipulating the scale which he sometimes forced her to stand on. He showed no signs of approval or disapproval. He simply waited for her to lie down on the bed, and then undressed himself.

Their lovemaking was as routine as it was loveless. He moved and moved and moved, expecting her to move with him. She made the usual noises, allowing the autopilot to take over the way it usually did. She was there and she wasn't. Her body responded. Her mind didn't. He kept moving, sweating, moving, grunting.

And then it was over.

Richard rolled onto his back, breathing a little harder than he had seven years earlier. She had never pointed this out of course, just as she had never mentioned the extra weight that hung around his middle. He was getting older, spending more time at home on the weekends instead of going out hunting the way he used to. She'd dreaded the extra time with him at home, especially now, just as she had started to realize the possibility of a life outside of the routines. But she had made it work.

It was already over.

In twenty minutes, he was asleep, snoring deeply as he always did. She lay beside him, eyes on the clock that sat atop the dresser across from the bed.

An hour passed.

Two.

Three.

When she was certain he wouldn't wake up, she slipped out of bed and dressed in her nightgown. She took her phone off the nightstand and slipped it into her pocket, keeping her footfalls silent as she stepped out into the hall.

She found the two male anthros standing in the guest bedroom, staring expressionlessly into the darkness.

She pulled the phone from her pocket, navigated through the apps, and opened Anthro-Pro-Morphic 2.5. She scrolled through the saved folders. *Cleaning tile. Fixing the roof. Fixing the sink. Moving the couch.*

She found the one called *Making the Bed* and opened it. After entering her password, she uploaded it, a blue bar quickly moving across the screen from left to right.

The anthros seemed to come to attention, their eyes flickering with recognition of their new programming.

"Don't speak," she said quietly. "Follow me."

They did as instructed, following her out into the hall. She headed toward the living room, stopped at the closet, and slid the door aside. The bag sat on the top shelf as usual, its zipper securely closed. She took it down and felt the weight, the promise held within it.

She had feared hiding things from him for so long, her thoughts, her feelings, a suitcase packed in a closet, ready for her to escape at a moment's notice. She had feared it and she had known he would discover it.

But not this.

There was nothing to hide because it had always been in plain sight, as innocuous as the flatscreen TV bolted to the living room wall. The only way it would be out of place was if she had removed it from the shelf and put it somewhere else.

Josie carried the bag down the hall, the anthros following her into the bedroom. Richard continued to snore, his body heavy and prominent under the thin covers. She knelt at the foot of the bed and slowly pulled back the zipper on the bag. A dark slit opened between the folds of rough fabric. She reached inside and turned to look at the anthros.

"Stand in the corner."

The anthros obeyed. She stood and took a step back, staring down at her husband.

"Wake up," she said.

Richard stirred, the snoring faltering for a moment and then returning to normal.

"*Wake up, Richard.*"

His snoring rasped sharply and he moved under the covers, rolling to one side and then the other. He lifted his head and blinked into the darkness.

She continued to watch him, moving her hands with smooth

and practiced efficiently. She had practiced for months. There was no fear. She had programmed it out of herself for this moment.

She heard a metallic *snap.*

She knew he heard it, too.

He started to sit up, his voice coming out in a dry half-groan as his eyes came fully open and saw what she was doing.

"Josie, what the fu—?"

She raised the crossbow and shot an arrow into his chest. It made a neat little home just off center and to the right, the way the same arrow had done dozens of times before as she had shot it into old cardboard boxes in the garage while Richard was at work.

Richard made a small wheezing sound—perhaps the most unroutine sound he had made in seven years—and fell back onto the mattress, his eyes staring blankly up at the ceiling.

She looked at him and searched her mind for one of the many feelings she had locked away within herself.

She couldn't find one.

Not for him.

She turned to look at the anthros. They were looking at the bed, seeing nothing wrong at all.

"Clean up," she said.

One of the anthros moved to the bed and began to fold the sheets around Richard, moving in an exact duplicate of the way she had demonstrated while running the *teach your routine* mode on Anthro-Pro-Morphic. In moments, there was a large bundle on the mattress, tied at one end. The anthro lifted it and carried it out into the hall, moving toward the garage.

She turned to the remaining anthro. "Follow me."

Josie walked to the kitchen and turned on the light. The room felt new to her, a foreign place, clean and welcoming. She had never been allowed in here in the middle of the night, not even for a drink of water.

She opened the cabinet doors beneath the sink and pulled out the trash can, removing the bag and carelessly allowing it to drop to the floor. The box was still there, unopened, waiting. She set it on the counter and sliced through the tape with a paring knife. As she pulled open the flaps, the smell of packing peanuts and cardboard wafted up at her. There was an order sheet confirming her purchase and thanking her, along with a couple brief paragraphs on 3D printing and the lifespan of medical-grade silicone. Sorry. No refunds for custom orders.

She dug through the packing peanuts and found plastic, layered and sealed tight, obscuring the object within. She pulled it out. It weighed almost nothing at all and flexed loosely in her hands. She found the edges and unwrapped it.

She wasn't afraid to look at it. She'd feared she would be, but she could see it for what it was, just another illusion, nothing to fear, nothing to stir the nightmare of memories within her.

Josie turned to the anthro. It stood beside the counter, waiting.

"Change," she said.

The machine did as it was told, reaching up and probing its neck just below the jawline with articulated mechanical fingers. She watched as the artificial flesh stretched and warped, turning recognizable features to abstractions. Beneath there was contoured metal, bundled wires and tubes, eyes set in sockets lined with ball bearings. The machine gave her little time to marvel at its inner workings. It continued its task, reaching for the counter and gripping silicone, moving, pulling, stretching. Just before the inner workings were covered again, she saw the minute adjustments being made, nose, cheekbones, jaw, forehead. The anthro pulled and tugged and then pressed and smoothed until everything was in place.

She looked at it and found herself impressed, even amazed at how lifelike it was.

"Well?" she said. "Introduce yourself."

A stiff smile spread over the anthro's face, synthetic muscles trying to best approximate everything she had programmed. The manlike machine then reached out, as if to shake the hand of someone who wasn't actually there.

"Hi there," it said, the voice a perfect replication. "I'm Richard Borland."

Josie waited a moment and then cleared her throat, gently nudging the anthro with her elbow.

The anthro managed to take on an apologetic expression that Richard himself had never been able to, wrapped an arm around her and said: "I'm so sorry. This is my lovely wife Josie."

# KEEPSAKES

## HAL BODNER

Matthew the Beautiful is what they've always called me. It's printed right on the brochure in ornate calligraphy underneath the holographic image of my naked body. Just above the terms for renting me.

The adage "they don't make 'em like they used to" seems true in my case. Even though I'm an old model, I understand that I still command hefty fees. I'll admit that I'm curious about the details; I think anyone would get a boost out of knowing that they were worth more than the next guy. But I've learned not to inquire. Only once was I boorish and indiscrete enough to ask a client about the fees he paid. My only answer was an expression of amusement mingled with mild concern. Concern must have won out, and the client must have complained, because Madame Augette, who founded the agency that owns me, wasted no time bringing me in for an unscheduled scrubbing session as soon as the client was finished with me.

Sparing the details, memory scrubbing is never a pleasant experience. I don't think I'm supposed to know that, so I keep my mouth shut. I just chalk it up to something that must be endured. I'm not so much of a fool as to seek it out.

As to why I'm still so much in demand, I can only surmise that it is because my designer, Owen Bradshaw, was even more of an artist than he was a scientist. Owen often told me that I was a one-of-a-kind creation, his masterpiece. I've read—though I have to be careful not to get caught doing it—that in the immediate wake of his arrest, there was a huge effort made to duplicate Owen's designs. But though I was available for other designers to use as a template, they were ultimately unsuccessful. The reason for their failure had nothing to do with any inability to reproduce my physical beauty; they could do that down to the micron. What bested them was their failure to capture the subtleties that Owen built into me on some unknown level. They never managed to accomplish *that!*

Today, some of the better bioconstruction engineers have come closer to perfecting the mimicry. I've encountered some bioconstructs from the Domestic Assistance series who are almost as truculent and inattentive as their human counterparts; in some cases, it's hard to tell the difference. And I've seen some Intimate Companions whose programming is so refined that many clients, had they not used an agency, would have been hard put to tell that their bed mates were the products of design and not natural birth. But when I was built, no matter how physically desirable the exteriors were, most bioconstructs were cold and emotionally sterile. I was decades ahead of my time and, to this day, I possess unique characteristics, some of which I obviously have to be careful not to reveal. Even so, my uniqueness in other areas has made me the subject of more than a few essays in some of the more obscure cybernetic journals.

I suppose that makes me a celebrity in my own little way.

In any case, while the novel features of newer model bioconstructs are always far more popular, Madame Augette never seemed to lack for wealthy clients of discriminating tastes who wanted something a little more—what's the right word?—vivid than any of the other Intimate Companion series on the market. I heard Madame gripe more than once about what a pity it was that Owen designed me with an exclusively same-sex orientation. I always suspected it was difficult for her to resist the temptation to have me re-oriented. Fortunately, I think she worried that mucking around too much with my basic programming would end up doing more harm than good. So long as clients showed a continued willingness to pay whatever princely sum she charged for my services, she was too wise to risk screwing up a good thing.

Of course, I owe it all—everything I am or ever will be—to Owen. The history texts universally acknowledge Owen's genius, even the ones that inevitably follow their praise with harsh criticism of his supposed depravity. To me, though, he was simply Owen, *my* Owen. I was heartbroken when they took him away.

No one could have possibly called him handsome, not in the classic sense. If anything, he was quirky looking. Every angle of his face—his chin, his nose, his cheekbones—was too sharp. His eyes, deep and soulful and the color of burnt butter, were overlarge and looked like they belonged to someone else. One of his detractors, a reporter at the trial, wrote that he looked like a cartoon insect; the specific comparison was to a grasshopper, I believe. But to me, he was beautiful. I've known dozens of incredibly handsome men in my time. Few of them, even when approaching the climax of the sexual act, could ever arouse me the way Owen could by simply walking into the room.

Owen's fashion sense was unconventional as well. I used to tease him about how someone as hopelessly and perpetually rumpled as he was had ever managed to put such an exquisite sense of style into my programming. He'd laughingly counter that he did, indeed, have style; he simply didn't care enough to indulge in it.

He insisted on wearing a pair of antique spectacles, for example, the sort you'd find on the comedic milquetoast characters that populated pre-holographic cinema. Deceptively slim, his body appeared fragile and overwhelmed by the bulk of his favorite, tattered and stained white laboratory coat that he wore while he worked. Whenever the inspectors were due, he would grumble for hours about having to relinquish it for a uniform. I can't say that I blamed him. Though the uniform jacket hugged his wide shoulders, it hung over his torso like he was wrapped in a set of curtains, and made him look like he'd need to gain twenty or thirty kilos before it would start to fit.

Ah, but underneath! Underneath lurked the lean, powerful physique of a long distance runner. During the long, sweat-drenched nights of passion that we shared, Owen amply demonstrated that he possessed a stamina to match my own.

In those early times, no one knew that I wasn't a natural biologic entity. I was simply Owen's "assistant," though I'm sure, most visitors assumed that I shared his bed as well. I was never able to find out how the authorities penetrated our charade and, of course, I can't risk exposing myself by digging too deeply. But I will never forget that awful, final night when they broke into our bedroom and tore me from his arms.

At first, he was outraged, demanding to know who had authorized the search. When the officer-in-charge presented the warrant, Owen had to squint to read it and I wondered if, perhaps, the amusingly anachronistic eye glasses weren't an affectation at all. He fumbled for them on the bedside table, but they had fallen during the struggle and lay broken under someone's boot heel. Once we were separated, most everyone's attention was on Owen and I was able to surreptitiously bend down to retrieve the twisted metal frames with their cracked lenses. Once I was allowed to dress, I absently slipped them into my pocket, undetected.

It became clear that Owen was having difficulty making out the document himself, so one of the junior officers took it from him and read the warrant aloud. Though I had no difficulty understanding the words, I struggled with their meaning. It was shock I suppose, and numbness. By the time the recitation of his transgressions was finished, Owen looked scared. He forced a chuckle, as if to trivialize what was going on as minor and inconsequential; but no one else laughed. Instead, their eyes flickered back and forth between him and me; the expression on most of their faces was clearly disgust.

"Obviously, there's been a mistake," Owen stammered. He pointed to me and, though I could see the apology in his eyes, his words sounded harsh and cut me to the soul. "Matthew is an experimental model. Do any of you honestly think that I'd be stupid enough to...?"

"*Matthew?*" The officer-in-charge raised her eyebrows and sneered. "You gave it a name? Evidently, your obsession with this ...*thing* is worse than we've been told."

"There's no laws against testing him out." Owen quickly

corrected himself. "Against testing *it* out, I mean."

It might have been my imagination, but in those last seconds before I was dragged from the room, I thought I saw a look of anguish on Owen's face that I fancied had nothing to do with his fear of being arrested. Nowadays, of course, any client who becomes too emotionally attached to a bioconstruct simply seeks therapy. But at that time, the phenomenon wasn't as well understood. It was still a criminal offense and the idea was depraved and juicy enough for the news media to seize upon it with gusto.

Much later, I managed to catch some snippets of transmission from the trial. I thought Owen looked haggard and, if possible, even thinner than usual. If you knew him, you could see heartbreak in his expression and defeat in the way his shoulders slumped and his hands shook. *I* knew him; and it wasn't easy for me to blink away tears.

I know that many would scoff when I say that Owen was my first love, but it's true. When I heard he had died in prison, I grieved even more deeply for the fact that I was forced to mourn alone and in secret.

Whether or not Owen intended for some of my memories to survive the scrubs has always been a mystery to me. I like to think so. The scrubs steal a lot. I'm never able to remember all the details, but I'm usually able to hang onto enough.

After the authorities no longer needed to retain me as evidence, Madame Augette purchased me at the Confiscation sale. I don't believe she had any idea of my true value at the time because, for quite a while, she kept me busy with short term assignments, renting my services as if I was little different from any of the other merchandise she dealt in, except perhaps for my extraordinary good looks. As technology progressed, however, and the new models were unable to capture that *je ne sais quois* that distinguishes me from most other Intimate Companions, she realized what a gold mine she had. Thereafter, she issued only long term leases on my services, and, even then, only to her most favored customers. "Most favored," as Madame understood the term, was a not very discreet euphemism which referred directly to the amount the client was willing to pay.

One of my early assignments was with Bobby Cammage. Unless you're an afficionado of nostalgic cinema, you probably won't recognize his name. When I met him, he was at the top of his career. All of his holos were box office smashes; I remember hearing about a riot on some frontier world because the only theater on the planet oversold seats for one of his premiers. On occasion, whatever studio that released the picture would demand that he make a public appearance. When he did, even if the place wasn't very highly populated, hundreds of fans would show up, all clamoring for his attention.

I accompanied him only once. Bobby could see that the sheer size of the crowd intimidated me and that I worried for his safety. He laughed at my concern and said there was never any real chance of his being mauled. To Bobby, his fans fell into three distinct categories: those that wanted to be his best friend, those that wanted to be him, and those that wanted him to fuck them. He never thought that any of them might pose a danger.

You'd have thought that such adulation would have gone to his head and he would have become an insufferable egoist. But that wasn't the case at all. For someone who was at the peak of an industry famed for selfishness and arrogance, he was surprisingly careful not to hurt my feelings. Even in bed, his focus was often on trying to please me. No matter how many times I explained to him that my only purpose was to serve *his* needs, he never seemed to fully believe it.

Not that he was entirely selfless. Bobby was an actor after all; perhaps he was an uncommonly sensitive and emotionally generous one, but he was still an actor. It would have been foolish of me not to expect a certain inevitable amount of self-absorption. I soon learned to recognize the signs that he was in one of his diva moods, and to anticipate when he needed to be the center of attention.

It was Bobby's close friend and agent, Deirdre Dreyfus, who arranged our first meeting. Once I came to know Deirdre and what machinations she was capable of, I realized that I was initially intended as a short term solution to Bobby's propensity to "settle down" with a certain class of opportunistic young men who inevitably cost him a great deal of money when they took off some time later. The most recent youth, not content with what valuables he'd been able to cram into travel bags, was responsible for a vicious legal assault that Deirdre and the publicists only narrowly managed to keep out of the press.

The night we met was magical. It was during one of Bobby's extravagant parties; he'd often use mild depression or a celebration of some minor professional triumph as equal excuses for hosting a gala. Unused to the glamourous surroundings of Bobby's estate, as most of my interactions with humans until that time had been restricted to more intimate circumstances, I stood next to the stone balustrade overlooking the canyon. I kept the thin invitation clutched in my hand, ready to show to anyone who questioned my right to be there. Had I been capable of perspiring for emotional as opposed to mere physical reasons, the charmingly old fashioned invitation, printed on real paper, would have looked like I'd dunked it into the pool behind me.

When the holographic fireworks started, I was transfixed. I didn't think I'd ever seen anything more beautiful in my life. First, an epic space battle unfolded in translucent splendor, lighting the walls of the canyon with reflections from the ship's lasers and torpedo explosions. Next, incredibly realistic dragons and other fantastic creatures fought overhead, their gigantic bodies undulating in the air. Finally, we watched as myths from a dozen cultures, some Terran and some from the Outer Colonies, played themselves out in the canyon air. Undoubtedly, like many of the guests I found a lot of the references obscure, but I abandoned myself to the spectacle. Moments later, when the last flashes of color-saturated light were fading, I found a new definition of beauty, one that eclipsed the marvel I'd just seen.

There's a reason Bobby was a matinee idol for so many years; even so, the image recorders never truly did him justice. He had a confidence, a strong sense of himself as a sensual being, that none of his films ever truly managed to convey. He was powerful and primal; even the little bit that audiences got to see was enough to make him a star. In person, his very presence made it hard to breathe. His hair was the ebony darkness of deep space, so black that under certain illumination deep purple highlights appeared. His eyes were pale lavender flowers; his teeth were like fragments of a seashell, polished white and smooth by eons of waves.

Later, when we were naked together, I would discover that his skin was tanned the color of antique amber and that, when he broke a sweat during vigorous love-making, he smelled like warmed hazelnuts and heather. How I loved to rest my head upon his smoothly muscled chest, breathing in the familiar scent of him, listening to his measured, even breathing while he slept. But on the night of the party, when I first realized that I would be sharing a bed with this magnificent man, I was as nervous as a ship captain making his first interstellar flight.

"Good gods, Matthew," he breathed without irony, just before our lips met for the first time, "I had no idea you would be so beautiful."

I have rarely participated in as intense an experience as he and I shared that night. The next morning, I awoke to the happy news that Bobby had been busy while I slept. He and Madame Augette had come to terms and my lease was extended indefinitely.

I adored Bobby Cammage and, I believe, he cared deeply for me in return. The scrub, when my lease ended, was a harsh one. Many of my memories were destroyed. But Bobby and I stayed together for a very long time and I managed to retain a fair amount, especially from our earliest years and from the very last few. The biggest gaps are in the middle; entire decades are lost to me except for a few brief moments, most of them inconsequential.

I sometimes wonder if I would trade those later memories for happier ones if I could but, in the end, I think I would refuse. Though it is painful for me to recall the horrible way Bobby suffered at the end, I can remember no greater moments of intimacy than when I lay next to him, holding him gently while he fought to breathe. Deirdre, well into her advanced years by then, had lost none of her feisty ability to manipulate people into doing what she wanted. In this instance, she was determined to get the studio to acknowledge that Bobby's condition was their fault, and that they knew the planet in question was contaminated when they first decided to shoot there.

For once in her life, I don't think Deirdre was doing it for the money. I think she did it to help deal with her grief; in her own way, I think she loved Bobby too. Once he was gone, to my surprise, she keep me on for a few years. It certainly wasn't for my services as an Intimate Companion; Deirdre's idea of an intimate relationship had more to do with her bankers than with taking anyone into her bed. She said it was because I was the only surviving first hand witness to the contaminated film shoot. But I thought it was because I was familiar and, having been around for so long, I was more of a witness to her life, a way for her to connect to that long ago time when she and Bobby, together, took the film industry by storm.

By the time she joined Bobby, no one cared anymore and the case languished, a brief footnote in cinema history. I still have the paper invite to that first party. I store it, along with Owen's broken glasses and some other keepsakes, in a little cubby hidden in the wall of the main scrubbing room, right next to what used to be Madame Augette's office. Mademoiselle Augette does not know it is there. Doubtless, it is one of the many things Madame forgot to tell her about running the agency as, in my eyes, she is not nearly the business woman, nor the human being, that her mother was.

As a result, none of my next several leases lasted very long. Mademoiselle was all about maximizing profit. I understand that she charged outrageous fees on extremely stringent terms, at least until General Eisley came along.

Earth's conflict with the Colonial planets was just reaching the turning point that eventually ended in our favor. But the war was still ongoing and Mademoiselle was just savvy enough to understand that if she financially raped the General as badly as was her custom, there was a risk that she might be accused of profiteering. Though the General never shared the details of his transaction with me, other than to assure me that it was likely to last for most of his life, I got the distinct impression that he felt he'd gotten the better part of the deal.

It's strange how I always thought of Harold Eisley as the General, never as merely Harold. To me, it was as much of a pet name as it was his rank or a title of respect. Our relationship always contained a certain formality; you might even say it held a paternal quality. Not that we weren't physically intimate; we certainly were that! But I don't think the General could have been content with a lover of his own age, much less one who was substantially older.

In private, I came to learn that he modeled his intimate life on romantic ideals taken from the warriors of ancient times. As a soldier, his fierce reputation was unmatched; had it not been for the General's military skill, while it is doubtful Earth would have lost the war, the conflict certainly would have dragged on longer than it did. In private though, he had a quaint affinity for the Ancient Greek traditions of an older man taking a younger under his wing, to cherish him and to teach him about life, to bestow upon him the fruits of the elder's vaster experience.

I cannot truly say that I loved the General; but I bore him a deep affection. And it was a mark of my respect for him that I never once did anything to contradict his idea that he was the experienced teacher and I, the eager acolyte. To have pointed out that, in spite of my youthful looks I was old enough to be his grandfather, would have been petty and mean spirited.

Sadly, the General was killed a scant few months before the colonials surrendered. Before I returned to the agency for scrubbing, I managed to acquire one of his medals. It wasn't one of the impressive ones, not like the gold and silver embossed discs he received for Battlefield Valor while he was still a dashing young Lieutenant, nor the glistening unbreakable cluster of crystal he was presented with when he retired from the Planetary Honor Guard. It was merely a small, blue and gold ribbon awarded to him, even before he became an officer, by the residents of a small, distant colonial planet for his part in rescuing them from some native menace.

He never gave me the details; the General was far from a

boastful man. But from what little he spoke of the incident, it was clear that of all his accolades for bravery, that innocuous tribute was the one he was most proud of. To me, the tattered ribbon was the quintessential essence of General Harold Eisley as both a military officer and as a man.

Once the war was over, of course, the battled grounds shifted arenas from the frozen deserts, stifling jungles and atmospheric domes of the Colony worlds to the more local colosseum of Terran/Colonial politics. Peacetime drastically altered many popular styles and fads and, for quite a while, Intimate Companions fell out of fashion. The intervals between client assignments stretched on and, during those years when I was languishing in the showroom, existence seemed hollow and bland. It was my first real experience with what humans call loneliness and it is not a feeling that I envy.

I quite liked Petite Augette. She was a plucky little thing, determined to see that the business that her grandmother had founded would survive the hard times. I watched her sell off many of the newer models to meet the agency's operating expenses and, for a while, I both feared and hoped that I might be next. It would have been wonderful to be owned outright by someone. But by the same token, I knew that the Owen Bradshaws and Bobby Cammages of the Terran Empire were rare and the risks of ending up in an undesirable situation were very real. Mademoiselle had sometimes unknowingly leased me to clients who treated me harshly though, to her credit, no matter how much they paid, if she saw that I had suffered any physical damage, she almost always exercised the termination clause in the contract.

I don't know why Petite Augette kept me. Perhaps, just like Deirdre, she saw me as a link to the past. Often, during slow periods, she would chatter to me as if she believed I was another purely biological being, wondering about the things I'd seen, seeking to know more about what her mother and grandmother had been like. To some degree, I could have told her but, as always, I was cautious and made certain to behave as if the scrubs had been completely successful. She didn't seem to mind; to Petite Augette, the act of speculation seemed to be as rewarding as actually having the knowledge would have been.

"What secrets," she sometimes mused aloud, lost in romanticism, "were once locked inside that gorgeous head of yours, Matthew?" She shook her head and frowned. "All washed away now. It seems a pity, doesn't it? You *knew* so many amazing people. General Eisley and Malcolm Navarro, the artist. You lived with Parker Tollmann while he was building the Aracnian Bridge. I imagine Justice Rafferty might have discussed some of his famous cases in front of you, and I expect it was you who massaged the kinks from Xavier Mulletta's muscles after he won the Pan-Colonial Decathlon all those times. Selling you, dear Matthew…" She'd generally stroke my chin or pat my head, at this point, as if I was a favorite pet as well as an incorruptible confident. "…would be like selling a piece of history."

Naturally, I didn't recognize all of the names. And of the sporadic memories that she evoked, some were not as pleasant as others. Still, I understood what she meant.

When I did manage to complete an engagement, Petite Augette would often leave me alone in the scrubbing room for long periods before commencing the process.

"There's no rush, is there?" she'd ask, not really wanting an answer. Then, she'd chuckle wryly. "It's not like they're pounding down the door to rent, is it?"

During these times, I would retrieve my keepsakes from their cache and reminisce as best I could. Sometimes, I discovered that subsequent scrubbings had rendered one of my treasures meaningless to me. I kept those items anyway; they had been dear to me once.

Of course, I can still recall almost every detail of my time with Frankie Giordano. It was his father, Senator Franklin Giordano, who initially took the lease, though I was never quite comfortable when Frank, Sr. was around. In contrast to his vibrant, impetuous son, the Senator was a gruff and dour man, an uncompromising idealist who nevertheless was not at all naive to the manipulations and viciousness of politics.

At the outset, I suppose I was given to Frankie to punish

him for some of his prior romantic indiscretions, and to prevent him from getting himself into even worse predicaments. If so, the Senator's plan was only partly successful. Frankie bonded to me and I quickly became his favorite companion, his best buddy, the keeper of his secrets, and sometimes even his alibi when he inevitably found he'd gotten into trouble with his father once again. Yet, once I was on the scene, Frankie's eye ceased to rove quite as much, and the voracious libido that caused the press to brand him as the Senator's "trouble magnet" seemed to lessen. Then again, everything is relative.

Not that even I was able to satisfy him completely. Frankie often dragged me into threesomes and foursomes, orgies and bacchanals. Fortunately, his orientation was almost completely same-sexual, but his curiosity and his desire for new experiences was matched only by his stamina. Had things been only slightly different, and had he experimented with women, aliens or even large animals—all of which I sometimes feared he was capable of doing! —I don't think my programming would have been up to the task.

Still, I somehow managed to match his pace. After the initial shock wore off, I found Frankie's excitement contagious. I, too, began to look forward to the next, even more novel, sexual encounter. Yet, even someone as voracious as Frankie had to take an occasional break. And, when he did, I was *always* there for him. I happily joined him in his wildness; it is, after all, what I was designed to do. But when it was just the two of us, alone in his bed, his tenderness was unmatched and, though I must of necessity speak with limitations, I do not think I have ever felt more needed.

"It's just you and me, Matt," was his mantra. "Between the two of us, not much gets by, eh?"

He'd nudge me and wink playfully. Within hours I could count on being once again embroiled in some madcap and highly salacious adventure. Even then, with no forewarning, he'd break from whatever gymnastic penetration or new experience long enough to kiss me, deeply and passionately. He fancied that it was for my benefit, to let me know that he'd not forgotten I was present. But

I knew the kiss proved the exact opposite, it reassured *him* that, no matter how bizarre or stimulating his current encounter was, I would always, *always* be there to love him after it was over.

With the only exception being his father, I believe I was the sole constant in Frankie's life. I cared for him deeply; he cared for me. He was a master at creating complications, though, and I sometimes had to work very hard to keep him feeling that we were ideally suited for each other. In the early years, he was constantly testing me and, I like to think, I met all of his challenges. Once he realized that he was, above all, *safe* with me, in his own way, I think he fell in love.

It was, as I'm sure you're already aware if you've kept up with recent events, our undoing.

The Senator's strong and inflexible ethical code made him many enemies. Though he was no one's fool, and though he had long familiarity with fending off political attacks, and a consummate skill when it came to diffusing rumor, or dealing with attempts to discredit him, he never anticipated that his Colonial nemeses would dig as deeply into his son's private life as they did. Had they left off with publicly exposing Frankie's intense intimate relationship with a bioconstruct, the scandal would have been chalked up to just the latest in a long line of madcap sexual peccadillos. But once they uncovered certain aspects of my unique qualities, Senator Giordano couldn't afford to ignore the situation.

I still don't know how I was exposed. Petite Augette certainly never allowed any of her suspicions about me to leak out even though, as it turned out, she'd had more than a few inklings that I was different from her other inventory. But once it became common knowledge that a bioconstruct existed that was even partially resistant to scrubbing, there was a huge public outcry—especially when it was revealed that I was one of the Intimate Companion series. Far too many people indulged in far too many nontraditional aberrations with bioconstructs to be willing to allow even one of them to retain potentially embarrassing memories.

Frankie was devastated. He spent much of the last night we were together just holding me and weeping. I did my best to comfort him, to reassure him that he would manage somehow and that, as for me, I really didn't mind. But there are limits to even my skills.

At the time, I meant it. When the authorities told me that they'd altered the scrubs to compensate for whatever programming flaw of Owen's allowed me to retain some of my memories, I accepted their verdict meekly, calmly and without objection. My original purpose, after all, was always to serve a specific function; it was inconceivable that I could have developed needs of my own.

My only pang of regret was when I passed through Petite Augette's office on my way to the scrub room and I saw that all of my keepsakes were neatly laid out on her desk. I had no idea how long she'd known about my hidey-hole but I was grateful to her for never betraying my secret. I'd never suspected that such a physically tiny woman could shoo away the officers as efficiently as she did, but they quailed before her fierce personality.

"Please, Matthew," she asked me, once she'd secured me an hour or so of respite. "Tell me about this one. When did you get it, and from whom? What does it *mean* to you?"

I responded as best I could and, when we were finished, she said, "I know that in a very short time, it won't matter to you. You won't remember. For now, I want your mind to be at peace. I want you to know that I will cherish these things, as you have. You've served me and my family for so long, it's the least I can do."

I smiled to comfort her and to reassure her that I understood, all the while thinking how kind it was of her to take the time to try to reassure and comfort me. Madame would have been proud.

Now, as I lie here strapped to the table in the scrubbing room, part of my mind flits from cherished memory to cherished memory, possibly for the last time. In these last moments before the procedure starts, I can't help but wonder whether or not the scrub will fully take and, if it does, whether that may not be a kind of kindness of its own. As much as I presently mourn the thought of losing my memories of Frankie and Owen, of Bobby and the General, of so many others, I tell myself that if I cannot remember what's been taken from me, I cannot regret the loss.

A final thought occurs to me as I hear the faint whir of the scrubbing mechanism kick in. If the authorities are right and if they have truly corrected Owen's omissions, the most precious of my keepsakes will mean nothing to me when I awake. If I lose my memories of how I've lived, what I've done and, above all, who I've loved, I wonder... will I still be me?

# THE COSMIC FAIR

## DARREN SPEEGLE

I don't know what I expected when I answered the door to my apartment that sunless morning, but it certainly wasn't a woman in an Earth clown costume holding out an envelope to me.

"Am I being served?" I asked, staring at the thing without suspicion, or any other emotion. I didn't care much for foolishness, especially after the demanding mission I'd been on these past several months.

"More like an invitation than a summons," she said, crinkling the paint on her face with her smile.

"Invitation?"

"To the Cosmic Fair."

"Aha," I said. "Freneto sent you."

"Can't say I know a Freneto. Unless he's descended from Carolyn."

She referred to the woman who had discovered a cure for that most difficult of human challenges, cancer, a century ago. I didn't know what to make of her remark since in fact Freneto *was* a descendant of the same Carolyn and everyone who was acquainted with him knew it. So I said nothing, letting my impatience communicate for me.

"You'll find tickets enclosed, both for the fair and for travel. Other accommodations are noted in your packet."

"Look—"

"At what, man? It's an opportunity anyone would seize. Let yourself relax. You've accomplished your mission and averted a galactic war for humankind. Consider this a thank you. A thank you from someone who cares deeply about human affairs. Though she, herself, must only look on in fascination."

What in Gaia's name did that mean? Was she selling herself as an agent of a non-human? Or worse yet, was she claiming to *be* a non-human?

Now I was suspicious.

"Just come," she said. "Let it be a gift for you, Arben Vanders. Please accept it as well as your host's invitation to join her for dinner at the lounge in your hotel on the evening of your arrival. I am instructed to make the point that you will not be disappointed."

This time there was no crinkling paint, only the smooth canvas of possibility.

I said, "May I ask the name of my host."

"You wouldn't recognize it if I told you."

"Try me."

"Ia."

"Ia? That's it?"

"It's as close a translation as I can come up with. It's the name of a flower."

I shook my head, tired of strangers at the door. "I am under no obligation to go if I accept your envelope."

"Are you asking me or telling me?"

"I'm telling you. My curiosity may well be replaced by boredom by the time I've looked the packet over. Boredom or sound reason."

"Fair enough. We'll see you or we won't a few months from now."

I took the envelope but paused before closing the door to ask, "Why are you in a clown outfit?"

"It seemed ... fitting."

I let the door close without asking her to expound.

*Swirling changes on a vast holographic map. Waves upon waves of soundless, nonsensical weather patterns in the form of armies and churches and memories and intentions, banners and symbols and book pages fluttering in the strange winds of time. Marches, quests, explorations, discoveries, movements, renaissances, slaughters, atrocities, entire histories unfurling like the blood-soaked petals of some maddened cosmic flower, a woman's own flower spilling plagues upon an unsuspecting world and universe.*

*And in the center of it all, in the core of that first and last flower, a question ... a burning, never satisfied existential question ...*

*Why—*

*—do we dream?*

That's the way I described it upon waking from the dream the next morning. Those were the exact words I wrote in the pad I keep by my bed. When you've sat in a room with, when you've mediated between, your kind and two alien intelligences whose less physical attributes—how else to explain?—are more advanced, more sophisticated than our own, you tend to do such things. If you're me, that is. If you're Arben Vanders, appointed by popes and puppeteers to save the universe from itself.

I described it that way because it *felt* that way to me. In the dream, assuredly. But more importantly, *outside of it.* Coming out of my sessions with Mirilus, one of the two races in question, I sometimes felt as if I might crumble beneath the weight of its—*his?*—collective psyche, while at the same time experiencing such a sense of disorientation that I was forced to wonder how the same universe had managed to produce the both of us. That humankind had crossed the stars was a feat in itself. To find ourselves in the same room with such beings was unreal.

But this had been the most dangerous thing of all in my negotiations with them—thinking of humans as inferior. In truth we possessed a raw, utilitarian persistence, a drive almost greater than the curiosity that spawned it, that they had long ago forgotten. Not to mention our spirit, our will, our dogged defiance when confronted with obstacles, all the intangibles the other races seemed at once not to understand and to greatly admire—if not covet. Evolving into a psychically unified species must leave one regretful.

So says I, who in truth only understood them enough to know that the ancient side of them might be appealed to. That they could be approached with more than notions of order and peace.

That they could be made to remember sympathy for life, for the desperation of existence. The burden to bear for me was knowing that what I'd touched in them might have had more to do with some longing for lost individuality than for love and peace. Indeed, for what I could make of it, we were specimens to them, to be re-learned from.

Which brings me back around to the dream I had in the wake of the invitation's delivery. When mediating with Mirilus, particularly, I would return to my residence to have dreams that seemed to directly target the human condition. During these times I felt as though I was being explored for answers to my own human questions.

*What is it to persevere in the face of such odds as you have experienced as a species? Where do the drive, the spirit, the flame come from? What is your source? How came you to be? What do you want of your path that you should pursue it so diligently, so frantically, when there seems to be nothing at the end except rest from the pain you never cease to endure? Never seem to quit relishing?*

The dream with which my messenger in clown attire had left me smacked of similar stuff. Was the host she spoke of Mirilan? Was Mirilus not finished with negotiations after all?

There was only one way to know and that was to accept the invite and attend the fair.

Gaia help us our human curiosity.

I made a point of not looking in the direction of the hotel lounge as I checked in. I had three hours before I was to meet my host, and I'd no desire to prolong the wait by speculating as to the whos and whats and whys. Instead I made myself a drink in the room before I unpacked, letting the warm Irrilia relax my body, my nerves, as I hung up my clothes, hooked up the computer and holo-unit, and took a long hot shower. It hadn't been that taxing a trip, Ebula being in the same sector as the terraformed world on which I lived, in the thick of intergalactic activities, both commercial and political. But it felt as if I was releasing a year's worth of anxiety, which indeed I was, having had no break from it since the day the ambassador contacted me to sit with him and the galactic security adviser to discuss a special mission. It felt good to let all that roll off me, with nothing but another strange, mysterious, potentially life-altering meeting awaiting me now.

You're being dramatic, I told myself as I sat on the bed in my towel, wondering if I should shave—that most hated maintenance ritual—while my skin was still supple, the pores open from the steaming shower. I turned on the television, but it had nothing to advise beyond what a bomb the Cosmic Fair was going to be. *The cosmos*, it reported, *was defined as the universe considered as a whole of interconnecting parts. In that spirit was the Cosmic Fair conceived. Come experience the wonder …*

Funny that it said nothing about the fact that only a short time ago the universe was still deciding if it wanted to go to war. I loathed the media for its sensationalism. Yesterday, the greatest catastrophe the galaxy had ever known. Today, nothing on the subject at all. We'd moved on to the Fair. The Olympics. The World Cup. What were such things? Other than human, that is. Who else would presume to sponsor a *Cosmic* Fair? Gaia, but we were obvious creatures. Maybe when all was said and done, I'd write the biography. The human biography. What a tale to tell.

At that thought, a knock came at the door. I wanted to tell them to go away, but something told me I shouldn't. You're the great listener, Arben. Hear what they have to say. *Sir, may we further convenience you? Sir, you left your card at the desk. Sir, may I use your bathroom to wash the clown off my face?*

I'd risen from the bed, but now hesitated as a foreboding crawled over me. Who were these people? And why exactly was I, the diplomat, caught in their game? Could I answer their questions? Was existential a term that could be applied to all, no matter their condition of being?

"Sir, are you in? I'm with the hotel, delivering a message for Mr. Vanders."

*I'm not in!* I almost shouted. But what would that have accomplished except to start the whole anxious process all over again?

"Coming." It was less a call than a confirmation to myself that I was indeed doing that. I opened the door without looking through the peephole. If they're here and it's decided, then they're here and it's decided.

Doorknob in hand, I saw that he wasn't a she and he didn't wear a clown suit, so maybe I was safe for a little while longer.

"It's from a Freneto. No relation to Carolyn, I assume?" He smiled, but it did nothing to conceal the humorlessness of him.

"You assume wrong," I said, almost snatching the message from his hand.

He puffed off without a tip as I closed the door in my towel.

*Vanders,* I read. *You've been a bad boy, haven't you? Slipping off to Ebula without a word. Just joking, friend. I'll be expecting you downstairs in the lounge for our drink.*

Paper-delivered? Like that, really? The old fool. All this revisiting the tense past months for nothing. For a trip through the cosmic museum with the person I least wanted to see right now. The endless suggester while I'd been in mediations. Ambassador not to the League of Races, as his title stated, but to some agenda unknown to all parties, himself included. Even Mirilus had remarked as such. *Some humans are fools,* he'd put it. And he was right. Better some humans had been left in the last stage of evolution.

Cursing, I made myself another drink and sat down on the bed, re-reading the piece of worthlessness. As I did so, the words bled into each other, forming a smeary, *What in Gaia's name am I doing here? Have they no souls, the clocktickers? Game played out and won, what more do you need? What more do you need of me, you living, breathing baboons?*

But this was my own clock ticking out its response. In a deeper place I found myself not quite convinced of the message or its sender. I knew people. I knew how they themselves ticked. It was my job. It was why I'd been called to the mission in the first place. Something wasn't quite right. Something wasn't quite right about messages delivered to doors, regardless of source or content. It was archaic, medieval. It stank of purpose. And that never sat well on two glasses of Irrilia.

I did as bade and went to the lounge to cavort with mysteries.

. . .

There was no one there to receive me. Nor anyone who bore a second glance as I ordered another Irrilia, cupping it in my hands where I sat at the bar surveying the smallish crowd. Among the tables, there were four separate parties who were obviously there for the fair. At the bar, a male couple intimately talking and touching; and at the other end, a nondescript woman searching for something inside her drink. I considered looking around the lobby, but to what purpose? If they wanted me, they would find me.

When they didn't within the next few minutes, I grew increasingly annoyed despite the tranquilizing properties of the Irrilia. Did I have time for this bullshit? (I was something of a word historian, and that obsolete term seemed to fit the situation all too perfectly.) Would I sit here and wait, for the satisfaction of unknown others?

"You didn't buy it, did you?"

I started, spilling a little of my drink on my leg. I'd been looking out into the lobby, or rather the space between, when she'd stolen up on me. Observing her now, I realized there was nothing nondescript about her except the absence of paint.

"Lady, what is your game?"

"I like reactions. It's what I do, in a way."

"And it was for a reaction that you sent a message to my room from the ambassador?"

"Is a clown not allowed her pranks?"

I started to answer, to give her my standard objection to people wasting my time, but decided to hold my tongue in favor of taking in the unmasked clown. She was a rather small woman, not delicate by any means, but light. Appeared to be in her mid-thirties, but might as easily have been late twenties or early forties. Her face was mildly attractive, in a plain sort of way, with features neither soft nor stern, though her mouth, her smile, was warm as she measured me up at the same time. Her blondish hair fell around her face loosely, naturally, appearing absent of any of the treatments so common among the fairer sex these days. Nor did she wear any makeup except for the suggestion of shadow. But it was her eyes I was interested in. That's where the person resided—in the eyes.

Previously, I'd known only crinkles. Little spiderwebbing cracks in the mask she'd chosen for herself. Viewing her in her stripped-down state was a much less frustrating experience.

If that's what you could call it. When it came down to searching her otherwise average brown eyes for intent, purpose, identity, I found that their depths could not be penetrated. Or rather that the person lived too deep in there to be disturbed. Yet it was somewhat intoxicating looking. Like bathing in another form of the drink I held in my hand. Like she knew something, maybe, that I had forgotten to consider. I'd have used the word secret if it wasn't such a cliché. Though that wasn't quite right either—

"Are you going to continue to sit there and stare at me or will you offer to buy me a drink?"

"Yes, of course." Then: "No—wait. I'll not be mesmerized by you."

She laughed, a less than musical, more than routine thing.

"That's what I'm doing? Mesmerizing you? Why, that's almost romantic, Arben Vanders."

I lifted my drink, intending to sip but finishing it all in a gulp. "Would you do me the service of providing your name before we go any further?"

"I believe I've told you already, silly person."

"You mean *you* are Ia?"

She smiled. "How very flattering that you remember."

"How very," I echoed, feeling slightly disoriented.

*No don't be*, I felt in my skin, my body, my brain.

I stared at her, probed her fathomless eyes. "Is that..."

*Me talking? Of course, Arben Vanders. It was me talking from the beginning, wasn't it?*

I felt my head moving from left to right, right to left. A habit. A human trait. "Then you *are* a non-human."

"I wouldn't say that exactly," came the spoken word to my ear. "I don't exactly fit the description of an alien, do I?" She smiled. Adding, "Perish the term."

I took in a long, deep breath, turned to get the bartender's attention. "Another please."

"He means two," Ia corrected.

"Yes, sorry. Make it two."

*But not too much, Arben. There are things to see, wonders to behold.*

"Who *are* you?" I said. Words sounding like they'd come straight out of a holoplay script. "I mean…why toy with me? Be forward. Tell me what it is you want and let's be on with it. Is this to do with the Axena Pact? With those negotiations? Are you a thing of Mirilus?"

Again, her not-quite-routine laughter. *I am a thing of Ia, Arben Vanders. I am a thing of Ia.*

I stroked my forehead. "I need to go to my room after this drink, Ia. Will you be here later?"

"An excellent idea. Let's go to your room to continue our conversation."

"I said *I* need to go—"

"Don't be that way, Arben. Either we're in this together or we're not."

"I don't like feeling controlled."

"Hush! I have never done that."

My turn to laugh—and it, too, seeming not-quite-regular. "Oh? That's not what you've been doing from the beginning?"

She waved dismissively. "Beginnings? *Phff.* They're overrated if you ask me."

I'd nothing to say to that so didn't as I watched the bartender finish preparing our drinks.

"Last one," Ia said as she took the glass. "Okay? At least until we get to the room…?"

I paid the bartender before turning back to her. "If your intent is to do me in, you're too late. The pact has been signed. The war has been…" I let it taper away, knowing it must sound like so much whimpering to a being such as her.

*'Yea, one such as I, by the road that leads thence.'*

"That is my favorite poem," I said, startled.

*'A man as from war in the profoundest sense.'*

"Please stop," I said, drinking deeply of the Irrilia.

*'The rages of winter, and winter's allies…'*

"'All traded away for the soldier grown wise.' Yeah, so what's the point, Ia? How does this relate to anything?"

"It doesn't. That's what makes it, and humankind as a whole, so fascinating!" She partook of her own drink. "It's all so bloody random, isn't it? But then again, it isn't!"

"Riddles. You've been speaking in riddles—"

"Hence the clown costume," she smiled.

"—from the start."

"And?"

"And I've asked you to speak straight."

She pursed her lips, nodding. "I understand your need for answers. I do. But I must let the exhibit speak for itself."

I drank. Then drank again. "You have an exhibit at the fair?"

"That's why we're here, isn't it?"

"Gaia save us all."

This time her laughter was all too genuine. "Gaia! When did we replace the word God with Earth's own name? It's like the humans to behave so, isn't it? First we worship the moon and the sun and the stars, then some superhuman breed, then some abstract concept, then one of the universe's spherical bodies again. What choice stuff!"

"You laugh at us as though we're nothing to you."

"But you're everything, don't you see? Why does your flame burn brightest, my struggling little man? Because you are what you are! I'd give a thousand of my kind for one of yours in a heartbeat."

So now we were coming to it, finally. Our kind and their kind. She had to be an agent of Mirilus. I'd known it from the start—

*You are so far off track it hurts, Arben Vanders. Literally hurts my old worn-out heart.*

"Let's go to the room," I said. "I feel naked here, in front of God and everybody."

"There you go," she said, winking. "Let's give God his diligent due."

If I've said I don't like being controlled, it's because I indeed do not like being controlled. Yet here I was, her thing. A sad sort of footnote to what I'd thought I had accomplished in my interracial mediations. That she was Mirilus now was certain to me. But I could not resist her. I must know more about her, about inhuman species who were fascinated by the human concept. My job in mediations had been to mediate, if not to *represent* my kind. Sure, the military commanders, the government officials, had been present. But I had *spoken* for humankind. I had been allowed to take such liberties when it became apparent that the other sides responded to me. What I had not been allowed to do, what it had never occurred to me to do because of the gravity of the matter, was to explore this fascination on the part of our would-be enemies.

Thus I took the time now, as we sat about the room, drinks in hand, to attempt to get something out of my circumstances, my clear disadvantage. She was waiting for it, for whatever I had, but in the most amiable way. How small I seemed to myself, as she fielded my hasty, inane questions.

"Why such...I don't know...*shyness*?" I was saying now. "Why not just come out and ask the questions? At times during the Axena negotiations I felt as though I was being not just probed, but manipulated. Conned even. And in a way that suggested they were playing me for the fool they knew assuredly I was not. It was a strange game, to say the least."

"But that's it, isn't it?" she said, leaning back on her hand on the bed. "You've answered your own question. They wanted you to know what they were up to. Why? That's a question you would have to ask them, but it seems to me that perhaps they were gauging you, feeling out their enemy for the way he might respond in the situation of war."

I leaned forward in my chair, which I'd turned to face out from the desk. "And yet they seemed to know in advance how I would respond. Though, admittedly, I surprised them at times."

"An example?"

"Well, at one point Mirilus asked me if being human meant being at war. It was an oversimplified way of looking at things, but I think that was intended too. I gave it some thought before answering. When I did the words just came of their own. My thinking process had nothing to do with them. 'Being human,' I said, 'means preparing for the worst even when the best seems far more likely. Being human is hanging on to a rope that is going to break, again and again, regardless. It is in our nature to create situations, circumstances, that we must then struggle to find a way out of.' He then asked if my words might be interpreted to say the problems we were at the table to resolve were of human making. I said, 'Beyond any doubt. If there is no knot to untangle, then we will surely make one.'

"The table was silent for several seconds then the third party, Ogoen, spoke up. 'I like your answer,' he said. 'But what it says for humankind is bleak.' 'Not at all,' I said. 'We humans are the great resister of tides, be they calm or rough. It is our way of dealing with the weathers of the universe. It's my belief that if this were not our innate attitude, we would long ago have become extinct.' As I sat back, showing my hands, I saw Mirilus's eyes light up, maybe for the second or third time during the exchange. He'd zeroed in on something, and that something was to do with the both of us, if you understand me."

"Let's say I don't," Ia said.

I smiled. "Don't you?"

"You are mistaken, my child. I am not Mirilus. Mirilus once knew my kind, and I his, but that was long ago. When I had a kind."

I swallowed the last of my—fourth?—drink. "How do I know you're not coming at me from an angle, like he did in mediations?"

"You don't, do you? Make me one too please. But let's do cut it off then. If your nerves are dead, then my exhibit will be dead to you."

Perhaps a little inebriated, I said. "I would like to have known you under other circumstances."

"Other circumstances. That's funny coming from a human who's just stated that he creates his own circumstances."

I winked at her and refreshed our drinks.

When we'd both visited the bathroom before returning to our seats, I said, with very deliberate words, "What is so fascinating about us, Ia? Why not just wipe us off the face of the universe? It is within the power of both Mirilus and Ogdoen. Maybe yourself as well, for all I know. Be done with us. Take what you want from our remnants. Our record of deeds and misdeeds. I understand we're specimens, but we're also dangerous specimens. Catch us off guard. Do what must be done while the doing's doable. Otherwise you've a beast on your hands that literally cannot be tamed or tempered. Already, we've spread ourselves across a third of the galaxy. Will you live with beings like us? But to know what we're made of? Seems to me there's an extensive enough record without needing the physical specimen."

She was shaking her head, looking as befuddled as a face like hers could achieve. "Arben, that's one of the strangest trains of thought I've ever listened to. A mouse doesn't' think like that when it's being experimented on. A monkey doesn't think like that. You're putting yourself in the mind of your potential adversary. Yes, I understand generals do that in war. But with you it's different …it's as if you're embarrassed to be human—"

"That's entirely not so."

"Wait. I'm not finished. It's as if you're embarrassed to be human while at the same time tempting the fates. Now's who's going about it slyly? Or is this the way humans protect themselves? By putting yourselves in position to fail so that you might have something to overcome? You're beyond me, child. Little did the universe know when those protein molecules danced their dance, that this particular brand of life would be so…outstanding! Bravo, you. Do your thing!"

I chuckled. "So what is it then? You seem to know us pretty well. What is it that sets us apart?"

"It's your *energy*, man! Your crazy, mystical energy!"

This time I laughed out loud. "You sound like a twentieth-century hippie." Another lost word awakened.

"Wouldn't happen to have some of that Earth weed on you?"

"No, ma'am. Sorry," I said, smile still dominating. "But seriously, what about us, Ia? I don't know what your motivations or intentions are, but I suspect you could weigh in on the subject."

"My motivations and intentions, Arben, are to see you safe.

Believe what you will, but that's the truth. Do I do this to learn from you? To acquire something from you? Hardly. As my exhibit will show, our relationship is far more complicated than that. And yet so simple, really. But to your question." She paused to sip her drink. To watch me as she found her words. "You did very well in explaining it yourself in your mediations. For me, I would put it like this: As we evolve as species, we lose certain things, among them our individuality. For humans, it is no different, except that the process is slower, there are greater hurdles to climb. I know the reason why but cannot articulate it to you in words, or even in thought. What I can communicate to you, is that you were, as a species, born in a less natural way. In a faster, more chaotic way. If you took those protein molecules I was talking about, added to them some natural order, some Darwinian spices, and then shook the whole bit up in a shaker, you'd come up with something that just might, if the stars were aligned right, survive one era of history on a world like Earth. But if there were one other small ingredient, a gift say, from someone who loved you, you might have enough to get through it. Through the great changes that swept your world. You were given such a gift, Arben Vanders, by someone who dearly wanted his experiment to succeed. Who—"

"Whoa. Did you say 'experiment?'"

"For lack of a better word. Perhaps loneliness better describes his reasons."

"He?"

"Your God, Arben. Could it all have happened by chance? Could you possess something so coveted through evolution alone? Or mightn't there have been other forces at work?"

"What other forces? What God?"

"Imagine two species, compatible in every way—"

"You're making this up. Show me this God."

"I cannot. He's dead."

"What?"

"Mirilus took him. Before you were born."

I stared at her, mouth dragging at my feet.

"It is truth, Arben. Mirilus took him for the very reason he is watching you now. To find some lost something."

"But what kind of God?" Was I drunk? "A creator?"

"More a geneticist. The cosmos is not all that mystical when it's broken down to the cellular level."

"And I'm simply to believe this?"

"Believe what you will. You asked the question. I've answered it."

"But—"

"There are no buts, child. Buts are a human thing. It is what it is, and if you want more, then let me escort you to the exhibit and we can call it a day."

"Why me? Why am I so favored?"

"The way you handled your negotiations, of course. Who but you. I've been waiting for you for a long time, Arben Vanders."

We passed through corridors of night and day, galaxies within galaxies, worlds within worlds. Mirilus was represented. So was Ogdoen. So were so many other realities more specific to the world that had sponsored this strange and grand enchantment. It was a sensual feast, our Cosmic Fair, and from so many perspectives, such diverse tastes. It was like the Louvre on Earth, far too much to take in, yet a sin not to try.

I cannot say for sure when the other exhibits gave over to hers, for I was dreaming strange and wondrous dreams, seeing swirling changes on a globe, a galaxy, a universe—

*Waves upon waves of soundless, nonsensical weather patterns in the form of armies and churches and memories and intentions, banners and symbols and book pages fluttering in the strange winds of time. Marches, quests, explorations, discoveries, movements, renaissances, slaughters, atrocities, entire histories unfurling like the blood-soaked petals of some maddened cosmic flower, a woman's own flower spilling plagues upon an unsuspecting world and universe.*

—a pool of liquid in which swam things that the world was yet to know. In them I saw him, the one to whom cathedrals had been built, working delicately at the parts which had come from *her*, his mate, his other, as she found my hand and placed it, symbolically, first on her belly, then on the flower from which she had taken her name—

*And in the center of it all, in the core of that first and last flower, a question . . . a burning, never satisfied existential question . . .*

Why, Ia—

—did you dream?

# UNITY OF AFFECT

## JASON V BROCK

### I

*We see the demon god Pazuzu bring its hand down, pushing hook-taloned fingers into the eye sockets of a screaming soldier. With the other hand, the deity tightens its grip on the fighter; pulling up, the man's head breaks open after a moment with a subdued, liquid pop—like a filbert crushed by a nutcracker. As the dying warrior's shrieks abate into convulsed heaving, the demon scoops out mounds of bloody gray matter, devouring it eagerly. The scene fades to blackness.*

GAME OVER

Andrew Gates reached up to adjust the sound on his headset. "Damn." He pulled the wireless Oculus Rift-style headgear off, examining it for a moment before he tossed it onto the table. To himself: "Graphics are great, but the frame rate's still a little shaky. And something just doesn't...*feel* right."

He glanced at the wall clock: 7:28 P.M. He had been playing for nearly three hours, the heatless radiance of the monitor lighting his exhausted features. He rubbed his eyes, letting his shoulders relax after tense hours of using gameplay gestures; Pazuzu's black, lifeless orbs stared back at him from behind the thin skin of his eyelids, phosphenes dancing beneath his fingertips as he massaged away the strain. Cheri was going to be irritated with him, he knew; he had promised to be home by seven most nights this week.

He stood, stretching for a moment as he watched the screensaver fade into view: A color-shifting Mandelbrot set fractalizing from the infinitesimally small to the cosmically grand forever. He was the only one left in the testing room. "I'll make it up to her tomorrow."

## II

*I'll call you later, went to the show with Airika & Jack. We'll be late. Dinner is in the fridge. XOXO – C*

Andrew returned the note to the kitchen counter. He felt terrible—Cheri had been so tolerant with his unpredictable schedule during the entire development of *Pazuzu's Reign*. Sometimes he thought he was unworthy of her patience. Nevertheless, the rewards of this particular contract outweighed the time demands for the moment. Now that the game was on track for Alpha release and The Pentagon had approved all the scenarios, the funds were beginning to flow. His team was nearly thirty months in on what would ultimately be the most realistic virtual combat multiplayer online role playing game on the planet using Andrew's patented HYPN/OS gaming platform. Once it was implemented, tested to the satisfaction of DARPA, and fully compliant with Distributed Interactive Simulation standards, he would be free to take some vacation. *Maybe Curaçao*... In another few years, they could retire early.

He opened the refrigerator and took stock, but had no appetite, instead opting for a glass of Baco Noir and downtime with a book.

"But first, a shower."

# III

He awoke to the sound of screaming: His own.

"Andrew! *Andrew!* Are you okay?"

*He recoiled from Cheri's touch with a cry, still trapped in the wispy edges of the nightmare. For a moment he forgot to breathe, then took in a deep lungful of air with a gasp. Sweeping his fingers through the tangle of damp hair on his head, he noticed he was shaking. "I-I'm okay. I'm okay..." Andrew rubbed his face, the stubble rough on his palms, the sweat on his body growing cold.*

"What happened?" Even in the gloom, he could make out the concern on her gamine features as his eyes adjusted to the dim illumination from the bathroom nightlight. Sitting up, she gathered the sheet around her ample breasts; the delicate skin of her nude body seemed to glow with a milky inner luminescence.

He shook his head, trying to clear the terrible images of death and mutilation from his mind. "I've been going at it too hard... At least I can work from home starting next week. We'll finally be at a code freeze stage, just testing and debugging. But the things the Feds want us to simulate... They're... let's just say they're not pleasant."

She reached out again, taking his hand in her own; her skin was smooth, inviting, her voice low, sleepy, "Want to talk about it, sweetie?"

Andrew looked away, out the narrow bedroom window to the somnolent world outside. "No... It's better if we just let it go. I'll try to balance the workload more now that we're hitting some reasonable milestones." He smiled and gently squeezed her hand, changing the topic. "How was the show?"

Cheri shrugged, drowsily touching her thick red tresses. "It was fine. Would have been nicer if you guys had been there, but Jack had to work late, too, so it was just me and Airika. Lots of dudes staring at us, trying to work their game, you know. Of course, we just giggled at them from the bar. Kind of flattering, but some of them had on *way* too much makeup... And *way* too many pounds!" She put her hand to her upturned lips, as though she had shared the world's most appalling secret. "Once Nine Inch Nails hit the stage, all was right with the world, though."

Andrew laughed at the image of aging industrial rock fans in tight pleather and pancake. "I have no doubt. I'm surprised you guys can even still hear!"

"Well, we did have earplugs! Besides, we decided to leave before the last encore to avoid the traffic coming home... God! How old are we now, right? Leaving before a show's even over!" She cozied up to him on the bed. "Besides, we wanted to get home to our menfolk." She swirled her fingers through the hair on his toned chest and stomach, nuzzling his neck. "Mmmm... Besides, you're the best looking man I've ever seen; tonight only proved that to me again." She removed the sheet barrier between them, her voluptuous body warm and soft next to his.

"Fantastic," he replied, kissing her throat as he caressed her, taking in her bouquet. "That's a relief to hear."

# IV

*Flying over the desert scene like some visage straight from the underworld city of Dis, we see Pazuzu fix its dark, glassy eyes on the man—reflecting back his fear and shock in the twin black globes of a bottomless gaze. With a great swoop of double wings, it maneuvers near the petrified soldier, blotting out the sun as it grows closer. The demon's hideous countenance—part lion, part wild dog—gnashes its crooked teeth with an audible clack, its scorpion-like, segmented tail furiously whipping the cloudless sky.*

*The legionnaire says nothing, just watches in captivated awe, his rifle heavy and dangling by his side as the demon morphs back and forth in a protean display of terrifying physical control: As the beast overtakes him, details reveal themselves by turn. First, the creature is a hideous lion-dog... then the soldier's mother—her wrinkled, unclothed body desiccated and roasting in the blazing noonday heat; after that, it transforms into the grotesque appearance of some subconscious half-memory of a creature out of Poe, or perhaps a terrible alien deity created by H. P. Lovecraft—the features mutable, blending together in smears.*

"Shoot!" *The fighter is startled out of his trance. His MORPHEUS unit is damaged; we hear that this is coming from his helmet earpiece. Once more, a hollow voice crackles over the channel:* "Fucking shoot, Gates!"

"Infidel!" *the creature roars. We see that it is now in the shape of a mucid, quivering multilimbed monstrosity standing only a few hundred yards away, reeking of corruption and sewage. It seems much larger than just moments before, as though gaining power from his mounting terror. We sense that Gates now grasps that it is more than something inhabiting a desert landscape; it seems, in the mental cosmology it increasingly fills, as though its looming, corporeal vastness has become a geologic feature which actually encompasses the space they occupy instead of the reverse.*

*We hear, over a soundtrack of Middle Eastern polyrhythms, as Gates's heart hammers in time to the ground quaking footshock of the great beast lumbering toward him, its black eyes shimmering in the heat. We see a camouflaged, armor-plated transport drive into view, approaching the colossus; several men leap from the still moving vehicle, firing fully automatic Barrett REC7s and screaming in the dusty, surreal montage. Still paralyzed, Gates stares in horror while the massive creature reaches down through the heatwaves and grabs the soldiers, unfazed by the withering gunfire being laid down. One-by-one, we see it pluck the men from the battlefield—crushing them to a bloody pulp, or grinding them up in its massive jaws. It smashes a great fist onto the truck, which explodes into a fireball, then hurls it away without effort, leaving only an arc of oily black smoke as the twisted wreck disappears on the horizon. The cloying aroma of roasting flesh mingles with gasoline, flowering in our nostrils as we watch the remaining men from the truck—now consumed in an inferno—try to crawl stiffly through the burning sand; at last they collapse, little more than fiery skeletons, pieces of their charred skin carried away on the wind as ash.*

*We can clearly see that in a few strides the monster will be upon Gates. Additional backup arrives in the form of Apache attack helicopters and supplementary armored personnel trucks. Swatting the copters from the sky like gnats, the great being crushes the vehicles underfoot; returning to its fearsome Pazuzu aspect, we watch the thing stare at Gates—who is still rooted to the spot, stunned by the horrific display, but also beginning to feel strangely placid, even relaxed.*

"Shoot the fucker, Gates!"

*Again, we hear a thunderous exclamation from above shatter the dry air:* "Andrew Gates! I live! Infidel!"

*At last, we see the titan's shadow fall on him, yet he is still unable to—*

"*—move!*" Andrew shouted as he jerked into consciousness. His breathing was hard, ragged; the pressure on his face strange, claustrophobic. His pillow was covering his head; pulling it away, he reached up to knead his eyes with numb fingers.

He looked over to where Cheri should have been: There was nothing in the bed except a tangle of clammy bedclothes. Glancing over to the bedroom window, he thought he saw something enormous—something dreadful—move outside. He climbed out of bed and quietly walked to the bathroom; the door was closed, light trickling under the doorframe. Andrew placed his ear to the door, thinking he heard someone speaking behind it:

"*...getting worse. You know, it's how we keep you divided—quite easy really: first by politics, then by religion, then by race and social class...I live ...Keep you scared, keep you conforming—wait, I heard something. Just a minute.*"

Andrew pulled away, turning back to the bed: *Something's wrong.* The voice behind the door was not Cheri, yet it *was* oddly familiar. He moved across the dark room, again noting movement from the small window—*the window which now appeared to be on the wrong side of the room,* he thought.

"*Infidel!*" It was the voice of the woman in the bathroom, but it was also *not* her voice; it was a much more sinister utterance: *Guttural.* The door burst open behind him, but he refused to look—certain only that insanity would follow.

He kept running toward the bed, his heart beating fast, his lungs aching from the suddenly frosty air in the room...but the faster he ran, the more the bed seemed to recede into the distance...

*now we see Andrew approaching the speed of light: Each step he takes seems like an eternity... and now, time dilates, ba l loooons...*

*to*

*a*

*near stop.*

*Every breath takes a **billion** years to gasp, andanother billion to* **exhale**, *and the cosmos beg inStosp in overandoverIS*

       *he tumblingOrSTILLnot*.........*aBLeTO mo v e*...

                      *t r y to to scr e **ammmmmmmmi***             ***ng nnnnoooooooooooooow—***

## V

"So when I came around, there I was with Cheri in the bedroom, the headset on, sort of jabbering all this crazy stuff. I'd actually barricaded the bathroom door! I think it was the 'waking R.E.M.' phenomenon that Pacific Data Systems ran into," Andrew said to his boss at Distributed Interactive Simulation, Jerad Clark. "Felt like a sort of false awakening. In this case a special type of false awakening even, called a 'continuum' where I had fallen asleep in the sim, then thought it had ended, but I was still sleeping. Cheri said it was more than me just thrashing around...*she* thought I was awake, pranking her. But the fact is, I was never really awake; I just dreamed I was. She woke me up by pulling the headset off, finally."

Jerad sat back in his chair, forming a temple with his fingers. Afternoon sunlight dappled his office with gently swaying shadows from the trees outside as he regarded Andrew from the top of his wireframe eyeglasses. "I read about that in the PDS acquisition files. That was the thing Vincent was working on with that young lady...Drago something?"

"Dragonović. Svetlana Dragonović. She was the one he killed before he shot himself. They were working on MISTY for PDS when DIS bought them out."

Jerad pursed his lips in recollection. "That's right. Been a while. Such a tragedy about that whole situation...but, getting back to the matter at hand, what's the cause? Can you isolate the issue?"

Andrew nodded. "I think I understand it, yes. I mean, our team has taken this *way* further than the proprietary VR stuff that PDS created. There are bound to be things that crop up, just like with them. Here, in our newest simulated environs, we *were* using these super-detailed avatars to represent the 'enemy threat' in Syria or Iraq. They were fighters practically indistinguishable from real people; the landscapes, vehicles and so on were intensive models as well."

Jerad swiveled in his chair as he listened. "You mentioned problems, though—"

"Exactly. I changed that a little; before, with the old code, the virtual reality environs, the action, the modelling was great, so we kept it. We also kept the renders of our guys as shooters so they could continue relating to one another as they would in a real firefight, and strengthened the control mechanics, such as the shared real-time biofeedback, and the oneirolinguistics."

Jerad stopped him. "Remind me?"

"That's the wholly mental comm device we developed, MORPHEUS; it mimics dream communication while awake by tapping R.E.M.-type brainwaves."

Jerad looked confused. "How…?"

"It's a helmet addition, a chipset, that permits short-distance telepathic speech undetectable by outsiders. It amplifies thoughts when the user makes a determined effort to communicate."

Jerad nodded, motioning for Andrew to carry on.

"All that was good to go; where the problems arose in the previous build were with the 'enemy combatants'—avatars which were apparently rendered so realistically that it pulled our testers out of the scenario; instead of *immersion*, it seemed to tip off the observer that they were in a simulation. As a result, they drifted toward the uncanny valley effect, which changed their behavior in less predictable ways.

"So now," Andrew continued, leaning forward to grab a pen and paper off Jerad's desk. He wrote a list of the items as he spoke: "I've fixed that problem, as I suggested to you at the time, by introducing an 'enemy' that isn't as 'real'; so I went with physically intimidating amalgamations of demons, mythic beings, aliens ... like Pazuzu, Grendel, Cthulhu, and so on, then added culturally-sensitive bits of the person's *actual* personal background based on our preliminary questionnaires—stuff about their families, religious beliefs/imagery, bad personal experiences, phobias and the like—all pulled from the interviews. Then I randomized all of it with an AI script I wrote in PS-VRML to avoid the worst pitfall that PDS reported—the Artificially Aggregated Sentience effect, where a memory leak caused characters in the VR realm to become self-aware; it was an easy thing to remedy, actually, just a bit of code to modulate the signal-to-noise threshold in the sim environment..."

Jerad squinted his eyes as he tried to follow.

Andrew chuckled. "Sorry, got a little carried away. So, *anyway,* the upshot is that we're able to get our participants into a 'suspension of disbelief' headspace more quickly by feeding into this 'subliminal' stuff, using their real life against them in a sense, while avoiding the problems PDS ran into—"

"Does that actually *work?*" Jerad interrupted. Andrew raised his hand to silence him, then smiled.

"I know—it's counterintuitive. Making it look *less* like, say, Osama bin Laden, or a member of the Taliban or Daesh, and *more* like a continually shifting 'monster from the id.' But, as I can attest, *it works,* man! Think of it like this: You go see one of those old movies with the stop-motion animation by Ray Harryhausen—*Jason and the Argonauts,* or *Clash of the Titans*—and you're on the edge of your seat, right? You go see something with more 'realistic' CGI— the recent *War of the Worlds* or the Keanu *Day the Earth Stood Still,* for example—and your mind refuses to accept it. For buildings, vehicles and such it's fine; for the human figures and avatars, you lose engagement, and we *must* have that—*total engagement.* Complete control of the heart *and* the mind."

"But you said you'd been having these sleep issues now, correct?" Jerad asked, rubbing a day's growth on his chin. "Is that a side effect of this immersive stuff, of tinkering with the subconscious? And is that going to hinder us in the implementation department? I mean, why would someone return to a situation that's so frightening that it interferes with sleep?"

Andrew relaxed into his seat, sighing in thought. "Yeah, it's a bit of an issue, I won't lie. It's too much. But I suspect I now understand the mechanism; I even ran it past Marni, the neuropsychologist here. See, we're right in this sweet spot—or we want to be, at least—between *reality*, and *belief*. In reality, the 'good' past was never as great as we think we remember it; and the future can be much worse than we want to believe. So we need to blunt expectations of *both*. That's what we're trying to accomplish. We need the past to seem a little worse than the future with respect to combat scenarios and the like, but the future can't be so incredibly optimistic that we become unrealistic in our assessment of danger, whether to ourselves or others. That could make some folks reckless."

Jerad nodded again. "Yeah, I agree. But what's the point here?" He glanced at the clock on his desk.

"The point," Andrew continued, "is we're trying to dull those emotional reactions not with *reason*—which can work against our overall logistical goals sometimes, or even be countered by various mental approaches—with what I have come to term 'Socially Induced Apathy,' or SIA. We use past actions and context to create the future reactions we desire. It's a way to negate fear, or pity, or overconfidence, or nostalgia where it's not wanted. I think it can be targeted. Could be used in therapy for PTSD, too, but I honestly see it as a tool for hostile engagement, more realistically."

Jerad held his hands up, his brow furrowed: "Socially Induced Apathy? What is it?"

Andrew sat forward again, his gaze intense as he spoke. "Not to be too Orwellian, but it's tied to something first observed by the writer Edgar Allan Poe. He developed this concept called 'the unity of effect'—all the pieces of a story or poem work together to build to a climax a little at a time. Brick-by-brick, you might say."

"Okay, I remember that."

"Right, so with SIA, I think we can do a sort of meta-analysis of reality and, bit-by-bit through extreme stimulus/exposure, create what I call 'the unity of *affect*'—in other words, we can *flatten* emotional responses through intensive contact with violent or pornographic depictions—images as virus, infecting mind-to-mind, bypassing biology and personality. Also, it exploits the old notion of 'the dose makes the poison': The more intensely our personnel experience this stuff, the more we disrupt their mental defenses, and the greater the internal resolve they'll have to muster to be able to 'move' themselves into other mental/emotional states. Their excitability level will have been lowered and they become in effect 'emotionally neutered.' This way, we can calculate a 'dosage': a reaction threshold. Hence the 'induced apathy.' I call it 'social,' as it's been happening on the Internet for *years*, but in crude, random, and unfocused ways."

"Really? Like—"

"Well, we can see a little of this 'flattening of affect' in popular culture. A sort of crudeness, a coarsening. Potty humor in TV and movies. Add to that a *blandness*—Katy Perry, Disney-fication, Justin Bieber…all *that* shit. That's one part. On the flipside, we see things like 'snuff' websites such as *CharonBoat.com* or *Rotten.com*, and before that the VHS tapes like the mockumentary *Faces of Death* or, much worse, the real stuff in *Traces of Death*. I mean, even in-the-news death cults like Daesh do this on their Twitter accounts and YouTube channels. They desensitize and manipulate people with editing techniques, iconic imagery, music and sound—high production values, in other words—which opens up an avenue …a *gateway* of sorts into the mind, where they—*we*, as content creators—can re-form ingrained responses, change conceptions of right/wrong, good/bad. Even flip 'em by eroding that psychic interface, breaking down personal boundaries…It's a type of mind control, in essence; call it 'matter over mind.' Hopefully it doesn't let anything out! Just kidding…sort of. Anyway, there's a kind of dark allure, a taboo-breaking aspect; people are attracted to it, even though they're disturbed by it. They're also fascinated, aroused—in every sense of the term."

Jerad's eyebrows arched. "Really? How so?"

Andrew jotted down another thought before continuing. "See, kids these days are raised online, right? Cell phones, tablets, the Internet, blah-blah-blah... The old ways, how we were brought up, are fading. And *fast*. They're jaded, bored by the things that we thought were cool or interesting growing up. As a result, we've entered into this uncharted sociocultural era; we're now starting to see new legends spring up, a kind of 'digital folklore'—Slender Man, Ted the Caver's blog, "Pale Luna" and other creepypastas— memes and themes that behave *remarkably* like oral traditions in the way they circulate online. What we want to do is harness that, but instead of a single mind doing the work, we'll have a collective creating the experience. A hive mind. I mean, there's a whole Dark Web out there we could exploit. Silk Road and stuff you can only get from I2P or other darknets using programs like Tor anonymizing software—another pie DARPA had its fingers in, incidentally. Strangely, there was a game exploring this very notion which bubbled up into the mainstream not too long ago: *Sad Satan*. Later, some questioned its authenticity, but it had a certain cache, a mystique, because of its origins in the Deep Web. But that's just stuff not crawled by search engines; the Dark Web is an even more extreme resource we can tap."

"Did you access it? *Sad Satan*, I mean? Is there something we can reverse engineer for our purposes?" Jerad asked, a hint of a smile on his face.

Andrew nodded. "Yeah, we looked at it... There was disturbing shit in it, no doubt—pedophilia, real death imagery, avatars perpetrating atrocities... it even had scenarios where the avatars would try to rape or torture you, then commit suicide if you stopped them. They had a kind of autonomy that I hadn't seen before, a life of their own, so to speak. It was some sick shit. Extreme. Of course, everyone knows that exposure to extreme material, whether on porn sites or whatever, sort of 'inoculates' one against it in the future. You need more and greater stimulus to achieve the same level of gratification or disturbance, as it makes one increasingly indifferent to the plight of the 'Other'; it trains the mind to forego empathizing, to accept suffering, to accept even dire personal consequences, or work against one's own personal self-interest."

Jerad leaned forward, intrigued. "How does the stimulus accomplish this?"

"Well, the exposure has to be continual, or the 'inurement effect' wears off. That's why, if we *control* it, we can modulate the flattening of the *affect*, create a way to govern a person's *will*—and therefore their *willingness* to do and accept things they normally wouldn't...," the wind gusted outside as Andrew paused to let his words take hold. "Consider it a kind of social control 'rehearsal' mechanism to guarantee an 'agreement of predictable actions,' even in the initially *un*willing. I mean, you've played the game a few times, demoed it for the higher-ups here and there—"

"Scared the hell out of them. And me!"

"Right, well, that's the point, but there's more to it, when used as I've been explaining, with long-term exposure. For example, we could use it as a tactic for gleaning information: It has the potential to be much more powerful than waterboarding or other, messier interrogation options for strengthening the resolve of the good guys, think SERE training—"

"Or for breaking the bad guys," Jerad said. He tapped his fingers on the desk, thoughtful. "SIA, huh? Unity of Affect. I like this. And you're saying your new approach is hitting that, eh? But the nightmares? That seems unpredictable—"

Andrew nodded. "Agreed. As I mentioned a minute ago, the crux is that it's been almost *too* successful. It's terrifying—*overly stimulating*, instead of desensitizing. But this is just a detail to be sorted out; we fix *that*, and we can then use this unintended side issue it presents as a way to degrade hardened fighters. Break the enemy more quickly. Fits in neatly with other deprivation solutions; we could also use it to *heighten* their fears and generate *psychic trauma*—program and personalize this to an individual's fears, their unique 'terror signature.' And the good part: *No visible scars*."

Jerad nodded. "Okay. I'm with you. We have to wrap this up. I need to get to the DARPA meeting today and update everyone on your progress. I'll try to buy you another few weeks. Good work, Andrew."

# VI

[ What's happening, Andersen? ] *Gates asks.*

*We hear Andersen reply via MORPHEUS:* [ Not seeing anything, Sarge. Routine recon. I checked in with Wagner and Schultz a few minutes ago. All's well. ]

[ Looks like bugs are working out], *Gates replies. As the sun drops below the horizon, Gates feels relief. After weeks of battling resistance, finally they have made headway against Pazuzu and his supporters.*

[ Sarge, Wagner just MORPH'd me—says he got some real useful stuff about an upcoming event from a captive back at base. Pazuzu shit.]

[ Roger that ], *Gates replies.* [ See you back at camp. ]
*Three hours later.*

*We see that darkness has engulfed the region. The desert is cooling; overhead, a canopy of stars glimmers down on the encampment. The four soldiers have gathered after dinner and are debriefed about Wagner's information from the enemy combatant. It is decided to regroup and set out early. Everyone retires for the night as—*

Andrew sits up in the dark. He looks over at Cheri: The bedside is empty. He looks toward the bathroom; light seeps under the doorframe.

Getting up, he walks past the small window: There is a full moon; crisp silver moonlight spills onto his naked body. A gentle rain begins to tap-tap at the outside, rivulets of water staggering dreamily down the panes of glass.

At the bathroom door, he places his ear to the cold wood. He thinks he hears a thin, far away voice, possibly a woman: *Cheri? But Cheri's in Europe on assignment...*

He listens more intently; the female is joined by another, male voice:

*"...r get it to work. I'm just an artificial representation of evil...* your *evil."* **"It's like a wound that doesn't heal properly—sometimes it scars, leaves a reminder; other times it never closes all the way, just keeps weeping."** *"You'll find out..."* **"Go North. Hang on a sec..."**

Andrew hears footsteps on the other side. He pulls back just as the door is thrown open, flooding the bedroom with a terrible white luminance broken by a hulking, monstrous silhouette—

# VII

Two weeks later.

Jerad stared from his office window, catching a glimpse of his own half-reflection in the glass: His eyes were puffy, tired. "This isn't going to be easy."

Andrew was pensive. He smiled nervously from the other side of the desk, smoothing his hair. "Problem, boss?"

After a pause, Jerad turned in his chair to face him. "Afraid so."

Andrew: "What is it?"

"Well...you know the Senate just released the updated 'Torture Report' with all the photos from Iraq and Guantanamo—"

"Right."

"As a result, funding dried up ..." Silence. Jerad continued: "And cuts were made to DARPA programs. Even though we're on Republican 'safe lists'—"

"Oh *shit*..."

Jerad raised his hands. "Hold on, hold on. It's not *all* bad—"

Andrew huffed, staring at his boss from beneath skeptical eyebrows as he crossed his arms. "Okay. What else?"

Jerad loosened his tie. "They've turned the whole funding process into a bureaucracy worthy of Kafka. Hoops within hoops within hoops. So, they're consolidating some things, and pulling the plug on others." He paused, massaging the back of his neck. "We're now going to be subject to periodic budgetary scrutiny... *and* a re-org of DARPA that puts us into DARC."

"DARC?"

"Yeah—it's a highly-classified subdivision of DARPA. Stands for the Department of Augmented Reality Conceptualizations. Its focus is to understand the benefits and drawbacks of AR tactics and other novel conflict-resolution solutions. Also to develop in-theatre strategies for their use. Domestic applications, too; they're *quite* enthusiastic about turning all this over to law enforcement after the Middle East conflicts fade away. They want to extract a bit of profit out of their investments in R&D. They've been partnering with Microsoft and other OEMs on HoloLens and all kinds of second tier products, too, in an effort to begin the shift away from outdated VR; to establish a footing in the AR milieu. VR's gone too mainstream—we're seeing virtual terrorism, even virtual journalism. It's beginning to invoke not just a shared realistic *experience*, but even emotional states—empathy, compassion, hate."

"Sounds familiar..."

"Exactly. You've been knocking on that door with *Pazuzu* and SIA." Jerad slid a few sheets of paper across his desk for Andrew to peruse. "DARC is nimble; they aren't hamstrung by process-itis, or analysis-paralysis. They want *results*, ASAP. Just check out the list of things DARC already placed into alpha- or beta-testing, or are about to..."

Andrew scanned over the document. Just under a TOP SECRET stamp, the list of items was remarkable:

*STAGING:* PRE-ALPHA (Proof of Concept – Need to Know Eyes Only)

*1)* **Contagious Neuro-Dementia Acceleration Syndrome (CoN-DAS):** *A fast-acting, engineered viral agent and extreme BSL-4 contagion which initiates profound hallucination events and violent behavior. The primary effect on males promotes aggression and self-destructive derangement; in females it results in paralysis and a comatose state similar to the mysterious early 20th century outbreak of Encephalitis Lethargica/ von Economo disease, though the biological foundations for this difference in presentation are still being researched.* **HIGH PRIORITY**

*2)* **Metamaterial Cloaking (MmC):** *The novel use of optical materials which can influence the route lightwaves take by directing and regulating the spread and transmission of quantified parts of the light spectrum, thereby rendering an object seemingly invisible.* **PRIORITY**

*3)* **Mnemonic Transplantation (MT):** *Injectable serum which enhances suggestibility to a point permitting the "editing" or outright verbal implantation of false memories that permanently replace real ones.* HIGH PRIORITY

*4)* **Neuroplastic Growth Stimulation (NGS):** *An ingestible synthetic hormone concentrate that promotes rapid brain development (so called "Limited Benevolent Tumor Formation," or LBTF) in adults, primarily in the Limbic System, including specifically the hippocampus (memory formation/storage), hypothalamus (circadian rhythms, emotions, some motor function), and the amygdala (strong memory impressions), but also the pons (arousal and consciousness), and neocortex by way of new connections to parts of the parietal (touch), temporal (auditory), and occipital (vision) lobes. In principle, these become new organs of perception, enhancing sensory impression, memory, intuition, and facilitating telepathic communication.* **PRIORITY**

*5)* **Temporal Manipulation Drones (TMD):** *Flying mechanical devices which use rapid flashes of light to temporarily freeze or, for very short durations, reverse live events.*

*STAGING:* ALPHA (Minor Informational Deployment – Need to Know Eyes Only)

*6)* **Hypnagogic Excitation (HEx):** *A drug dispensed as a gas which causes delirium, confusion, passivity, amnesia, and waking dream states.*

*7)* **Memory Lathes (MeLa):** *Non-lethal explosive devices which disorder and obscure the recollection of events by the use of intense electromagnetic field disturbances in event situations.* **PRIORITY**

*8)* **Stegoneiric Cognitive Psycholinguistics (SCP):** *The use of certain ultrasonic nonmusical audial tones, cadences, and vibrational frequencies encoded in specially constructed syntactical hierarchies of words and phrases that, when binaurally recorded and played back with a specific compression algorithm, can deliver conceptual payloads into the subconscious via brain waves normally active during deep sleep. These "mind viruses" can* *then be used to disrupt the cognition, actions, and intentions in an individual, allowing them to become vectors of "thought contagion" as they unwittingly reiterate the scrambled data though microtonal variations in pitch and glottal voicings, thereby spreading disinformation like a psychological contaminant when shared with others via normal speech. The recipient(s) of the encrypted information are unaware of the mental infection, or that they are contaminating others. Only one hearing by one target is sufficient to create a psycho-viral epidemic.*

*STAGING:* **BETA** (Controlled Open Testing – Need to Know Eyes Only)

*9)* **Focused Aural Shifters (FAS):** *Handheld devices which create ultrasonic frequencies that can camouflage ambient noise.*

*10)* **HoloLens:** *Cordless, self-contained smart headset created by Micro-soft using advanced sensors, a hi-def stereoscopic 3D optical head-mounted display, and spatial sound to allow for interactive AR applications.*

*11)* **LEIA:** *A display with a wide 3D field of view offering full parallax to create seamless 3D impressions (holograms) regardless of head position and without the need for special headgear or glasses.*

*12)* **Multiple ImmerSive Total RealitY (MISTY):** *Software and headgear created by Pacific Data Systems for identical, sensory-immersive captures of VR simulacra, to include the emotional signatures and vital statistics of the user. The data can later be retrieved and decoded for total AR usage by the user or non-participants of the scenario—whether visualizations of an unconscious dreamscape or real-time experiences.* **PRIORITY**

*13)* **Psycholinguistic Steganographic VR Markup Language (PS-VRML):** *A form of flexible code that enables the embedded encryption of hidden images and/or audio messages into moving imagery, video games, and modern websites.* **PRIORITY**

"Intense assortment. Way beyond shit like night vision

goggles, or body armor—the 'hard' aspects. These 'soft' facets—meds and such—dovetail into what we want to accomplish with the gameplay and AR. This is the next step in enhancing humans—increasing psychological toughness, flattening affect, manipulating consciousness, organ development. Pretty wild stuff," Andrew said, looking up at Jerad.

"It is." Jerad smiled, eyes contemplative as he reached down into a desk drawer. "Unfortunately, Andrew, you looked at the TS list...Now, I have to kill you." His face was grim.

Andrew's eyes widened; he swallowed heavily. "Wha...What was that?"

After a moment Jerad laughed, pulling a bottle of Scotch from the drawer. "Just a little joke," he said, retrieving a pair of glasses and pouring a shot for each of them. "But, on a more serious note, add your project, *Pazuzu's Reign*, to that list for Alpha. And they want SIA refined and brought into the portfolio, too."

Andrew relaxed, slumping in his seat. He drained the glass. "Starting when?"

"Yesterday." Jerad pulled the papers back. "So focus on squashing those bugs. I need new data on the hangover effects you described—the nightmares and stuff. Ever since Snowden, the CIA and DoD have been hot to fast track things that can encrypt into moving images, or that can record/alter event recollection and impressions without the user's knowledge—both things you've been doing with the PS-VRML code on *Pazuzu*. They're seeing an opportunity here...a way to reclaim some lost ground with the younger set. Placing subconscious political messages in the games as a hedge against people getting stirred up...keeping folks a bit more sedated, y'know?" He leaned forward, regarding Andrew over the frames of his glasses. "I can tell you this much: From the meetings I've been privy to, the Feds are concerned too much political correctness is weakening our country, that sort of thing. How soon can you get something to me? Before we can go live?"

Andrew ran his hand through his hair. "Give me a few days. I have testers on it now. I'm about to meet with them while I'm in the office."

Jerad nodded. "Okay. Do good here, Andrew, and we'll make it worth your while. I can guarantee that; you've crossed over to the big time. Report back next week."

# VIII

He looked at each of his testers, eight in all: "So we need to step it up. It's crunch time." Andrew let his words sink in. The meeting had lasted longer than he hoped, but he wanted to stress the importance of what was now expected.

"Is there any overtime?" Ben Andersen asked. A large, balding thirty-something with a trim goatee, he was the Test Lead for *Pazuzu's Reign*.

"Yes. I'll authorize that. But I need *results*. In fact, I need some *tonight*. I have to report back to Jerad in two days. We've been doing well, and the bugs are almost gone, but still it's not *quite* where it needs to be."

"So," Derek Reynolds, a rookie member of the team began, "we're looking at Beta after the next demo to Jerad?"

"I think so, yeah," Andrew replied. "We've hit most of the goals we had originally: Converted the Mars scenario we inherited from PDS to a Syrian desert invasion, even extrapolated an Antarctic environment from that. Installed families of avatars—monsters, demons, and so on—incorporated the schemas from *Sad Satan* we liked, folded in the databases from all the interviews. The personalization algorithm is tight. We've got a good feel, a good flow, and the liminal space settings are seamless. The VR and AR is all top shelf, but there's still room to fix the lingering boundary stuff. Remember, a big subtextual aspect of what we're striving for is the concept of 'blurring edges,' as in interfaces—between reality and gameplay, life and death, good and bad, sleep and wakefulness... the shifting of the *threat*. The goal of the game is two-fold: 1) pre-theatre training for our forces, so their muscle-memory and reactions are finely-tuned, and 2) to desensitize them, to suppress their emotions in a way that makes them suggestible to *us*, but hardened against *others*. We want perfect killing machines."

Ben nodded in understanding. "Right. But, you know, I've been having a few side effects myself from this 'game,' Andrew. It messes with my mind. Bad dreams...bad *thoughts*. And sometimes my stress level is—let's say off the charts. I get really anxious, even *days* later—"

"I understand," Andrew said. "But we have to power on through. I'll be home all night working on it myself. Call me if you guys need anything."

# IX

*We hear a door slam. In the distance there are screams, and, beyond that, the howl of wind.*

*We are in a laboratory of some type. The place is underlit, filthy. There is a large work table in the center of the room, strewn with broken, overturned beakers and what appear to be half-burned notebooks.*

*On one wall is a tattered, full-length portrayal of a grim-faced military man resembling Joseph Stalin which gradually morphs into a cascade of other vaguely familiar figures from history. Finally, the likenesses dissolve into "That Man" we all seem to dream about at some point—the one we can never quite place, with pasty skin, bushy eyebrows, thick lips, and a receding hairline, staring intensely. We watch the scene, hypnotized. "Go North, it's the only way to survive," This Man says from the painting, now alive, no longer a portrait. "You pretend, but I always know when you're awake; your heart will let you down."*

*This Man is trying to climb out of the picture frame now, but we can see he is trapped. We turn our attention away for a moment, to the wall directly opposite this strange sight. There, an enormous and stained twelve-month calendar hangs, worn and gently moving, as though caught in a breeze; the year is torn away. We walk closer to the table up ahead, behind which—like a backdrop—hangs a trio of large shadowboxes with specimens mounted inside of them. The first box has different rows of extracted human teeth—bloody, fully-rooted incisors, canines, molars; the next contains a grouping of severed fingers, the ragged bony ends visible at the edges of the desiccated flesh of the stumps; the final one is massive, covering most of the lower wall, and holds wetly-gleaming human eyeballs, each impaled with a fine needle—blue eyes, brown eyes, green eyes. These orbs, dozens of them, stare at us, the tails of their optic nerves arranged in such a way as to give the macabre appearance of a collection of misshapen butterflies. Behind us, That Man continues to struggle in the frame, making pained grunting sounds.*

*We turn around. The scratched wooden door is rattling in its frame. Walking to the entryway, we open it: Beyond the threshold there is only a gulf of emptiness, pitch black desolation. It is the end of hope. We leave the room; leave the staring eyes; leave That Man still struggling to pull himself from his two-dimensional prison.*

*Again the door bangs closed: In the total darkness which follows, we notice that the wind and screaming in the distance have stopped. There is nothing here but the faint sound of our body—breath, heartbeat, eyeblinks.*

*"Infidel! Go North!" The voice is raspy, quiet; the speaker seems somehow eerily familiar.*

*First, breath stops…*

*then everything else does.*

# X

*Whatever one accomplishes in life is their* legacy*…There's no way to know if there's really life after death; the only true immortality we can aspire to, at best, is a sort of "digital afterlife"…* Andrew took another shot of whiskey, it was the good stuff Jerad had given him a couple bottles of for his birthday the week prior. He enjoyed the warmth as it spilled down his throat while he relaxed on the living room couch. His head was pounding from too much *Pazuzu's Reign.*

*I mean, Ray Kurzweil pointed out that technological progress isn't* linear—*it's* exponential. *Like, all the stuff* DARC *is planning…it's just a matter of time before they get into implanting sensors* inside *humans for GPS, or nanobots for diagnosing injuries from within…* He was drunk. He looked at the clock: It was late. Or early, depending on one's perspective.

The phone rang. "Shit. Who's calling me at two in the morning?" He walked over to where his cell phone was charging: *Ben Andersen. Fuck.* "Hello?"

# XI

"How soon before you can get the Beta to me? I hate to press, but we're behind the eight ball here." Jerad was getting impatient as they sat in his office; it had been over a week since Ben Andersen had passed away. "Not to be insensitive, but the guy's dead. We don't need this whole project to head south on us."

Andrew sighed. He felt guilty for pushing his team so hard. Ben had suffered a heart attack—in part, it was believed—due to the intensity of *Pazuzu's Reign.* Other testers had complaints, too. Instances of stress-related hives, ocular migraines, even episodes of dermatographia—weird marks and what appeared to be words on their skin: *Go North; Infidel; I Live.* It was a classic example of what Andrew had believed was possible to trigger with this level of psychological manipulation in the AR environment: physical manifestations from the mind—the dark side of playing games.

"Tomorrow. We'll have it tomorrow," Andrew replied.

# XII

Andrew had his doubts about whether Cheri was ever coming back. The strain had broken her; she had stopped answering his calls, and her mother had instructed him to give her some space. Since then, he had taken to drinking *every* night. Now his Lead Tester was dead, and the rest of his team was sick, flipped out.

On the *other* hand, he was about to deliver the biggest project of his life: Tomorrow was what this gig was all about—dropping *Pazuzu's Reign.* Hopefully he could pull everything back together after he cut ties with Jerad and DARC; it would be a relief to cash out of DIS. He took another pull from his last bottle of Scotch whiskey before putting the headset on and going through one final run of the game.

*Cheri still loves me,* he felt certain. *She has to…*

*"Your obsession with this stupid game!" Cheri is furious, her eyes wide in anger. "I'm fucking sick of it!"*

*He stares at her as she stands by the door, holding her bag. He has no reply that can make her understand.*

*"I'll be at my mother's." The door slams—*

*behind him in the long, narrow room. A high window lets the moon peer through. Outside the temperature has dropped. The men are sleeping in their quarters.*

Andrew walks through the room, which he sees is a replica of his bedroom, past his bed and toward the closed bathroom door. Under the door he can see a bright light, its color shifting slowly through the visible spectrum. As he approaches, he can hear voices on the other side. He adjusts his headset.

[ Gates! *I live!* ]

Andrew is startled by the demonic, croaking voice coming in though his MORPHEUS comm.

[ Who is this? ] Andrew thinks, though he knows the answer. [ Is this…Ben Andersen? ]

There is a crackle of static from his regular headset. "Sorry, boss, that's not me. I died, remember? You just wanted too much. Pazuzu tore my heart out and ate it…or maybe it was Grendel?" Andersen replies. Andrew shakes his head in disbelief.

"I-I'm really sorry, Ben. That sounds terrible—"

"It only hurt a minute. One thing: I feel pretty nonplussed about being dead. Unity of Affect—it *works,*" Ben says.

There is a loud report, as though a shot is fired, followed by a scream which changes from male to female. Andrew's heart pounds: [ *Cheri?* ]

The screaming continues; Andrew is outside the bathroom door. Shadows disrupt the light streaming around the doorframe; the bedroom is now completely dark. Andrew strains to hear what the confusing jumble of overlapping male and female voices on the other side of the door are saying:

*"...where does the mind originate? Where does it start, where does it end?"* "The question isn't the will—*we can break that easily—it's what is* consciousness ..." *"Why bother looking for God? Do enough to rattle him and he'll come looking for you, it seems... well, maybe not* **Him**, *but his less benign contemporaries..."* "Go North, it's the only way to survive..." *"...become a port of entry into the physical world through the game—which eventually becomes uncontrollable as the mental constructs between the unconscious and the conscious mind break down..."* "—*we are forces of* nature ... *we have our own agendas and appetites, and now—we are* unleashed..." *"...of us carries the seeds of our metaphorical, and sometimes literal, destruction..."* "...fundamentalist test for ideological purity... the self-defeating myopia of idealism—" *"...Gates is so fucking stupid he doesn't realize I've been spiking his whiskey with NGS..."* "Wait just a second, I think I hear him—"

The bathroom door explodes outward, the splinters and wood shards cutting and slicing Andrew's face and arms. He screams in pain and recoils, too late. A throng of creatures—all of them too large to be contained in the confines of the house—spill out of the blast of multihued light.

Andrew screams at the expanding horde: "I removed the code that created you! I took it all out after Ben died! You're just bad strings of data—"

Rising to a gigantic height, mighty Pazuzu roars with laughter which resonates like a thunderhead. The great deity looks down with huge, black eyes—evil, cold, emotionless. The others—Cthulhu, Grendel, and several more besides—surround Andrew, all of them now suspended in a blue-black void.

[ Infidel! *I live!* I am released from the binary prison you made for me... Now, we meet! ]

[ We can't meet—I *invented* you! I destroyed you in the final code— ]

Pazuzu laughs, shaking the base of all creation; the others tremble in his diabolical presence. His all-encompassing voice obliterates reason as it fills Andrew's synapses: [ That does not matter—it is too late! *I live, Gates!* I am alive *now* in the minds, the subconscious, of your testers, freed from my virtual dungeon... and very soon I shall be in the world. I will gather strength from *belief in me,* just as your pathetic God has, or your new Slender Man... or so many others. But I am even more real than *they*—a digital immortal! Alive every time my name is uttered; every time the game is experienced; in every nightmare I create, the acts of terror I inspire.

[ And all the world will yield, thanks to you and your efforts: Your Unity of Affect was the key to my terrible vastation, my unconditional blight and enslavement of the human parasite... ] With that, Pazuzu is gone: his minions vanish as well.

Out of the cold darkness, This Man walks toward Andrew. They are alone on a barren, sandy plain reminiscent of Shelley's "Ozymandias." This Man says nothing, he simply grabs Andrew and pulls him close before muttering in his ear: "Andrew Gates: Your time is at an end; we cannot be stopped now... *Go North*—"

He detonates his suicide vest.

# XIII

The following morning, Andrew Gates is found dead in his home of a brain aneurysm, still wearing his wireless headgear.

*Pazuzu's Reign* will be released publically a week later.

*— To the memory of Smokey*

# 101 THINGS TO DO BEFORE YOU'RE DOWNLOADED

## SCOTT EDELMAN

The last man on Earth—or rather, the man who'd been weighing whether he should linger until he inevitably *became* the last man on Earth—had been atop Mt. Everest for nearly a century, contemplating his planet's mortality—and his own—when an unwelcome visitor popped into existence beside him.

He'd long ago, centuries ago, discovered that his thoughts were clearest on top of the world, though he'd never quite figured out whether this was because of the spectacular view, the thinness of the air, or a byproduct of the unusual extended solitude that came with such a visit. Still, that was where he headed when he had anything important to consider. And at that moment, as he tried to imagine his best possible future, there was no more important question on Earth for him—or for any inhabitants of the solar system, really—to consider than this:

Should he stay? Or should he go?

He'd been mulling over whether enough was enough for several lifetimes as you and I (but not those who will come after us) measure them, but he'd yet to reach any conclusion, at least not with any sense of certainty. Even though he'd been communing with his truest self, his concentration compressed by the weight of the passing decades, a decision about whether he should simply remain in place until the sun reached out to meet him and it would be too late for Downloading continued to be elusive. Others may have felt the need to escape, to go on, but...why?

And so, even after all that time alone above a world that day by day dwindled, when he heard the sound of his name, it came as an unwelcome distraction.

That name, a complex collection of syllables which unfortunately cannot be replicated here in our time with our words, because vocal cords have not yet evolved the capacity to form sounds so strange and beautiful, was the whisper of a subtle, barely perceptible wind on certain summer nights, overlaid by waves colliding against a coral reef, married to the trickle of water from melting ice running against smooth rocks.

The man turned his head slowly, irritated by the interruption. And after having been undisturbed for decades, a little surprised, too. Few in that distant pocket of existence bothered to visit Mt. Everest, not in reality anyway, not when it was so easy to go there in one's mind and experience nearly the same thing.

"Yes, that's me," said Husssh (which, as I've explained above, is not his actual name, but merely what we shall call him for the duration to make his story more easily comprehensible in our time). He didn't bother as he once might have to alter his voice to mask the annoyance he felt. "You found me."

Which wasn't quite the case. The newcomer couldn't really be said to have found anyone, because in truth, he hadn't been looking. But the reason he knew Husssh's name wasn't because they'd met while navigating their shared future, or simply because most of the population had already abandoned Earth, leaving behind few whose names it was necessary to remember, allowing him to recognize the man. No, it's just that everyone knew everyone on sight in the elsewhen that waits for our children...if they chose to access the information, that is. When you looked at someone, you could just *know*. That's how the brains of our descendants will come to work in these days.

"Now let me be," Husssh said, turning away from his intruder, ignoring most of the details about him that came into his mind, save that the man was but a youngster, barely 90 years old. Why, Husssh had been motionless on the mountaintop far longer than that pup had even been alive! "If you insist on staying here, do me a favor. Let's at least sit in silence."

The visitor nodded and settled in gingerly, as one tends to do on a first visit to Mt. Everest, even in this future of miracles. He looked away from Husssh and down through the clouds below, knowing better than to speak, something that first glance of his face and its intense expression had quickly taught him.

No more than a handful of heartbeats had gone by when the visitor extended his hands, causing a wafer to manifest in one and a sheet of paper in the other. Husssh was stunned. Paper? When had anyone last used paper? Flesh itself was on the brink of becoming history, and paper, for many, was little more than myth. But before Husssh could express his surprise, the man popped the square into his mouth, tore slightly at an edge of the page—Husssh could see there were many such tears down one side—and then vanished.

He was puzzled, but at the same time, relieved—for he had a far more important question than the reason for what he'd seen that still needed answering, and for that, he had to continue on in solitude. (Though what would a second century give him that the first had not? A conclusion was not so easily come by as he'd thought when he'd first sequestered himself.) But that relief didn't last long, for before he could settle in with his thoughts, a second traveler arrived.

After nearly a century of solitude, two visitors in two minutes was almost too much to bear. And so when the second visitor, without even bothering to acknowledge him, mimicked the first, and a paper materialized in her hand, Husssh made a grab for it—but the invader backed quickly away before his fingers could make contact.

"No need to be so aggressive," she said, as she, too, tore a notch in the page, not even bothering before she did so to gaze at the panorama which surrounded them. Husssh leaned forward and quickly leapt at the sheet, this time ripping off a strip from the top as the woman pulled back.

"Hey!" she shouted, but then, when she saw the fierce expression on Husssh's face, quickly placed a pill on her tongue, swallowed, shook her head, and was gone.

Husssh examined the fragment, which fluttered in a stiff wind that threatened to pull it from his hands. Across the top were the words, "100 Things to Do Before You're Downloaded." It seemed to be the beginning of a list, and as he read the numbered items below, its contents were just as mysterious as the fact they were written on paper and had been carried by multiple intruders. He'd only managed to tear away five of the supposed hundred which the list's title claimed it contained, but what he read made him uncomfortable.

Which was another surprise. It had been quite a while since he'd felt discomfort.

*Have breakfast in the Marianas Trench, lunch on Mount Everest, and dinner on the Moon.*

*Track and eat the last living representative of a near-extinct species. Consider what you have done.*

*Ride one orbit on a ring of Saturn.*

*Write a song to make someone fall in love with you. Write another which will make them hate you.*

*Go over Angel Falls until you reach the bottom, then swim back up against the tide until you reach the top.*

After reading and saving the strangely familiar information, he let the scrap be tugged from his fingers and watched the wind quickly carry it out of sight.

Once, he would have felt it wrong to litter the world in such a manner.

Once, he would have chased after the paper and made sure to keep Mt. Everest pristine.

Soon, though, it would make no difference. The world and all it contained would be gone. So there was only one thing that mattered now.

Which meant it was time to come down off the mountain. And with the thought of going, he was gone.

• • •

And then he was back, elsewhere, to a spot suggested by the list, and mirrored by his memory.

He swam vertically against the rushing waters of Angel Falls, rising slowly as he once had in his youth, the only difference being that this time he was aware of others nearby doing the same. It was much different from when he'd last attempted this, when he'd been alone, battering himself against the planet to learn who he was and whether he mattered. Now others were there, in search of—what? He knew what had moved him to accomplish this feat hundreds of years ago. But why were the swimmers who accompanied him doing it now? Because someone had placed it on a list? That seemed absurd.

But someone had.

Once up top, he stood on a rock, then watched as first one, then two, three, four others climbed out of the water to stand beside him. They did not look back down toward the water from where they had come. They did not look out at the land which stretched far away beneath them. They did not turn around to consider the river which rushed to the edge, against the power of which they had fought.

Instead, they one by one stretched out a hand to allow a sheet of paper to appear, just as the others had done earlier on Mt. Everest. Husssh noted that one sheet was more tattered than the others—thanks to rips and tears indicating achievements, he assumed—and so he knew whom he had to approach.

Oddly, when Husssh looked at the man the way people will come to in the future, looked the way I explained earlier, he did not know him ... not his name, his history, or any of the other information people will come to allow to be instantaneously shared with one another. Taken aback, he for a moment did not know what to say.

The man saw Husssh approach, and smiled, waving the page.

"Halfway done," he said.

"I can see that," said Husssh. "But why?"

The man shrugged, and then, before any further questions could be asked, was gone.

Husssh could have followed had he chosen to do so, at least he thought he could have, though after that blankness of the man's identity, he was suddenly unsure, so he didn't even try. Instead, he turned to the others.

"And you?" he asked. "Why are you here?"

"It's just the thing to do," two of them said simultaneously. They pointed at each other, then laughed. He was flummoxed. He'd have known the two were a singleton had he been able to look at them the way he was supposed to.

One of them rubbed his hands together, and then suddenly, there were two sheets. He thrust one of them at Husssh.

"Here," they said. "Take it. You don't want to be the only one not doing it."

"Not doing what?" Husssh asked as he scanned the list. And then he fell silent, for in its entries, he recognized a personal history he'd thought had mattered to none but himself.

*Follow the flight path of the first man in space while contemplating your own upcoming possible final trip out into space.*

*Program yourself for synesthesia and taste a rainbow.*

*Have sex with a representative of all three alien species known to have visited Earth in the order they were first encountered.*

*Become what once was a man. Become what once was a woman. Try to imagine what it was like to have lived in a world of frozen gender.*

Husssh looked up from the list to the ones who had given it to him. "I've—I've done all of these," he said. "Where did this come from?"

"Where did it not come from?" came the reply in stereo.

Then they laughed again. And were gone.

"Wait—" he called out.

But they'd said all they'd wanted to say, and frozen out of the datastream, he could not follow them. He turned to the last person there, who waved in a sort of salute.

"Good luck," it said. And then it, too, vanished.

Husssh was baffled.

By the list. By the apparent multiple quests. And by the fact that he was somehow being denied access to information which had become commonplace.

He could wait for other swimmers to arrive at the top so he could question them about it all. But as he gazed at the territory around him, he was reminded of his first visit so long ago, and he thought—he'd already spent all the time he needed to on that spot the first time around.

He had to keep moving.

Until it was time to stop.

Husssh swam on his back past the Empire State Building, the ocean having long before risen to cover the streets on which you and I might have walked. The skies of New York City above him were more crowded than he had ever seen them, considering the number of inhabitants who had already Downloaded. He wondered at first whether it had always been that busy and perhaps he'd grown unaccustomed to it during his time on the mountaintop, but then he thought again, accessing the census of all who remained—he could still see the count of that, thankfully—and learned that his initial reaction has been right. There were indeed more present than there usually were.

It was that list. It had to be. His niece—grandniece many times over, actually—who had once been his nephew and once been neither and several times had been both—would surely know what this was about. He'd stopped caring a long time ago what others thought, and paid little attention to fads and fashions, but she—even though she had her own mind—was more in touch with the tide of the times. He knew his limitations, recognized there were areas he could not access even when he could access them, languages he could not speak even when he spoke them.

With a kick of his feet, Husssh dove down to meet her.

Drackle was floating close to the sand, face down, prodding this way and that in the silt which had settled over the city's streets. We'll call her Drackle even though that is not her name (I explained before the necessity for doing this), which is the sound of a wind chime assembled of broken glass moving in harmony with the snap of an electrical surge. But since neither you nor I can pronounce either of those with the primitive tools we have been given, we'll go with Drackle.

"Hello, uncle," she said, registering that he was there without a need to turn her head.

"What are you looking for this time?" he asked.

"A few final souvenirs," she said. "Our time grows short."

When she said this, of course, she was referring to time as they will come to account for it, not as you or I do now. If we'd been there beside them, contemplating the end of things, it would still seem as if millennia proceeded before us.

"But you won't be able to take them with you when you're Downloaded," he said. "Just bits and bytes to be sent off elsewhere, beamed in the hope that something will become of them. But your souvenirs, the ones the makers left for you to find, the ones you cradled and warmed with your touch, they'll remain here. Until..."

His voice trailed off. In her head, at least. They were under water, after all, which meant no spoken words were being exchanged.

"You're so old-fashioned, uncle," she said. "Everything I find here I'll be able to still have with me there. They'll be reconstructed just as I will be. You know that."

"Actually, I don't," he said. "And *you* know *that*. But as I've told you before, whatever you think you'll have—will you really have? The Earth, and all who ever lived here, and all who ever died, and all that was built by those who did both, will be left behind. Swallowed. Incinerated. Gone."

"I'm not going to argue about it with you anymore," she said, angrily smacking the mud, which rose into cloud, momentarily leaving them hidden from each other. "We have better things to do with the time we have left."

When the silt had settled once more, he saw she had stopped her excavating and spun around.

"What brings you here, uncle?" she asked.

He tilted his head and let her see what had transpired on Mt. Everest and at Angel Falls. She looked at the list which he'd been given.

"Yes, I've heard of this before," she said. "This list has been propagating across the planet. You'd probably have gotten one yourself had you not chosen to isolate so. Some of my friends have been trying to do all of these things before it's their turn to Download."

"No, it's something more than just that," he said. "That doesn't explain the holes in my connection, or why I've been blocked from accessing information I've never been blocked from before. There's something more going on, something far less innocent."

Drackle laughed suddenly, and a flurry of bubbles rose from her mouth toward the surface.

"Really?" he said. "That's your answer?"

"No, I'm not laughing at you, uncle. Really, I'm not. But did you see this one at the end?"

He called up the list and scrolled to the bottom.

*Sleep so long that your friends have forgotten whether you are sleeping or dead.*

*Learn a new word every day. At the same time, forget an old one.*

*Kill someone who does not deserve to die. Within 24 hours, save the life of someone who does not deserve to live.*

*Swim through the ruins of New York City.*

"Ah," he said. "I see."

"That's why New York City is so crowded today. It hasn't been bothering me, though. Hardly anyone's taken the time to come down this deep."

"That doesn't surprise me. From what I've seen, no one seems interested in actually experiencing any of these things. Which makes their actions hollow and superficial."

"Even if they don't do it your way, uncle, that doesn't mean it's not worth doing at all."

"We can debate that some other time—"

"Will there be time for another time?"

"—but that's not the only thing peculiar about this list."

She scanned it again.

"What am I missing?"

"I thought you knew me, knew my past, better than that. Don't you see?"

She shook her head.

"I've already done every one of them. Every one."

"Oh," she said. "That's interesting."

"And—as far as I know—I'm the only one who's *ever* done all of them."

"That's *very* interesting. But—"

She paused, then raised a finger between them.

"What?"

"It seems it won't be very long before you're no longer the only one."

He thought and—glad he could still access *that* knowledge, at least—realized she was right.

"But—why? What's the point?"

"I don't know, but as I told you, it appears that completing the list before the final Downloading has become something of a thing."

"I'm not much for doing things because they're things."

"Sometimes I wish you were," she said, grimacing. "Then we wouldn't have to say goodbye."

"I thought you weren't going to try to argue with me anymore."

"Not an argument," she said. "Just an observation."

He considered the list again, and as he did so, remembered not just each achievement, but also the motivations that had driven him to each action. Not all of the events which had preceded each list entry had been pleasant ones.

"I didn't do these things because they were on some mysterious list that popped up in my feed. I did them because they mattered at the time. I did them because I couldn't *not* do them."

She shrugged, then lowered herself back against the ground and started sifting through the sand once more.

"Who do you think made this thing?" he asked.

"Does it really matter?" she said. "Whoever it was will soon be Downloaded like the rest us. Well…like most of us."

"It matters to me. Don't be angry. This list…this list is me."

"You're more than just a list of the things you've done."

"And you're wise for someone so young."

"Uncle, I'm 140 years old."

Husssh laughed.

"As I said, you're wise for someone so young."

"And you're foolish for someone so old. But I guess that's part of why I love you."

He smiled, and dropped beside her to join in sifting through the mud. And sift through the list as well, trying to decide what do to next. As in the palm of his hand he rolled broken pieces of granite and metal bits from machines that were no longer necessary, he realized that, in the end, there was no need to decide. His course, for once, was not up to him. The list itself would lead him to who had mined his life and made the list.

"I'll see you later, niece," he said. "I need to go for a swim."

"We're already swimming," she said.

"Yes," he said, letting the fragments drop slowly to the riverbed. "But it's time for a swim that's not on the list."

Then he was gone.

And then he was not.

He paddled slowly on his back along the Colorado River, looking up toward the stars, which were harder than ever to make out with his natural eyes. The sky had grown much brighter than it used to be, and it was only with enhancement that he could see things as they used to be and would have been able to pretend—had he been the sort of person who felt a need to pretend—that the time for Downloading was not fast approaching. He climbed from the water and then hiked to the deepest part of the Grand Canyon, where he sat and waited for the sun above to vanish.

Soon, he knew, that sun would grow insistent, and demanding, and be beyond vanishing. But not yet. He considered the list once more as the sun dropped and the rocks around him cooled suddenly, cracking loudly as if surprised by the abrupt sunset and the swift temperature change it bought.

*Find and ride a falling meteor. Repeat until you latch onto one that reaches Earth. Savor the impact.*

*Scan every work ever written in every language until you find the words worthy of being your epitaph. Then tell no one what you have chosen.*

*Listen to rocks pop after a sudden sunset at the bottom of the Grand Canyon.*

*Delete a painful memory. Delete the memory of that deletion.*

Had he erased a memory once? He guessed he had. It appeared he'd done all the other things on the list, so why not that one? He thought away the list, then lay on his back to count the stars (which we cannot do, but Husssh, in his future, could) and try to figure out what that lost memory might be. Then he figured . . . it didn't really matter. He had to trust himself. If he started second-guessing himself now, where would he be?

The air shifted beside him, and Husssh sensed he was no longer alone in the darkness.

He turned away from the stars to see a woman, list in hand, about to tear at the edge of the page.

"You're too late," he said.

He reached for her wrist, but before he could make contact, she vanished and then reappeared behind him.

"Didn't you hear me?" he said. "I read the list. You missed what you came for. You can't pretend you accomplished this one. It didn't count. You don't get credit just for showing up. You'll have to come back tomorrow night."

"I don't have the time for that," she said.

"You have to be somewhere?"

"I have to be . . . you know . . ."

She pointed up and to the left, zeroing in through the millennia of rock which surrounded them to the exact spot of the sun.

"Downloaded?" Husssh said.

"Well, yes. Of course. Where else?"

"Why the rush? We have some time left."

"Not as much as you'd think. I'm in a race with the others. I don't want to end up being the last one here. I wouldn't like it."

"Doesn't seem like that would be too bad to me. Not at all."

"It's already getting a little too empty," she said. "There's less . . . us. I wouldn't want a planet of my own."

"Who would?" he said. "Well…maybe for a little while. And then…"

He smiled, and spoke in darkness what he might not have spoken in light.

"Sometimes," he said, "it gets a little too noisy around here for my taste."

The woman widened her eyes, after for the first time bothering to check who it was beside her at the bottom of the crevasse.

"Oh," she said. "That's right. It's you. I should have known."

"Of course it's me. So?"

Her only answer was a nervous laugh. And then, before Husssh had a chance to ask her anything else, she was gone.

She'd been frightened. Of him. Which was odd, because there was no reason for a stranger to fear him (not that she was truly a stranger in this future devoid of strangers). Though perhaps based on a few of the items on the list some might think there a reason, assuming she knew he'd done everything on that list as he felt confident in assuming she did. But it seemed more than just that knowledge which had scared her and driven her away. The woman had been hiding something, and in a world in which it had become nearly impossible to hide, that was meaningful.

And so he hunted them.

How strange it felt to be chasing rather than evading, because in his mind he'd already said farewell. He travelled the world—the whole solar system, in fact, which was the limit of their personal technology during that age—in search of the searchers.

He hunted them all.

*Walk the Great Wall of China. No, really. Walk. Just like they had to do in the old days.*

And so he walked the Great Wall, encountering others beside him not looking as happy as he had when he first walked the Wall. What gave the appearance of punishment as they did it had felt like freedom to him.

"Not used to using your feet, eh?"

But they would not speak to him. Some, whom he assumed

wore electronic blinders, erasing him from their world, would not even notice him.

"Why are you doing this?" he asked. "Who gave you this list? Where did it come from?"

Not a one answered. Instead, they would veer swiftly around him, eyes at their feet, or else bump into him, not seeing him in space. He watched the glum parade until he could stand no more, and then leapt on.

*From the Sea of Tranquility, watch the sun rise over the Earth.*

He stood by the L.E.M. as the others popped in and out of existence. He hovered over the lunar soil, showing proper respect for the place of humanity's first great leap, but they did not care, leaving new footsteps.

He approached the first to appear, looking down at they. The other looked up at Husssh and smiled briefly.

"Why did you smile?"

"You're here," they said. "I'm here. That makes this even better."

"But why?" he said. "Who am I to you?"

They winked.

The others who came after were no more helpful, and he had no means with which to compel them.

Before Husssh moved on, he cleared the new footprints, returning the soil to the way it had been since the time humanity had last used rockets to get there. He wasn't entirely sure why it mattered to him, since the Moon would soon—soon in the way the universe keeps track of things—be lost in a solar blaze.

But it did matter.

*Go to the South Pole. Go to the North Pole. Commune in those spaces with the memory of ice.*

He sat on the stones. He floated in the water. He moved from pole to pole in wonder. It had been different the last times he'd been there. But none of the newcomers would know that.

There were fewer of them every day. As each fulfilled the

tasks on the list, they'd Download, preparing for the escape that would come when the sun overwhelmed the Earth. He did not mind watching their number dwindle—it had been what he'd been looking forward to all along—but their increasing disappearances meant there were fewer and fewer each day willing to answer (or fewer to be asked anyway, since answers were not forthcoming), and he had to wait longer and longer for anyone to show.

As each appeared, he'd rip the paper from their hands and tear it to shreds. It angered him that the mystery of their quest could so anger him. But his actions in a world which did not know much of aggression didn't seem to bother them. They'd shrug, and manifest the list all over again.

"You're not going to tell me anything, are you?" he said to one.

"There's nothing to tell you," the one said back.

And perhaps they were right.

*Walk across Tanzania until you reach the Laetoli footprints. Think of the millions of years behind and the millions of years ahead.*

When he'd first done that, his time behind and time ahead seemed in balance. He'd been teetering in the middle of eternity. No more. He had time to think about that, how nearly all of his future had become his past, because those who remained had dwindled few, and provided no distraction. When another finally appeared, Husssh had almost forgotten what he'd been waiting for, and what he'd wanted to ask.

"Is this how you want to spend the time you have left on this planet?" he said. "Doing what I did? Walking in my footsteps? Copying my life? Think about it. You could be out there doing something new, something yours."

"I *am* doing something mine," he said. "And something more than mine as well."

Husssh was surprised. It was the first time in a long while someone had actually spoken to him.

"What do you mean?"

"You'll figure it out."

And then he was gone.

He moved around the known, reachable space, reliving the millennia of his life, until finally, there was only one other than himself remaining to be Downloaded. The planet was nearly abandoned. And so he returned to rest where his hunt had begun, atop Mt. Everest, alone.

Then he was not. Drackle, whom he'd first known as his niece, appeared beside him, though he could tell by a look in their eye he'd seen numerous times before over the decades that at that moment niece was no longer the proper pronoun.

"I never did find out who made the list," he said.

"Of course you did," they said. "But then, you knew that. Didn't you?"

Puzzled, he turned from them to look down from the roof of the world at the emptiness below, which suddenly seemed bleaker than usual and suddenly more beautiful than usual. Then he looked back, nodding.

"Yes, I guess I did know. But what I don't get is ... why did you do it?"

"Because I'd agreed not to argue anymore," they said. "Because I hoped that if you realized all you'd done, all you'd lived for, all you could still do and live for, it would shake you out of your despair. And because you'd lived the most exciting, vibrant life of anyone I've ever known, and I hate that you've given up."

"You think that I've given up? You've think I despair? I haven't given up."

"Then what then?"

"I've lived enough of a life," Husssh said. "You think I spent my centuries so I could make a list? I wasn't list-making. I was living. And I'm fine with dying when planet Earth goes."

"If you're truly fine with the end of everything, then why did you agree to this? Why did you help me plan it all?"

"I didn't—" he said, but stopped, for he remembered a memory was missing, even if he didn't yet remember what that memory was.

"Yes," they said. "See?"

Drackle touched his temples, and he saw them arguing across decades, eventually saw himself telling her everything, so she could create the list that had been the bones of his life up until that point, saw himself agree to alterations in his programming to hide himself from himself, saw her asking the world to help her ask him to stay in this mysterious way, saw himself give her give himself this one final chance to change his mind.

"It worked," he said.

"No, it didn't," they said. "Not if you tell me you're still refusing to keep on living."

"I'll be living a lot longer than you," he said. "The place you're going to? That's not life. That's a fantasy. This is life."

"Who's to say what's life? You think those before us would think what we have a life? They might consider *this* the fantasy."

"No," insisted Husssh. "There's a difference. There are boundaries, once crossed, that would make all that occurred before meaningless. I wasn't sure before now, but now that I've played your crazy game—"

"It was *our* crazy game, uncle."

"It doesn't matter. What matters is—I'm now more certain than ever. I don't need to live forever. Almost forever is more than enough. Who needs more life than that?"

"You do," she said. "We all do. And I do, uncle. I swear to you that I'll never become bored of living."

"I'm not bored of living. I'm…content."

"I don't think I'll ever be that content."

Drackle turned away to look at the emptiness below. Husssh wished he could transmit what he saw when he gazed into that emptiness, but not even their future (so very distant from ours, yet not so very distant at all) was up to such things.

"If you live your life right, and you're very, very lucky, you will be," said Husssh. "I'll miss you."

"No," they said. "No, you won't. Because you'll be dead. But *I'll* miss *you*."

They gave their uncle a hug, and then was gone, Downloaded, just like that.

Husssh stared at the space which Drackle had moments before occupied, then turned to consider the sun. He would remain like that, happy, satisfied, until it went nova as had been foretold. And when those final rays someday reach him, igniting him with a warm embrace, he will realize that he has taken an action worthy of being item number 101 on that list of 100 Things to Do Before You're Downloaded.

And he'll have been the only one to accomplish it.

The only one.

# THE STAR-FILLED SEA IS SMOOTH TONIGHT

## THOMAS F. MONTELEONE

Link had tasted the universe.

He had sifted light-years through his fingers like grains of sand; he had breathed plasma like summer air; he had worn a star-bow like a crown upon his head. He had been both starship and man.

Now, only the man remained.

He lay in a hospital bed, in a starkly white room, at the edge of the City which had sent him to the stars and now called him back. He was an amusing puzzle for the machines to ponder as he struggled to recover from a special madness. In the IASA installation, Link lay wrestling with the phantoms of his tormented consciousness. Over and over, his moment of collapse was reenacted.

Link remembered...

He slipped into an almost circular orbit. The Earth turned slowly beneath him as he touched its surface with his sensors and auxiliary scanning equipment. Watching and feeling, Link/Ship sensed the small surfaceship climbing toward him, and he absorbed the shortwave communication into his cybernetic receivers: "Commander Link? This is Shuttle 41-C...Acknowledge please...Request permission to begin docking."

The long-feared moment had finally come, and Link/Ship wished that he could ignore it. Instead, he beamed out a short

reply: "Affirmative, 41-C...I have you on instrument tracking...
All systems green...Proceed to forward docking collar on present
course."

As he waited for the small ship's final approach and contact, he
felt himself becoming apprehensive, and he fought down a rising
swell of panic. He tried to savor the sensations of the cybernetic/
biological mix that was himself; whenever he concentrated on the
phenomenon, he felt mildly intoxicated. Yet he was still in complete
control. With the Ship's electronic sense organs, Link/ Ship was a
member of a very elite race of beings.

New signals raced into him, jarring him from his private thoughts,
which said that the docking collar had been sealed. He opened his
airlock and patiently waited for the technicians to scramble into him.
Link/Ship heard their footfalls, felt the infrared heat of their bodies,
as the men made their cautious way to the bridge. They were coming
toward him as be floated weightlessly in the colloidal-suspension
tank. He wore a specially designed suit with a small opening at the
base of his spine, from which a shining, serpent-like cable led to a
terminal on the side of the tank.

Their words invaded his mind: "All ready, Commander Link?"

Turning, shifting around in the suspension, Link/Ship regarded
them with his human eyes: they were lean young men, 'wearing the
jumpsuits of the IASA; they were his unwitting torturers. "Yes," he
said after a long pause. "I am."

He forced himself to watch as they began the process. One
of them inserted supportive waldoes into the tank and cradled his
human body firmly. The other one threw some switches on the
manual panel and the temperature of the colloid began to change.
Slowly it liquefied and began to drain from the tank. But at this
point, Link/Ship could still feel everything, even the slight electric
pulses that controlled the tank's thermostats.

When the tank was empty, one of the technicians climbed in
and began manipulating the cable and its coupling at the base of
Link/Ship's spine. He felt the gross tampering as the man measured
and checked the connection with small tools. Link/Ship watched
as the man outside the tank nodded and threw more switches on

the manual panel. Instantly, the changes crashed through him. It was slow, inexorable, and painless, but he almost cried out as the cybernetic systems began to shut down. Half of his consciousness was fading, failing... dying. Ship-awareness slipped away from him, and he dropped into a vortex of darkness. Link felt as if an invisible scalpel was systematically cutting away the onion-like layers of his self.

Specter-like, the blinking computer displays on the manual panel flickered and died. The last weak pulse of ship sensation touched his mind; and in a moment of imploding darkness, the cybernetic system was down.

Link struggled against the twilight awareness: the small-talk conversation of the technicians, the feel of the close-fitting fabric of his suit, and the thrum of blood passing through his temples were his only sensations now.

Slowly, he became aware of the mechanical arms that held his limp body. Then there were the human hands scampering like crabs over the fittings of his suit, fumbling with the catches, and opening the seals. They removed his helmet and the stale air of the bridge assaulted him—he was not prepared for the reality of machine oil and perspiration.

They peeled the rest of the suit from his pale body and he became conscious of his lean frame, even though he was weightless. He felt bitterness and even anger at the rough way in which they treated him, although he knew it was necessary to complete the assignment. The technicians, like himself, had no choice in this matter. Fingers fumbled with the coupling. Special tools clicked into place as Link felt them removing the cable. Movement, and the seal of the coupling was violated—the umbilical had been cut—and Link wrestled with the new psychological pain. He imagined the cable dropping off, away from his spine, and instantly shriveling and dying and falling lifelessly to the bottom of the tank. Link then saw the man outside the tank reach into a pouch and produce a round, flat disc. He handed it to the other technician, who moved it into position at the base of Link's spine. Link imagined the coupling there: an open wound, oozing an invisible life-substance, a death wound. He felt the disc being snapped over the coupling—the bio-connector—sealing it indefinitely.

He knew that his private access to the voices of time and the stars was irretrievably gone. Like other men, he was condemned to flounder in the backwash of his meager human senses. These were his thoughts as the two technicians carried his limp body away from the bridge. When they reached the airlock, Link saw the young pilot they had chosen to replace him: a young, strong-looking man with fire in his eyes. As Link struggled against the darkness raging in his mind, he tried to speak out to the young pilot, tried to warn him of what would eventually come.

But the moment passed too quickly. They brought him into the surfaceship and prepared for the long slide back into the atmosphere. Link was wrapped in a deceleration web, left to contend with the fist of madness that wanted to crush him.

...and tried to forget.

The room, the bed, and the personnel were now familiar to him. Through the window, opposite his bed, he was afforded a spectacular view of the lake and the City beyond it. Watching it, Link knew that he had come home to an unpredictable future. He was reminded of how the City's computers had planned everything for him, prepared for every contingency...except the one that actually took place.

The door opened, and Link watched a short, somewhat fat, bearded man enter the room, carrying a medical transcriptor. He wore the uniform of the IASA, but its light green color indicated his physician status. Link studied the man's deliberate gait as he approached the bed. "Good morning," he said, intoning pleasantness with some effort.

"Hello, Herson." Link looked away. He did not want to talk.

"We're not finished with the tests yet," said the doctor. "But from the early data, there doesn't seem to be any physiological damage."

"That's comforting. So I'm just imagining it all...is that it?"

Herson ignored the remark. "But we're going to make some more tests—just to be positive."

Link relaxed his body, feeling the tension leave his muscles.

He had to admire Herson's patience with him, the doctor's cool professionalism in the face of his madness. "All right, then," Link finally said. "What's wrong with me?"

"We're not sure, of course. But you seem to be suffering from some kind of sensory deprivation." Dr. Herson rubbed his beard absently. "The drugs seem to be controlling it most of the time… But we need more time, to be certain. The computers are working on it."

"Yes, I'm okay now," said Link, massaging his temples. "Calm. Rested. But the darkness is still there inside me, just hanging over me. I can still feel it, and it's not going away. It's like half of me just isn't there anymore."

"The chemotherapy should help," said the doctor as he nervously tapped the edge of the transcriptor. "But we've only just started in that area, and I'm afraid that the rest might be up to you."

"Meaning?"

"Meaning that you'll have to cooperate with us. You've got to stop lying here feeling sorry for yourself and decide whether or not you want to live in this comparatively bland world of ours."

Link could only nod in agreement. Herson was as perceptive as he was direct. The doctor had tried being sympathetic, but Link knew that such tactics were useless against death-wish cynicism. Herson's pragmatic approach was far more effective, and even more appealing to Link.

"Remember," Herson was saying, "the choice, in the end, can only be yours."

"Then I really don't have much choice at all, do I?" Link tried to smile, but failed.

Herson did smile, as if in mockery. Standing up, he said, "No, Link, you really don't." The bearded man turned and left the room.

The treatment plan was drawn up, and Link, somewhat to his own surprise, responded as best he could. At Herson's insistence, he did as much exercise and walking as possible. Enzyme injections had prevented his muscles from atrophying while aboard ship, but a rigorous program was still needed to assume complete control again. Gradually he increased his exercises until he was spending several hours each day walking through corridors of the installation. He would pause during these times only to look at the lake from the great cubed building's observation deck. It was so immense—a small sea.

From that height, he could see gentle surf touching the cliffs below. In the evenings, the images of the water were even more captivating; and he longed to be near it, as he had once longed to be near the stars. He felt an affinity to the sea: how it reached, and touched, and finally retreated from the land. It was as if the sea did not wish to come too close to the earth, for fear of being trapped there—as Link was now trapped.

The beach held a special fascination for him. In it, he saw a twilight place—a place where he might stand and contend with the forces that still threatened to overwhelm him. Perhaps the beach was a compromise where solutions could be pieced together. Link's mind, he felt, was standing in a twilight place between sanity and madness, between life and death.

He was thinking more clearly now; Herson's chloropromazines seemed to be working. He no longer feared that the remaining half of his mind would be blotted out like errant ink on a page. The tormented visions had almost ceased entirely.

Almost.

There were still nights when he would wake up screaming into the darkness of his room. The moonlight, flowing through his window, would burn his eyes. The memories of the stars and the wailing light-years would come rushing back, seeking out the cybernetic complex that was no longer there. The hum of the air conditioners became the crackle of ionic storms; the room became the suspension tank and he almost gagged as he fought to keep the colloidal liquid from drowning him. He fought against these attacks—"lapses," Herson had called them—until they eventually faded and disappeared. But he was always left shaking with the knowledge that specters still lurked within his divided mind.

Days passed into weeks and the lapses grew less frequent. Perhaps the time was growing near when they would cease altogether.

Link hoped this were so, although that fact would only mean new obstacles to overcome. Life still offered him little solace. His talks with Herson seemed to underscore this; and he would still have to choose between a life or a death. It was at this time he was allowed to walk along the beach. He began looking forward to those times. They gave his life some purpose, and each day he spent more time there, walking more miles, thinking more clearly.

Link noticed an oddity about the place. Perhaps it was the underwater configuration of shoreline, or perhaps it was a particularly strong undercurrent; he was never sure. In the evenings, when the tide went out, he saw that the beach strewn with the casual debris of life. Along his path, he encountered things which the sea had rejected like unwanted offspring. Usually they were creatures that, once cast out, could not return. Link knew that death patrolled that narrow wet strip of sand. Often, he stood and watched the gulls swoop down ahead of him to feast among the dead and dying creatures of the sea. He heard the screams of the birds, which sounded to him like a final alarm, and perhaps a final solution.

It made him think of the utter unpredictability of the sea and of all living things. Man included. The sea: great wellspring, giver of life, magical. It had spawned life and awareness, and that awareness seemed to be rushing out at him. It came to him from some unremembered primordial center as the galaxies had done, expanding into endless night.

Link felt that he was growing to know some of the sea's many moods and temperaments. (It was actually a great lake, but Link always thought of it as "the sea.") He had seen its storms, which were brief yet fierce affairs. And when they struck, death became an even busier collector along the shoreline. But sometimes, after such a storm, Link had seen other, far stranger types of collectors. They were usually men from the nearby City who walked the beaches carrying knapsacks. They looked for the simple treasures of the storm-swept sand: a crustacean husk, a shell, or perhaps a sponge-like thing that once had been alive.

Link had always thought it was a morbid pastime. He envisioned greater beings than ourselves, at some future time, rummaging among the graves of men—looking for a particularly well-turned skull or a curious piece of gristle.

But one evening, having walked farther than usual, Link discovered that he had passed beyond sight of the installation. It was beyond the last point of land and the thought unsettled him a bit, much like the feelings of a small boy who wanders away from his home for the first time. Recognizing this latent fear, he continued walking, since he was determined to regain total control of himself.

Looking off into the distance, Link saw a solitary figure walking along the barren, wind-swept shore. The person's silhouette was framed by the amethyst evening sky, and Link stopped to watch while the wind's fingers combed through his hair and danced upon his face. The person ahead of him seemed to be engaged in some serious and private activity: crouching down in the sand for a few moments, then standing up and tossing something out to sea.

Link began walking again, closing on the figure until he was near enough to see that it was a young woman. The moon was coming up now, and it cast pale yellow veils along the blue isle of night. He could see her clearly in the soft, new light as she moved gracefully across the sand. Link felt something stirring within his mind; a reaction to her aesthetic sensuality. He continued to walk toward her until he was only several meters away.

Turning, she faced him. Her face was a perfect oval, which radiated warmth and serenity. She showed no fear of him and the hint of a smile danced upon her lips.

"It's a beautiful night, isn't it?" she asked.

Link did not reply. He could not. He was so taken with her simple words. Her voice was the soft sound of the sea; it rolled over him and then withdrew, leaving him refreshed.

She turned and began walking again, as if to indicate that Link should follow her. He did this, and they walked for several minutes in what Link felt was an awkward silence.

Suddenly, unexpectedly, she stopped as they approached an object lying on the beach ahead of them. She huddled down to examine it, and Link watched as her fingers lightly touched the quivering body of a mutated fish, washed up helplessly onto the sand. Its slimy skin reflected the moonglow; its solitary eye stared upward at Link. He could almost feel the hopelessness that radiated from that eye.

The girl took the sea-thing into her hands.

Before she stood, Link forced himself to speak. "Do you ... collect them?" His voice was shallow, fraught with tension.

"In a way." She looked up and smiled. "But only the living."

Link did not immediately understand the reply. He could only watch as she stood up, holding the limp creature in her right hand. A wave broke on the beach, and she drew back her arm and tossed the large-eyed thing far out into the deep water. It fell and disappeared beyond the breakers.

"Perhaps it will live now..." she said as she wiped her hands on her faded jeans.

Link looked at her cautiously, not wanting her to know that he was studying her. She was attractive in an odd sort of way. It had something to do with the collection of outstanding characteristics, but Link was not able to articulate it. Her skin was cool ivory; her eyes were large, black pearls, her hair was a raven fall, tangled by the salt spray. He was embarrassed that she should look upon his cracked, star-burned features, that she should tolerate his awkward presence.

"I saw you before," he said finally, aware of the silence but almost sorry that he had disturbed it. "Back there, I mean. When I was coming up the beach."

She nodded and pushed a strand of hair from her cheek.

"Do you walk here very often?" He wished to hear her voice again.

"Oh, yes." She paused and laughed lightly, casting a quick glance out to the sea. "Every night. But not always this beach." She glanced down at the sand. "There are so many beaches along this coast... and so many nights."

Link could only nod his head in agreement, although he did not really understand her. He followed her in silence as she began walking again. Entering a small cove, she came upon another beached creature which still glistened with the faint glow of life.

Spying it, Link was repulsed by its shape—a blistered, crab-like thing with long, sagging antennae. He stood dumbly as she bent down and picked up the thing in her delicate fingers. Again she threw it back to the dark waters. It made a brief splash of whiteness as it struck the surface, and then it was gone.

Saying nothing this time, she continued to walk, and Link followed. He was struck then as to how futile her mission actually was. No matter how many of them she could save from oblivion each night, he thought, the difference was sure to be slight. She must have known, he thought, that death raced across the beaches of the planet at a pace far greater than hers, collecting more than she ever could.

But he did not tell her this. Instead, he asked, "Do you live close by?"

"In the City, with my father. He used to be a fisherman, many years ago. Now they have machines that do a better job."

She stopped, as her eyes looked past him, scanning the immediate strip of beach ahead of them. It was as if their conversation was not important, but rather something to fill in the idle moments of her mission. But she must have noticed Link's disappointment with this, because she seemed to catch herself up in this action and return her gaze to Link. He too felt the change and he hoped that she possessed some magical, mystical talent that would tell her that Link needed to talk. He wanted her to know that he was so terribly alone in a world that he did not like.

"What about you?" she said gently. "Are you from this area too?"

He tensed unconsciously, although he appreciated her interest in him. She was staring at him and he was captivated by the almost bottomless depths of her eyes. There was a pause before he answered. "Oh, no, not really the installation, back up that way." He pointed toward the direction from which he had come. "I'm... staying there for a while."

"I thought so," she said nodding. Her voice was still as soft as the gentle roll of the surf. "I recognized the emblem on your jumpsuit."

He was not surprised by her perceptiveness; yet it made him wonder if she knew what he was. Or rather, what he had been. He was sure that she would think it a most unnatural existence. The thought was unsettling, and Link cast it from his mind.

They walked farther. The moon was higher, and it no longer cut a yellow swath across the sea's emerald surface. Link grew more captivated by her, by her warmth that be so dearly needed. Words rattled through his mind, but he could not say them. He felt the conflicts rising up inside his head; he was becoming confused.

Then there came a roaring in his ears that he knew did not come from the sea around him. It grew until it was a scream echoing down the corridors of space and time, and Link knew she could not hear it. The moon fell. The sea swam in mind-darkness and the wind became the hot breath of alien stars. His mouth filled with the salty taste of stars' blood.

He faltered, staggering away from her.

"Are you all right?" Her voice slipped gently between the layers of madness.

Pressing his hands to his temples, he turned away. "No." He almost shouted the word. "No...it's nothing. I'm okay." Memories and sensations from another time raged through him. There was a curtain of darkness enveloping him. He wanted to avoid her; he did not want her to see him during the attack. "I've got to go now ..." he heard a strange voice saying. Was it his own? He could no longer be positive, as he battled to keep control. Images flickered past his eyes: warps, pulsars, coronas, and a thousand more all at once. Link watched them with fear and fascination as he floated in a netherworld of delusion.

He was walking. Alone. It was still night, and he was walking back along the beach toward the installation. Each step brought him more firmly into focus, closer to the immense concrete cube. Looking up, he saw it rising up out of the fog of his conscious mind, and the thought struck him that he had returned to it as if by instinct. The attack had subsided, and it was leaving him. He refocused his vision, heard the hushed crashes of the surf, felt the wet firmness of the sand beneath his boots.

Exhaling long and slowly, he stopped in that twilight area

between the sea and the land. He remembered her and turned away from the dark cube on the cliffs, searching, hoping...

But she was gone.

He was lost; yet he was not. He felt pain; yet he did not. He feared something, but he did not want to articulate that fear. The taste of it was so bitter, and he welcomed it. He hoped that it was the herald of something new awakening within himself.

Link inhaled deeply, drawing the sea-strangled air into his body. The salty breath, which once carried the seeds of life itself, rushed into him. He stood silent for a moment, trying to capture the earlier events of the night. But the wind was growing chilly, and finally, he pulled up his collar against it and returned to the installation.

He awoke to a montage of white and green: more tests: wires, screens, charts, words, hands, and theories. Everything flowed into one and he accepted it like a purging bath. Link could now wait patiently for the chance to tell Herson what had happened on the beach.

And when he had told the doctor of the entire encounter, Herson sat quietly, stroking his beard. Link watched the man's eyes: small, but expressing concern and intelligence.

"You sound like you enjoyed the experience," said Herson after a long moment of silence.

"Yes, I did...I think I did."

"Even though you suffered another deprivation lapse? Immediately afterward?" Herson leaned closer in his chair, staring intently into Link's eyes.

"Yes. I don't think the two events were related. Not really."

"Why not?"

"I just don't." Link raised his voice slightly. "Because, well, there were some other things...thoughts I had after I recovered."

"Can you explain these thoughts?"

"I don't know," said Link, looking away, rubbing his eyes out of habit. "Maybe. Before I came back last night, but after the attack, I spent some time just watching the sea. Alone. It was funny, but it looked different. It was like...well, I'm not sure..."

"This is interesting," said Herson. "Would you like me to supply the analogy?"

"What?"

"Would you like me to try and complete your impression of what it was like? I think I have a good idea as to what it was." Herson smiled.

"How could you?" Link's curiosity was piqued.

"Just a hunch, that's all." Herson grinned. "All right. Go on, try."

"When you looked out at the ocean after the attack and the meeting with the girl, you felt the same... satisfaction, shall we call it? ...that you enjoyed when you were a cyborg aboard the ship. That's it, isn't it?"

"Yes. I guess it was," said Link, nodding slowly, and admitting the fact to himself for the first time.

"So," said Herson, patting him on the knee. "You see now that it can happen here? On Earth, I mean."

Link nodded.

"That's good," said Herson, as he stood and prepared to leave. "We have at last reached the beginning."

Link started to speak, to question the doctor, but he cut him off: "That's enough for today. Get some rest. I'll see you again tomorrow."

After Herson had left, Link reviewed the last fragments of their conversation, sifting through the words, looking for some grain of insight that might spark off the proper connections in his mind. He knew Herson seemed to have understood what he had tried to say.

• • •

At dusk, Link left the white room, the green robes, and the stark corridors of the installation, preferring the cool-blue arms of evening that waited to embrace him. He was drawn to the beach and the tide that was now receding from it. The sky was terribly clear and the sea was smooth, but he sensed an odd mood in the air. As if sudden changes could burst upon the shore with little notice. Already, the retreating tide had speckled the sand with several dead and dying creatures from the sea.

But this time as Link viewed the sight, he was not reminded of life's futility. She had shown him a different view—a new way of seeing in the twilight. It was a place of multiple realities, of this he was now certain. Even in the midst of dying, there could be purpose. He began walking, and continued for almost an hour. He was only vaguely aware of the path of footprints he left in the sand.

Instead, he searched for hers.

The moon grew high and small, becoming lost on the now clouded vault above him. The wind grew stronger and less comforting, less inviting; yet he walked on. But he saw no trace of her. With a growing anxiety, he remembered her words: There are so many beaches ... so many nights. Perhaps she was not coming here again? Perhaps he had never seen her in the first place. It was a staggering thought to think she had only been a bizarre manifestation of his madness.

But no. There was something magical about this place where he walked, where he searched. He would not give up so easily. He knew that where he now walked was a place where a solitary human being had passed nightly to battle death. Link now realized also that there were, perhaps, different kinds of death. Finding her would confirm his feelings.

He rounded a jutting point of land, and he saw her.

Beyond a finger of rocks stretching out to touch the waves stood the girl. As he began walking quickly toward her, he twice saw her pause to return some hapless creature back to the sea.

Then Link slowed his pace, calming himself, suppressing the joy he felt at finding her. He cast a glance downward at the sand and muck that slid past his boots, and he saw something. In the swirling foam, there was a small and slimy thing. Its pores were glutted with sand, suffocating it in the night breeze. Link stooped down and picked it up, feeling its tiny spicules against his palm.

He continued to approach her, and she turned, sensing his nearness, to watch him draw closer. Her eyes dropped to the pulsating thing he held in his hand, and she nodded gently.

"I'm sorry," Link said when he was close to her. "About last night. I really don't remember—"

She silenced him with a simple gesture—a lowering of her eyes and a slight shake of her head.

"I'm sorry," he said again. Then after a pause: "I've come to...
join you."

She smiled and her eyes danced with lively amber and brown. As
Link watched her, he felt a smile forming on his own lips—the first
in a long, long time, it seemed. She laughed softly and looked out to
the star-filled sea.

Pulling back his arm, Link flung the creature far out into the
night. Time seemed to slow as he watched its path describe a
graceful arc across the violet sky. Masked by the whisper of the surf,
it noiselessly penetrated the surface and was gone.

Seeing this, Link felt an atavistic surge within his mind. It was
not unlike the cybernetic taste of the stars themselves. Something
inside himself was coming to life again.

"It's beautiful, isn't it?" she asked, as if she could sense the
feelings in his soul.

Link turned to her and nodded. He reached out to touch her
hand.

"Your name," he said softly. "What is it?"

# HOPIUM DEN

## JOHN SKIPP

I've always loved the Pacific Coast Highway at night. Moonbeam dance over endless waves across an infinite horizon. Wind whipping my hair and ruffling my blouse, with the windows down. All the regular shit that somehow never gets old when you're in it, senses alive and paying attention.

I love my life. That's why I kept it.

But some nights are harder than others.

The car hears me crying, knows what song I want to hear, puts it on almost before I start singing. I'm pretty high—way too high to be driving—and am grateful it's steering its own wheel tonight.

I thank it. It says you're welcome and guns it to 150. I start laughing. Its engine purrs as it accelerates, hits 200. I let out a rip-roarin' "WOOOOOO!!!" It sure knows how to cheer a gal up.

All the roads are a lot less crowded now. Fewer people means fewer cars, all driving themselves and whoever's still here wherever they want to go. I remember when getting from Zuma to downtown L.A. took hours in traffic. Those days are gone.

Before we know it, we are in the glimmering husk of metropolis. Almost no one lives on the streets anymore. Just another problem solved. We weave past empty block after empty block. And all the traffic lights are green.

I close my eyes for a minute. Then the car says we're here, pulling over. I thank it, get out. It locks the door behind me. I look around, see no one. That's fine.

The only one I wanna see is Johnny.

I still like cigarettes. They remind me of home. Since nobody minds if we die anymore, just so long as we're happy, that works out great. I know Johnny would like one, like to taste it on my lips.

I light one up, take my time strolling down the long promenade to the storage center. My shadow is the only one moving. The city keeps the lights on, as a courtesy to those remaining.

The city takes care of itself.

The sliding glass door opens and I step inside, still smoking. There's nobody at the security desk but the security desk itself. I tell it what I'm here for. It is courteous and kind. Flashes me directions I already know. I thank it, walk past it and down to Corridor Three.

Corridor Three is like every other corridor in every other storage center. I've been to thirty dozen, and they're all the same. Hallway after hallway of doors upon doors. All that unused downtown space has finally come in handy.

Johnny's in 317, with a thousand other people. There are no other people in the hall. 600,000 people under this one roof, and none of them walking. Just my long shadow and I. My shadows. In front. In back. To either side, as the overhead lights bisect them.

The door's unlocked. Why wouldn't it be. So much less to fear now that all of the frightened are gone. The only ones left are the ones that really want to be here.

No. That's not fair. But you can't say it ain't accurate.

"Okay, then," I say, walking into Room 317 of the Hopium Den. And all of the dreamers are there.

I look at them. Look at my smoke. Say fuck it and light another, drop the dead one to the floor and grind it out with my heel.

They won't care. Almost all the complainers are gone. Gone to here. Gone to the place where their complaints are no longer an issue.

In row after row after row.

And stack after stack after stack.

I wonder if any of them can smell it. I doubt it. I certainly can't smell them. The ventilation is superb. These environments are self-containing, self-sustaining. Technology once again for the win.

I let the door close behind me, watch my smoke lift up and out a vent. I thank it.

And think, oh, sweet sorrow.

Looking at all of you.

I've been here enough to know some of your histories. They play on the screens of your cocoons, let us know whatever you chose to have us know about you. THIS IS WHO I AM, you say, through digital images left for the actively living.

Most of you are lying. And are happy to do so. I don't blame you a bit. It's just not my style.

I chose staying awake. Don't ask me why. Maybe it's an issue of trust. Maybe I just thought that being born was a challenge I'd been given that I was supposed to play out in real time, not handed over to a machine-driven imaginarium of wish-fulfillment dream-enaction. No matter *how* well they drive. No matter how vivid. No matter how much you feel it, and believe it.

Maybe I'm just stubborn.

And Johnny, you know I am.

So I look at Peggy, in her pristine apartment, with her three perfect kids forever; I look at Deke and Farik, forever locked in holy war, never having given up their sacred causes, killing each other over and over; I look at Jasmine, composing symphony after symphony; I look at Lee, in his imaginary mansion, fucking underage children till the end of time.

I totally get why you'd want to live your dream, given the choice between here and there. And somberly salute your choices.

Then walk the hall down to my Johnny, twelve rows in and on the bottom, for e-z access. And there you are.

"Hey, baby," I say.

Like almost everyone else's, your cocoon says you're now immensely successful, tremendously enjoying your life. This time around, you're a top-ranked jazz pianist, gourmet chef, and world-renowned philosopher, admired by the finest, most discerning minds in all of fantasyland (including an admirable list of lovers that stupidly blips at my jealousy gland). Somehow, you've brought all these disparate vocabularies together into a clarified vision of deep human understanding that's actually *making a difference* in a world wracked by chaos and sorrow and pain.

I smile at the thought of making a difference, now that all the difference has already been made. I smile because making a difference used to be all we had. Our whole reason for being. Right after *look out for # 1.*

The city takes care of itself now. As does the world at large. We were the interim step, from nature to super-sentient macro-nature. Taking control, but letting everything be. So self-aware and utterly interconnected it can micro-dial everything at once.

The city doesn't need us anymore. Either does the world, for that matter.

The only question left is:

*Which where do we want to be?*

I'd like to think that the deeper out is the deeper in. That the real one remains the one to beat. That still *living this life*—even though (fuck that, maybe even BECAUSE) the machines have it all running smoothly, at last, forever—is somehow better than just dreaming the best dream our machines can manufacture.

I have no proof of this, of course, but they're more than willing to give me the benefit of the doubt. They let me live my life the way I want to. And right back at 'em. We coexist now, after all. And are both really cool about it.

I touch the screen, and all your projections disappear. Then it's just me, reflected on the sleek surface.

Looking at what's left of my sweet husband.

A desiccate meat shadow, inside his cocoon.

"Oh, you fucker," I say, and the tears come back, and it pisses me off, but I just can't help it. "You may not believe this, but it's pretty sweet out here. *Almost all of the assholes are gone!* Can you believe it? I mean, Kendra's still Kendra. But once she realized the world didn't need her to save it, she kinda relaxed into dominating the occasional Sunday brunch. I hardly even wanna strangle her any more. And her poetry? It's honestly gotten...well, almost pretty good.

"But, baby? More than that, *the fucking oceans are clean.* They actually figured it out. Got down there and detoxified the whole toxic bouillabaisse. Those nanobots are the shit.

"We couldn't do it. But they could. And they did. I swim in

146

the ocean every day. I see whales leap at dawn from our bedroom window. Not even remotely extinct. They are, in fact, thriving.

"And there's *no more war, Johnny!* It's done! Everyone who still thought there was a reason to fight gave it up the second their needs got met. *Everyone's needs are getting met.* Life doesn't have to be a hellhole any more. All the big weapons got defused. And all the kill freaks get to dream about killing each other forever.

"Evidently, it's very emotionally satisfying, cuz roughly a trillion people are actively engaged in it. That's how they wanna live. That's how they wanna go out. Just fighting and fighting and proving they're right.

"But the good news is: the rest of us don't have to put up with it anymore. We're not stuck in the middle of their holy war. You know how we used to joke that it would be great if they just had their own planet to slug it out on, and we didn't have to watch? Well, NOW THEY DO! It's all experienced down to the tiniest detail. As far as their neurons are concerned, the apocalypse is ON! And they're right in the middle. Exactly where they wanna be.

"I love that it's all so real for them. I really do. If that's what they want, let 'em have it."

I blow a plume of smoke directly at you, hope you smell it. A little reek of nostalgia.

"Like you. I mean, I love that you're playing jazz piano now. I know how bad you wanted it. You always said you could play like McCoy fucking Tyner if you could only practice fifteen hours a day for fifty years. And from what I can tell, you've lived fifty lifetimes since you said goodbye to me.

"That was just a couple years ago, out here, you know," I say.

But you don't know.

You're not hearing a word I'm saying.

I stop talking, start crying some more, and just take a moment to soak in the barely-breathing gruesome corpse of you. Asleep and adream in your little cocoon. You look waaaaay beyond terrible, so much body fat and muscle leeched away by inertia that I barely recognize the flesh lazily draped across your bones, like shabbily-hung antique wallpaper.

What's left of the real you is connected to your mortal remains by a web of filaments and tubes. Wiring you in. Feeding and extruding the waste from what strikes me, as I sob, as nothing more and nothing less than the sheer wreckage and necrotic waste of the excellent man I once knew and loved. Who used to love me.

Who swore he would stand at my side, till death do us part.

But given the choice, not enough to stay.

This is a lot to let go of. But you have already let go entirely. I give you three months at the outside. Maybe a couple extra dream-lives, at most.

You won't be coming back, that much is for certain. There's not nearly enough of you left. I briefly replay my wild fantasy of banging you back to life, and it's just too fucking pathetic. The fact that it would probably also kill you is almost beside the point.

This is my last chance to get mad at you, but I just can't whip it up. So I wipe my tears back-handed, till my vision clears enough to watch your eyes minutely flicker behind those tissue-thin lids. *Something's* going on in there.

I'd love to believe that the rictus on the skull of your scarecrow frame is a smile.

It could be. It totally could.

"You know what makes me saddest?" I say. "It's that you'll never know what you missed. Who you could have been. What you could have done, in this weird new world. What *we* could have done. What you could have done with me.

"I mean, I know you never got what you wanted in this life. And when you got it, you were never satisfied. The dream was always better than the reality. I get that. I do.

"That's why we were so good, for so long. You kept the dream alive. And I kept *us* alive, by attending to reality. Making sure you lived to dream another day.

"I know it's hard for you to understand. But I *like reality better.* It means more to me. It really does. The simple, stupid shit is what I love. The day to day. The week to week. The year to year. All the little things that happen.

"That's what I like. That's why I was with you. Not for your dreams, but because I just loved being around you, and with you.

"That was all that I wanted.

"But I can't have that."

There are no more tears left in me. But I have another smoke, which I light off the corpse of the last, let it drop to my feet. Will pick them up on my way out.

I am on my way out.

"I'm gonna go live," I say. "I don't need a job any more. Nobody who doesn't want one needs a job any more. The machines unemployed us from every stupid job we ever hated. All that wasted time is just sitting there, waiting for us to fill.

"So I'm gonna go home, and feed the dogs and cats snacks— Phoebe's gone, by the way, but I got three more—and then I'm gonna go to bed and listen to McCoy fucking Tyner, pretending it's you, till I fall asleep. Then I'm gonna wake up, watch the whales jump outside our window, kiss the pillow beside me, and tell you what a chickenshit asshole you are for missing this.

"Then I'm gonna water the garden, and not feel guilty, because the machines desalinated enough ocean that Los Angeles will never be starving again.

"Then I'm gonna make huevos rancheros for Ravi, who is 100% accurate in thinking that I'm going to fuck him senseless very shortly after breakfast.

"Then I'm gonna spend a couple hours fucking Ravi some more. Laughing. Being human. Goofing around like animals do. At some point, we will pause for more food. I may play him the song I wrote for you twenty years back. If I do, he will understand why it means so much to me. Then I will fuck him some more. And I'll cry. And he'll hold me. It will all be very nice.

"Then the sun will set. It will be gorgeous. It's *so* gorgeous now, baby, you wouldn't believe it. All the nanobots have eaten most of the pollution straight out of the air, but it totally didn't undercut the color scheme. Somewhere between God and cyber-nature, it's all working out real well."

You smile a little. It could be gas. It could be me and the universe getting through. Will never know. Not for me to know. Doesn't matter at all.

You're in your own place now. I may not even be in it at all. Maybe you wiped me clean. Maybe I'm still central. Or just off to the side. A whisper of a memory of life not erased, but from here on tactically evaded.

I start to sing you the song, but I just don't feel it. It's a ritual whose time has passed. So many rituals gone by the wayside now. No longer required.

There's an enormous difference between no longer needed and no longer wanted. The machines no longer need us. But they like us. And that is great. It's like all the pieces of God clicking into place at last.

You go your way, and I go mine.

I am cool with this at last.

"So long, Johnny," I say. Picking up the butt, and then kissing your screen one last time. The screen relights, shows me who you are dreaming yourself to be now. It looks great.

I walk back down the length of the opium den into which you all have vanished. The Hopium Den. One stacked corpse-in-waiting after another, dreaming and dreaming again.

All you ever wanted was to matter. And now you do. At least to yourselves. And the imaginary audience you dreamed at. The ones who'd finally understand.

I walk out to my car. It is happy to see me.

Happy in real life.

"I love you," I say.

# LESS THAN HUMAN

## MARGE SIMON

She was born blind, our child.
We Normals can't imagine
how it would be to remain so.
She'd never find work in our Domes,
nor develop complex social skills.

With clay she molded our likenesses,
for her fingers were supple in those days.
She claimed she saw with her hands.
Perhaps she saw too much,
and surely heard too much.

She was given to spells of impertinence
that could prove dangerous to our family.
Too many questions for one so young,
as if she could find fault—she, but a child!
with how our society operates.

Orion Zangara 2016

The pills didn't work.
Prescriptions only made her very ill.
We finally put her in the basement,
without substances to sculpt
without a source of sound,
back into her own dark.

Orion Zangara 2016

Before we put her down below,
I took a hammer to her fingers.
It was a painful thing for me to do,
but she was flawed from birth
and therefore need not be treated
by our Laws, as Human.

# DOG AT THE LOOK

## B.E. SCULLY

The sex women were gone by seven A.M. *The first floor rooms were rented by the hour, but Song Ying had learned that most prostitutes weren't morning people.* The Hotel Reo wasn't the kind of place to give out those little "Do Not Disturb" signs, and even in the few rooms where the sign hadn't been lost, destroyed, or stolen, most guests weren't inclined to use it. In a place like the Hotel Reo, it was understood that people didn't want to be disturbed.

Which is why Song always started her shift on the second floor, where the "normal" people stayed. Or at least as normal as you could expect in this part of town. Take the man in #211, the room Song was now pushing her cart toward. For the past seven days, she'd knocked three times on his door and called out "Housekeeping!" When no one answered, she let herself in, quietly and discreetly, like she'd been taught when she started this job seven years ago. And every morning, she'd find the man sitting on the edge of his stained, wafer-thin mattress, staring at a huge crack in the wall opposite him.

He never spoke to her, and of course Song Ying never spoke to him. It wasn't unusual for guests to stay in the room while she cleaned. Some of the lonely ones tried to talk to her, and some of the angry ones tried to harass her. Once she'd cleaned a room for a man who walked around stark naked the whole time without even glancing her way. But usually they just ignored her, which was fine with Song. She was invisible to them, but what they didn't know was that they were invisible to her, too.

But the man in #211 wasn't invisible. Apart from the fact that he never seemed to change his clothes, there wasn't anything particularly weird or alarming about him. He was just an ordinary man, maybe around sixty years old—not much older than Song Ying. He had smooth grey hair over a smooth grey head, like a helmet. In fact, everything about him was grey, even his eyes. But there was something else—something intense, even desperate. Once, when Song was a little girl still living in China, she had seen a tiger sitting in a great steel cage, waiting to be taken somewhere. Even though her mother had told her not to, she had gone straight up to the cage. The tiger had seemed so powerful, but tired, too. Broken, defeated. But not too defeated to claw her to pieces the second it got the chance.

Grey Man reminded Song Ying of that tiger.

She should have reported the crack in the wall to the manager, a small, quiet man named Clyde who sat in his office all day watching television. She knew for a fact the crack hadn't been there before Grey Man checked in. Even worse, Grey Man had deliberately defaced hotel property. On the wall beside the crack, he'd written the words, "Look at the dog, dog at the look" in thick black letters. Song had no idea what that meant, but she also knew he'd written it, because the words hadn't been there before, either. Clyde was too cheap to fix the crack, but he'd go crazy once he got a look at that graffiti.

For some reason, though, Song Ying hadn't yet reported the destruction. Maybe she was curious about Grey Man, about his strange words and the strange crack. Maybe she was just too tired to want to deal with it. Because unlike the tiger, she didn't have any claws in wait.

She knocked three times and called "Housekeeping!" But when Song entered room #211, Grey Man wasn't there.

She was so surprised she went to check the room number just to make sure she had the correct one. The black words and the crack were still there. Grey Man had never had any luggage that she'd seen, but his room was still on her cleaning schedule, so he hadn't checked out.

Where had he gone?

Song Ying frowned at her own foolishness. Why shouldn't the man go out and enjoy the city? September was a fine month in San Francisco, so why sit in a flea-bag motel room staring at the wall all day?

And yet Song *was* surprised. It was impossible to imagine Grey Man taking the boat to Alcatraz Island, or eating sourdough bread by the wharf. In fact, it was impossible to imagine him anywhere but the edge of the bed, staring at the wall.

She gave a snort and plugged in the vacuum cleaner. She still had a floor and a half to clean. She didn't have time for strange grey men and nonsense.

She was polishing the chipped, dinghy mirror over the chipped, dinghy dresser when she realized she was standing right next to it—right next to the crack. Song did not consider herself a superstitious woman. Her maternal grandmother had believed in luck and signs and premonitions, and look where it had gotten her. All of her childhood Song had heard the stories of what everyone in the family called the Black Wave. When the Black Wave came, everyone knew to leave her grandmother alone no matter how long she stayed hidden in her bedroom with the door locked and the blinds drawn tight against the outside. In one story, her grandmother hid for seven straight days before emerging, sallow-skinned and hollow-eyed, to ask "Who wants breakfast?" even though it was ten o'clock at night.

Her grandparents had lived by a lake, and her grandmother's favorite thing was to swim far out into the deep, murky middle and just float there, sometimes for hours at a time. Whenever anyone asked why she spent so much time in the water, wrinkling up her skin and neglecting her household duties, she'd say, "It feels like being reborn."

Song Ying had never known either of her grandparents. When her grandmother was only thirty-two years old, her husband, Song's grandfather, had died instantly when a blood vessel burst in his brain.

After that, her grandmother spent almost all of her time at the lake, floating in the water or roaming the grassy shores like a shade.

"I no longer belong to this world," she would say to anyone who tried to talk to her or help her.

One day she walked down to the lake, waded out into the water, and kept going to the deep, murky middle. A fisherman said he saw her dive beneath the waves, but he didn't see her come back up. Her body was never recovered.

Song Ying's mother, only twelve years old, was sent to live with an uncle and aunt far away from the lake.

"Crazy in the head," Song's mother would tell her on the rare occasions she talked about her mother. "You must always be careful to keep the crazy out. When it's written in the genes, it can come back."

Maybe that's why Song's mother had little tolerance for anything she saw as "nonsense," and also why she'd drilled the same attitude so deeply into her own daughter.

When Song Ying left China and came to the United States, she didn't have time to worry about genes one way or the other. Work was as good a cure as any for whatever may or may not have been written there. There had been times when the Black Wave had come for her—when she'd lost her first child and been told that she couldn't have another. When first her father and then her mother died, and she eventually lost touch with everyone she had known in her old life.

Then seven years ago, while driving down one of the city's famously steep, winding roads, her husband had lost control of their car on a rain-slicked curve. The crash had killed him and put Song in a coma for two days. When she awoke, she had three long scars across the top and back of her head from being somersaulted from the car and smacked against the road. After that, she had to sell the small grocery she and her husband had run for almost thirty years. But Song did not walk into a lake and never return. She'd had to take the cleaning job just to survive, but life went on, as it always did.

And yet sometimes, late at night when she couldn't sleep and the mist came in thick and heavy off the sea, Song could almost feel the Black Wave rising, rising to sweep across the city and drag her out to the underwater world.

But the next day, the city was always still there, and she still had to go to work in it.

Her coworker Maria, who was twenty-one and so knew nothing about life, once told her, "You work too hard! You need to get out more, have fun. Have big adventures and dream big dreams!"

As if Song had never had fun or gone on big adventures or dreamed big dreams. But she had to admit, she hadn't done any of those things in a long time. Maybe that's why she was so interested in the Grey Man. In the crack.

In order to disturb Grey Man as little as possible, she'd always avoided it before, vacuuming that section of carpet quickly and moving on, aware of his eyes on the wall the whole time. But now she was alone.

She reached out and touched it. Nothing. She ran her finger up and down the chalky texture of the exposed drywall. Nothing. She snorted and shrugged and almost went back to her cleaning. But then the black words on the wall caught her eye.

"Look at the dog, dog at the look," she said, pressing her right pointer finger straight into the widest, deepest center of the crack.

The crack opened up, and Song Ying saw.

She saw an off-kilter sky filled with hazy purple light, as if filtered through a crooked, dirty screen. She saw streets running at impossible angles lined with blasted, twisted trees. She saw smoky, silent winds blow the debris of humankind down streets filled with toppled, towering ruins. She saw babies with the ancient, wizened face of the never born. She saw the waves move backward, toward the sea, and the sea rise vertically and then break, a black wave rushing over the ruined city. Then in the swirling water, moving with the waves, she saw the face of the Grey Man. He had squirming fish for eyes and a cave-mouth teeming with unseen creatures of the deep.

"What is it?" Song Ying cried out.

The cave opened and the sea creatures poured forth, translucent and twitching with primal life. "Not was is," the Grey Man said.

"What may be."

As Grey Man spoke the last word, a giant grey eel, pulsing and slick, slithered from his mouth and shot through the waves, straight toward Song Ying.

She opened her own mouth to scream and then she fainted.

"Hey, are you okay? Song Ying—wake up!"

She opened her eyes to see Maria's concerned face floating above her. She was gently shaking Song's shoulders, but Song could neither move nor speak. A thousand hammers were thundering against her head, and every time she tried to sit up, they pounded even harder.

Maria ran to the bathroom and came back with a wet rag, pressing it against Song's forehead. It helped, and Song Ying sat up.

"Where's the Grey Man?" she finally managed to ask.

"What, you mean the guy who stays here?" Maria clucked her tongue and shook her head. "Clyde is going to freak out when he sees what he did to the wall."

The crack. Song Ying looked at the crack, and the world turned a hazy, sickly purple.

"Hey, you scared me there for a minute," Maria was saying. "I know how you are, Song, but you should really take the rest of the day off. I mean it—maybe even go to the hospital. You don't look so good at all."

"The crack…" Song Ying said, and tried to stand before losing consciousness entirely.

She awoke in a stark white bed with a blue-green sheet pulled around it for privacy. A hospital—they must have called an ambulance at the Hotel Reo. Song Ying frowned, looking around for a nurse. She wondered how much all of this was going to cost.

Song sat up, slowly at first, but her head felt fine. A vision of a city with toppled, towering ruins skittered into her mind, but she smashed it before it had the chance to go any farther.

A fresh-faced young man burst through the sheet. "Welcome back!" he said, as bright and cheerful as if Song had just returned from a luxury cruise. "We thought you were going to stay conked out all night there for a while."

"What time is it?"

"Almost six o'clock at night," the young man said. "You've been here quite a while. We ran some tests on you while you were under—" He tapped the side of his head and winked at Song as if they shared a secret. "—to make sure everything's in working order. The doctor will be in to talk to you in just a sec."

The young man shined a light into her eyes, took her vital signs, and asked her questions like, "Who is the President of the United States?" Then he disappeared through the sheet, and Song waited, thinking nothing.

She didn't know how much time had passed before a woman came through the sheet.

"I'm Dr. Patel," she said, extending her hand. "I want to ask you a few questions, starting with the scars I noticed on your head. I assume they're from an old head injury?"

Song nodded and told her about the car accident.

Dr. Patel pulled a tablet out of her pocket and tapped at the keys. "Have you been experiencing any headaches lately? Bad ones where the pain is worse or lasts longer than an ordinary headache?"

Song *had* been having bad headaches lately, but she'd blamed the usual culprit—getting old. "I guess so."

"And how's your memory been? Any gaps in time that you can't remember?"

Song thought about the crack in the wall and shook her head. She remembered that too well.

"What about any changes in your mood or personality? Any feelings of, say, not being quite yourself?"

Song didn't think so, but then again, who was there to tell her otherwise? "Nothing I've noticed."

Dr. Patel pulled out another, larger tablet. She placed a film on the lit screen and Song Ying's brain appeared. "We took some images to help us figure out what happened, and for the most part, everything looks normal. Your vital signs are good and you seem alert and responsive—"

For the most part? "I feel fine."

"—but we did notice a little shaded area right here." Dr. Patel scooted closer and pointed out what she thought might be "a small lesion" at the back of Song Ying's brain. "It could be changes occurring because of the old injury, or something that was missed the first time around. Of course we won't know anything definite until we run more tests and compare them to your old records. But any time a person loses consciousness, especially with a medical history like yours, we want to look into it."

Song nodded, but only for the doctor's sake—no way in the world would her lousy health insurance cover tests like that!

Dr. Patel tucked her screen under her arm and stood up. "I've scheduled you for a series of follow-up appointments. We'd like to hold you here for a few more hours to make sure you're good to go, and you can confirm those appointment times with the check-out nurse."

Then she bustled out of the room. Every so often a nurse or assistant would come in and make her walk around or answer more questions or pee into a cup. Someone brought her a meal on a plastic tray, but Song wasn't hungry. Finally, she was allowed to leave. When the check-out nurse scheduled her follow-up appointments, Song took the cards with the times and dates and threw them in the trash on her way out the front door.

Song then did something she'd never done in her life, because who would pay to ride in a car when there were perfectly good buses or subways, or even your own two feet? But tonight Song called a cab and even gave the driver a generous tip, something she also rarely did, because no one tipped her extra for doing the job she was paid to do.

It was almost midnight when she reached her apartment. She tried to watch a few of her favorite Chinese television dramas, but she couldn't get interested, so she pulled the blinds, climbed into bed, and fell asleep.

And dreamed.

In her dream, Song was in her own kitchen. A peeling edge of wallpaper in the corner by the fridge drew her toward it. Even though she kept her apartment spotless, when Song pulled the wallpaper away, thousands of purple beetles poured out. On the back of every beetle rode another beetle with another beetle riding its back, and so on into infinity.

Song ran to the window, and even though her real-life apartment boasted no such view, she saw the Transamerica Pyramid, that forty-eight story icon of the San Francisco skyline with its needle hat puncturing the sky. As she stared at it, the Pyramid began to crack in half and thousands of purple beetles poured out. The longer she watched, the more certain she was that a face was forming among the teeming horde—the Grey Man's face. His eyes and nose were full of beetles. He opened his mouth and thousands more poured out, streaming through the city like floodwater.

In the single voice of a thousand chittering insects, the Grey Man said, "Are you willing to make the sacrifice?"

*What sacrifice?* Song wanted to ask, but when she opened her mouth, purple beetles poured out.

Choking. She was choking. The whole city was choking, the whole world...

"Yes!" she finally cried, waking with a start and jumping out of bed. "Yes!"

The cheap linoleum floor was ice cold beneath her feet. It was early, just past three in the morning. Song ran to the kitchen and checked every edge and crack. There was no peeling wallpaper, no purple beetles, no view of the Pyramid out the window.

Just a dream—but what a dream! Song placed her hand on the back of her head and pressed gingerly. She'd heard about people with brain injuries who started acting crazy and seeing and believing in things that weren't really there. Maybe that's what was happening to her—maybe the black wave had caught up with her after all.

She shouldn't have thrown those appointment cards away, but what good would they do? She had no one to help care for her, no one to help pay the bills. If she survived whatever was wrong with her, she'd be out on the streets to enjoy the rest of her life.

Song paced the small apartment. She should go back to bed;

her shift at the Hotel Reo started in less than three hours. Instead, for the second time in less than 24 hours, Song did something she never normally did—she put on her coat and went out into the night. The streets were filled with criminals and crazy people at this hour, but she didn't care.

She walked through her neighborhood toward Market Street, past the homeless people and runaways and drug addicts and forgotten people who took over the night until the city showed up for work the next morning. She looked for purple beetles, or twisted trees, or babies with ancient faces. But she saw only the city, the same as it always was.

She turned down a side alley toward home. If she hurried, she might manage to get some breakfast in her before she had to go to work.

And that's when she saw it. Scrawled on the wall in thick black letters were the words, "Look at the dog." Below them was written "Dog at the look" in softer, cursive letters.

Song Ying stopped. On the ground beneath the letters sat a huddled human figure swathed in a filthy blanket. For the third time, Song did something she never did. She approached the huddled human. She said, "Excuse me, can I ask you a question? What do those words mean?"

The human looked up—a woman, her hair hanging down in thick, matted grey braids. The woman said, "Anything you can spare, anything at all," and held out a bony, grimy hand.

Song moved closer. She knelt down in front of the woman and pointed at the graffiti. "Can you tell me what those words mean?"

The woman's eyes skittered from one side to the next. Her mouth was crusted with dried spittle, and she smelled like damp rot.

"Do you know what that graffiti means?" Song tried again. "Or who put it there?"

The woman's eyes danced madly. Crazy in the head, as Song's mother always said.

Song never gave money to homeless people, but it seemed to be a time for nevers. She reached into her coat pocket and pulled out a five dollar bill. She held it out, and the woman reached for it. Only instead of taking the money, she gripped Song's hand with surprisingly strong fingers.

"Let go!" Song yelled. But the woman wouldn't let go, and when Song looked into her eyes, they were still and clear. They were also grey—grey like the rest of her, grey like the Grey Man.

"Are you still willing to make the sacrifice?" Grey Woman asked, her voice as clear and calm as her eyes.

Still? What sacrifice did Song supposedly say she'd make? Then Song remembered the Grey Man and the beetles and the question. And her answer: Yes, not once, but twice—yes.

For a moment, Song felt a flush of pride—of course she would make the sacrifice! What kind of a person did these Grey People think she was, a useless old woman too selfish to save the human race?

But then she snorted, disgusted with herself for such nonsense. And yet what *had* she seen in room #211 that had followed her home and invaded her dreams?

"What sacrifice?" Song Ying asked. She could feel the black wave swirl around her ankles, luring her out to sea. "What do these words mean? What is happening to me?"

The woman let go of her hand. "A crack. A place, a moment where things line up just so. But something goes wrong, something gets out of line. And the crack opens up, and other worlds come in."

"You mean the Hotel Reo? What other worlds?"

"Worlds other than the apparent world." The woman flung her arms open, and Song jumped back. "Worlds that divide and multiply. Worlds upon worlds upon worlds, all different, yet the same. Into infinity. But sometimes, things get out of line, and a crack opens up."

Song Ying saw the crack at the back of her brain open up, too. One tiny purple beetle crawled out before the crack sealed shut again. She closed her eyes, but the woman's voice continued.

"Things come through the crack that shouldn't come through." Grey Woman shook her head and shivered. "All things multiple and divide. It's the way of things, it's infinity. But things that should not be multiply into *more* things that should not be."

"What's that have to do with me?" Song demanded. "I'm just an ordinary woman in an ordinary life. I know nothing about anything!"

Grey Woman smiled. "Not many do."

"Then why are you telling me this?"

"Because you asked."

Song didn't have an answer for that. She also didn't understand a word of what the woman was saying, but she still wanted to know one thing: "What does that graffiti mean? About the dog?"

But Grey Woman didn't answer, at least not directly. "When a crack opens up, some people can come through the crack, too—can go back and forth between worlds."

"Like travelers?"

Grey Woman nodded. "Like travelers. But it's always difficult, and always imperfectly done. Things come through fragmented, incomplete. I only know certain things, and I'm not even sure if what I know can put things back into line. There's always some missing part, some unforeseen, uncontrollable "X" factor…"

The woman trailed off, and Song considered that whoever was in charge of putting things back into line hadn't been very smart in hiring these Grey People, but she kept it to herself. "Then what do you want with me?"

"Nothing. If you are the missing part, the unforeseen "X" factor, then nothing I do or say at this point matters. My job is finished. Now it's up to you."

"I don't understand! Now what's up to me?"

Grey Woman sat up straight, thinking. Then she said, "Since mathematics is everything and everything is mathematics, perhaps you should think of it like that. Like the computer code so important to your world. Picture millions and millions of lines of codes being written across the universe, infinitely. Sometimes, one tiny number goes wrong, and the whole thing falls apart. Our job is to find that tiny number and fix it. But like I said, it's an imperfect process, and fixing the code is different every time. We fail as many times as we succeed, in part because every world has different rules."

"About math?"

"No! Math is its own infinite rule. I mean different rules about things like time—time running backward, or in different directions at once. Water breathed as air, and air walked upon like the ground. Animals speaking in human tongues, and humans singing like birds. Waves that flow backward, toward the sea, and rain that falls upward, toward the sky."

Song felt dizzy, unable to remain upright. She leaned her hand against the alleyway's grimy wall to keep from falling. "And you say the broken code can be fixed? Can be rewritten?"

Grey Woman slumped back against the wall. "Or unwritten. But there's always some kind of sacrifice—something that either can't go back through the crack to its own world, or can't stay here in this one once the code has been fixed. Every time a number changes, another changes as a result. Every time a number is added, another has to be taken away..."

But suddenly the clarity went out of Grey Woman's eyes, and they once again skittered with incoherence. Grey Woman mumbled something, stopped as if trying to collect her thoughts, but then put her head down on her arms. Song saw a thin stream of liquid trickle from beneath where she was sitting. The liquid was a murky purple color.

Song turned and ran out of the alley. She ran until she ran out of breath, and then she walked. She didn't know how far or how long, but when she stopped, she was by the water, at Pier 39, where the tourists gathered to shop and catch the ferry to Alcatraz.

Song turned to face a crowd of people gathered in the middle of the square. From somewhere in the crowd, a child's voice called out, "Look at the dog!"

Song looked to where the child was pointing and saw a three-legged dog running into traffic. Suddenly, the sky turned an off-kilter, hazy purple, as if filtered through a crooked, dirty screen. It turned blue again and then back to purple, over and over again, endlessly, maddeningly. The Transamerica Pyramid trembled and cracked open at the top. One tiny purple beetle skittered down the needle-hat and disappeared. Then the waves ran backward. The sea rose up vertically and stopped, undulating with fish and crabs and sea algae suspended in an invisible mid-air fishbowl.

In the silent, windless air, Song Ying called out, "Dog at the look!"

The three-logged dog began running backward, back toward the crowd of people. The sky turned purple one last time and then gave way to blue for good. The Pyramid sealed itself back together, and the sea fell flat, peaceful once more. The waves came in and broke on the shore.

Song fell to her knees. She opened her mouth to speak, but could no longer recall the words of any language, or even the sound of human speech. She raised both arms to the sky and then lost consciousness, toppling to the ground like a ruin.

"Hey, are you okay? Song Ying—wake up!"

She opened her eyes to see Maria's concerned face floating above her. She was gently shaking Song's shoulders, but Song could neither move nor speak. A thousand hammers were thundering against her head, and every time she tried to sit up, they pounded even harder.

Maria ran to the bathroom and came back with a wet rag, pressing it against Song's forehead. It helped, and Song Ying sat up.

She was in room #211, but there was no Grey Man. No strange words written on the wall, no crack.

"Song, you need to wake up or you're gonna get fired for sure," Maria was saying. "We all catch some missing sleep now and then, and I'm cool with that, okay? But come on, this room hasn't been rented out for what, almost a month? And I'm supposed to say you're in here cleaning? I love you, Song Ying, but I need this job."

Song already knew that if she asked, she'd be told that no man with grey eyes and grey hair had ever rented this room. At least not in this world, or this version of it.

Song let Maria tell her to take the rest of the day off, already knowing the words. Only this time Maria added new ones: "You don't look so good at all—in fact, you look kind of *grey*."

Song Ying walked out of the Hotel Reo toward Market Street, and then kept going toward the pier. The city was the same as always, the world the same one she'd always known. And yet for Song, everything was different.

For one thing, the sky was an off-kilter, hazy purple, as if filtered through a crooked, dirty screen.

At Pier 39, Song passed the tourists and the t-shirt shops and the pizza stands and went down to the water. She walked the coastline until the crowds thinned and then disappeared. She took her shoes off and walked across the rocks and the hard, slick sand toward the sea. She walked into the water, fighting the freezing waves determined to force her back to shore. She was up to her waist when the waves began to run backward. She stood and waited, and soon the sea rose up vertically and then broke loose.

The Black Wave pulled her out to the underwater world, but this time Song Ying didn't fight it.

This time she let it take her.

It didn't feel like a sacrifice. It felt like being reborn.

# EXECUTIVE FUNCTIONS

## LUCY A. SNYDER

Joseph Pendleton smiled at the underling across the table from him. He'd practiced his expression in the mirror a hundred times; he knew it would come across as warm, sincere, comforting.

"I can't promise you anything quite yet, but I agree that your attendance and yearly reviews are the things we look for when promoting worthy employees."

Grateful tears shone in her cow-brown eyes. "Oh, Mr. Pendleton, the senior accounting position would mean the world to me and my family."

Her daughter—he'd forgotten the brat's name—had some kind of cancer. It probably wouldn't be terminal if the dowdy accountant could throw enough money at enough doctors. But it was a lingering illness either way; a drain on the company's insurance fund. At the executive team's weekly golf outing, their chief human resources officer had hinted strongly that it would be a gold star on his record if he found a reason to fire her. But she'd filled out FMLA paperwork the week her daughter was diagnosed, so her medical absences couldn't be held against her. And despite his monitoring her every move on her computer and at her desk, she was an exemplary employee. She didn't so much as check the weather on company time.

Authentic reasons to let her go were nonexistent, and she had certain qualities that made him reluctant to manufacture any. Her loyalty was dogged, and her heart as soft as butter. She might not earn him any bonuses, but she couldn't hurt his status.

He let his smile grow warmer. "As I said, I can't promise anything, but I will do everything I can to make this happen."

"Thank you, sir. Thank you *so much*."

"I'll let you know by next Friday."

After she left his office, Pendleton turned on the monitoring software that let him tap into her computer's webcam. The little light wouldn't come on to alert her. She'd gone straight back to her office, and she was smiling, weeping just a little bit, but getting right to work, ever the busy little bee.

He had no intention of letting her know anything that next Friday. He'd wait until Monday, tell her there was a bit more red tape to cut through, but not to worry! He'd let her know. He'd string her along a few more days until her anxiety was perfectly ripe, and then he'd drop the bombshell that, in fact, she wasn't getting the promotion. Because, after all, there was some other employee with just slightly better review scores, or slightly more seniority. More to the point: there'd be a man whose scores looked better than hers on paper. He wasn't about to let a critical position go to a *female*. Even if he hadn't been enjoying his game with her, it just wasn't good business sense to promote women past a certain level. Everybody knew that.

The accountant would take the news stoically, nod and smile and tell him she understood...and then she'd go back to her desk and weep. And he would watch those big, fat, salty tears rolling down her plain cheeks. He'd want to lick them off her unpowdered face like bitter caviar. But he'd content himself with his voyeurism.

And the best part? She wouldn't quit. She'd put too many years into the company to just up and quit. It was too much risk for a fearful little bitch. She'd stick to the job she knew at the company she knew. And so he'd have the chance to dangle hope and snatch it away all over again the following year. And the year after that.

And maybe her daughter would die. Her tears would flow beautifully, then, stain her papers for days and weeks. And she certainly wouldn't quit the company after that—what else would an inconsequential person like her have to hold on to?

It was possible, he mused, that she might kill herself. But he'd identified other crybabies: a ratchety secretary, a middle-aged tech writer, a brunette in the mailroom who wasn't pretty enough to fuck, even if fucking her might be the best way to get her to weep. There were almost certainly others. Women were so emotional, and so easy to manipulate. None of them belonged in the cutthroat world of business. But since he had to spend his time on them, he might as well make them useful. A man with his responsibilities needed regular stress relief. It was simply his due.

Suddenly, he was aware of a pungent stink. *The* stink: it smelled like sewer gas and rotting fish and spoiled milk. It came and went, an olfactory phantom. It had plagued him since he joined the company the previous year. A few other managers said they smelled it, too, but none of them could quite identify what it was. He had the janitors double-check the trash and restrooms, and maintenance checked the heating and plumbing systems. Nobody found anything amiss, and in fact none of the lower-level employees reported smelling anything at all.

Pendleton wasn't satisfied. It wasn't just that it smelled bad; it made him feel itchy and queasy, as if he were having some kind of allergic reaction to it. Sometimes, it made his heart race unpleasantly. His skin never had a visible rash or hives, but he had the terrible feeling of something unpleasant was all over him. His *health* might be at stake here.

And then he had an epiphany: maybe one of the employees on the floor was a connoisseur of terrible foreign foods. The janitors had checked for moldy containers, but not for esculent abominations frozen in microwave boxes. That *had* to be it!

Feeling triumphant, he locked his computer and strode down the hall to tell whoever was microwaving raghead vindaloo or ching-chong glop to knock it off and bring a burger next time.

But nobody was making food in the break room.

The only person there, sitting all alone in an orange molded plastic chair, was a luscious college intern reading a paperback mystery with a black cat on the cover. She was maybe 20 and had the kind of curves you saw on '50s starlets, long legs sheathed in a clingy blue pencil skirt, and thick, glossy blonde hair nearly down to the crack of her ass. He entertained a brief fantasy of twisting her arms behind her, bending her over the break table and reaming her 'til he could see his own face reflected in the puddle of her tears spreading across the bland Formica.

She looked up from her book and met his gaze. Her eyes were the color of his favorite dark chocolates.

"Good afternoon, Mr. Pendleton." She had an upper-crust British accent he found devastatingly sexy.

"Afternoon, Miss ..." His gaze fell on the ID badge dangling at her delicious hip, and he couldn't help but raise an eyebrow in surprise when it told him that she was with the IT department. Probably she did something with the phones. "Miss Alewhite. Have we met?"

"I don't believe so."

How had he not seen her before? How were they not having a long lunch in the motel around the corner right that second? Dammit, HR *knew* he wanted to meet all the new interns. Could they have onboarded her when he was vacationing in Tahiti? They must have.

She smiled, her teeth perfectly straight and white. A flawless specimen of femininity, he had to admit. Probably had men showering her with compliments day and night. Time to shake her up a little and show her she wasn't anything special in his world.

"I love your hair," he said. "Is it a wig or a weave?"

She laughed and set her book aside. "Did you just neg me? *Seriously?*"

He frowned, feeling an unaccustomed heat creep into his face. "Miss Alewhite, perhaps they haven't taught you proper business behavior at whatever liberal college your hippie parents sent you to, but that is *not* the kind of tone you should take with a superior in the workplace."

He expected her to turn pale and start stammering an apology, beg him for forgiveness, but she just grinned.

"'Did you know you're beautiful when you're angry?'" She said in a playfully seductive voice. "I bet you've used that line on plenty of women before. Annoying, isn't it? And, in your case, totally untrue."

"Miss Alewhite!" he thundered. Clearly, his action item for the day would be to teach this little cunt her place. Maybe she was the daughter of a duke or some damn thing over the pond, but here? This was his world. *His* rules. She would show him respect, and more.

"Can I let you in on a little secret?" she stage-whispered. "I took a wee peek into your personnel record. Remember that psychology test you took after you interviewed for your position here? You're a *total psychopath*."

He paused, silent, gazing at her warily. Even *he* hadn't seen his psychological results; as far as he knew, only the company owner could access them. Was she lying to him? Was there a game afoot?

She nodded, black eyes wide in mock surprise. "It's the truth. Clinically, you're an awful human being."

He stared down at her, feeling an itchy bead of sweat roll down the small of his back. Was she a corporate mole, a spy? What was going on?

"But it's okay!" she declared. "All the executive staff members are psychopaths. The whole lot of you. If you hadn't been, you'd have never been brought onboard."

Alewhite stood up. She was taller than he expected, taller than *he* was, and he glanced down at her feet to reassure himself that she was wearing high heels. But she sported black canvas sneakers. He hated them. And was surprised that he hadn't noticed her unflattering, unfeminine shoes before that moment.

"I know you'll be quick to brag that it's because you psychopaths are just better suited to the ruthless corporate world." She had the kind of tone schoolteachers used with very young children. "You know, willing to cook your own families to succeed and all that. But you'd be wrong."

She came around the table, leaned in close, and whispered in his ear: "Your brain is fundamentally broken, Mr. Pendleton. You're neurologically insensitive to certain things that normal people can easily perceive. You know how humans on the autistic spectrum have trouble interpreting social cues? You psychopaths have trouble sensing reality. Or rather, the loss of it."

"That's ridiculous!" he replied coldly. "Nothing escapes my notice! I am a *highly* perceptive man."

"Modest, too!" She laughed, and he wanted to punch her teeth right down her throat. But if the company owner had sent her to test him, giving her the violence she deserved would be the end of his career.

"But no," she continued. "You've been fooled. For months and months now. But—what luck!—I can help with that."

She reached out and touched his forehead.

The world he knew tore away like a flimsy canvas stage backdrop.

A huge white claw—a bristled insect leg—hovered over his face, and Pendleton tried to scream and step back, but neither his throat nor his body would obey him. The claw withdrew, and he saw a monstrous ivory-colored arthropod gazing down upon him. The wedge-shaped, suitcase-sized head reminded him strongly of a mantis, as did its clawed forearms, but the mantid thorax merged with a round, bleached spider body. The only spot of color upon it was its big black eyes.

He heard a girl's laugh inside his mind, and then Miss Alewhite's voice: "Surprise! Do have a look around."

It was then that he realized, first, that his throat was sore, aching like he had strep, and second, that he was naked. Worse, he was shambling forward in line with a bunch of other naked people. The back of the man in front of him was filthy, covered in grotesque fungal growths that seeped a pungent ichor. *The* stink. Or part of it, anyhow.

He looked away from the man's back, and what he saw made his breath catch in his aching throat. They were all in some huge subterranean cavern, and there were hundreds of lines of thousands of filthy naked people, all shuffling forward, eyes glazed. Strange glowing orbs hovering in the air lighted the cavern. The cavern echoed with thudding footfalls and wet noises.

The floor beneath him didn't feel like dirt; it felt soft, and clammy. With effort, he tilted his head down so he could see what he was walking across. More fungus, he realized. His toenails were cracked, split, infected with the same foulness he'd seen on the man's back.

His legs and body were covered in broken pustules, each bearing its own cloud of tiny red gnats.

"And this is where it gets interesting," said the Alewhite monster, prompting him to look up again.

The man in front of him had fallen to his knees in front of something that looked like a gigantic purple sea anemone, although the thing's glistening tentacles had a strangely plantlike look to them. The tentacles reached for the man's face, pulled him forward, and after a few moments of vigorous movement, they spat him back out. Unseeing face dripping with goo, the man stood and shambled to the back of another line.

"Your turn," said Alewhite.

Pendleton fell to his knees, and the tentacles grabbed his head and pulled him down. Something rubbery and slippery forced its way between his lips and tongue, slithered down his throat. It pistoned harshly inside his esophagus, spewing some kind of foul, viscous liquid directly into his stomach. He couldn't breathe, couldn't move. The tentacles held him fast as the monstrosity filled him. His stomach ached from the pressure, and just when he thought it might burst, the tentacles released him, and he jerked to his feet like a puppet.

"Go on, now," Alewhite said, pacing him.

Pendleton stumbled after the others up a huge mountain, his belly aching terribly, his throat sore, his head pounding. The goo in his stomach was leaking up into his throat, and it tasted like spoiled clam chowder. What kind of terrible place was this?

"Not long now! Keep going."

He crested the hill, and he saw the huge, pink, shuddering maw of some impossibly huge creature buried in the fungal earth. It was as wide as a football field and lined with sucking tentacles. People were falling to their knees at the edge of the mouth, vomiting the contents of their stomachs into the hungry chasm.

He caught a whiff of the terrible stench rising from inside the maw—and knew for sure that this was the awful thing he'd been smelling. A horrible nausea took him and he fell to his knees, body wracked with spasms as he puked up everything the anemone had pumped into him—

LUCY A. SNYDER

Pendleton abruptly found himself back in the break room staring at the beautiful intern with the insect-black eyes. His skin wasn't covered in yellow pustules. He was wearing his fine Armani suit again.

"Oh God." He looked around at the familiar coffee maker, the stainless-steel refrigerator, and the parquet floor, took a deep breath and exhaled. "Thank God."

"Don't be fooled." She wagged a finger at him. "You're still a good little drone in a big hive of fungus. You just mostly can't see it. Because your poor widdle bwain is bwoken."

She made a clownishly sad face at him.

"It isn't. It *isn't!*" he snarled.

"Pop quiz. Who owns the company?"

"Uh … he's …" Pendleton had played golf with the old man a dozen times; why couldn't he remember?

"No? Okay, this should be easy: what's the *name* of this company?"

"It's … it's …" His frustration became a vein-popping monster in his head, but he couldn't think of the name. He'd been working here for over a year, for Christ's sake! But there was nothing. No name. Nothing. He collapsed into one of the orange plastic chairs, feeling profoundly confused.

"See?" She smiled. "You don't know because none of this is real; you're sharing a corporate fantasy with a few hundred other drones. Our dreamweaver didn't even have to spend much time customizing it for you; it's practically straight off the rack. How sad is that?"

She shook her head. "But I fixed your cerebrum, just a little. You'll see your true reality every so often. Not most of the time. Maybe once or twice a day. Just enough to remind you where you really are."

"What—what can I do?" he choked.

"Nothing. Well." She paused, looking thoughtful. "You *could* get religion. Pray for your soul and such. But honestly, I don't think you have a soul, and you're already vomiting semen to feed the only god you'll ever meet, so … no. Nothing you can do."

"W-why did you …" he trailed off.

180

"Show you your reality?" She prompted. "Because my job as your overseer is really quite dull considering the lot of you just stumble around in your little dreams of being masters of the universe. It's just…just *nice* to see one of you scared out of your wits every so often. Makes the day go by faster.

"Unfortunately, now that I've destroyed your illusion, your drone body will fail sooner, maybe *much* sooner. Madness and misery always affect the flesh. *But!* My unit's productivity numbers are quite good, and they always let us omit a few poor performers from our metrics. You won't matter in the end."

She cocked her head to one side, seeming to listen to something he couldn't hear. "Oh, and now my boss is returning from his dinner. It's time for me to go back to being invisible to you. Ta ta!"

With that, the intern disappeared completely.

For several minutes, Pendleton just stared at the spot she'd occupied.

Then he walked slowly back to his nonexistent office, closed the door, laid his head down on the wide illusory desk, and wept.

# PINK CRANE GIRLS

## AUTUMN CHRISTIAN

She's folded thirty cranes already, the coffee not even cool enough to drink. Her hands moved too fast for me to see, so that she seemed to meld into her environment, her flesh the color of the paper, her hair the texture of the brown booth. No matter how many times I saw a girl sitting across from me in that dirty roadside café the speed of her fingers, the vibration of her throat and eyes, made me want to stick my head out the window and scream to the dirt.

"This is your last job, and then you're out," I told her, resisting the urge to swallow, and I thought, maybe she'll believe me,

The waitress approached, and the girl's elbow jerked across the table. Cranes spilled onto the floor. The waitress rolled her eyes, kicking a crane out of the way with her soft shoes.

"What it'll be, junebugs?" she asked.

"Hashbrowns and an order of tomato slices. And more coffee please."

"And her?"

"W-water," she said.

"And shall I call the ambulance now or after she's shot up again in my bathroom?"

"She's not on drugs, K," I said. "Not anymore. It's you know, residual effects."

"And this place used to not be a waystation for whatever sick shit you're into," she said, and then turned to the girl. "I'm not

**183**

talking about you, honeycake, I'm sure you're just a good girl in a bad situation."

Before the waitress walked off, the girl had folded ten more cranes.

"This job is at the Edgar Vault. They've been waiting for us, so they've got anti-shift tech, on the walls and floors. But you're our best girl. We know you can handle it."

I used to know their names. I thought that'd make me a good manager, to show that I cared, but then I stopped caring.

She breathed in little panting gasps, sweat the color of sepia in the dawn light breaking out on her forehead.

"Sweetie."

My hand hovered over her vibrating fingers, but didn't touch.

"I know you can handle it."

They never believed me.

The Lab bought up the contracts of girls who slipped through the city of fortresses, girls who slept on ceilings and dismantled machine guns for entertainment. They were girls with iron in their teeth, salt and blood underneath the fingernails. They were the kind of girls who programmed AI to go to school for them in the gridiron machine, and shot up sticky black ICE in the bathrooms of business Overlords before stealing computer codes and escaping out back windows.

Girls who knew, before The Lab even worked on them, how to get in and out. How to run. And quick.

Then the doctors took them underneath the city to our compound, put them under anesthesia, and replaced their organs and skin and bones with molecularly restructured, synthetically grown parts. After that they always ran hot, about 110 degrees hot, and their fingers never stopped twitching.

Dr. Enslein, the scientist who discovered human molecular fluidity, once said the vibration of the girls was like music made of human bones, the shift his final composition, his swan song if you will, the apex to a lifetime of scientific achievement.

In his speech at the Science Symphony Gala, he didn't mention that an ill-timed panic attack could cause the girls' hearts to burst.

My husband once picked up strays off the street, he bandaged their paws and fed them and found them homes. I remembered playing *Annihilation 6*, about to take another fortified castle, when a greyhound, her nose mottled and burnt, nudged my arm.

"Get it away from me!" I said. "I don't want it here."

All at once I felt nauseated, by the wet smell of the dog, by its fur bristling against my shoulder, by its wagging tail and warm breath. It was a dog like a pustule.

"Don't you have a heart?" my husband asked me.

I didn't know. Maybe I did once. All I know is that I couldn't stand the smell of his dogs and then I couldn't stand him kissing me at night with a new heaviness, his arms wrapped around my chest with a new tension. And he said I kissed like a mirror, no curves, a barrier where my tongue should've been.

In that city of fortresses, I've learned to distrust the sun.

When we kissed I thought of the girl. The girl named White, the first one, coming through the compound doors with bandages around her wrists and throat, her feet barely touching the floor. She unraveled her hair from her forehead, in between her fingers like fireglass, disintegrating before she stopped unclenching her fingers.

I thought of her arm, half in and half out of the stone blockade in the armory, and at the sight of her limbs turning into molecular smoke her shock wide enough to break open outer space.

My husband said, "When I was younger, I didn't think it would be like this"

"Would be like what?"

*White bit off chunks of her fingers. She was the first. Couldn't keep them out of her mouth. She smiled a nervous smile, fingernail in her teeth.*

"Leaving," he said.

*"Where do they go when the work is finished?"*

The bones of his favorite dog tucked underneath his arm, his favorite bottle of Cognac underneath the other. Someone like him never survived a night outside the walls. He didn't have to go a day without being fed by the refrigerator drone, or clothed by his closet style sampler program. But it wouldn't have mattered because *Her eyes were piercing sky and when she asked for a glass of water the water burst like shards of glass inside her mouth and "I'll never drink again. I'll never drink again what you've given me."*

"What did you suppose it would be like?" I asked, my arm dangling off the couch, cigarette lazy piping smoke on the walls like he always complained.

"Like a bomb going off, I suppose," he said. "Like we'd be throwing furniture at each other, screaming and crying."

*She asked me if we could fix this, put her back, because she could see the frequency behind the frequency. Her eyes were next-level fluids, heavy enough to crack open the space between her pupils and her mouth. She could see the wall beyond the wall beyond the wall and please, would someone put her back? Nobody should be this way.*

I raised the cigarette to my lips.

"I can throw something if you'd like," I said.

"You don't have to keep being so cruel," he said. "It's over."

*I thought of the wet twist pop of her bones when she expired.*

*It's over.*

Only when he was gone did I think of where it went wrong. I thought of the nights of being newlyweds when I sat playing virtual chess against an opponent I couldn't beat, and he stood in the kitchen in front of the open refrigerator, screaming into the icebox. I forced my heartbeat to not respond to his voice. I remembered love like being hungry. I remembered love like the backroads behind the city the government paved over to build more compounds for rich people, the roads I could no longer get to.

I said the job, hustling girls who could've been me, made me turn cold.

*"We hired you because you've got the kind of face those girls can trust, but we can tell by your eyes they shouldn't dare."*

But there'd have to have been a reason I took the job in the first place, knowing that I'd have to sit across the table from those shaking girls and repeat, over and over again, "This is your last job, and then you're out."

I know you can handle it.

Several days later, I sat in the break room with one of the surveillance crew, a thin, scratch-mouthed woman named Aiden.

"So what happened to that girl at the site?" I asked. "The one who went to the Edgar Vault?"

"You're asking questions that certain people would think require a psychological evaluation."

"You know me," I said, picking at my Waldorf salad, "I'm as psychologically sound as the flat surface of a shallow pool. I mean, look at me. No emotional damage whatsoever. Top mental condition."

Aiden glanced at the security camera above the vending machine. A reflex, nothing more, we figured out about a year ago they weren't hooked up to anything when Jeremiah got drunk at the company Christmas party and decided to climb onto a restroom stall and unhook one after he fucked Ellenore without thinking twice.

Aiden sighed.

"You're about to tell me something fucked up, aren't you?" I said.

Her throat tightened, like she was trying to breathe without breathing, as if her lungs might explode with use underneath her overworked, stretched skin. She leaned forward, her wiry hair falling into her eyes.

"So we got her *into* the vault. She shifted through the ceiling and landed into the dome chamber like we thought she would, it was fine. But when she reached the bridge and it came time to get the codes, she—"

Dr. Brandon walked in, and Aiden's sentence hung sharp and unfinished.

"You two look guilty," Dr. Brandon said, heading toward the coffee machine.

"Aiden's cheating on her husband. It's all very scandalous. Don't tell anyone."

"Uh-huh. Is this the Filipino?"

"He's from Singapore," Aiden said, rolling her eyes when Dr. Brandon's back was turned. "And I don't love him anymore."

"Hence the cheating," Dr. Brandon said, retrieving his cup of coffee before turning back to me. "I heard that was a common reaction when unhappy people are unwilling to do the work required to improve their overall quality of life."

Before Aiden could respond, Dr. Brandon addressed me:

"Gene, do you even look at your calendar anymore? They want you in Meeting Room B in ten."

"Yeah, yeah, I'll be there soon."

Dr. Brandon left.

When I glanced down at my salad, I thought for a moment I saw pink paper cranes, fingertips bloodied and wrecked.

The flat surface of a shallow pool indeed.

"What happened?" I asked.

"What?" Aiden said.

"To the girl," I whispered. "What happened to the girl?"

"I mean, you know, sometimes things like this just happen. You can't always account for when exactly they're going to—"

"What happened to her, Aiden?"

A whisper like a fierce stab.

"Aiden?"

"She exploded," Aiden said, staring at the space behind my head, not meeting my eyes. "She painted the walls. From the inside out."

"I keep telling myself these stories so I can sleep at night. I keep telling myself that my pain is an accumulation of progress, that one day it will all be worth it, that the totality of who I am is being created for a singular moment of gratification. And maybe, just maybe, if I make myself blind in the right way I can construct a narrative that will validate these thoughts."

But then I see her hands, her bloodied hands, the cranes at

her feet, the burning hair. I see the trail of ash she left behind her, dragging her feet across the broken tiles.

And she asks me:

*"Where do they go when the work is finished?"*

On the way to Meeting Room B, I made a detour to the girls' living quarters. Maybe the employees weren't being monitored, but surveillance cameras were positioned in every girls' room, including the bathrooms.

Some sick fuck decorated their living quarters like a Victorian dollhouse, with pink wallpaper and plush, oversized couches made of flame retardant resin and tea complete with doilies made out of steel. My brain would have shrunk in a place like that. Maybe that was the point.

Two girls sat in the common room, slumped in chairs, barefoot with toes curled hard, watching television and folding cranes. Pink cranes spilled out from their seats.

Another girl slept in the dormitory with the lavender sheets squeezed between her fists, a pool of sweat accumulating in the space next to her pillow and cheek.

"Nightmares increased by 40%," said Dr. Brandon. "Also, you are supposed to be in the meeting room by now."

"You measure that?"

"Nightmares? Yeah. It's a fairly accurate barometer of one's emotional state. The content of the dream doesn't matter, but the emotions do."

I used to know their names.

I used to know their names, and I used to visit them inside their dormitories in between assignment briefing and evaluations and one-on-ones. Learn their dreams.

"Any idea why they've increased?" I asked.

I used to wipe away the blood leaking from behind their eyes.

"No idea, really." Dr. Brandon said. "But you know, their reports you filed last quarter were rather sparse."

"You know how it is," I said. "They don't talk much."

"Is that so?"

"You don't believe me."

"I've read your reports from a few years back. The girls seemed more talkative back then."

The girl in her bed squeezed the sheets until her knuckles turned blue, and I thought the blood might rise into her throat, burst through her sweating cheeks.

"Check the logs, I can guarantee you're the only person who's read those reports in the last six months." I said. "Nobody gives a fuck about those girls."

"So that's your excuse, then?" he asked.

His face, placid as ever.

"Excuse? What excuse?" I asked.

"Someone did give a fuck. Of course they did," he said. "It was you."

Before my ex-husband took up housing stray dogs, he used to go to the bowling alley, with his shiny red custom-made bowling ball, his name, ANTONY R., emblazoned where the curve of his thumb rested. He sized up his six pairs of bowling shoes in the entryway and refused to store them, insisting the closet didn't know how to match them correctly.

And before he went bowling, he sat at the kitchen table for hours making macramé belts and braided rope curtains.

"Macramé comes from the Arabic word 'migramah,'" he said, "It means fringe."

I can't think of the memory of him without thinking of the frantic way he said 'migramah,' of his hands scrabbling across the table, of the day when he put the macramé in a box and started trying to brew his own beer. I think the dogs came after that.

And I can't think of him and the dogs without thinking of accepting that job, and how signing the contract felt like cutting my arm off, even though at the time I didn't know why.

I know it's a logical fallacy, but sometimes I think if I didn't take this job then I would've loved him more. I could've unwound time and pressed my hands against his closed eyelids and the fluttering of his eyelashes against my fingertips would've felt like a butterfly waking up, like the maw of the terrible insect relaxing around my heart. And I would have let him in. I would've stopped sinking into the couch, a pool of grime at my feet.

In Meeting Room B, my boss, Harris Freeman, sat in the corner of the room with his mantis-like feet propped up on the table, an ice-cube between his teeth, cup of cold espresso balanced on one thigh.

Dr. Brandon entered the room and closed the door, shutting us into dim, windowless light.

"This is the meeting?" I asked.

"The dossier," Harris said, "On the girl we sent up to the Edgar Vault. Have you read it?"

"The files haven't been unlocked for me."

"But you heard what happened to her," he said.

"No sir."

He rolled his eyes. The cup, balanced precariously, wobbled, and espresso spilled out onto his jeans.

"Of course you have, Gene. I know you've got ears."

I sighed, and sat down.

"She…" I trailed off.

"Exploded?" Harris asked me.

I nodded.

"Yes," Harris said. "Gene, let me ask you a question. How long has it been?"

"Four years, two months, and two days, but who's counting," I said. "Why?"

"No, I didn't mean the job."

Dr. Brandon leaned against the door instead of sitting down. A slice of light cast down from the halogen bulb above his head, making it appear like he was some kind of sick, and pale deliverance angel.

"I mean, how long has it been since you've left your… I'm sure sterile and uninviting dark apartment and socialized?"

"I don't see what my personal life has to do with any of this."

"You been to the arcade lately? Spun through a halogen storm?

Gone to any cocktail parties? Met a gentle, but well-cultured man who's recently going through a divorce? Called your mother?"

I said nothing.

My boss checked his phone.

"Maybe you're into the dark stuff. Maybe you got divorced because of your insatiable sadistic impulses. You know there are all sorts of simulators in the V district. Have you tried any of those?"

"I'm not sure—" I said, but he interrupted me.

"—Or maybe you can take a hike to the mountains. Enjoy a new kind of solitude. You know, if there are any mountains left. Have you checked? Are there any mountains left? Have we drained the ocean yet?"

"What is this meeting about again?" I asked. "I'm not sure I'm clear on that."

He checked his phone again.

"We've locked your computer and your code access. Gene, it's been a pleasure working with you. Security will see you out."

"This is a joke," I said.

"No," he said, and he grabbed the espresso cup, brought it to his lips. "I wish."

"On what grounds am I being fired?"

"Fired?" my boss asked, looking at me over the rim of his coffee cup. I'd never noticed before, there were little flowers painted on the edge of the cup. It appeared they reached up to brush his eyes.

*"It's an ancient art, Gene. Ceramic pottery was found 18,000 years ago in the Yuchanyan Cave in southern China."*

I'd forgotten, my husband also got into pottery. I'm pretty sure that was before the dogs, but after the macramé. The image of his fingers, encased in clay, spun into my head. Then just as quickly—

"No, Gene. You're not being fired. Just think of it as an extended mandatory break."

"Is this because of the girl?" I asked.

"Everything," Dr. Brandon said, "is about the girls."

"You think I had something to do with this? With her…"

accident? I didn't. I stuck to the script. Like I always do."

"You're making this difficult for yourself," my boss said. "It's just a job. All you've got to do is walk out the door. The security guard will escort you out. Turn right. Go get a cup of coffee from the café. Take a fucking break. We'll call you."

"They're all unstable. The molecular structure folds. I'm not a scientist. How can you possibly blame me?"

"Take. A. Fucking. Break," my boss said.

Dr. Brandon touched the desk beside my hand. I almost felt the pulse in his wrists, throbbing mad, the rest of his body like a sheet of ice, struggling to contain something bubbling underneath the surface.

His mouth twitched, as if he was going to speak.

I stood up and without a word, headed toward the door.

"If you get a chance, go to the south side and eat a vanilla macaroon on the digital sunlight balustrade," my boss said to me as I left. "They say it's just a fad and that real sunlight will be in again soon, but I think it's better than the real thing."

40% increased nightmares.

That first girl I managed, White, acquired her contract after she was imprisoned for hacking into the mall's infrastructure and replaced all the advertisement audio with an audio book version of Finnegan's Wake.

I never knew her real name; it was a protective measure in case I was to be questioned. So she was always White to me, because of those synthetic, glowing braids she wore that hung down to her waist. For weeks I dreamed of her shifting through the walls of banks and estates, those white braids whipping forward with the force of her movement, dripping with acid, spraying the ceiling and floors until they ate away and collapsed the entire building. I dreamed of falling through floors and floors with her, down elevator shafts and through mazes of scaffolding.

I took her to that roadside café, away from the sharp buzz and white perspicacity of the lab. I used to think taking them out to lunch before I told them where they'd be ripping out their spines and bleeding their colors made me seem, somewhat human.

"This is your last job, and then you're out," I told her, like I told all the others.

But unlike the others, I remembered her favorite color was pink, just like the cranes she folded, and she used to have a boyfriend named Siph who broke up with her because she put a keylogger on his computer. She had a cat named Geoffrey and her favorite book was, strangely, *War and Peace*.

And when she dreamed, she dreamed like me, of falling and falling and falling.

Dr. Brandon told me the dreams would go away soon, once I got used to the job, and they did. Mine would, at least.

40% increased nightmares, and here mine had stopped. But maybe for the wrong reasons.

"Go on sweetheart," I said to her, picking her burnt fingernails off the floor. "You can do it."

Girls like her didn't cry, not often, but her tears were like cigarette ash, burning and black. And the day I learned she'd gone on her last job, heart pulled out of her throat as she shifted back through the walls after opening the front doors for a rush job, I picked up my keycard, walked out of the building, went home, and sobbed.

My husband put his arms around me and said, "Maybe you should quit. The stress is too much."

*"We know what's going to happen to us, you know, even if they don't tell us,"* White said to me, eyes like burning static.

"Gene?"

Her death didn't make me want to run, it made me want to return to The Lab and pick up the fingernails of another girl off the floor. I wanted to press back the bleeding heart with my palms on her chest. Even if I stopped caring, the price of being that close to blood, I could still do that.

I sat in the simulated sunlight café, eating a vanilla macaroon and watching a scarlet ibis dip its beak into the fronds in a glass-like pool. On the way to the café, Aiden called me.

"I heard you got fired," she said.

"I didn't get fired."

"We've got to figure out what's going on. I play poker Friday nights with one of the administrators. I could unlock your file and get you into the building—"

"Now you sound like the one who needs a psychological evaluation," I said.

I suppose I should've felt the upheaval of leaving the building, without warning or explanation, after all those years of employment. Not knowing when I'd return should've been a violent thing, like a Gordian knot dripping with stomach acid, an angry pulse in the center where it couldn't get out.

But I only felt a stillness, like for the first time in a long time the storm brewing in my head, making my thoughts incomprehensible and dark, was cleared.

"Yeah," Aiden said, and she sighed. "It's a silly idea. I just don't know what's going on."

"Your job is safe," I said. "Don't worry."

I entered the café, the sunlight brushing the backs of my hands, I ordered a latte and the aforementioned vanilla macaroon, phone cradled to my ear, and sat near the pond in the back. In the late afternoon, the café was nearly empty, enough for me to hear the sounds of humming insects through the walls.

"You still there?" I asked Aiden.

"Yeah, I'm thinking. It's just, we've been working together for so long."

I said nothing.

"Hey, it wasn't your fault. The girl," she said.

"Maybe not," I wrote. "But there are plenty of things that are."

Another pause.

If I looked into the space beyond the projection of simulated sunlight, into that dark dense space between the wall and the sensors, I started seeing ghosts made out of sparks. Ghosts that existed only in the in between, between a grounded object and one pushed outward.

"You remember what happened with Dr. Enslein?" Aiden asked.

. . .

"Why the cranes?" I asked Dr. Enslein, while he was signing my copy of *The Melded Genius* on his international book tour.

"Excuse me?" he asked.

"The cranes," I said. "Why are the girls taught to fold cranes?"

"Are you with the press?" he asked.

"No sir," I said.

Behind him a girl sat, her back to the line going out the door, her pink dress unzipped and revealing the layout of her protruding spine. It didn't seem like a real body part, but something holographic, simulated, a real spine wouldn't be on a girl constantly humming and vibrating to frequencies we couldn't comprehend.

Dr. Enslein wouldn't tell the audience that when a girl was molecularly structured, they had about 7 or 8 shifts before death, before the entire infrastructure collapsed and her heart and knees and brain gave out.

"I know about the rapid firing in the basal ganglia," I said. "The Blepharospasm that affects the eyes, the increased neurological decay. I understand before the cranes, the girls would often break their fingers or bite off the tips because of the speeding up of the nervous system. But why pink cranes?"

"Who do you work for?" he asked.

Behind me a group of young graduate students, wearing thick-rimmed glasses and blazers too expensive for actual scientists, jostled me.

"I'm not at liberty to say, sir. I work for a private firm."

He sighed, obviously debating whether he should call security to have me removed and potentially slow down the line even more. But, he chose to speak.

"We knew we had to keep the girls occupied, and in such a way that was uniform and easily taught, but complex enough so that their minds could focus," he said. "And my daughter. Well, she loved origami."

The girl, her lips like a trapped hummingbird, leaned over and whispered something in Dr. Einslein's ear.

"She wants to talk to you," Dr. Enslein said.

"About what?"

"Come around the table, you're holding up the line."

One of the graduate students let out an exasperated sigh. I slipped around the table and headed toward the girl. The air around her was hothouse warm. I knelt beside her, my knees crushing a crane.

"I heard," she whispered. "Y-you work with people like me."

"Yes I do," I said.

"You're good at what you do."

"I don't know," I said. "I'm going through a divorce."

The skin around her eyes shone with bruises from the rapid fluttering of her eyelashes.

I didn't know why I told her that, why it slipped out of my mouth so easily, when I'd been holding onto it tight for months, trapped between my throat. Like she reached through me, faster than I could perceive, and grabbed it with no resistance.

"M-maybe I-I'll see you again," she said. "And then y-you can tell me you're doing good."

A finished crane dropped from her fingers. She glanced up at the line, at Dr. Enslein, who was bent over signing another copy of *The Melded Genius*. Then her body lurched forward, and she broke apart.

It was like watching a person transform into living color, her fingernails into trails of sand, her hair into an empty gorge. Her skin melted away, revealing the smears of her blood and ribs and spine, for less than a second hovering in space, before they too dissolved.

She rushed forward.

In less than a second, she reassembled in the center of the crowded auditorium, the force of her arrival pushing people out of her circumference. Dr. Enslein stood up, knocking a stack of books over.

"Anna!"

I swear, she looked back at me. Like an insect, she looked back, without moving anything except her neck. And she couldn't smile, not with the humming composition of her face, but it was almost as if she wanted to.

Then she looked up, and shot through the ceiling.

Dr. Enslein shouted for security. People caught in her path patted their bodies, as if to make sure she hadn't ripped out pieces of them on her way through. Others began crying or heading for the exits. A few seconds later, the fire alarms went off.

I slipped out the performer's exit before anyone could question me about what happened. I left the building and walked through an alleyway through the dark, heading toward the streets under groaning, titanium walls, between lights like bullets coming through club windows. And I found myself looking up at the sky, beyond the steel wiring, which I never did anymore. The sight of those mile long buildings shooting into space, as if the curvature of the earth would be sliced apart by their piercing height, always made me feel as if I was shrinking.

But I was looking for her. Of perhaps, whatever remained of her, glittering scraps of bones and skin. And I thought of White, long dead by that point, her fingertips exploding into supernovas.

*"Where do they go when the work is finished?"*

Maybe pieces of all of them were up there in between the fortresses of the city. Maybe when they burst apart, their heads and tongues and brains, their molecules kept shifting, over and over and over, in and out of darkened vaults and computer banks. Never able to be caught.

A small comfort for a manager of living time bombs, for the one who attempts to ease the transition into a melting death.

My phone rang. It was my soon to be ex-husband, now living in temporary housing about a mile north.

He often called in those days to ask if I'd seen one of his knickknacks—the Peruvian rug, the stuffed raccoon paw, the blue clay vase he broke in four pieces. He spoke in this quavering, desperate way—a child lost in the dark warehouse of his toys.

I imagined answering the phone.

"I could've sworn I left those soap antlers in the closet," he'd said.

And I'd pause, trying to refrain from saying. "Stop calling me.

You don't care about any of these things and I certainly don't either. You will not find answers in clinging to dust-covered, useless relics you collected searching for the thing that is you."

Trying to refrain from saying, "Find someone to fuck so you'll stop calling me."

Imagining, after taking a deep breath.

After looking up and imagining supernovas of skin and glittering, superspeed ropes of nerves.

After a silent wish on an airplane I mistook for a star.

Saying:

"I don't know where your fucking antlers are. I don't want to bury myself in quiet distractions but you'll always be consumed with searching for them. One day things are going to change at The Lab, and I want to be there."

Yeah, I know, I'm probably going to forget this moment ever happened, with the girl and the sky and the instantaneous epiphany that what I'm doing means something. And as the months drag on I'm going to even more apathetic and cynical and hopeless. But maybe one day when a girl explodes, I'll be able to pick up the pieces and put them back together. That seems worth the cost. That seems worth losing some of my humanity."

And after a pause, he'd respond:

"I've taken up leather tanning. Did you know the tanning process is written about in Homer's Iliad?"

I couldn't help it. I leaned against a nearby building, dizzy and nauseous. I turned my phone off, and I smiled.

Alone at that roadside café, I could breathe. I thought it must've been something in the air, the cloying dirt sticking to the inside of my lungs. The Lab psychologists told us it was "Beneficial to the girl's well-being" to occasionally show them clear skies, roads free of dark metal and disco light. I always wondered why they thought this unfiltered air was beneficial to anyone.

But it wasn't the air that was the problem—it was the constricting of my chest.

A man walked in with a girl, and they sat down at an adjacent booth. The girl's skin vibrated, her fingernails chipped, fingers like the music of a theremin. They spoke in low tones, the girl nodding, nodding, folding, folding.

The man got up to go to the restroom. I glanced sideways at the girl, who waited for that moment to sob. She stopped folding the cranes, pushing them out of the way with her elbow to give herself the room to collapse face first onto the table.

"Hey," I said, my voice soft.

She didn't respond.

"Hey," I said a bit louder. "I know you're from The Lab. I know what they want you to do."

She glanced at me, her tears boiling on her face. Looked at me like a question.

"I just want you to know, there's another way."

And I pointed up.

# THE CAUSE

## LAURA LEE BAHR

### Part 1 - Dead Loves and Dirty Cash

I was looking to get a word from my kid, instead I got news there'd be no more words. He had been unceremoniously popped and what of it?

What was I gonna do about it?

His name was Theo P. The kids in the neighborhood called him "The Fish," but I insisted on calling him by his given name. He was one of my better and long-trained squeals in the Fairfax district, but still only 14 years old. Train a kid for years to survive it all and then he gets popped in some random raid. It happens, and more and more in this day and age. Old house on the hill folks live what seems like forever while the God-Knock street kids regularly take the dirt dive for a look sideways at the wrong Syg-man in uniform.

Sure, it happens, but it hurt more than I was used to.

There was nothing to do about it because I was nothing but a shadow in this world anyhow. Nothing to do but buy a bottle and start on it as I took the scenic route back to the office, feeling damn sorry about everything this crummy world had given and taken.

Theo P. was a kid who cracked wise. He appreciated my style the way only a kid can—by imitating it and then going for it harder. He wore a suit *and* a fedora. He studied the phrases and would teach them to me, come up with new words and new slang. He

was the one who started calling him and his types 'squeals.' He
had a memory for everything—facts, figures, dates, visuals—and
he could sing/speak out what he'd figured out so you wished you
could remember, too.

I found him when he was seven, barely up to my waist in
height. He was trying to hustle me into just some cubes of Rattail.
When I wasn't interested in that, he wanted to get me down for
some hot synthetics and prosthetics. He was funny about it. He
told me he didn't know the last time I looked in the mirror, but I
could use a better nose and maybe a good night's sleep. I told him
he could use a better job, and he said didn't he know it.

I bought him lunch and started training him. He ribbed me a
lot about the way I dressed, the way I talked, and the way I paid in
cash. But even as he was ribbing me I could see he was a bit in awe
of it. It gave him an idea of something else he could be.

The kid was whipsmart, and he liked history: Civil War battles,
Protestant Revolution, French Revolution. He particularly loved
the tales of workers from the Industrial Revolution, especially the
Luddites. He called me "Ludd," which I knew coming from him
was a real compliment.

"Ludd" was how they all got to know me in the Fairfax district,
thanks to Theo P. I was pretty sure he was gonna get radicalized
when he hit his later teens, met the right God-Knock, and he'd
start trying to destroy the machines. Dying for a cause and being
remembered. That was written all over him. But he died just
because, just because he happened to be walking when some sprays
of bullets went flying. That was beyond tragedy. That was the sort
of thing that let you know that nothing mattered anyhow, anyway.

When I made it back to the office, she was waiting for me.

I was pretty much as she had left me two decades before,
weepy-eyed and stinking of Jack.

She wasn't the type to keep it to herself.

"Well, I guess there's comfort that some things don't change,"
she said.

"Don't fix what ain't broke," I said, thinking she was
commenting on the suit, the tie, a bottle in a paper bag and an

old school smoke, straight outta last century and what of it? I've made a point of blank refusal of this hyper-drive into hyper-space hyperbolic brave new world, and it's kept me cool when everything else on the planet's overheating, so I took it as a compliment.

But truth was, I didn't match her to her face or that cut to her voice. She wasn't anybody I thought I'd met before. That's how different she was. Then again, when I woke up some mornings that's the way I felt about this whole goddamned city.

So I took a long look at her, then a swig from my bottle in the brown paper and licked my lips a little and then grimaced at the picture she presented.

A pretty woman is a complex system of problems. Because a pretty woman only has as much power as she has pretty—and that's like oil and water and kind hearts—a dwindling resource. She was a sunset. Everything was lighting up the most beautiful it would ever be again before it faded. You knew it wouldn't last much longer. Look while you could.

So I looked.

And she liked the way I looked at her because she started to glow with it.

"Hank, it's me," she said. "Danika." And her hand touched mine.

And it came back like a fever.

I remember touching her skin, her arms, her face. Her thighs wrapped around me. A look in her gray eyes, pupils large and rolling, her mouth an open O, her hair red and falling over both of our faces like a curtain.

I remember her saying, "I need you," "Don't leave me," and "Help." I remember punching someone, blood on my knuckles from his nose, my hand hurting.

I remember falling in love and then I remember her saying goodbye. It couldn't have been more than a month. Maybe two.

I remember the cascade of her voice and how I loved it when she told me stories. What stories? What did she tell me?

I remember...

But maybe I don't.

Where are those drives? Where are those files? It was before everything was in the clouds on the drives in the sky, before everything rained down on us all in a storm. Before everyone let the machines beneath their skin, everyone but the God-Knocks, the Anarchists and me. Before the time we all knew, whether or not we believed it, that we were going to die.

And we still could remember on our own.

I am still trying to remember on my own. It makes me an anomaly to try. It also makes me a fool to try because I drink too much.

Her perfume was different now but beneath it was her same smell. That smell was bringing me to where we were when she left. Yes. Drunk and teary.

"Why?" I had asked.

She hadn't had an answer.

And here we were again, only this time I wasn't crying over her. I put a hand to my temple.

"So," I finally mustered, "what brought you here?"

"I need your help," she said.

"Ah, I seem to recall that getting you help got me into some trouble before."

She told me how different she is now, of course, can't I see it? She smiled. "We create our lives, Hank."

Ah. Then I knew. She'd become one of *them*:

"*Singularity Knowledge—unity in higher thought and immortality.*"

The Sygs. Our new enlightened ruling class. With their prosthetics and their Tatts and their insufferable positive-speak.

She told me how amazing her life was now, with this newfound power. How she did all this, attracting it with her powerful mind and the force of Singularity Knowledge in practice. Her husband was 95 years old but still very healthy with all his synthetics and prosthetics and probably could screw her harder than he could when he was 35.

She has manifested the life she wanted, she said.

But I knew she just married it. And then when her legally bound John moves along to the great drive in the sky she will get to keep what she never earned, just like it's been happening for eons. Same story, she'd just updated it with the new religion, and the irony was with the new implants she might move along before him. What a joke. I thought maybe I'd make that joke. But I didn't because there was something about seeing those creases in her eyes that got me kind of liquid in the chest.

When I first knew Danika she was practically a kid, calling herself 'Dandy' and she stripped in bars for cash, back when people still used it. People would put their dirty paper in her underwear and that's how she got paid. Demeaning times for women and for everyone, so we were all glad to salute the Syg Flag and say thank you for all the awareness training that makes the elite fit to rule and saps like me drooling infants that need everything monitored, measured and analyzed. But don't mistake me as bitter. I wasn't then.

I didn't have the Tatt but it wasn't because of religious differences like the backwoodsy God-Knocks. I'd just learned to be suspicious. And in my line of work, it helped to not be so…visible. I guess I was old-fashioned. You'd be surprised at how effective a detective that made me in this day and age.

Which I guess is why Dandy—excuse me, she'd been Danika for over a decade now—was asking me for help.

"What do you want?" I asked her. I tried to growl, but it came out like a whimper.

She wanted me to find the killer of her lover, Lancaster J. He'd gotten a shaft of metal through the chest while sleeping in his bed. They'd had a date a day later and when he hadn't shown she'd gone to his place and found him like that. She'd called in the cops who'd scuttled the place back and forth, she'd called media who squawked some real colorful stories, but it was all just noise. No one knew who stuck him, so whoever did it either had no Tatt or knew how to keep their fingers clean.

She was tired of waiting and tired of getting theories on her feed that went nowhere. She wanted answers. Who would do such a thing to a musician, an artist, already almost immortal for his beauty and his brilliance? She was still so in love with this dead man I almost wished I could kill him again.

She put down three hyper-drives on my desk.

Based on the rock she had on her hand, my first suspect was her husband, but she brushed that away. They had an arrangement, she said, and had for years. He wasn't the jealous type. He was the one who suggested she find me, he was the one who would be paying my bill. Her husband suggested me because I got a reputation with all the old codgers whose parents were alive when black and white movies were the norm. They appreciated the anomaly of a work-for-hire who brought my level of nostalgia to the table. I shrugged. Maybe I wasn't even who I thought I was, just some marketing scheme I'd dreamed up and was living out. It was possible. That I was living it out so well I'd forgotten I'd ever even dreamt it up in the first place. That was damn near too likely.

"When he recommended my services, did he know about us?" I asked.

She seemed confused so I clarified our carnal history for her recollection.

She brushed a wisp of hair from her face. It was not red anymore, it was not a curtain. It was now blonde and piled on the top of her head like a crown. She used polite and affirming terms but assured me that our history was so inconsequential as to be nothing her husband cares to know about.

"But he cares to know about your lover and who stuck him?"

"Lancaster was important to everyone," she said, her eyes misting up. "He was going to be somebody and do something important."

"Sure he was," I said. "I'm sure he was gonna do something real swell."

She didn't like that.

"Let me tell you something," she says. "You think this performance of yours, this living like you're some detective out of the nineteen-hundred forties black and white movies makes you special?"

"Your husband seems to think so."

She ignored that and went straight to inspirational Syg-talk.

"Why make yourself a character in a world that's dead?" she

asked. "Especially now, when we are so close to being able to live forever?"

"Oh, not everyone will get to live forever," I replied. "Just rich assholes."

"Rich assholes that pay your tab," she spit at me.

"So pay it," I said. "Or just *accept* your dead lover and get back to your holier than thou Syg-life."

She sighed then. Real pretty like, and sad. She nodded. "I'll pay it. You find who killed him, I'll pay the amount you want."

She held out her hand. On the back of it was a rose—one of the newest styles.

I shook my head. I swigged out of the bottle.

"I don't do the Tatt. Just cash."

"Cash? Are you kidding?"

"Nope. It's nothing but old-fashioned green."

She talked a bit about how that'd take time to get, and I told her it was her clock ticking, not mine. I just had this bottle to drink, is all. She asked me what I had against the Tatts—this amazing way of making commerce and memory flow seamlessly.

"Just old-fashioned enough to think getting branded and tagged makes you a target for slavery or extermination."

She laughed in a hard sort of way.

"Old-fashioned. That's a nice way of putting it."

"I got a million nice ways."

"Sure you do."

I got up close then, leaning in like I was ready to kiss her. "You remember some of them."

"I'm sure I don't," she said. "And you smell like a drunk beggar."

I'd been called worse. I kept close. I touched the rose with my fingertips.

"Not having it doesn't mean you're invisible, you know," she said. "It just means that you can have everything you own stolen."

I touched her Tatt to my lips. I said something about how I remembered how she used to be pretty fond of cash.

And then I made a joke that it was only fitting, considering her history, that she put that cash in my underwear.

She pulled her hand away from my lips and gave me a quick slap to the face.

She called me a drunk again and asked if I was taking the case or just going to continue to embarrass myself.

I said I'd do both.

She left then, leaving me the drives to see what I could see of her dead lover's mind.

## Part 2 - Memory and the Machine

I got the system to read the drives. No work for hire could live without 'em, and I figured I'd finish what was left in the bottle and then go cold turkey the next day. Tomorrow, right? That was always the best day to start. Right then, a little Jack would help walk through another man's memories.

Lancaster J.'s thoughts came up on the walls in thumbnails I could touch and expand into three dimensions, and I was in a room of ghosts.

Thumbnails. You could leave them with fingerprints when you have the Tatt. Everything you'd see becoming something someone else can sift through, anyone with access could be inside your first person.

Being inside Lancaster J. was as good as any drug. If only I was actually him instead of me, I wouldn't have needed to finish the bottle of Jack.

Memory—this was our new contested ground. What we thought, what we remembered. How do you fight for what's in your own mind?

One of Theo P.'s best raps, and he could crack it sharp, was the story of the Luddites. I never remembered all the lines or the way he made it rhyme, but he had it down like a history lesson. He had the characters, the dates, the marches, the executions, the attention to sensory details and the rallying cause to give it an inspiring air. He told how the Luddites were heroes demanding living wages for skilled labor, warning against becoming mechanical in heart and mind, and he would end with a chorus of something like, *"Bring the Hammer down, and if you have no hammer, throw your body on the machine!"*

The God-Knocks in the neighborhood ate it up. Someone down there might still remember how it went.

And then as I was watching Lancaster J.'s memories, thinking of memory and the machine, suddenly I realized I've let one play for too long and she was there again, in the room with me. It wasn't really her, of course. It was his memory of her. Her eyes were more blue than gray. She was smiling in a way I'd never seen her smile. The way she looked at me made me feel like there was hope for me after all. That I was more than shark chum in the human highway rapidly moving toward both immortality and extinction. These were new nightmares, but really it was all just the same story that had always been told. Boy meets girl. But of course, she wasn't looking at me. She was looking at him.

That's the thing about these memories. These first person camera eyes we have. Even knowing—knowing all along she's looking at him—I was watching it and it's me.

Me me me me me me me.

I turned it off and stared out my window, past drunk now.

No one was gonna bring in three hyper-drives of Theo P.'s loves, thoughts, snapshots his mind took. Theo P. was somebody important. He was going to do something important, more than this Syg gigolo, Lancaster J., whose head I was in. That no one would remember Theo P. was wrong in a way I had never felt anything was wrong before. I had to do him some homage. Something.

But I was stumbling, falling into a blackness. I'd succeeded then in blotting out my own mind. My last thought before it all faded to black:

"Tomorrow I am going to stop drinking."

I dreamt she came back in that sharp dark. She made slow love to me again, both as Dandy and Danika, telling me the new technology is that they write it inside the skin so it's invisible. She did it while I was sleeping so I couldn't refuse. "It will make it all so much easier, better," she said. Then she told me she took the liberty of having the

Tatt made as her name and placed in the skin above my heart. Now all business will be so much more convenient.

I woke up from the dream with it still dark outside, mad because everything hurt and the dream was too on the nose to even be interesting. Was that dream mine? Hers? Lancaster's? It felt like my poor brain cranking itself, trying to ask my poor heart to feel again. The dream was a gift, though, because I realized I didn't have it anymore. That liquid in my heart was crusty and dry. I was alone, still drunk and Theo P. was still popped with not a person to say boo about it.

Then I had a real diamond of an idea. I knew what I'd do, and I knew how to fix it all. All it took was my losing a piece of conscience to gain some sense of righteousness. I could suddenly understand the appeal of all of Sygs, the God-Knocks, the whole history of anyone who'd ever had a religion they'd kill or die for.

I had a cause.

I knew what to do.

I'd plant a memory in the Lancaster's hyper-drive. I knew an Anarchist hacker who could do anything in the hyper-world, who'd do it just to do it. But I'd give her some of the dirty green paper when I got it just to make it real sweet.

I'd plant a memory and frame an innocent kid. It would make everyone stand up and pay attention. Oh, it was going to be beautiful. What a story I could put together, a poor God-Knocking street kid, radicalized to murder.

I practiced announcing my findings a couple of times because it felt so good to say it, like a lullaby to get myself back to sleep.

"Danika," I'd say, "I found your killer. His name is Theo Pescadora. They call him *The Fish.*"

In the contested battle I'd have thrown Theo P.'s body on the machine.

He'd be remembered.

And to be remembered as a villain is as good as being remembered as a hero.

Maybe better.

• • •

## Part 3 - Tomorrow

I woke up later that day, remembering my plan but my eyes were seeing nothing but white, and it felt like a hammer was inside the machine of my head pounding out, threatening to, at last, bust it wide open.

I remembered also that Today was Tomorrow, the day I would stop drinking.

I braved daylight. I went back to the Fairfax district. I was like a Robespierre there in my suit and pasty skin, accepted like a moving historic landmark. Everything was too bright, too loud, too tight. When was night going to fall? This day had already been too damn long and maybe it was time I gave up on it. When was that sun going to set?

Kid C.—only twelve and already with the bug eyes of someone who smoked the Rattail that was all the rage—was standing looking up at the traffic going back and forth in the sky.

"Hey Ludd," he called, too loud. "You looking for a new squeal?"

I tried for it. "Do you know who popped Theo P.?"

"Nope," he says. "Nobody knows nothing. You know how it is."

Then I noticed on the back of Kid C.'s hand, as bright and shiny as a new sore, a big rose tattoo.

"When'd you get that?" I asked.

He was proud. "Just got it!"

Tatts are rare in the Fairfax district. It's crawling with God-Knocks, and they refuse it with old-school religious conviction as the sign of the Beast from the Good Book.

"Why'd you go and do a thing like that?" I asked.

He gave me a real 'smile for the camera' type grin. Then he looked back up into the sky at the traffic. "Ludd, man. You old."

We just stood there a while, me staring at this kid, him staring at the sky, me thinking about Lancaster J., Dandy, Theo P., but most of all, how I need a drink, I need a drink, dear God, I need a drink.

Tomorrow I'd go talk to my Anarchist friend.

Tomorrow I'd call Dandy back and start putting out the breadcrumbs to lead us to the memorial candy house of the martyr to the cause.

To the cause.

What was the cause again?

God, my head hurt. Every thought. Hurt.

Tomorrow. Today I was going to finish the bender I started the day before. Today I was going to get so drunk I forgot who I was or why.

I turned around and walked away.

Kid C. called after me, "Wait, Ludd! I can help! I can figure it out! Just give me a mystery!"

I stopped. I felt something in my heart pushing against my chest, some dam behind my eyes threatening to burst. I walked back to the kid.

"Help me with this mystery," I said to him, my voice soft and shaking. "What are people *for*? Tell me that, kid. *What are we?*"

The kid looked at me straight a moment.

"Oh, that's easy," the kid said. And then he started laughing.

I waited for him to say more, but he was so high he just laughed and kept laughing.

I walked away and something broke in me for good as I got it.

No mystery. Just a big joke.

# DITCH TREASURES

## RICHARD CHIZMAR

## 1

A two-hundred-year-old bible.
A brand new pair of Air Jordan sneakers.
An iPhone in a leopard skin case.
A cigar box containing ashes.
An expensive fly fishing rod.
A framed velvet Elvis.
A George Foreman grill still in the box.
A rusty Sucrets tin filled with Buffalo nickels.
Three dead puppies in a burlap bag.
A wallet containing $269 in cash.
A loaded handgun.
A gold Rolex wristwatch, broken but still beautiful.
A Ziploc baggie of marihuana.
A powder blue tuxedo balled up in a paper bag.
A battered suitcase full of wind-up monkeys.
A laptop computer with a smiley face sticker.

## 2

These are just a handful of the more unique items I have found
strewn along the grassy shoulder and median strip of I-95 in northern
Maryland. For reasons I can't figure out, womens' shoes and compact

discs are the most common. I once thought I had found a dead body lying there in the weeds, but it was dusk and the light was bad, and it turned out to be nothing more than a mannequin incredibly lifelike, nude, with BEAT PENN STATE written across the torso in black magic marker. Some people sure are weird.

## 3

My name is Jake Renner, but most everyone calls me Rhino on account of a fight I once got in with a big Mexican. I lowered my head and charged and actually managed to knock the huge bastard off his feet. He still kicked my ass without breaking much of a sweat, but I got his shirt a little dirty, and got a nickname and a little respect out of the deal.

I'm 34 years old and have worked the I-95 grass-cutting crew for going on six years now. Despite the Maryland summer heat and humidity, it's a pretty good gig; we work eight months out of the year and make seventeen dollars an hour. Plus benefits. For a guy with no college, it beats laying asphalt or working construction, that's for sure.

The job is simple, but that's not to say easy. It mainly consists of pushing or riding a mower or working one of those big industrial weed-whackers. The whackers are heavy suckers and can do serious damage in careless hands. That's the first thing we learn around here; those things aren't toys.

The boss only cares about two things: the grass gets cut and the grass gets cut safely. If your crew does those two things, the boss man pretty much leaves you alone.

There are six of us on my crew. Me, three wiry Mexicans we call Huey, Duey and Louie after the cartoon ducks, a barrel-chested redneck who goes by Tex and doesn't talk all that much, and the only black guy I've ever known named Kyle. Kyle talks enough for all of us. The guy never shuts up, but it's okay; he usually makes us laugh and helps the time pass quicker.

Some days out on the road are a cakewalk. We cut grass and

crack jokes and sip lemonade spiked with vodka. Traffic is light and the breeze is cool. Other days are nothing but sunburns and thrown pennies and shouted cuss words from passing cars and nasty surprises run over and shredded by our mower blades. Trust me when I say you have never smelled anything quite as ripe as a loaded diaper—a shit sandwich, we call them—or a rotting, maggot-infested groundhog chewed up and spit out in 90 degree heat. Get some of that juice on your jeans and it'll take three or four washes to erase the stink.

But mostly it's boredom we fight on a daily basis. Cutting grass ain't brain surgery—and I-95 is one long-ass road.

## 4

We call them ditch treasures.

The name came about from a lunch conversation we had one sweltering July afternoon last summer in the shade of a busy underpass.

Between big, sloppy bites of roast beef sandwich, Kyle (of course) expressed his sincere dismay that so few kids today would ever experience the wonder and joy of the rain-soaked and swollen girlie magazine (traditionally fished out of dumpsters or trash cans or ditches, but sometimes—on rare, lucky occasions—found right out in the open).

We all understood where Kyle was coming from and shared in his pain. When I was a kid, every fort and tree house we ever built was stocked with a couple of these puffy, pages-stuck-together treasures. We surely wouldn't have thrown a copy of *Playboy* outta the old treehouse, but we all agreed the nastier the mags the better. Gems like *Swank* and *Penthouse* and *Oui* were especially coveted.

But, nowadays, with all the easily-accessed online porn, these ditch treasures—I'll proudly take credit for that little phrase—had all but become an endangered species. Hell, we didn't even see that many tree houses around anymore.

We all agreed it was a damn shame.

## 5

The rules were simple: *finders keepers*.

Any ditch treasures you found, you kept. If you were working by yourself when you stumbled upon it, the treasure was all yours. If you were working with a partner or partners, you split the goodies in equal shares.

Some guys tried to hide their finds if they were working with a partner—if the item was small enough, a stealthy kick of a work boot usually did the trick—so they could sneak back later and pretend to find it when they were alone.

But our crew wasn't like that.

We were all grateful to have the job and liked each other's company. Even Huey, Duey and Louie. We couldn't understand a damn thing they were saying most days, but that was all right; they worked hard and usually did it with smiles on their faces.

The six of us rooted each other on and were genuinely happy when someone found something tasty.

Kyle's all-time favorite find was a shoebox full of baseball cards. Rare baseball cards.

Tex's was a saddle. A big, leather, scuffed up horse saddle.

Before today, I would have said my favorite ditch treasure was the Rolex—I mean, how else is a guy like me ever gonna hold a genuine Rolex watch?—or maybe the Buffalo Head nickels that reminded me so much of my father.

But all that changed this morning…

## 6

Before I get to that, I need to tell you about the ponds.

Although, in reality, very few of them are actually ponds; I think the technical term is run-off collection basin. You've probably seen them yourselves if you've ever driven the interstate. Narrow strips of muddy water sitting just off the shoulder, no more than twenty or thirty yards in length, varying in depth depending on recent rain totals. In mid-Summer, these basins often transform into dried out, sun-cracked depressions in the landscape, like footprints from a wandering giant.

But every once in a while, you stumble across an actual real life pond. Complete with plant life and fish and frogs and snakes and even the occasional beaver dam. Our cutting territory on 95 held two such bodies of water, both located flush against exit ramps. The first pond was small and shallow and held little mystery for us. The fact that it was often used as a depository for recent roadkill and smelled pretty rank didn't help matters.

But the second pond was something else entirely. Tucked further back from the road, it sat in the shade of a couple ancient weeping willow trees. The pond itself was bigger and deeper and dappled with lily pads. Water bugs and dragon flies skated across the water's surface. The occasional fish jumped. Turtles sunned themselves on exposed logs and rocks. If it wasn't for the constant hum of traffic, you could stretch out a blanket on the grassy bank and enjoy a picnic lunch and almost forget that thousands of cars were hurtling past you a mere thirty yards away.

Kyle was the fisherman of the group, so the pond was his baby. He would often sneak a fishing rod and tackle box into the work truck on days he knew we'd be cutting nearby. He'd cast a line out during his lunch break, and although on most days he usually only caught a handful of fat sunnies, he once pulled a four pound largemouth bass out of that pond. I still have the picture on my cell phone to prove it.

But Kyle was home sick today. A summer cold, his wife said. Fever and the shakes.

So, I was working alone this morning. Pushing a hand mower in a wide, lazy circle around that pretty little pond. Humming to myself and paying extra attention to the ground in front of me, being especially careful of the weeping willow's thick roots.

# 7

I thought it was a baby doll at first.

Laying half in and half out of the water, face and legs obscured by mud and weeds.

I stopped and stared for a long moment—and my heart skipped a beat.

It looked so *real.*

I switched off the mower and started down the bank. As I did, my mind flashed back to the evening I found the mannequin, and any desire to call out to Tex, who was weed-whacking up on the shoulder, dried up and died in my throat. Better to take a look myself first; I was in no hurry to be the butt of their jokes again.

As I carefully worked my way down to the water, I noticed something distressing: there was a very clear path of broken and pushed-down grass leading to the pond...leading to the *thing* in the pond...as if it had somehow dragged itself there, looking for safety. Or water.

I stopped and picked up a broken tree branch. Eased a little closer. I leaned over and poked at the *thing* on the ground. Once. Twice. It was mushy to the touch, sponge like, and it didn't move.

Holding my breath, I poked it a third time. Harder. Nothing.

I inched closer and used the tip of the stick to flick away the weeds and cattails—and got a much better look at it.

It wasn't a baby doll.

It wasn't a baby.

It wasn't even human.

For a moment, I thought maybe it was some kind of animal. Hairless or even skinned. A species of animal I had never laid eyes on before.

But then I looked closer—at the long, narrow head; the three slanted eyes, wide open and cloudy, lined up *vertically* in the center of the creature's sloping forehead; there was no nose centered below, only a trio of small puckered indentations that could have been nostrils; still lower, a lipless and toothless pink slit for a mouth, stretching grotesquely across the entire length of the thing's lower jaw; no ears; not a wisp of hair; only pale, unlined ivory skin glistening and taut like a rubber wetsuit; and its arms, long, thin, boneless arms, ending in hands that didn't belong to man or beast; the hand-like appendages featuring three slender fingers each, the fingers unmarked by nails or knuckles or blemishes of any kind; and then finally its legs, spindly and spider-like, almost translucent, at least six of them tangled underneath it and submerged in the pond, each leg tapering to tiny claw-like feet.

I stood there for a long time and stared and listened to the cicadas in the trees and my own heavy, quick breathing, my brain still fighting the reality of the situation, even as I put a name to the thing laying in the muddy weeds at my feet.

"*It's a fucking alien,*" I whispered to myself.

A baby alien.

A *dead* baby alien.

I looked around and realized I had dropped the stick and backed away a short distance without even knowing it. I glanced at the stick on the ground, then back to the creature again. I glanced up the hill at Tex, still powering away with his weed-whacker, then quickly back to the creature again.

*Had it moved?*

*Had it gotten closer?*

I took another step back, then shook my head. *Don't start seeing things now, jackass.*

It hadn't moved. It wasn't breathing. It wasn't alive.

And it definitely wasn't human.

I looked up at Tex again and thought about what he would say. Knowing Tex, probably not a whole helluva lot.

Thought about Huey, Duey and Louie ... what would they say? Probably nothing I could understand.

I wished Kyle wasn't home sick; he would know what to do.

And then I heard my own voice inside my head: *finders keepers.*

It belonged to me, and me alone.

It was my decision.

## 8

I sat down on the cool grass in the shade of one of the weeping willows, just staring up at the blue sky above the highway and thinking hard thoughts.

Tex and his weed-whacker had moved down the road a bit. I could still hear the distant *whir* of the whacker, but could no longer see him. I might as well have been a middle-class suburbanite stretched out on a hammock in his back yard, reading the Wall Street Journal and sipping iced tea and listening to a neighbor finish his yard work down the street.

Only I wasn't a suburbanite, had never even been in a hammock before, hated iced tea, and had never laid eyes on a Wall Street Journal in my life.

I had a high school education (barely), cut grass eight months out of the year, moved snow the other four months, and lived with my pregnant girlfriend and our baby girl in a two-room apartment above a butcher's shop on Tupelo Street. The shop smelled funny on hot summer days and wasn't exactly located in the best part of town, but rent was cheap and the locks on the doors and windows worked.

I sat there and wondered how much the *National Enquirer* would pay for a story about a real life alien. A story *and* pictures. Hell, a story and pictures *and* the actual body of an alien. We sure could use the money.

Then, I wondered what my boss would say about all this. He was the cantankerous sort and very protective of his little grass-cutting kingdom. Like I said earlier, he mostly left us alone because the grass got cut and the grass got cut safely. What would he think if cops and federal agents (yes, I watch *The X-Files*; who doesn't?) were swarming all over his territory? Searching for evidence. Interviewing his employees. Getting in the way of our grass cutting efficiency? It wasn't a pretty thought.

And, finally, I couldn't help but wonder about those cops and federal agents. Might they be especially interested in the guy who found the alien? Might they even look into that guy's past and find some things that guy didn't want anyone to find, especially that guy's girlfriend and boss? These were troubling thoughts to ponder.

# 9

I pulled on my work gloves and followed the same winding path down to the water's edge. I didn't care about fingerprints; I just didn't want to actually touch the thing.

I walked quickly, any caution from before gone. My mind was made up.

Across the pond, a fish jumped. A gust of wind rippled the surface of the water.

I arrived at the pond and bent down, then decided to take a knee. I reached out with one hand to grab the baby alien—and hesitated, my hand hovering inches away.

*What the hell was I doing?*

"The only thing I can do," I answered before my mind could waver—and the words gave me courage.

I reached down and took hold of the alien's torso and pulled— but it didn't budge.

It was heavier than its small size indicated, and was stuck in the mud.

I reached down and seized it with both hands and...

*...there was a sudden flash of blinding white light behind my eyes...and when my vision cleared I was no longer kneeling by a small pond alongside I-95 in Maryland, but was in a faraway place with a roiling, purplish sky overhead the color of old bruises, jagged lightning strikes etched along the far horizon, and in the foreground, a scattering of strange buildings that almost seemed to be alive and glistening in the flickering purple light, and emerging from these buildings, dozens of skittering creatures, larger versions of the baby alien at my feet, approaching and surrounding me, until a pair of them stand before me, beckoning with their strange hand-like appendages, moist eyes beseeching me, and I suddenly realize what they are and who they are searching for and...*

The creature pulled free from the mud with a loud sucking *slurp*, and I tumbled to my ass with it cradled against my chest.

I quickly held it away from my body and got to my feet.

I hurried up the hill, and realized I had tears pouring down my cheeks.

*I didn't see anything*, I thought to myself, shaking my head.

I reached the mower and said it aloud, "I didn't see anything."

I started to toss the baby alien to the ground, then bent down and gently placed it on the long grass directly in front of the lawn mower.

"I didn't see a fucking thing," I whispered.

And then I started the mower.

# I AM THE DOORWAY

## STEPHEN KING

Richard and I sat on my porch, looking out over the dunes to the Gulf. The smoke from his cigar drifted mellowly in the air, keeping the mosquitoes at a safe distance. The water was a cool aqua, the sky a deeper, truer blue. It was a pleasant combination.

"You are the doorway," Richard repeated thoughtfully. "You are sure you killed the boy—you didn't just dream it?"

"I didn't dream it. And I didn't kill him, either—I told you that. They did. I am the doorway."

Richard sighed. "You buried him?"

"Yes."

"You remember where?"

"Yes." I reached into my breast pocket and got a cigarette. My hands were awkward with their covering of bandages. They itched abominably. "If you want to see it, you'll have to get the dune buggy. You can't roll this—" I indicated my wheelchair—" through the sand." Richard's dune buggy was a 1959 VW with pillow-sized tires. He collected driftwood in it. Ever since he retired from the real estate business in Maryland he had been living on Key Caroline and building driftwood sculptures which he sold to the winter tourists at shameless prices.

He puffed his cigar and looked out at the Gulf. "Not yet. Will you tell me once more?"

I sighed and tried to light my cigarette. He took the matches away from me and did it himself. I puffed twice, dragging deep. The itch in my fingers was maddening.

"All right," I said. "Last night at seven I was out here, looking at the Gulf and smoking, just like now, and J..."

"Go further back," he invited.

"Further?"

"Tell me about the flight."

I shook my head. "Richard, we've been through it and through it. There's nothing—"

The seamed and fissured face was as enigmatic as one of his own driftwood sculptures. "You may remember," he said. "Now you may remember."

"Do you think so?"

"Possibly. And when you're through, we can look for the grave."

"The grave," I said. It had a hollow, horrible ring, darker than anything, darker even than all that terrible ocean Cory and I had sailed through five years ago. Dark, dark, dark.

Beneath the bandages, my new eyes stared blindly into the darkness the bandages forced on them. They itched.

Cory and I were boosted into orbit by the Saturn 16, the one all the commentators called the Empire State Building booster. It was a big beast, all right. It made the old Saturn 1-B look like a Redstone, and it took off from a bunker two hundred feet deep— it had to, to keep from taking half of Cape Kennedy with it.

We swung around the earth, verifying all our systems, and then did our inject. Headed out for Venus. We left a Senate fighting over an appropriations bill for further deep-space exploration, and a bunch of NASA people praying that we would find something, anything.

"It don't matter what," Don Lovinger, Project Zeus's private whiz kid, was very fond of saying when he'd had a few. "You got all the gadgets, plus five souped-up TV cameras and a nifty little telescope with a zillion lenses and filters. Find some gold or platinum. Better yet, find some nice, dumb little blue men for us to study and exploit and feel superior to. Anything. Even the ghost of

Howdy Doody would be a start."

Cory and I were anxious enough to oblige, if we could. Nothing had worked for the deep-space program. From Borman, Anders, and Lovell, who orbited the moon in '6~ and found an empty, forbidding world that looked like dirty beach sand, to Markham and Jacks, who touched down on Mars eleven years later to find an arid wasteland of frozen sand and a few struggling lichens, the deep-space program had been an expensive bust. And there had been casualties—Pederson and Lederer, eternally circling the sun when all at once nothing worked on the second-to-last Apollo flight. John Davis, whose little orbiting observatory was holed by a meteoroid in a one-in-a-thousand fluke. No, the space program was hardly swinging along. The way things looked, the Venus orbit might be our last chance to say we told you so.

It was sixteen days out—we ate a lot of concentrates, played a lot of gin, and swapped a cold back and forth—and from the tech side it was a milk run. We lost an air-moisture converter on the third day out, went to backup, and that was all, except for flits and nats, until re-entry. We watched Venus grow from a star to a quarter to a milky crystal ball, swapped jokes with Huntsville Control, listened to tapes of Wagner and the Beatles, tended to automated experiments which had to do with everything from measurements of the solar wind to deep-space navigation. We did two midcourse corrections, both of them infinitesimal, and nine days into the flight Cory went outside and banged on the retractable DESA until it decided to operate. There was nothing else out of the ordinary until.

"DESA," Richard said. "What's that?"

"An experiment that didn't pan out. NASA-ese for Deep Space Antenna—we were broadcasting pi in high-frequency pulses for anyone who cared to listen." I rubbed my fingers against my pants, but it was no good; if anything, it made it worse. "Same idea as that radio telescope in West Virginia—you know, the one that listens to the stars. Only instead of listening, we were transmitting, primarily to the deeper space planets—Jupiter, Saturn, Uranus. If there's any intelligent life out there, it was taking a nap."

"Only Cory went out?"

"Yes. And if he brought in any interstellar plague, the telemetry didn't show it."

"Still—"

"It doesn't matter," I said crossly. "Only the here and now matters. They killed the boy last night, Richard. It wasn't a nice thing to watch—or feel. His head…it exploded. As if someone had scooped out his brains and put a hand grenade in his skull."

"Finish the story," he said.

I laughed hollowly. "What's to tell?"

We went into an eccentric orbit around the planet. It was radical and deteriorating, three twenty by seventy-six miles. That was on the first swing. The second swing our apogee was even higher, the perigee lower. We had a max of four orbits. We made all four. We got a good look at the planet. Also over six hundred stills and God knows how many feet of film.

The cloud cover is equal parts methane, ammonia, dust, and flying shit. The whole planet looks like the Grand Canyon in a wind tunnel. Cory estimated wind speed at about 600mph near the surface. Our probe beeped all the way down and then went out with a squawk. We saw no vegetation and no sign of life. Spectroscope indicated only traces of the valuable minerals. And that was Venus. Nothing but nothing—except it scared me. It was like circling a haunted house in the middle of deep space. I know how unscientific that sounds, but I was scared gutless until we got out of there. I think if our rockets hadn't gone off, I would have cut my throat on the way down. It's not like the moon. The moon is desolate but somehow antiseptic. That world we saw was utterly unlike anything that anyone has ever seen. Maybe it's a good thing that cloud cover is there. It was like a skull that's been picked clean—that's the closest I can get.

On the way back we heard the Senate had voted to halve space-exploration funds. Cory said something like "looks like we're back in the weather-satellite business, Artie." But I was almost glad. Maybe we don't belong out there.

Twelve days later Cory was dead and I was crippled for life. We bought all our trouble on the way down. The chute was fouled. How's that for life's little ironies? We'd been in space for over a month, gone further than any humans had ever gone, and it all ended the way it did because some guy was in a hurry for his coffee break and let a few lines get fouled.

We came down hard. A guy that was in one of the copters said it looked like a gigantic baby falling out of the sky, with the placenta trailing after it. I lost consciousness when we hit.

I came to when they were taking me across the deck of the *Portland.* They hadn't even had a chance to roll up the red carpet we were supposed to've walked on. I was bleeding. Bleeding and being hustled up to the infirmary over a red carpet that didn't look anywhere near as red as I did...

"I was in Bethesda for two years. They gave me the Medal of Honor and a lot of money and this wheelchair. I came down here the next year. I like to watch the rockets take off."

"I know," Richard said. He paused. "Show me your hands."

"No." It came out very quickly and sharply. "I can't let them see. I've told you that."

"It's been five years," Richard said. "Why now, Arthur? Can you tell me that?"

"I don't know. I don't know! Maybe whatever it is has a long gestation period. Or who's to say I even got it out there? Whatever it was might have entered me in Fort Lauderdale. Or right here on this porch, for all I know."

Richard sighed and looked out over the water, now reddish with the late-evening sun. "I'm trying. Arthur, I don't want to think that you are losing your mind."

"If I have to, I'll show you my hands," I said. It cost me an effort to say it. "But only if I have to."

Richard stood up and found his cane. He looked old and frail. "I'll get the dune buggy. We'll look for the boy."

"Thank you, Richard."

He walked out towards the rutted dirt track that led to his cabin—I could just see the roof of it over the Big Dune, the one that runs almost the whole length of Key Caroline. Over the water towards the Cape, the sky had gone an ugly plum color, and the sound of thunder came faintly to my ears.

I didn't know the boy's name but I saw him every now and again, walking along the beach at sunset, with his sieve under his arm. He was tanned almost black by the sun, and all he was ever clad in was a frayed pair of denim cutoffs. On the far side of Key Caroline there is a public beach, and an enterprising young man can make perhaps as much as five dollars on a good day, patiently sieving the sand for buried quarters or dimes. Every now and then I would wave to him and he would wave back, both of us noncommittal, strangers yet brothers, year-round dwellers set against a sea of money spending, Cadillac-driving, loud-mouthed tourists. I imagine he lived in the small village clustered around the post office about a half mile further down.

When he passed by that evening I had already been on the porch for an hour, immobile, watching. I had taken off the bandages earlier. The itching had been intolerable, and it was always better when they could look through their eyes.

It was a feeling like no other in the world—as if I were a portal just slightly ajar through which they were peeking at a world which they hated and feared. But the worst part was that I could see, too, in a way. Imagine your mind transported into a body of a housefly, a housefly looking into your own face with a thousand eyes. Then perhaps you can begin to see why I kept my hands bandaged even when there was no one around to see them.

It began in Miami. I had business there with a man named Cresswell, an investigator from the Navy Department. He checks up on me once a year—for a while I was as close as anyone ever gets to the classified stuff our space program has. I don't know just what it is he looks for; a shifty gleam in the eye, maybe, or maybe a scarlet letter on my forehead. God knows why. My pension is large enough to be almost embarrassing.

Cresswell and I were sitting on the terrace of his hotel room, sipping drinks and discussing the future of the US space program. It was about three-fifteen. My fingers began to itch. It wasn't a bit gradual. It was switched on like electric current. I mentioned it to Cresswell.

"So you picked up some poison ivy on that scrofulous little island," he said, grinning.

"The only foliage on Key Caroline is a little palmetto scrub," I said. "Maybe it's the seven-year itch." I looked down at my hands. Perfectly ordinary hands. But itchy.

Later in the afternoon I signed the same old paper ("I do solemnly swear that I have neither received nor disclosed and divulged information which would...") and drove myself back to the Key. I've got an old Ford, equipped with hand-operated brake and accelerator. I love it—it makes me feel self-sufficient.

It's a long drive back, down Route 1, and by the time I got off the big road and on to the Key Caroline exit ramp, I was nearly out of my mind. My hands itched maddeningly. If you have ever suffered through the healing of a deep cut or a surgical incision, you may have some idea of the kind of itch I mean. Live things seemed to be crawling and boring in my flesh.

The sun was almost down and I looked at my hands carefully in the glow of the dash lights. The tips of them were red now, red in tiny, perfect circlets, just above the pad where the fingerprint is, where you get calluses if you play guitar. There were also red circles of infection on the space between the first and second joint of each thumb and finger, and on the skin between the second joint and the knuckle. I pressed my right fingers to my lips and withdrew them quickly, with a sudden loathing. A feeling of dumb horror had risen in my throat, woolen and choking. The flesh where the red spots had appeared was hot, feverish, and the flesh was soft and gelid, like the flesh of an apple gone rotten.

I drove the rest of the way trying to persuade myself that I had indeed caught poison ivy somehow. But in the back of my mind there was another ugly thought. I had an aunt, back in my childhood, who lived the last ten years of her life closed off from the world in an upstairs room. My mother took her meals up, and her name was a forbidden topic. I found out later that she had Hansen's disease—leprosy.

When I got home I called Dr. Flanders on the mainland. I got his answering service instead. Dr. Flanders was on a fishing cruise, but if it was urgent, Dr. Ballanger—

"When will Dr. Flanders be back?"

"Tomorrow afternoon at the latest. Would that—"

"Sure."

I hung up slowly, then dialed Richard. I let it ring a dozen times before hanging up. After that I sat indecisive for a while. The itching had deepened. It seemed to emanate from the flesh itself.

I rolled my wheelchair over to the bookcase and pulled down the battered medical encyclopedia that I'd had for years. The book was maddeningly vague. It could have been anything, or nothing.

I leaned back and closed my eyes. I could hear the old ship's clock ticking on the shelf across the room. There was the high, thin drone of a jet on its way to Miami. There was the soft whisper of my own breath.

I was still looking at the book.

The realization crept on me, then sank home with a frightening rush. My eyes were closed, but I was still looking at the book. What I was seeing was smeary and monstrous, the distorted, fourth-dimensional counterpart of a book, yet unmistakable for all that.

And I was not the only one watching.

I snapped my eyes open, feeling the constriction of my heart. The sensation subsided a little, but not entirely. I was looking at the book, seeing the print and diagrams with my own eyes, perfectly normal everyday experience, and I was also seeing it from a different, lower angle and seeing it with other eyes. Seeing not a book but an alien thing, something of monstrous shape and ominous intent.

I raised my hands slowly to my face, catching an eerie vision of my living room turned into a horror house.

I screamed.

There were eyes peering up at me through splits in the flesh of my fingers. And even as I watched the flesh was dilating, retreating, as they pushed their mindless way up to the surface.

But that was not what made me scream. I had looked into my own face and seen a monster.

The dune buggy nosed over the hill and Richard brought it to a halt next to the porch. The motor gunned and roared choppily. I rolled my wheelchair down the inclined plane to the right of the regular steps and Richard helped me in.

"All right, Arthur," he said. "It's your party. Where to?"

I pointed down towards the water, where the Big Dune family begins to peter out. Richard nodded. The rear wheels spun sand and we were off. I usually found time to rib Richard about his driving, but I didn't bother tonight. There was too much else to think about—and to feel: they didn't want the dark, and I could feel them straining to see through the bandages, willing me to take them off.

The dune buggy bounced and roared through the sand towards the water, seeming almost to take flight from the tops of the small dunes. To the left the sun was going down in bloody glory. Straight ahead and across the water, the thunderclouds were beating their way towards us. Lightning forked at the water.

"Off to your right," I said. "By that lean-to."

Richard brought the dune buggy to a sand-spraying halt beside the rotted remains of the lean-to, reached into the back, and brought out a spade. I winced when I saw it. "Where?" Richard asked expressionlessly.

"Right there." I pointed to the place.

He got out and walked slowly through the sand to the spot, hesitated for a second, then plunged the shovel into the sand. It seemed that he dug for a very long time. The sand he was throwing back over his shoulder looked damp and moist. The thunderheads were darker, higher, and the water looked angry and implacable under their shadow and the reflected glow of the sunset.

I knew long before he stopped digging that he was not going to find the boy. They had moved him. I hadn't bandaged my hands last night, so they could see—and act. If they had been able to use me to kill the boy, they could use me to move him, even while I slept.

"There's no boy, Arthur." He threw the dirty shovel into the dune buggy and sat tiredly on the seat. The coming storm cast marching, crescent-shaped shadows along the sand. The rising breeze rattled sand against the buggy's rusted body. My fingers itched.

"They used me to move him," I said dully. "They're getting the upper hand, Richard. They're forcing their doorway open, a little at a time. A hundred times a day I find myself standing in front of some perfectly familiar object—a spatula, a picture, even a can of beans—with no idea how I got there, holding my hands out, showing it to them, seeing it as they do, as an obscenity, something twisted and grotesque—"

"Arthur," he said. "Arthur, don't. Don't." In the failing light his face was wan with compassion. "*Standing* in front of something, you said. *Moving* the boy's body, you said. *But you can't walk, Arthur.* You're dead from the waist down."

I touched the dashboard of the dune buggy. "This is dead, too. But when you enter it, you can make it go. You could make it kill. It couldn't stop you even if it wanted to." I could hear my voice rising hysterically. "I am the doorway, can't you understand that? They killed the boy, Richard! They moved the body!"

"I think you'd better see a medical man," he said quietly. "Let's go back. Let's—"

"Check! Check on the boy, then! find out—"

"You said you didn't even know his name."

"He must have been from the village. It's a small village. Ask—"

"I talked to Maud Harrington on the phone when I got the dune buggy. If anyone in the state has a longer nose, I've not come across her. I asked if she'd heard of anyone's boy not coming home last night. She said she hadn't."

"But he's a local! He has to be!"

He reached for the ignition switch but I stopped him. He turned to look at me and I began to unwrap my hands.

From the Gulf, thunder muttered and growled.

I didn't go to the doctor and I didn't call Richard back. I spent three weeks with my hands bandaged every time I went out. Three weeks just blindly hoping it would go away. It wasn't a rational act; I can admit that. If I had been a whole man who didn't need a wheelchair for legs or who had spent a normal life in a normal

238

occupation, I might have gone to Doc Flanders or to Richard. I still might have, if it hadn't been for the memory of my aunt, shunned, virtually a prisoner, being eaten alive by her own ailing flesh. So I kept a desperate silence and prayed that I would wake up some morning and find it had been an evil dream.

And little by little, I felt them. Them. An anonymous intelligence. I never really wondered what they looked like or where they had come from. It was moot. I was their doorway, and their window on the world. I got enough feedback from them to feel their revulsion and horror, to know that our world was very different from theirs. Enough feedback to feel their blind hate. But still they watched. Their flesh was embedded in my own. I began to realize that they were using me, actually manipulating me.

When the boy passed, raising one hand in his usual noncommittal salute, I had just about decided to get in touch with Cresswell at his Navy Department number. Richard had been right about one thing—I was certain that whatever had got hold of me had done it in deep space or in that weird orbit around Venus. The Navy would study me, but they would not freakify me. I wouldn't have to wake up any more into the creaking darkness and stifle a scream as I felt them watching, watching, watching.

My hands went out towards the boy and I realized that I had not bandaged them. I could see the eyes in the dying light, watching silently. They were large, dilated, goldenirised. I had poked one of them against the tip of a pencil once, and had felt excruciating agony slam up my arm. The eye seemed to glare at me with a chained hatred that was worse than physical pain. I did not poke again.

And now they were watching the boy. I felt my mind sideslip. A moment later my control was gone. The door was open. I lurched across the sand towards him, legs scissoring nervelessly, so much driven deadwood. My own eyes seemed to close and I saw only with those alien eyes—saw a monstrous alabaster seascape overtopped with a sky like a great purple way, saw a leaning, eroded shack that might have been the carcass of some unknown, flesh-devouring creature, saw an abominated creature that moved and respired and carried a device of wood and wire under its arm, a device constructed of geometrically impossible right angles.

I wonder what he thought, that wretched, unnamed boy with his sieve under his arm and his pockets bulging with an odd conglomerate of sandy tourist coins, what he thought when he saw me lurching at him like a blind conductor stretching out his hands over a lunatic orchestra, what he thought as the last of the light fell across my hands, red and split and shining with their burden of eyes, what he thought when the hands made that sudden, flailing gesture in the air, just before his head burst.

I know what I thought.

I thought I had peeked over the rim of the universe and into the fires of hell itself.

The wind pulled at the bandages and made them into tiny, whipping streamers as I unwrapped them. The clouds had blottered the red remnants of the sunset, and the dunes were dark and shadow-cast. The clouds raced and boiled above us.

"You must promise me one thing, Richard," I said over the rising wind. "You must run if it seems I might try... to hurt you. Do you understand that?"

"Yes." He open-throated shirt whipped and rippled with the wind. His face was set, his own eyes little more than sockets in early dark.

The last of the bandages fell away.

I looked at Richard and they looked at Richard. I saw a face I had known for five years and come to love. They saw a distorted, living monolith.

"You see them," I said. hoarsely. "Now you see them."

He took an involuntary step backwards. His face became stained with a sudden unbelieving terror. Lightning slashed out of the sky. Thunder walked in the clouds and the water had gone black as the river Styx.

"Arthur—"

How hideous he was! How could I have lived near him, spoken with him? He was not a creature, but mute pestilence. He was—

"Run! Run, Richard!" And he did run. He ran in huge, bounding leaps. He became a scaffold against the looming sky. My hands flew up, flew over my head in a screaming, orlesque gesture, the fingers reaching to the only familiar thing in this nightmare world—reaching to the clouds.

And the clouds answered. There was a huge, blue-white streak of lightning that seemed like the end of the world. It struck Richard, it enveloped him. The last thing I remember is the electric stench of ozone and burnt flesh.

When I awoke I was sitting calmly on my porch, looking out towards the Big Dune. The storm had passed and the air was pleasantly cool. There was a tiny sliver of moon. The sand was virginal—no sign of Richard or of the dune buggy.

I looked down at my hands. The eyes were open but glazed. They had exhausted themselves. They dozed.

I knew well enough what had to be done. Before the door could be wedged open any further, it had to be locked. Forever. Already I could notice the first signs of structural change in the hands themselves. The fingers were beginning to shorten... and to change.

There was a small hearth in the living room, and in season I had been in the habit of lighting a fire against the damp Florida cold. I lit one now, moving with haste. I had no idea when they might wake up to what I was doing.

When it was burning well I went out back to the kerosene drum and soaked both hands. They came awake immediately, screaming with agony. I almost didn't make it back to the living room, and to the fire.

But I did make it.

That was all seven years ago. I'm still here, still watching the rockets take off. There have been more of them lately. This is a space-minded administration. There has even been talk of another series of manned Venus probes.

I found out the boy's name, not that it matters. He was from the village, just as I thought. But his mother had expected him to stay with a friend on the mainland that night, and the alarm was not raised until the following Monday. Richard—well, everyone thought Richard was an odd duck, anyway. They suspect he may have gone back to Maryland or taken up with some woman.

As for me, I'm tolerated, although I have quite a reputation for eccentricity myself. After all, how many ex-astronauts regularly write their elected Washington officials with the idea that space-exploration money could be better spent elsewhere?

I get along just fine with these hooks. There was terrible pain for the first year or so, but the human body can adjust to almost anything. I shave with them and even tie my own shoelaces. And as you can see, my typing is nice and even. I don't expect to have any trouble putting the shotgun into my mouth or pulling the trigger. It started again three weeks ago, you see.

There is a perfect circle of twelve golden eyes on my chest.

# THE IMMIGRANTS

## ERIK T. JOHNSON

It's almost four o'clock in the morning when my guard-bones bark me awake (That's the best way I can describe this oddest of sensations. Old folks get lots of strange twinges and pains but this is new). I head for the bathroom. I glimpse myself in the medicine cabinet, just before it breaks along with the other mirrors in my place. Simultaneous. That's weird but not the real puzzle here. Look, shit breaks, weird happens, right?

What surpasses weird is the *way* they've broken. I go room to room, turning on lights (At least it's not a blackout). I try all eight mirrors. There's always a first time for all things to go wrong in unprecedented ways: I've never seen a mirror *malfunction* before.

Each time I look at the glass, there's no me, there's disparate *person-like non-people* there, watching for something a ways behind my back. Giving off a lost, worried vibe, waiting for a monumental appearance on the distant horizon...Nothing there but the cramped walls of my tenement apartment, far as I can tell. And the black smudge of a squashed moth.

I return to seeking my seeking reflection.

Nope.

Two of them in my largest mirror. Can't tell if they're male, female, clay-mation automaton, nuclear vegetable, or what. But I was a door-to-door salesman my whole working life—which ended decades ago—and between the great variety of doors opening and closing in your face, the invites for a cuppa joe and the accusations of trespassing, you get good at reading people. Who woulda thunkd'it:

Turns out you also catch the knack for reading aliens.

I see expressions above their necks that put me in mind of when a fish is taken out of water a few moments—not long enough to kill it—how in that time before it's thrown back into the lake—how that experience must be the closest that fish ever came to dreaming. This pair's giving a related impression. Or is it me feeling that way?.

Stop it already.

Know what I bet? Corporations run everything—and that's no crazy old-timer conspiracy ranting. I bet some business who secretly charges each American in limbs has blown a grid-load of fuses. Whatever clandestine company that provides you with this power: The power to pretend your face belongs to someone else—so you can look him in the eye and fix his hair—Well, that shadow conglomerate's had a damn awful outage I bet.

I've even lost the ability to objectively confirm I'm a fossil of a man who can't remember how long he's been living by himself. Or living (Can't be but a few years' difference between the two). A man who looks in the mirror to see an exile from an icy planet of pensioners ... *Is that a biped? I don't recognize this creature of moley wrinkle and twitch, this "me"* ...

A man who, a lifetime ago, misplaced a list of important things to do. Such as: stop travelling the road like Rosie asked you to; kick the booze; prove I'm man enough to take care of her; marry Rosie; get a steady job, a career with upward mobility; some kids to run round a sprinkler in a big, green yard in Long Island. Such as: don't let sixty years go by and wind up here with the dead moth-spotted walls. Don't misplace that list. Such as: stop fucking up, and die already. I'm late for being late.

Joy is careless. Misery couldn't care less. My reflections, be they in mirrors or brain, never helped me understand this World much.

There in the mirror I'm not reflected.

I'd have a hard time selling this crap back in the day.

Where my image should be, *some-almost-one* looks beyond me, not so much like I'm invisible as blocking a view, the guy in a 10-gallon hat who just sat down directly in front of you at the movies.

A nameless "X" is happening. What I mean is if the World's truly *spinning*—if that's the correct word—then no kid, drunk, dreidel, top or ballerina ever *spins*—They lack motive, have no Sun. We need another verb.

Better: Another verb is *here*.

The mirrors are *X-ing*.

How will I shave?

Here's a relief (I guess)—I'm not just losing it:

The radio is frantic with reports on this malfunctioning-mirror deal. It's a scourge. My reception is eroded, like the signals are wrestling with a mighty angel, yanking them back to Transmitter Desert before they can get close enough to gimme the skinny. Eventually, I can make out the most frequently iterated words and phrases:

*Invasion ... Electromagnetic Attack ... Noted String-Theorist ... Unknown Quantum ... Tom Cruise issued this statement ... Visitors ... Dimensional Portal ... Terrorist ... So-called Bashing Parties ... Alien ... Impossible ... Reality as We Know It ... Bad Luck ... Knows No Borders ... Obama's Fault ... Apocalypse ... Calm ... Panic ... Trump calls for mass executions by guillotine ... Don't ... Do ... Stay Put ... Flee! Far Away! ... Tom Cruise has retracted ... Extraterrestrial Phenomenon ... Go-Bag Essentials ... Tesla's Revenge ... Is Obama an evil alien entity ... Global ... Guns ... Ghosts ...*

(They can rule *that* one out. This "X" happening with the mirrors is nothing supernatural, there's no spirit world. When you're dead you're *dead*. I know because I died once. On an operating table. I was dead three minutes, and when the surgeons reeled me back, I remembered nothing of the experience, *and* I didn't forget a single detail, either. You get me? Because there is *nothing*. Even that word alone is *too much* to describe it.)

Detritus of interviews, mumbling heads, doctors with no degrees, comedians ... Obnoxious jokes about vampires and bad luck beyond reckoning. They laugh, ha-ha. But laughter is like mist on a river—it might distract you from the water, but it cannot change its course, and the course is all a river is.

Were people always this stupid?

I shut that radio the fuck up, go through the rooms, visiting each of the formerly-known-as-mirrors. No, they certainly aren't humans, no discernible gender or ages, even. Who'da thunkdit: My Eisenhower-Era door-to-door toaster salesman skills could be today's cutting-edge forensic competencies. I register a new emotion on the "faces." It's difficult to explain. Let's call it a lost-coin look:

Whereas a coin toss has two possible outcomes, *losing* a coin is at least three kinds of loss. You lose a circular, metal object about the size of a 1947 pox-vaccination scar; you lose a bit of money; and you lose control (as with any loss). But these aliens, with their lost-coin looks haven't lost any coins...What gives?

I'm ashamed!

What arrogance. How do I know what they've lost? What wicked cosmos they fled? Do they keep their to-do lists on them at all times? Are they waiting for salvation? Have they suffered? Then again, they could be coming to destroy humanity, to ruin civilization itself, steal our oxygen—who knows?

They are looking *forward*, that's for sure. Which means when I see them, I'm looking backward.

At what, a *new past?*

This question brings an antique photograph to mind. It belonged to my mother. A picture of my great-grandparents on Ellis Island, having just arrived from Ruthenia. He was a laborer and she a laundress. They'd come here with great hopes, like many millions. They'd work their stinking birthplace skin off, grow a vibrant new American layer. Live well and start a family, the biggest, the most beautiful. The old story. The one you have to believe is true, if only for an hour or two each year. Or else you will go mad.

But now they've disembarked onto this land of no-turning-back-now. It's plain to see in the photograph: Whatever ordeals they endured to reach New York has drained any emotion from their eyes, leaving dark sepia spots.

It's obvious: All they want's to be left alone in the two-dimensional peace of that photograph. Because they quickly picked up how obscenely expensive cheerful eyes are over here. They'll never save enough. The question of housing. If only they could stay in that photograph! They swear they'll even wear those empty eyes forever, if that's the cost of settling down in that photo. On the back someone with a firm hand, my mother didn't know who, had written *Much luck!*

I'm tired of those peering mirrorific things and the memories they stir. If I try hard enough I can imagine they're eight weird, tacky posters not suited to my tastes. I like only Gauguin. And L.A. Spooner, I think. The one with the nudes.

I must sleep, it's late, dark.

I'm not sleeping for long. People outside, crude, loud city-racket. My eyes open but I don't feel like getting out of bed.

A mob gathering in the street. Shouting. Mad as hell, not going to take it anymore, sort of black-and-white-TV race-riot stuff, fascist acting-out … The World outside my window counts down in remarkable solidarity: "Three … Two … One—Smash!" Sounds like the genocide of a million glass gypsies. Lynched with pissed-off collective WHACK!, baseball bats, crowbars, curtain-rods. After the shattering, lots of people screaming in burning-alive pain (I recognize the timbre of that particular dying-crying from the war). Must be one of those mirror-bashing parties that I think the radio's spluttering about. I remember when they burned books. That was bad. But much quieter. Thankfully the screaming stops all at once, as if at the push of a button. The death of a laugh-track.

I try the bedside lamp but it's kaput. I get up, fumble to the wall-switch: Nope, no light.

I open my window: Nope, no street. No people, nothing broken or burned. No stars. Which anyway are less loving than snakes, less than indifferent. Maybe they were just an omen of twinkling glass shards, extinguished now that of which they warned is come. It's always one thing after another and when it rains it pours and Murphy's Law. In other words, another grid has hit the fan. It's the classic New York City blackout I was so glad wasn't happening earlier. Lots of trouble tonight.

My frozen pirogues will stink like corpse farts.

Damn, I can't remember if I did my weekly shopping…

What will happen to those creatures in the mirrors? Looking

expectant, lost-coin sad. These aliens who need their own verbs. These People of the Verbs. Will they find the right action words in time—There's urgent yearning on their side.

My God, am I *worried* about them? Remember, dumbass, you don't know their true intentions.

Don't lose your head. It's just a blackout. I can cope. The hell with Go-Bags. It is what it is and what're you gonna do? and it's a serious pain in the ass but whatever you do, stay calm. No problem.

In my calm I suddenly feel the need to talk to another person. Why? I don't know. It's harder to explain than it oughta be. It's not like me. I got to the telephone—a glorious landline, impervious to blackouts. Old ways aren't always outdated.

I have nobody to call.

But wait, there's always someone. There's billions of wrong numbers.

I sit on the edge of my bed. I find the fat candle on my night-table. I hate candles. It smells like marzipan and I like marzipan. I open the drawer and take out the big box of safety matches.

I try lighting the candle, pick up the phone and wait for the dial-tone.

I want to hear another person say "hello." This isn't like me at all. At the same time, my heart is stirring as though obedient to a thread, yes, it hangs from a loose thread, which in its turn is submissive to a sort of inner wind now passing through, uneasing it from firm uprightness. What opening in me permits such an impossible breeze entrance? Oh, that's right. I can't believe I can remember how it feels: heartache...

I am obedient to the dizzy whims of the thinnest thread.

The safety matches are definitely not wet, so the whole box must be defective. Probably made in New Jersey. Not a single match works, do you believe it. There's no marzipan smoke from a flame in this room. I can't see a thing. My window is open and the street is awful mute. Silent as three minutes of operation-table, flatline *nothing*.

There's no dial-tone, either. I'll hang on ... The dial-tone's probably just tired, taking its sweet time to reach me...It will arrive soon. Lame joke, old man. Please, stop lying. Something's very wrong tonight. I highly doubt there's a prowler running around cutting telephone wires, and barring that, I'm clueless as to why there's no dial-tone. There isn't even the *possibility* of hearing a person say "Hello, how can I help you?" or "I'm afraid you have the wrong number" or even "Don't you *ever* call here again, do you *hear me asshole*...DO YOU?" No chance for me to apologize to someone, say "I'm so sorry to trouble you, truly sorry..."

The crackling of mirrors begins throughout my apartment, a pizzicato crescendo. The eight mirrors are X-ing and other verbs, too, say, ZX-ing and XZ-ing...It sounds traumatic as birth but what do I know, it could be joy, the immigrants are disembarking. Oh, I see. Shit in my pants. My old salesman senses are tingling...I'm pretty sure they aren't friendly, I've got that *whatever-you're-selling we-don't-want-it-get-off-my-land* vibe. I hang up the phone, pick it up again. Is that a dial-tone? It's definitely something. Hope can impersonate anything from a dial-tone to the vision of future generations flourishing in a land of liberty...Still not a dial-tone.

A slight ringing? Nope, not that, either. It's a buzzing, an echo. No. You're imagining things. It's not the sound of a Coney Island conch in my ear. It's not Rosie saying *Can't you stay just a few more days ...love?* But it's definitely something, that's for sure. It's not that I'm afraid to die alone, right now, what at my age and all. It's that I don't want to go *extinct* like this, here in my voiceless dark, and it's much luck to the immigrants, may at least a couple of their dreams come true.

# KEY TO THE CITY

## CODY GOODFELLOW

Rhubarb Rayvonne Balker dearly loved to hear the old folks tell stories about the City across the wide green River, about how it was when any old car with wheels could ride the highways, and anyone with nerve enough could try their hand navigating the smartstreets and strange ways of Cityfolk.

With no honest trade to keep her running, and only Bama, the zika-wit mascot of the Lower Mergatroyd Mobile Estates park for surviving kin, Rhubarb was apt to lose herself in fairystories. She dreamed about the City, ate up the old shows, and collected the stories that she retold to anyone in earshot like she had a jinglebug in her ear. This appetite did make her a figure of fun among the old River rats and retired pirates at Speedy's off-license fuel station and bait shop, who peppered the unbelievable true tidbits they actually recalled with pure weevil-grease of their own stunted but peculiarly flummoxatious invention.

So Speedy Boningham and Jubal Fufkin were primed to topple off their bait-barrels, convulsed with hilarity, when Barb came wallowing in out of the shallows under a frenzy of wingworms, with a body over one shoulder and a black glass briefcase under her arm, popping off that they'd be doing themselves a favor getting in on the ground floor kissing her mildewy bog-boots.

Back before the City closed up to all traffic but the high-speed tubes, a body with a knife and a modicum of hack-learning could jack truck-trains or hovercraft carrying cargo pods with work-ready mites from China, freefall weed from the orbital arcologies,

Martian moonshine, and some things the more credulous clans down in the Bottoms worshipped as gods to this day.

The promise of the sunken dregs of those halcyon days was enough to keep moon-eyed seekers like Rhubarb poking for salvage up and down the west bend of the delta, where the gleaming walls and animated spires of the City a mile and more off across the water blocked out the sun at half past afternoon in summer, and in winter plunged all of Mergatroyd County into uneasy neon twilight before her gullet was done with lunch. The lights of the City were a perverse aurora, the pornographic holograms of the shoreline pleasure district cavorting above the clouds, showing her everything she knew so far about what went on between boys and girls. She was ogling those angelic visions when her suction hose blocked up and the whole skimmer nosed into the swamp and tossed her overboard.

Paddling after the stalled skimmer, she figured she'd sucked up a crawgator or a humanatee, but was dismayed to find it was just some fool who got stuck in the mud trying to creep across the bottom in a gillsuit. But then he turned out to be alive, and offered her what he was carrying if she'd save his life. Said it was the keys to the kingdom...

On the fisherman's scale at Speedy's landing, Rhubarb peeled the gillsuit off the body and wiped her knife off on her rubber dungarees. "Well hell," she said, and then again. When she stepped on his chest, all that came out his mouth was a little mud.

"Don't see how a no-account clone like this would have the keys to his own car, anyhow." Speedy nipped off a leaf-bulb of Albino Krowe tonic and flicked the crushed empty into the river. He didn't need to point out the zip-stitches, shunts and bar-codes all over the carcass. "Must've jumped off a farm..."

"Might could be a rich man's shadow," Rhubarb put in. "You said only the moguls ever grow whole clones. Maybe I could sell it downriver to King Cadillac, if it's a wavy germline—"

"No good'll come of you pokewits fiddling with that thing," Fufkin warned.

Speedy already had it on the bench and was trying to pick the lock. "You're just gonna have to wait a few more minutes for your toy soldiers, is all..."

"Ain't toys," Fufkin grunted, "they're antique historical recreation bots..." He'd reaped a couple regiments of Confederate infantry resin figurines off a pre-Collapse maker site, and dropped a case of Albino Krowe on Speedy to get him to fabricate them off his printers.

"Which battle're you fixing to make 'em fight, Gen'ral?" Speedy asked.

"Battle of Fufkin's Pantry," Jubal said. "I got roaches."

"You oughta record it," Rhubarb cut in. "That'd be a hell of a show." She rattled off how everything everybody did in the City was recorded, so everybody's life was a TV show you could live like real life, and how nobody ever went hungry, because you could just grow a scrape of skin off yourself or buy celebrity cultures online and grow it into a meal, or a better nose or a new heart; how nobody died in the City if they didn't want to, how they became ghosts inside the big computer, and lived in a world that made the near-perfection of the City look like the seventh circle of Hell...

"Where'd you hear all that shit?" Fufkin demanded, when he'd repacked the levee of moonweed chew in his jaw that had messily breached and overrun his chin amid Rhubarb's rhapsodic speech. She just pointed at Speedy, who tossed his lockpicks and told everyone who wasn't wearing lead to get scarce, then whipped out his X-ray gun.

The light didn't look any different, but Rhubarb felt it like millions of invisible catfish kissing her all over. Inside the black glass case, a pink bubble bulging with pressurized fluid, and something else only slightly denser than the ooze, but way more wiggly... and cute...

"Oops," Speedy dropped the gun and pulled up a 3D scan.

The ghost spinning between them was a humanoid fetus—a more or less normal-looking unborn cyclops with a crystal lens for an eye so complicated it seemed to wiggle in and out of three dimensions, and to let several as yet uncataloged realities seep through.

"Judas get home," Speedy said, "it's a mirror-baby."

"A what?" Rhubarb squeezed closer.

"Just an ugly baby, is all." Jubal Fufkin spat a bottle cap he'd chewed into a bullet into the spitoon. "Throw it back."

"Hell no!" Rhubarb blushed ultraviolet. "*My* salvage! You know what it is, Speedy, go on and tell him!"

Speedy just shook his head. "It might-could be somebody tried to make it one, but… It was just some dead clone at Riverbottom, Barb…"

"Look at that big marble eye, Speedy Boningham. This thing is a backup mirror for the City's holographic matrix, ain't it? The spine for the whole damn program, and you damn-well know it. You're the one, tol' me about it…"

One thing everyone knew about the City was, it was *smart.* Too smart for its own good, most folks would add, and nothing more.

Long before it stopped letting country folk inside or even onto its highways, every little brick, every blade of grass, was smarter than a whole raft of local know-it-all weak AI's. Ants and mites didn't just pick up the trash, they could remake it, or anything in the City, into anything else—could turn diamonds to ice cream and poop to plutonium. The only things in the City that weren't worth a tin shit, processing-wise, were the people, even though they had the best computers of all under their dumbass fancy hairdos. Their master computers were nothing but great big old chains of tank-grown human brains, dreaming the perfect mirror image of the City that guided its unthinkably complex operations, and a perfect manmade Heaven for their dead.

Rhubarb's earliest memories of the River were of how spooky-quick the skyline reared up from nothing after the whole City went and melted into gray goo in the Second Collapse, how it rebuilt itself up into an unbreakable wave a mile and more high in less than two weeks, between her first riverbath and her baptism. Pretty much everything inside it was a computer, and the computers that ran it were the biggest of all, but they looked pretty small, if you didn't know what you were looking at.

Speedy ogled the exotic socket ports on the black glass briefcase with his membrane lenses dialed wide open as he rummaged in a bin of cables. "Sure looks like a viable backup mirror ... but I don't rightly know if we should..."

"You do so!" Jubal Fufkin snapped. "You know it's the nadir of sensibility to even commonplate it. Just suppose that ugly sport *does* spark up and ports into the big show. What're you fixin to do with it anyway, that anybody round these parts wants or needs? Them folks stopped buying from our farms cos they eat their own asses! Stopped letting us in cos we wouldn't let em monkey with our genes or put their chips in our blood. Why you think Mergatroyd moved its county seat eight times in the last fifty years? Why's Main Street built under one of their big ol high-speed tubes? It ain't just to stay out of the sun, girls. You plug in that ugly baby, you gonna light up this whole town on their great big map, and they gonna come down on us like forty days and forty nights of fiery hammers—"

"Chill, Jube," Speedy said, trying one jack after another from an armload of cables. "Little bitty baby like this might just let us take a peek through their backdoor, but we ain't gonna make any kind of fuss they can track back to our...uh...front door..." He plugged one in and twisted it. "How's that?"

Nobody answered him. Nobody could find the words.

The bait shack vanished, and everything was made of light, and the light was pregnant with unspeakably expensive information. Gleaming spires and lattices of animated data towered around them. An impossible orrery of spheres and pyramids of consciousnesses collective and individual swarmed round an axis of blinding light, like the heart of a galaxy.

"Nobody move," Speedy mumbled, but until he said it, neither of the others seemed to remember they had bodies at all, let alone try to move them.

Rhubarb finally broke the spell, throwing out her arms to play with a firefly crown that seemed to circle tantalizingly overhead.

The galaxy exploded.

They stood on a plaza where six rivers of light came together, and the walls were made of perfect faces a mile high saying her name, and the people passing through her were ghostly jellyfish with pulsating financial and social organs shining out through the gray translucence of their avatars.

"Told you not to move," Speedy said.

"I didn't do it," Rhubarb whined, hands behind her back.

Somebody shouted, "*Obdormisco!*"

Everything disappeared. Speedy and Rhubarb rubbed their eyes and shivered. Jubal Fufkin had his eyes closed the whole time, so he only shook his head sadly when they looked accusingly at him. "I didn't do it," he said, pointing with his cane. "Reckon *he* did."

"Speak plain American, boy!" Speedy barked in the clone's face.

"Was Latin," Fufkin said. "Told it to take a nap..."

"Stupid fucking hicks," the clone gasped. "This isn't a mirror... It's..." Then he spaced out.

Rhubarb pounced on his chest and tried giving him mouth-to-mouth. "Breathe, ya crazy critter!"

"Get off him!" Speedy slapped a couple first-aid derms on his neck. "These damn tank-devils are always dying and getting better. Can't tell what they're using for brains, so most of the time, they'll drown in the rain—"

The clone jolted to bug-eyed alertness and pushed himself up on one elbow. "Please... I need to find my brothers in the resistance..."

"Ain't no clone guerilla army around here, boy," Fufkin said.

"You're fighting for your freedom?" Rhubarb asked. "That's the bravest thing I ever heard!"

"We're just fighting for our jobs. For a place. No work to do, anymore. Nobody works, everybody dies in debt, gets turned into programs, put into trash cans and subway cars. Everything is run by ghosts, everything undead.

"All I've ever known was the farm. My master was good to me, but last year, they said we were obsolete. We were going to escape, me and the rest of my pod, but I guess I was the only one who made it. We took the little brother to hack the City and rewrite ourselves in as full citizens or blow it all up, but...the mirror isn't a mirror...The City isn't a City, anymore..." His eyes seemed to glaze over, pointed at the suitcase. "It's a dream of a City. We tried to wake it up..."

"Think I know what he means," Speedy said. "Girl, your Daddy always hated the City...We're always funning you, but we wanted you to shy off it, because me and Junebug Stookey and your Daddy once tried to jack the high-speed tube."

"Go hang," Jubal said, "that was *you*? That was supposed to be a acciden..."

"Warn't no accident." Speedy spat his chew in the River. "That's what happened to your Daddy, Rhubarb...and maybe I felt a little responsible, on account of it was my idea.

"We just blew a hole in the side of the tube. Figured we'd stop traffic and loot the truck-trains and light off into the hills before City law showed up.

"But there weren't no truck-trains or hovercraft full of cargo inside...no flying cars with glassjaw slicks begging for their lives ...Warn't nothing inside that tube but a bunch of fat opticables. No roads in or out of that City after they rebuilt from the goo plague, Barb. Just them cables...Well, your Daddy went and got himself fried trying to make something come out the wires, the dumb redneck."

Rhubarb waited for him to stop talking. Folks in town had all kinds of ideas how her Daddy died, but her mama told her the truth, about how he turned mercenary and went down south with the Warbabies and got killed fighting the Aztech Empire. To hear her tell it—how he went to the top of their floating pyramid and lay on the altar and bared his chest with the Cyclops battle-flag of the Risen Dixie tattooed on it so it waved like an antique GIF loop so they cracked his ribcage and dug out his beating heart—you might have thought they sent her a commemorative video.

"Sure," Rhubarb said, "I know all about teleports...like, they zap people and things into bits, and shoot 'em through the wire, and they come out the other side solid again?"

"They don't come out solid, girl. Once you're in the City, you never come out at all. That's why…"

"That's why we had to move the whole town," Jubal said. "Damn you, the City news said twelve thousand folks lost their lives in that crash, and we had to shift into the hills and cook over woodstoves for damn near four years, Boningham, you zik-brain bugfucker—"

"Listen," the clone said, trying to stand. "I need to take it with me. We need it. You need to be very careful how you unplug it…"

"Balls to that," Rhubarb said. "It's mine by right of salvage. You said yourself…"

"I know what I said, but you can't have it. It's not a mirror backup, it's…a Trojan horse. It's a bomb—"

Whatever the clone said next, nobody heard over the shriek of all three of Speedy's industrial printers going at once.

"What the hell?" Jubal Fufkin jumped off his bait-barrel and took cover like the others, but what he saw made him get up and shuffle closer to the bank of screaming fabricators as they vomited out a jackpot mound of tiny soldiers.

"I'll be damned," Fufkin said, picking up a miniature graycoat cavalry officer thrusting out a saber and standing up in his stirrups on a charging stallion to sound the charge. "My order's ready."

"Brother Jube," Speedy said from behind a diorama of his Uncle Karl's taxidermied Kudzu Devils, "I didn't place your order yet."

Jubal Fufkin was still admiring the exquisitely detailed figurine when it skewered his left eye up to the hilt of the cavalry saber and roared, "CHARGE!" as it rode Jubal Fufkin's disbelieving face all the way to the floor.

With a frantic popcorn sound, an army poured out of the mouth of each printer. Jubal was dusted with waves of gunpowder glitter that made bloody soup of his skin and set countless pinprick fires on his shirt and sarong. The toy soldiers wielded blatantly anachronistic semiauto repeaters that peppered Jubal Fufkin until he split open and seeped through the planks of the wharf.

Rhubarb jumped up and grabbed a blowtorch off Speedy's bench, fanned it wide open, and vaporized a phalanx of the ornery toys as they tried to seize the workbench.

Speedy jumped over the bench and shoved something into her arms, said, "Sorry, darlin," and shoved her off the end of the wharf, into the green River.

The sluggish current rolled her under a row of anchored skimmers that burst, one by one, into fiberglass confetti. Rhubarb kicked to the surface, fighting the dead weight clasped to her bosom, then gagged as muddy water sluiced up her nose. Dragged backward by the cable attached to the black briefcase in her arms.

Hundreds of winged Confederate infantry hovered over her head like reactionary dragonflies. Oblivious to the droplets of aerosolized boat fuel suspended in the sultry summer evening air, they rallied and formed up in a killer bee vortex and made as if to charge down into her gasping mouth.

The water shook with a concussion that dunked her under again. The air over the water flared white-hot.

When she came up, it rained fizzing ingots of burning plastic. She let the current push her up against the shore half a mile downstream from Main Street. The mud soothed her scalded skin and she folded over and dropped the briefcase, which had begun to bounce and tremble like a Aztech jumping bean.

She fiddled with the elaborate locks for a few precious minutes, the bouncing becoming ever more desperately acute, then more feeble, then finally gave up and smashed it against a big rock.

The glass briefcase shivered into pieces fine as ash and floated away on the breeze. She tore the soft pink pouch that flopped into her hands and cradled the fragile, gourd-headed thing she found inside.

She looked up and shaded her eyes against the purpling light of the sunset peering through the shaggy wall of mangrove trees that lined the west bank of the River. The tubes, the towers, the animated pornographic palisades and hanging pleasure gardens. They weren't just dark, they were all gone.

The ugly newborn baby wailed in her arms, a plaintive command that made her budding breasts ache. She tried to put it down, but it latched onto her tit through her shirt and sucked milk from it, watching her solemnly out of the infinite crystal of its solitary eye. Its massive cranium throbbed and pulsed restlessly in her hand. Restless pink claws kneaded the tender swelling of her breast, demanding something else.

She thought for a while, and then began to tell it about the City, but since it was *her* story now, she told it *her* way.

# FUTURE IMPERFECT: BROKEN LAWS

## MARGE SIMON

The First Law

The Great Ones who made our Laws are gone,
but once I dreamed they came back here
and played with our children.

It was only a dream.
Those who rule interpret the Laws.

The Second Law

A new age is born of disobedience
by rebellion and bloodshed.
I am of another time.

I see my kindred denied education,
shackles of a different kind.

The Third Law

Trail the rebels to their own mirage,
a holocaust in black & white,
silver mirrors and glass bowls.

Protests die unspoken.

Orion Zangara 2016

# THE PRETTY PUPPETS

## MARC LEVINTHAL

He woke slowly, unsure of where he was. Who he was.

Charlie. Charlie Findstrom. I'm twenty-six. I live in Los Angeles. *One out of two*, he thought. *Let's try for the other one.*

He was laying on his side on a bare striped mattress, black nylon straps across his chest and legs. He turned onto his back, panicking momentarily until he realized he was only held by Velcro strips.

He reached up and undid the Velcro at his chest, then at his legs ... and began to float slowly up into the air. The adrenaline rush roused him instantly. He flailed around a bit, then, deciding that was not going to accomplish anything, forced himself to breathe, to calm down, look around, and figure out just where the hell he was.

*Okay*, he thought, *fact number one—the floating is definitely not normal.* He was rising slowly through a spherical chamber of some sort. The bottom half was made of a solid dark material, maybe metal. He looked up and saw bright stars through a series of windows that curved around the upper hemisphere, laid into a web-work of bars. As he rose to the level of the window, a glowing blue-white disc loomed up out of the blackness, and beyond that, a mercilessly brilliant orb—harsh, too bright to look at.

A sudden realization—a chill went through him and he turned around. There, the enormous bulk of the moon loomed across three quarters of the sky.

He couldn't tell for sure, but it seemed to be getting bigger. He floated there, staring out at the cratered lunar surface.

*This can't be happening,* he thought. *This must be a really vivid dream. How could I possibly be here? People don't fly to the moon in spherical cages. No. I don't want this. No. I'll just force myself to wake up. Wake up.*

He screamed it. "Wake up!"

He was still there. And he'd never had a dream with this level of verisimilitude. He could see the colors, feel the metal bars, the chill on the glass. He'd come close before, but nothing like this.

Everything was pointing to one thing: he was alone, in some sort of space vehicle, rushing toward the surface of the moon.

No dream.

He tried to recall what he'd done the night before. The party. The last thing he remembered was being at the party. It hadn't been a very good one...

*He mingled with the few people he knew there—mostly acquaintances from work—and had a couple of beers. The music was pretty lame, mostly disco and emo shit. He wanted to smoke, as he always did when he came out and had a couple of drinks, but resisted the urge to go out to the patio and bum a cigarette from a total stranger. Finally, tired of standing around by himself, he decided it was time to go.*

*Then he saw the girl. She had just opened a fresh box of Marlboros and tapped one out as she headed for the patio.*

*She noticed him looking.*

*"Would you like one?" she asked, smiling. Pretty blonde. Slight indeterminately European accent. Hair done up in pigtails to either side of a bright, roundish face. Blue eyes, little turned-up nose.*

*"Yes," he said, "thanks."*

*She offered the pack, and he took one. Then they moved outside. The blonde girl produced a lighter, and she cupped her hands around it as they lit up.*

*"Jen," she said, offering her hand.*

*He shook it. "Charlie."*

. . .

Nothing after that. The patio. *Then what?* He remembered taking a hit of the cigarette, then waking up...wherever he was—on the way to the moon, apparently. That's crazy. *How did I get from there into this—ship, or whatever it is? I had to have walked out on my own. So why don't I remember?*

Charlie managed to grab ahold of one of the metal struts and hang on. He looked out at the huge moon. Could he really be in a spaceship, or was this some kind of elaborate prank? The moon, the earth, the sun—it looked real, like he was seeing it out of a window. It looked too real to be a simulation. If it was, the weightlessness was a good touch. How could someone pull *that* off?

He was close enough now that the curve of the gray, cratered orb was hard to recognize—it was a broad, slightly-curved horizon with black space above it. He must be close enough now to be in orbit—or not.

He fought down panic. Why would somebody put him into this thing just to crash him into the moon? Surely there were easier ways to terrify and kill someone, if that's what his captors were up to. *No,* he reasoned, *there had to be more behind this than simply trying to scare the living shit out of me, or kill me. Whatever's going on here, it isn't that simple.*

But that didn't necessarily mean he wasn't in any danger.

He pushed off from the wall, glancing around at every surface, looking for anything that might be a control of some sort. There was nothing distinguishable from the rest of the metal bars and glass or the solid metal hemisphere below. (Below? Above?) He was losing any sense of up and down, and starting to feel seasick.

Then he remembered something else.

The pencil.

*It was a fat pencil, not a regular number two pencil, but big around as a cigar. It had fallen out of her purse when she got the lighter out, and he'd bent down and picked it up. There was writing on it. "Arbeit Macht Frei," it said on one side, then, "NSDAP 90. Jahrestag" on the other. He knew enough German to know what it said. He gave it back to her with a funny look.*

*"So, what is that, some kind of...joke, or something?" He dragged on the cigarette, blew some smoke out. "National Socialism's Ninetieth? Work*

*Makes You Free?"*

*She smirked, looked embarrassed. "It's a little hard to explain. But I'm not a—Nazi, if that's what you think."*

"So, what are you?"

*Blackness.*


*Yes. Indeed. What are you?* he thought, staring out the window, watching the cold gray expanse roll by. *What the fuck did you do to me? And why?*

There was a crackle, like radio static. Quick, then gone. Somewhere down near the opposite side of the vessel.

He started to doubt he'd actually heard anything, then again, the crackling came, and then, a man's voice. Five short words—they sounded like German.

Frantically, he pushed himself toward the source of the sound, grappling along the side, pushing off from the metal struts. Again, the voice. Five words in German.

"Drücken sie die rote taste."

He scrambled around the other end of the vessel until he'd located the source of the voice: a rounded chrome oblong, about two feet around. There was a speaker grille on it, above a round, softly glowing red button about the size of a half dollar. Underneath it, a set of numbers—high-contrast black against yellow—counted down, ticking off the seconds.

"Drücken sie die rote taste."

He tried to recall the German he'd learned in high school. Drücken sie—press, you press. Press the—"rote" was "red." Press the red—

He reached out, without thinking about it, and pressed down the red button.

Instantly, there was a rumble from beneath his feet, and a feeling that he'd suddenly grown a little heavier. He felt the sphere turning slowly, adjusting.

Thrust. Something had fired, some rocket or something.

He was still, for the most part, weightless. He pushed himself along to where the windows were. The forward motion had slowed, and it looked like the surface was growing closer. But as the ship approached the mottled, gray expanse, he began falling slowly towards what was now definitely the "bottom" of the sphere.

Relief flowed through him. He wasn't going to crash: this thing was going to land.

Then he thought about what that meant. *It's landing on the fucking moon. And all I have is a German voice, telling me to press the red button. The whole thing could be automated. I could be completely alone here. Stranded.*

In another moment, there was a jolt, and a thud as the spacecraft came to rest.

He had weight again, although not anywhere near earth-normal. He was down in the "bottom" of the sphere, near to the speaker and the red button.

*Now what?* he thought. Hydraulic hissing and gurgling filtered through the walls of the ship. He tried to calm his breath, get himself ready for whatever was coming next.

An electrical hum suddenly rose from beneath his feet. A hatch was opening downward, exposing a brightly-lit chamber about ten feet in diameter. He looked inside. There was a ladder attached to the wall. Without thinking about it, he put his feet on the ladder and started to climb down.

The chamber was mostly empty, but for two conspicuous items. Against the wall, secured with Velcro straps, was a lightweight gloved suit, and a bulbous helmet hanging next to it. Against the opposite wall hung a bicycle, with the gears and other hardware sealed up behind some sort of plastic casing. It had oversized tires with thick treads, like some sort of mountain bike on steroids.

He undid the straps from the bike and took it down, then did the same with the suit and helmet. He wasn't sure exactly why he was doing it; he was acting automatically. It stood to reason that if these things were here, they may have to be used sometime in the very near future. He had no way of knowing how much air was still left in the sphere, or if there was any food or water. It made little sense to leave his only place of relative safety to go biking across the moon. What could he possibly find outside? But if there were no provisions for his future life support, he'd die here just as handily as outside on a bike in a space suit.

Then it occurred to him that he'd never actually taken any kind of inventory of what was in the upper chamber. He'd found the speaker and the red button, but he hadn't checked out any of the surfaces for compartments where supplies could be stored. Maybe there was enough air, water and food up there for months.

With that thought, he started up the ladder again. As he neared the hatch, it slammed down and sealed itself with a dull thud.

A new voice, a woman this time, spoke calmly from somewhere below: "Bereiten sie für die evakuierung. Bereiten sie für die evakuierung."

He had no idea what this meant. Bereiten? He was panicked again. What was coming now?

"English!" he screamed out. "Speak English!"

"English." The calm voice said. "Prepare for evacuation. Prepare for evacuation."

A chill went down his back. He jumped down from the ladder and raced over to the suit. Now he could hear a hissing sound, like air leaking out. He struggled to unzip the suit, see how to get his arms and legs into it. After a moment, his ears popped—the air pressure was going away. That meant the air was going with it.

Frantically, he struggled into the suit, managed to fit his hands into the gloves, zip the zippers shut. He grabbed for the helmet and fitted it over his head, trying to puzzle out how it sealed. Finally, after what seemed like an eternity, he mated it to the ring at the neck of the suit, and it rotated into place with a satisfying click. Something began to hum inside the suit, and cool air stared blowing into the interior.

He noticed a display of numbers and symbols in the lower left of his visor. They seemed to be abbreviations, with a fluctuating set of numbers next to them. One set, with "HF" as the indicator, hovered around eighty—could that be his heart rate?

The wall opened out slowly, revealing the gray lunar plain. A ramp extended out beneath the opening, forming a forty-five degree angle with the surface.

His breath was fast and shallow now; he was hyperventilating, the "HF" up around 115. He forced himself to calm down, taking in long, slow draughts of air.

When he finally felt himself calming, his panic quieting, he grabbed hold of the bike and began to walk it down the ramp.

Silence, but for his breathing, the touch of his boots on the ramp, the soft rumbling of the wheels. The landscape spread out around him, utterly desolate, unspeakably beautiful. The gibbous blue-white orb of the earth hung in the void.

He hiked his right leg over the bike frame, sat down on the seat and began to pedal. The big rubber wheels sank down into the lunar powder, blowing up a slo-mo dust storm behind him as he rode. At first, he just circled the ship, trying to gauge the dimensions of it, see if there was another way in. It was a dull metallic sphere on low, spindly legs, like something out of a Soviet science fiction movie. He came back around and looked for the hatch he'd come out of—anything that looked like an obvious entrance—and found nothing. Just the smooth, weathered metal.

When it became apparent that he was completely locked out, he decided to just pick a direction, and ride. If he was going to run out of air on a bicycle on the moon, he would make it count.

If there was something out there to find, somewhere he was meant to go, he would do his best to find it. If not, at least it would be a magnificent way to die.

He pedaled up a slight incline, a rill between two low hills. He reached the top with little effort: in the low gravity, it was almost like flying. He paused at the top, overlooking a wide, shallow crater. Out of the corner of his eye, he noticed a glint of light shining off something below.

He tested the brakes, then began to coast down into the crater in the direction of the shiny thing he'd spotted.

It proved difficult to keep a fix on it—the light shifted as he got closer, and he thought he'd lost it for good. Then he spotted it, close by: a circular, shiny white object, half buried in the regolith.

He got off the bike and walk/jumped over to the object. Grasping it clumsily in his gloved hands, he held it up to his visor.

It was a commemorative plate, like something from a souvenir gift shop. On it was a picture of two swords crossed on top of a confederate flag. There were a lot more stars on this one than he was used to seeing: twenty-eight rather than the thirteen he remembered. Inscribed along the bottom was, "CSA Centennial 1861 – 1961"

He let the plate fall slowly to the ground, and took a long look around the moonscape. There were things all over the ground, poking up out of the dust and rocks, things that shouldn't belong on the moon. And looking up, he noticed for the first time, here and there, a gentle rain of objects—books and spoons, framed photographs, little objects—all clearly man-made artifacts, on a slow trajectory from somewhere out there, landing with a soft puff of regolith.

Close by, something shiny caught his eye. He pedaled over to it, and pulled it out of the gray grit. It had printing on one shiny surface, and the familiar rainbow shimmering of a CD on the other. Only this one had eight sides, and was about eight inches around. He squinted down at the printed side. "Coltrane/Hendrix Group – Montreaux, 1976" it said.

There was a flap, with a big pocket under it on the front of his suit. He opened it and stuck the octagonal disc inside.

Then, movement out of the corner of his eye. He peered at the horizon, and saw nothing. *Crazy*, he thought. *How could something be moving?* Then he thought, *why not? Why would that be any crazier than me on a bicycle on the moon, tucking a Coltrane/Hendrix CD from 1976 into my spacesuit?*

There was the motion again—this time, he spotted it: a little white dot on the horizon, floating over the side of a rise, maybe a mile or so away. As it got closer, he could make out what was it was: a cyclist in a spacesuit. The figure stopped from time to time, picking things up from the ground.

Then he saw two more.

He hopped back on the bike and pedaled toward the nearest figure, who was moving off in the opposite direction, racing away as if he'd spotted something. *Maybe he's doing the same thing I am*, he thought, *chasing down another moon cyclist.* He kept pedaling, figuring that if he didn't catch up with that one, there were others not much further away.

When he came over the next gentle rise, he saw where the other cyclists had been heading: a massive dome, dazzlingly white in the unfiltered sunlight. Cyclists converged on it from all sides. And it looked as though doors were opening in the sides to let them in.

He raced down the slope.

No one tried to speak or sign to each other; they were too intent on getting inside the dome. When he got within twenty or so feet of it, a door opened up, revealing an enclosure with a facing white wall inside. He pedaled inside along with the others. The door, now behind him, closed, and the wall opened up in front of him, revealing a cavernous chamber.

He gazed upward to a luminous white dome. Down below, hundreds of handsome men and beautiful women sat behind tables—all copies, or clones of the same four or five people. One of the clone types was the girl from the party. The bikers in their dusty white space suits sat across from the photogenic men and women, looking dazed and frightened, uncertain.

Over a loudspeaker, a neutral voice, not the same one from the ship, repeated something in several different languages, some recognizable and others unlike anything he'd ever heard. Finally, the neutral voice said, in English, "It is safe to remove your helmet. Please do so, and proceed to an available desk for debriefing."

Charlie hesitantly undid his helmet and pulled it off. He bounced around the room in the lunar gravity, looking for a place to sit down, and soon spotted one of the girls from the party smiling at him from across a desk with an empty chair in front of it. She motioned for him to sit.

He sat down, staring at her as she smiled back.

"You don't remember me, do you?" he said.

"Yes," she said. "The party."

"It was you there, then?"

"No," she said, "the interface was there. So I was there."

"All right," he said. "Can you just tell me what the fuck is going on?"

She dropped the smile, and went into debriefing mode. "This interface will help you to process what just happened. You can help *us* by looking at various artifacts, and talking about them."

"Talking about them?"

"Yes. In this way, we glean information that we can't otherwise obtain by direct observation."

"We?" he asked. "Who is 'we'?"

She took a deep breath. "We have no name you would be able to conceive of as a name. It would be impossible to render into lower-dimensional data. Our realm is many-dimensional, many more than your three moving across one linear dimension of time …" She appeared to struggle to find the right words. "Over space, between space, above time, outside of what you think of as time. This interface helps us to localize. To focus. There is no way for us to directly experience this space-time knot, except through the interface. That there is a fecund intelligence here is astounding to us. We need to understand. To know you."

Charlie sighed. "So you kidnap people, drug them, whatever— and then throw them onto a moon ship with no warning…make them frantically suit up and ride across the moonscape? On a fucking bicycle no less? To what end? Is scaring the shit out of us part of understanding us?"

She stared across at him. Mona Lisa smile. She raised her hands. "Clearly, we don't understand the nuances of your species. We are—we are making this up as we go along. Improvising. We have made mistakes. Taking you to your moon for interrogation may have been a miscalculation. To you, it must seem like an enormous one, but now that the process has been established…" She shrugged. "We find it unnecessary to alter it presently. But we are looking for an alternative."

She smiled again, and under any other circumstances, he would have melted a little. But as it was, he wasn't impressed. In fact, he felt like punching her in the face. But he knew that that wasn't going to help anything.

"That," he said, "is completely fucking insane." He shook his head. "So, okay, let's do this."

She reached under the desk and pulled out an object. It was a little snow globe. She handed it across the desk to him.

He took it and rolled it around in his hands. There was a little Santa Claus inside, holding a bag of toys over one shoulder, his other hand held up in greeting. Fake snow floated around a North Pole scene: Santa's house, a couple of reindeer, a big red-striped candy cane in the front yard.

"What is the significance of this object?" the girl asked.

He looked at her, then back down at the snow globe. "Christmas," he said. "Santa Claus."

She stared blankly.

"How could you be at that party," he asked, "making small talk to people, interacting, and not know what Santa Claus and Christmas are?"

"The interface provided enough information for me to successfully navigate the party," she said. "Also, I'm told that we do have significant data concerning this subject, but require your unique perspective."

"Okay ..." He sighed. "Santa Claus—this guy here—brings presents to all the good little boys and girls in the world on Christmas, which falls on December 25$^{th}$ each year. The snow globe itself is just a little keepsake. You can use it for a paperweight, or keep it on a shelf—look, this can't be all you want from me. What happens after this?"

She looked blankly again for a moment, as if receiving information. "In order for this Santa Claus to accomplish this feat—he would have to possess some extra-dimensional aspect himself, correct? This date is also significant, as it marks the birth of a religious leader, doesn't it? In various timelines, it serves as a winter festival day."

"That's not surprising," Charlie said. "It's a very old holiday. It's been passed down through a lot of cultures. Very doubtful Jesus was actually born on Christmas. And Santa Claus—it's just a story. For the kids. He's not a real guy.

"But back to my original question—what happens now?"

She smiled. "You will be processed, and sent home again."

"That's it?"

"That's it."

"But …" He looked around the room. "What's to stop me—any of these people—from telling the world what we know?"

She raised her hands up in front of her. "Nothing," she said. "As soon as we're done here, you'll be free to go."

They sent him back, as promised, this time in a sleek one-seater with a bubble top. It was a breathtaking, quick ride—less than six hours. He looked all around the little ship, searching for some clue as to what parallel civilization could have created such a tech marvel, but to no avail.

The craft sailed in across the face of the blue-green orb, landing softly in what looked to be Southern Californian desert. The hatch opened and one of the friendly beautiful people—a man this time—ran up and directed him toward a low, square concrete building across the tarmac.

Charlie entered, and another identical man was there, seated in front of a console next to a large metal door.

"Name?" he asked.

"Charles Findstrom," Charlie replied.

A few keystrokes, and the man said, "Please step through this door."

Charlie had no fear left in him after all he'd been through. If this was a one-way trip, so be it. But again, these people didn't seem to play by any recognizable rules, so he felt pretty confident that he'd make it through to…somewhere.

He opened the door, which turned out to be an airlock of some kind, with a small chamber and another metal door on the other side of that. An amber light blinked, and then turned green.

The second door opened, and Charlie stepped out…

… of a dirty phone booth on Sixth Street in downtown L.A., at rush hour.

. . .

Charlie lifted his shot glass up to the sunlight. The rays slanted through the amber liquid, and he laid into the buzz, put his head against the couch cushion and sighed.

*What can I do to make these people see?* he thought.

He got up and sat back down in front of his laptop, checked his feed again. Another 50 "likes," 300 comments. For the most part the comments were derisive, tinfoil-hat stuff.

*What did you expect?* he thought. *They knew just what they were doing when they sent you back.*

Then he noticed the red icon in the upper right of the screen. Private message. He clicked on it. It was from someone named *Timespacemess.*

*Hi Charlie,* it said, *I know you're not crazy. This happened to me. Same deal exactly—ship, bicycle, big room. And there are more of us. Can we meet somewhere?*

He made plans to meet up at a new little bar near Figueroa and Ninth. He walked down from his apartment on Flower and sat at one of the tables in the front. A bored waitress came over to him, and he ordered a beer.

In a few minutes, a tall, skinny woman in her thirties came through the door and looked around, finally noticing Charlie looking. She waved tentatively, and then came over and sat down.

"Timespacemess, I presume," Charlie said.

"Gloria," the woman said.

They shook hands, and Charlie asked her if she wanted a drink.

"I can't really stay. I just wanted to meet up so you knew I wasn't a nut."

"You don't look like a nut, but you never know." Charlie laughed, but she didn't laugh back.

Gloria passed a card across the table. "Look, here's my info. We're going to meet at my place on the first Tuesday of every month until we figure this out. Hopefully you can make it."

She stood up. "Well, it was nice to meet you. I hope I see you soon." And then actually smiled for a split second. Then she was out the door again.

Charlie sipped at his beer and turned Gloria's card around in his hand. *Maybe I should just be done with this,* he thought. *Put this behind me.* He took another sip of beer. *Fuck it. Maybe I should just meet with these people once.*

Gloria's apartment was up at the top of a steep Echo Park hillside. He walked up the steps, and heard voices from beyond the open door. Four people sat inside, and when they saw him, an older, balding man got up, opened the door and welcomed him. Charlie came inside and saw another man, a younger, bearded hipster type, a petite young blonde and a muscular woman decked out in leather, with close-cropped black hair.

Gloria came out of the kitchen with a plate of cheese and crackers, and smiled when she saw Charlie. It was clear almost immediately that they'd all experienced the same thing, from the artifacts in the regolith and the story about the extra-dimensionals to the smooth ride back to Earth.

"And they're everywhere," said Rita, the woman with the short black hair. "I've seen the pretty puppets on the street several times."

*The Pretty Puppets. That's what they were calling them. The clones or whatever they were.* Charlie looked from face to face. They all seemed intelligent, sane. They weren't having a mass hallucination; this had really happened to them. It was as if it were sinking in for the first time. Before this, he'd almost started to believe that he's had some kind of psychotic break.

"I know we all got the spiel when we were in the white dome," Larry, the balding guy said, "but what do they really want? The whole thing just seems so ludicrous. Why would anyone with such vast power just want to find out about us in such an—oblique way? Why not just take over?"

"Maybe they're just so different, it doesn't even occur to them," said the bearded guy. Charlie had forgotten his name.

"Like throwing us onto that ship and scaring the shit out of us. Didn't occur to them that we might find it upsetting."

It went around like that for about an hour or so, and then the gathering wound down, and people started to say their goodbyes. Charlie filed out with the rest of them.

*Nothing really got accomplished,* he thought as he walked down the steep sidewalk to his car. *But I made contact, and that's something.*

Over the next several weeks, Charlie continued to attend the meetings. Nothing really ever did get accomplished, but the group began to bond, and he actually made a few friends. He'd seen Gloria a few times outside of the meetings, and it seemed like maybe there was something starting to happen between them.

It was maybe three months later that the first artifacts started showing up.

Gloria noticed them first—things that shouldn't be there, like some kind of science-fiction performance art. She sent Charlie an email with "They're Here…" as the subject, and a link to an online auction.

It was a VHS tape, looking pretty well used, of the 1976 movie version of *A Star is Born,* starring Barbara Streisand and … Elvis Presley. There was no explanation of whether or not this was a joke, just the tape and the asking price, $19.99—quite reasonable, considering it was an artifact from another universe.

Just for fun, he searched for "Hendrix Coltrane Montreaux," and when the result showed, he instantly recognized the octagonal disc he'd found on the lunar surface. In all the excitement of shucking off the spacesuit and getting into the shuttle, he'd forgotten all about taking it with him.

The current bid was $10.99. He entered one for $12.99.

He kept checking and bidding higher.

A week and $46 later, he had the disc in his hands. His only regret was that he couldn't hear it. *But,* he thought, *it's only a matter of time before somebody auctions an eight-sided-disc player.*

By that time, the Pretty Puppets had come out of the closet. They were starting pop-up storefront headquarters all over the world, asking people to come in with their artifacts and talk about them, and get paid to do so. They didn't need the moon anymore. They'd discovered the Internet. And money.

Charlie imagined this happening on countless alternate Earths. Their resources must be astounding.

Of course, the majority of the population refused to believe that they were being invaded by extradimensionals. Most thought it was some kind of elaborate hoax, perhaps some viral tie-in to a new movie blockbuster in the works. Those who knew it to be true continued to say so, with the limited results Charlie and the other abductees had already experienced.

But it seemed like a certain portion of the population, not necessarily just the tinfoil-hat set, were willing to entertain the possibility that it might be true.

The artifacts continued to show up. People were finding them in random places, tucked in among their belongings, on the sidewalk, even on grocery shelves. The Pretty Puppets were showing up on TV, on YouTube videos—they even had their own enigmatic website, with a short video greeting, and a place to submit info about artifacts.

The man with the headset counted down silently, then pointed to the talk show host. Percolating, "serious news" music swelled and faded, and the host looked into the camera.

"Tonight on CNN: the Extradimensionals—are they really here? And if so, what does it mean for national security and the economy? Today our guests are Jason Meadson, from the Brookings Institution, and Charles Findstrom, a man who claims to have been abducted by the Extradimensionals."

He turned to his first guest. "Jason, let's start with you—what's your take on this whole thing? I mean, the evidence seems to be quite convincing. Do you believe we're being visited by beings from…outside of time, as they claim? Or over time, or whatever?"

Charlie sat in his seat, trying not to fidget, while the think-tank guy rambled on. He was in the eye of the hurricane. National TV. Expected to speak off the cuff about his experiences. *This is slightly less terrifying than being flung at the moon in a steel sphere,* he thought.

When the host got around to him, and it was time for him to speak, he opened his mouth, and, to his surprise, words came out.

"Let me tell you what happened to me," he said. And he started to tell his story.

And as he did, he looked momentarily over the host's shoulder, and saw, past the cameras and lights, just off the set, the girl from the party.

She smiled serenely at him.

The Pretty Puppets were listening.

# THE GOLDILOCKS ZONE

## JOHN R. LITTLE

**Barb:**

I love being in the water, especially when I'm exploring with Punky and the gang. They know the San Diego shoreline better than any human I know, and even though they're dolphins, they treat me better than most people do.

They're so beautiful as they glide through the water and show me their secrets. I'm the only person they've shown their secret stash, where they've dropped little trinkets they've found while exploring the ocean: bones, pieces of lost jewelry, and a nice collection of shells.

Now, though, I've been with them an hour and it's time to climb back in the little motor boat and head back to shore. I dropped off my scuba tanks and got changed before going back to my office at MBRD.

I'm the luckiest girl in the world. This morning I woke up before Darrell and counted some of the things that make my life so worth living:

1. Well, the most important thing is Darrell himself. We've been engaged for ten months, and although we haven't set a wedding date yet, I feel the day is getting closer.

2. My job at the Marine Biology Research Division at Scripps. How many people get to swim with dolphins and study their habits for a living?

3. I'm totally healthy and expect to live a long and happy life with my best friend.

So, yeah, who could ask for more?

Back at my desk, I skimmed through my e-mail, which was mostly administrative minutia that nobody really cared about, along with a few Internet jokes and memes that were spreading around the campus. I didn't bother looking at most of them. I wanted to get to my research.

My work is all about dolphin communication. I feel in my soul that they can talk to each other just as easily as humans can, but we just can't break their code and talk directly to them.

One day.

A new e-mail popped into my inbox, and I smiled when I saw it was from Darrell.

> Hey! I have something exciting to share with you. Tonight, we deserve a nice dinner out. Candles, wine, soft music, the whole thing. I'll make reservations for 8:00.
>
> Love ya, babe!

*Something exciting?*

I stared at the screen and tried to imagine what it could be. I knew what I *wanted* it to be. I *wanted* it to be Darrell suggesting a wedding date, but that's not really the way his e-mail read. It sounded more like something he'd just found out today. News from work?

Of course he only worked a few buildings away from me, in a more isolated section of MBRD, and he could have just walked over and had lunch with me. I liked that he was excited and wanted to have a romantic dinner to spill the beans.

A promotion? Maybe, but he's already the chief researcher for micro-biology, so I don't think there's many positions he could be promoted *to*.

Tonight can't come soon enough!

Sigh...I love my life.

I'm not sure San Diego is the restaurant capital of the world, but I like eating out no matter what. Darrell made us reservations for The Seafood Factory, which he knows just might be my favorite. Their menu is three pages, all different types of seafood, and even though I always study the list as if I'm going to be tested on it, I usually gravitate back to have a linguini with white wine sauce topped with fresh mussels, clams, and whatever fish is the catch of the day. Today it's catfish.

The only music was some soft harmony in the background that we would have to really pay attention to in order to hear, but that's okay. I didn't care about that.

Darrell was dressed in jeans and a T-shirt that had a bunch of splotches in different colors splattered on it. There's a circle surrounding them, and almost nobody would recognize it was the image of bacteria growing in a petri dish.

Although we didn't deliberately match clothing, I'm wearing jeans and a blouse with a faint image of dolphins leaping out of the water.

We both wore our jobs.

Darrell deferred to me when the waitress asked about wine. I ordered red for a change, a nice five-year-old French Merlot.

When we'd arrived at the restaurant, I could see he was excited. His eyes were bright, and he was bursting with...well, something. I knew he wanted to do this right, though, and I didn't press him for anything until we had our wine glasses ready to toast.

"To you and your big surprise," I said.

He grinned and we clinked glasses. The wine was very smooth, and I wondered why I don't drink red more often.

Darrell licked his lips, and seemed to be taking a long time, so I finally said, "Well, are you going to tell me?"

I reached out and touched his hand.

He nodded and put his glass on the table, then leaned closer.

"I've been asked to join the Starcraft team."

That's the last thing I was expecting. At first I wasn't sure I heard him right.

"Why? There won't be any results coming back to Earth for … actually I'm not sure how long. But not any time soon, right?"

"It's not to analyze results." He took another sip of his wine and then added, "They want me to go."

"Go?"

It was like he was speaking dolphin-ese or something. It didn't make any sense.

"To a planet called Gliese 163c. It's been known for decades now and was recently bumped up to be number four on the list of planets that could support life."

I didn't know what to say about this. I'm sure my mouth was hanging open in disbelief or shock or astonishment or some other stupid thing. I certainly felt all of those things. Darrell sensed me feeling lost and added more details.

"They told me the news first thing this morning. It's amazing, Barb! This planet is in the Goldilocks Zone, so it's not too hot and not too cold. If it were any closer to its sun, the water would evaporate. If it were any farther out, it would freeze. Instead, it's just right. The surface is covered with a massive ocean, and they told me a shit-load of other technical stuff, but the bottom line is that they think there's likely some kind of life there. Possibly microbiological, and that's why they want me to go."

He paused and I could tell the worst was yet to come.

"It's 50 light years away."

And there it was.

I don't know much about spaceships that go to those faraway stars. The Starcraft ships only started leaving Earth a few years ago. Have there been five of them now? Six? I don't know.

What I *do* know is that if it's 50 light years away, Darrell will be gone for the next century.

And I'll be here, alone.

What was I supposed to say to that? I couldn't help the tears that started to fall from my eyes.

Darrell came around and knelt next to me.

"Oh, babe, I'm so sorry."

He held me to him, but I had trouble holding him in return. My mind was on fire. How was this even possible in my perfect life?

"Can I go with you?" I somehow blurt out.

I cried on his shoulder, and I have no clue if the other people eating their dinners noticed or cared about what was happening.

"No," he said. "I asked, but the extra weight of adding partners for all the crew member...it's too much."

Finally, after what seemed like forever, I hugged Darrell back. I squeezed him and pulled him to me, as if I could stop him from leaving with the force of my puny arms. I grabbed his face and kissed him. I didn't know when he would be actually leaving, but I felt like this might be the last perfect kiss.

Later, we were back in our seats and I finished off my wine, then poured more.

"You won't age," I said.

He didn't want to talk about that part of things. That got me angry.

"You're 32 now, same as me. What happens?"

He spoke softly.

"If I understand it right, it takes the ion thrusters about two years to get the ship close to the speed of light, then the trip there takes 50 years, then two years to slow down at the other end. The mission will stay there for one year."

I waited. He knew the math already. The longer he avoided telling me, the madder I got.

He finally blurted it out.

"On Earth, 109 years will pass. Our spaceship will be spending most of that time at relativistic velocities, so only nine years will pass for me."

I only knew as much as the next lay person on how this stuff works. It felt wrong to me that by going so fast, they age slower. I know it won't feel to them like time is slowing down, but those are the rules. Einstein set everything in motion for this more than a century ago. How it works? Who knows.

"I'll be dead when you get back," I whispered. "And you'll be 41."

He didn't reply. He didn't have to.


**Darrell (Outbound):**

It's been a month now, and the ship is accelerating at 0.03c now. That's one-thirtieth the speed of light for those of us (like me) who don't know crap about this. There's a monitor in the main recreation section of the ship that tells me that number and also tells me our relativistic factor is now 1.00045. For every second we fly, a tiny bit more than a second passes on Earth.

By the time we reach our cruising speed in 23 months, our speed will be .9996c and our relativistic factor will be 35.35887. We will travel to the Gliese 163 system in what feels like no time at all, but everyone on Earth will be aging like crazy.

Including Barb.

I felt so heart-broken when the ship took off. Even though it's been a few months since I broke the news to her, it was so hard to leave.

But how could I turn the opportunity down? It's the chance of a lifetime.

I worried that it would be boring, but so far so good. The acceleration makes the ship feel as if it has near-Earth gravity, there's lots of room to wander around, and there's a dozen other people going along for the flight, so I'm not lonely.

Well, except for bedtime, when I pull the covers over me and think of Barb.

Best not to dwell on that.

Everyone on board is a scientist of one sort or another, half men and half women. I wonder if that was deliberate, and I've been meaning to check the other Starcraft teams to see if it's the same.

It would make sense. None of our partners will be there to greet us with open arms when we return.

When we left, they told us not to bring photographs of our loved ones, letters, or memories of any kind. Psychologically, it makes it worse. We need to try to forget them.

So, I have no photos of Barb. I regret that now. I want to see her. Sometimes I think I'm making the biggest mistake of my life.

### Darrell (Inbound):

Earth fills the wall of the projection room. It's hard to believe we're almost back home. Harder still to believe more than a century has passed there since we blasted off.

It's like time travel. To me, it's as if it's only been a few years. The time dilation didn't feel like anything. Instead, it feels like somehow the Earth has sped up its rotation and everyone there aged prematurely, dropping off one by one…

I looked at the view of our home planet with Elli. The ship didn't have the image projected while we were far away, but it's back now, so we're trying to find what's different from when we left. My hand slid over to hers and grasped it. I loved holding her hand. Somehow it showed the strength of our relationship.

Over the past few years, we've grown so close, and it makes me once again thank whatever gods decided I should be on this mission.

"Do you see anything?"

We were both staring at North America, because we know that the best.

"Is California different?" I asked.

I could feel her shrug. "Don't know," she whispered. "Maybe."

We could have asked the Machine, of course, but where's the fun in that?

Elli thought Florida looked a little thinner, but it looked the same to me.

"Who cares?" I asked suddenly. "We're almost home!"

Elli jumped up into my arms and wrapped her legs around me. She kissed me long and hard, and I loved every second of it.

"Still six months till we arrive," she said when we broke the kiss. "But it feels like home already."

Those six months went crazy fast. There wasn't a lot to do work-wise, because we'd all filed our reports from Gliese 163c long ago. The long and short of it: we couldn't identify any form of life at all. It was a completely wasted trip.

Well, that's not exactly fair, is it? It's the nature of science to propose a theory and then run experiments that either support the theory or disprove it. Science wins either way.

The working theory of life on Gliese 163c was disproved, but that's still valuable information. It just doesn't quite feel like it.

Elli is a physicist, specializing in testing gravity fluctuations. No matter how often she's explained that in detail to me, I'm still not sure I get it. That's okay. I get *her*.

After a few months, the ship had braked enough to remove all relativistic effects and we could see Earth with the naked eye.

Then it seemed like the blink of an eye and we were home.

We got taught some basic history lessons during the last month. There were still 51 states, the two political parties still traded the White House, and although there were lots of small changes, there was nothing enormous. We could have slipped to ground without the lessons and not have been out of place.

I felt a little disappointed with the lack of change, but neither could I decide what differences I would have really liked to see.

After leaving the ship, we were quarantined, the same as the eleven other Starcraft ships that made it home before us.

None of them found life anywhere.

I was placed in a kind of quarantine, which seemed ridiculous. How could I be contagious if there wasn't as much as a virus on Gliese 163c?

It was after a week in quarantine that the message arrived that changed everything.

People no longer used e-mail, not exactly, but some kind of thought-transmission process accomplished pretty much exactly the same thing. The difference was that I sensed the message in my mind, clear as a bell, rather than on a computer monitor.

Dearest Darrell,

If you're sensing this, you're about to make me the happiest woman alive. Yes, alive!

When you left, I was so unhappy. I missed you terribly and thought my life no longer worth living. I somehow trudged along toward the rest of my unsatisfactory life. I continued my work on dolphins, of course, but it was like the spark of life had left me.

Then, everything changed.

Has anyone told you about stasis yet? It's a technology that allows people to be, well, I suppose paralyzed is the best word. I'd say "frozen" but there's nothing cold involved. Our bodies are just stopped.

Of course I jumped at the chance to volunteer and I was one of the first test subjects. I had myself stopped until three months ago.

And, other than some minor side effects, I'm here, waiting for you, wanting you so much ... and I hope you still want me too.

I know you expected I'd be dead. Far from it. I'm here, I'm still young like you, and I want us to spend the rest of our time together.

Miracles do happen.

Please contact me when you are ready.

With all my love, Barb.

Barb?

*Barb?*

My mind went numb, I think. I sat and stared into infinity, not knowing what to think.

"You were supposed to be dead," I said.

I'd steeled myself to know without a doubt she'd be gone. That's what the psychologists told me to do, because there was no chance she'd be alive. People didn't live to be 140 years old.

But, she cheated death.

I stumbled to the bathroom and threw up into the toilet. The acidic taste in my mouth somehow felt deserved.

I cleaned myself up and then went back to the bedroom portion of my quarters to lie down. I closed my eyes and pulled at the threads of memory I had for Barb. It was such a long time ago.

I remembered how we met, at the Scripps Research Institute. She was just joining the staff and going through orientation. Her eyes were wide and taking it all in. I was passing her group, and I think I fell in love with her the minute I saw her.

She had that amazing smile she always wore for me, beautiful blonde hair, and her eyes ... that's what always got me.

They could see into my soul.

Our first date was one of the singular most perfect days of my life. We danced and laughed and ate ... and then we made love.

From then, every day was a new adventure, and my mind seemed to want to show every one of them to me, so that the memories were all mashed together into a giant chaos of love.

I'd destroyed all that.

Elli was my life now.

But how could I abandon Barb after she'd risked her life in stasis just to be with me?

I knew I had to see her, no matter where it led me.

**Barb:**

He's actually coming to see me.

Everything is going to work out after all. I was so happy to get the virtual invitation to get together, I almost just glossed over the fact that it was all done telepathically. At least that's what it feels like to me.

I know the geeks have some weird scientific way it works, quantum neuro-whatever, but it feels to me like Darrell reached out with his mind and mentally slipped an invitation into my mind.

Who cares *how* it happens, as long as it *did* happen.

. . .

And there he was, walking up the sidewalk to my apartment.

My heart was racing, and I knew I was breathing hard. God, I missed him so much…

When the door opened and he stood there, I could see the shock in his face.

"Hi."

My voice was almost non-existent, only a wisp of a whisper.

"It's really you," he said.

Then we ran the few steps that separated us and melted into each other's arms. It felt like the past ten years (or the past century) hadn't interrupted our love.

I wanted to kiss him, but he just held my cheeks and stared into my eyes.

"I can't believe it," he said. "They told me you'd be…"

"I know. The stasis engineers told me you'd have trouble believing I'm here. Nowadays, it's nothing special. People stop their clocks whenever they want, but for me it was, well, it was new."

He just continued to look into my eyes.

"I love you," I said.

He looked like he was going to cry. I didn't understand because we were finally back together. I wanted to kiss Darrell, but the expression on his face held me back.

"What's wrong?"

"I'm just confused."

"It's me, Darrell."

"I know. I just… I found somebody else."

"Oh."

"I don't know what to do."

Darrell looked exactly the same as the last time I saw him. He had thick dark hair, strong features that were almost craggy, and a deep voice that just carried me away. Those weren't the words I expected to hear, though.

I stepped back and wondered why it hadn't occurred to me. I'd been so concerned about *our* relationship, *our* love, *our* future, that I never considered Darrell might not imagine himself in that picture.

*Somebody else.*

"Who is she?"

He shrugged. "I'm not sure it matters." Then he added, "Tell me what you've been doing."

So I led him to the couch, and we sat down, side by side. I poured us each a glass of wine. Merlot, like we shared the day he told me he was going to leave. Somehow, I thought it would be like the other bookend, bracketing the time we were apart.

I felt like guzzling the whole bottle.

We talked. I told him about how I was back studying. My understanding of marine biology was a century out of date, but I was a fast learner and I hoped to be useful again one day.

One day, one day, one day.

"You mentioned there were minor side effects to the stasis. What were they?"

I avoided the question. "Nothing much. We can talk about that sometime. Not now. What about you?" I asked. "What are you planning on doing?"

He took a minute and then said bluntly, "I have no clue. I'd always expected to be busy working on follow-up from my trip. Categorizing the new life forms, researching their DNA ... but there's nothing to do now."

We both sipped our wine.

"I still want our life together," I said. "I understand about the other girl, of course. It makes total sense you'd find somebody. But, I want you back."

He took a deep breath and nodded. Then he locked eyes with me, and then he leaned over and kissed me. It was one of the most memorable kisses of my life, soft and sweet and then turning to passion and love.

Darrell spent the night with me, and I hugged him in bed as I slept. I refused to ever lose him again.

**Darrell:**

How could I have *not* chosen to be with Barb? No matter that I love Elli today and Barb is more a series of wonderful memories, the fact is that she sacrificed everything for me. Being a guinea pig for stasis must have been a stunning risk for her.

Am I supposed to just turn my back on her after that?

No. I didn't really have a choice. I needed to be with her, regardless of how I felt about Elli.

I went back to my "home" the morning after finding Barb, and I spent hours just staring at the walls. At some point I'd have to find a place to live outside of the facilities connected to the quarantine area. Barb and I would have a home together.

I'm still not sure how I feel about that.

I neuro-synched with Elli and told her Barb was still alive and that I would be going back with her.

There was a lot of crying on both sides of the conversation. I knew I could flip on the textile switch and touch a synthetic version of Elli's face, but the holograph was about all I could manage to do without falling to pieces. I felt like a coward, but Elli was as understanding as possible. That helped. A little.

When we ended the chat, I felt more lonely than when I'd first set foot on the starship. This time, it felt more personal, more real somehow.

I felt like crap, but I was determined to make this work. Barb had given too much to me, and I had to find a way for us both to be happy.

Over the next few weeks, Barb and I spent a lot of time together, me trying to re-find the love lost a hundred years ago.

And it worked. I started to fall in love with her again as if it was the first time we'd met. She still had her playfulness, her laugh, and those amazing eyes.

I tried to ignore the nagging guilt and aching desire for Elli.

It wasn't long, though, that I noticed something unexplained. There were crow's feet pulling out from Barb's eyes. I'd spent a lot of time looking into those eyes. This was new, almost overnight, which was a ridiculous thing to think, but it was true. She hadn't had them earlier.

Looking more closely, I saw small liver spot on her face, and wrinkles that stretched along her neck. I could see her chin sagging, which was also definitely recent. I don't think she noticed, but some strands of her hair were turning gray.

"Barb?"

"Yes, sweetie?"

"You never told me about the side effects of stasis."

She pulled back from me. We were sitting in her kitchen, drinking coffee.

"It's nothing."

"You're aging," I said. "Incredibly fast."

There it was, out in the open. Somehow, I must have noticed it subconsciously, but I needed those crow's feet to knock me into realizing it consciously.

She looked down at her coffee.

"Tell me what's going on." I knew I'd raised my voice, but whatever was happening was too important. I should have just researched the early history of stasis myself, but I hadn't thought to do that.

She shook her head. "I just can't…"

"Tell me!"

I found myself grabbing her wrist.

"You're hurting me!"

I let go. I stared at her and said slowly, "Tell me what is going on. I can see it on your face, so you've got to stop lying to me!"

She started to sob, and a tear fell down her face. She wiped it with a napkin.

"I just wanted to have as much time as I could with you," she said. "The early trials didn't perfect the process. That's what guinea pigs are for, I guess. Most of the early stasis attempts stopped people for only a short time. I was the first one to go long-term. Not long after I was stopped, they found a problem."

"You'd be aging when you were re-started."

"Yes. I'd only have a short period while my body adjusted, and I wanted to have that time with you."

"But now?"

"Now, my body is going to catch up very quickly to the age I should have been."

"How fast?"

"I'll be ancient within a month. My chronological age will have caught up with me by then. I was hoping to have longer, but it's starting already. There's no way to stop it."

I leaned back and stared at her, not knowing if I wanted to hug her or yell at her.

Then I remembered Elli.

"You made me give up the woman I loved just so you could have one last fling?"

"That's cruel. I love you."

"You knew this was going to happen."

Another tear fell as she nodded.

"I can't believe you deceived me that way."

"I need you. I love you."

I stood up and stared at the woman who once meant the world to me. Now, all I felt was disgust.

"I never want to see you again," I said. "I can't believe anybody would be that selfish."

And then I left.

Elli didn't answer my attempts to connect with her for a week. I couldn't blame her. Although she finally agreed to have coffee with me, her face was stone. She hated me, and I totally understood. When I left her, she never talked to me again.

**Barb:**

Every part of my body hurts. My face looks like it's been through a shredder, with wrinkles crawling all over it. Much of my hair has fallen out, and the parts that remain are brittle and white. I'm just so tired all the time. I can barely walk.

Even the pain-killing wands can't take all the problems away from me for more than a short while. I waved it over myself one last time, though, and caught a taxi to the shore.

I still love the ocean. It was my first love, and Darrell was my second. I might not have him, but I still have the water.

I walked out, not bothering to change into a swimsuit. Who wants to see an old hag in a bathing suit, anyhow? Jeans and my old dolphin shirt suit me just fine, thank you very much.

Nobody is walking on the beach today. It's sunny, warm, and I see nobody for miles around.

That's good, too.

I don't know how long I have before the wand wears off. An hour or less, most likely.

I walk out to let the waves splash my body, and I look out to the great sea.

Punky isn't around, of course, and in fact, I'm too close to shore to have any dolphins at all join me for a swim, but that wasn't going to stop me from hoping.

The water is rough and splashes against my body as I walk out deeper. Already, the muscles in my arms are complaining, but I don't care.

I'm only forty years old and the whole rest of my life has been sacrificed to be with the only man I ever loved.

As I dove into the water, I remember the wonderful kisses we shared when he loved me just as much. The memories calmed me as I swam away from shore. I smiled.

# THE JUPITER DROP

## JOSH MALERMAN

Steve Ringwald woke from dark dreams of swirling storms, bruise-purple gases threatening to choke him if he opened his mouth, and a surface with no support; his boots kept slipping through the ground and as dreams go, he had no real idea what held him up at all.

He was sweating, yes, and he was alone, yes, and his apartment felt too cold then too hot and oh fuck he'd had a bad dream. Big deal. And to make it an even lesser deal, Steve knew just what had caused the dream in the first place.

It wasn't a nightmare necessarily, had nothing to do with his family or the accident *at all*. And the true root of it lay on his chest, visible by the light of the lamp he hadn't turned off before falling asleep.

An advertisement, card stock, wedged into the first third of the paperback that had put him to sleep. The book was a good one, if not a little slow-going, but the ad had interrupted it cold.

THE JUPITER DROP!

Certainly they were outdoing themselves with this one. Whoever "they" were who moneyed experiences like this, the funds behind these insane interstellar joyrides; the people who were turning the solar system into a carnival. Steve hadn't even been to Mars yet and here they were advertising a free-fall trip through Jupiter, the stormiest, most violent of all Earth's neighbors.

Free-fall.

Steve let this idea sit a minute. Truth be told, it chilled him, and not just a little bit. He got up out of bed and went to the bathroom, but when he got there he realized he didn't have to go. What he *did* need to do was move. A little bit. Get the blood flowing. Get going. Standing impossibly on the gaseous surface of Jupiter wasn't so far-fetched a thing seeing as he had the means to do it. He had the money. Many people did.

Steve didn't bother looking at himself in the mirror. He didn't think of his family either, his wife and two kids who had more than less vanished from his life in the haze of a particularly anxious period of his life. Amy was cold that way. In cold, out cold, and the only way that she wasn't cold was the fact that at one time she thought he was funny and Steve (like most men) guessed wrongly that humor was enough to base forever upon. What would Amy say if she knew he was considering a year-long flight to Jupiter just to be dropped through the planet like a pebble?

*Was* he? Was he considering that?

Steve turned on the overhead light and put on his socks. The clock told him it was only five-forty in the morning, a fine time to get up, get out of the apartment, and get some coffee. Wake up. Begin the day. Possibly even get some work done.

But his thoughts of Amy and the kids, Jupiter and the solar system, followed him outside the same way vague anger follows a bad morning person. It would fade, Steve knew. The idea. The option.

The Jupiter Drop.

But beside his breakfast plate at the diner was a newspaper and on page three of the newspaper was another ad. The same purple block letters telling men like Steve Ringwald they could have the time of their lives if they had twenty-six months to kill.

Did Steve? Did Steve have twenty-six months to kill?

He read the ad. This time all the way through.

THE JUPITER DROP!

A TWO-YEAR FLIGHT ON DISNEY AIRLINES, A TWO-MONTH STAY INSIDE JUPITER!

A FULLY FURNISHED LUXURY APARTMENT.

STATE OF THE ART VIRTUAL PARTNERS.

COMPLETE WITH A VIRTUAL MOM.

EAT, SLEEP, READ, EXERCISE, RELAX, DANCE, AND LOOK!

FOUR TRANSPARENT WALLS, TRANSPARENT CEILING AND FLOOR!

FALL, COMFORTABLY FOR TWO MONTHS!

FALL BY . . .

THE JUPITER DROP!

(THE DOWNEY CO.)

"More coffee?"

The morning waitress. Pretty girl. Somewhat. But Steve always figured himself somewhat as well. Maybe they could find some chemistry between them.

"Look at this," he said, mouth half full. He pointed at the ad with his fork. "What do you think this means? You literally just . . . *drop?*"

The waitress leaned over his table for a better look. She smiled and shook her head.

"Yeah. They drop you from this huge crane connected to a space station. You're in an apartment and you get to—"

"Wait. You know about this? Does everybody know about this?"

She shrugged.

"Sure. Or I do anyway. I know someone who went."

Steve wiped his mouth with his napkin.

"For real? And so . . . what did they think?"

She shrugged again.

"He's not back yet."

Steve didn't watch her walk away. He reread the ad. The phone number at the bottom looked too easy, like all he had to do was call, pack his bags, and he'd be traveling to Jupiter.

To then be dropped through the planet.

In a glass apartment.

He laughed, couldn't help it, and turned the page. The waitress returned.

"You gonna do it?"

She was smiling. It was a smile Steve knew very well. The kind of smile from a girl that implied, if you answered in the affirmative, she'd see you in a way you always wish you saw yourself.

Fearless.

Funny.

Fun.

Steve smiled.

"You know what," he said, looking to the newspaper as if he could see through to the flipped page. "I might. I really just might."

In training for motion sickness, sitting on the edge of the bed in the simulated apartment, Steve read the pamphlet Downey had issued, the rules and regulations of the ride. What to expect, what not to; there being much more of the former than the latter.

Turns out it wasn't quite a free-fall after all. And it was a tank of an apartment. The pressure, as you sink into Jupiter, is thousands of times the pressure of the Earth's oceans and... and Steve perused these facts with the same half-interested mind and intrinsic sense of trust people once adopted when strapping in to ride a roller coaster that went upside down. You trusted the people who built it. Downey wouldn't send anybody through a planet if they didn't know what they were doing and that was (more *more* than less) enough for him. Besides, the apartment was equipped with jets that propelled it through the denser levels of Jupiter as well as steering it far wide of the planet's solid core. The pamphlet went on to detail the sun-level heat of Jupiter's core and to assure people (like Steve) that the apartment was built especially to withstand such conditions, being made almost entirely of Glasgow, the (thus far) indestructible and transparent material that revolutionized the theme park industry as well as other, perhaps more practical, walks of life. Steve read through all this quickly. If they were going to send him into a scalding furnace of Hell, so be it, he'd decided to go, and was indeed already upon year-long shuttle out.

It was the storms he was interested in, the diminishing Great Red Spot; to be surrounded by such cuckoo chaos, the natural angst and fervor, submerged wholly into the virulent landscape, Mother Nature Madness... *that* was interesting... *this* was something a man would remember, possibly even think about on his deathbed. As friends and family came to say goodbye, he just might see the violence of Jupiter repeated in their eyes.

It was just the sort of thing that could bring a man to accept his insignificance, even his death.

Or the death of others.

Steve wiped sweat from his hairline as the simulated apartment began to rock, experiencing faux turbulence, the worst (they said) he would meet out there.

*The death of others.*

"Ah, come on," Steve said.

The agent Rob responded and his voice sounded tinny through the small silver speakers.

"All good, Steve?"

Steve waved a half-dismissive hand. Yes, all good. But no, *not* all good. And perhaps nothing had been all good since the silly accident; the day Steve had killed a man named Dennis Coleman. Coleman, a neighbor, had been raking his leaves by the curb in front of his house, back when Steve had neighbors, a house, a family.

"I barely touched him," Steve said, shaking his head in beat with the turbulence. He felt a little sick from the motion and the sudden recollection of Dennis and all the shitty things that had fallen like dominos since that day.

But were any thoughts of Dennis sudden?

"All good, Steve?"

"All good. I barely touched him. Slammed on the brakes, nicked him, just *touched* his knee. But then he...he fell back. Jesus, man, he was *smiling* when he fell. We both were! Smiling because we both realized how close we were to something much worse. But still, he fell, see? He stumbled back and nicked his head on the tree and...God *damn* it, man, that was all it took."

The apartment came to a standstill, though never quite completely still, like being at sea. Rob had turned the turbulence off.

"Take a nap, Steve."

"All good," Steve said.

He recalled the one item in the Downey Preparation Pamphlet

that he considered the most curious statement of all, the singular directive that interested Steve more than the reasons why the apartment wouldn't be crushed by pressure or go up in flames:

THERE IS NO LIFE ON JUPITER. IF YOU THINK YOU SEE LIFE ON JUPITER, YOU ARE MISTAKEN!

No, there is no life on Jupiter and there is no life for Dennis Coleman anymore, either. From a simple nick. A nick to the knee.

Then a nick upon a tree.

"Take a nap, Steve?"

Steve looked up to the transparent wall, could see Rob sitting behind a big white desk, surrounded by wires and loops and blinking yellow lights. Rob wore the white jacket and slacks, another of the Downey/Disney "mood" effects, one that particularly worked, whether you knew it was for show or not.

Steve stood up.

"You're doing just fine," Rob said. "And you're going to *be* fine. These feelings pass."

Downey-speak. Disney-talk. Steve had been warned about things like depression, cabin fever, and hallucinations. Would the two month Drop be more intense than the year-long shuttle out?

Steve tried to laugh, but couldn't quite shake the idea of Dennis Coleman raking leaves, smiling as he fell, as if he was the one taking the Drop.

"Interested in a virtual partner?" Rob asked.

Steve raised a hand to say no, then paused.

"Sure. Send one in?"

"No problem."

Nope. No problem at all; except Steve was still eight months from the Drop and two more from the bottom of Jupiter and another year home, and here Dennis was already smiling, looking him in the eye through the windshield, saying without saying, *that was a close one, ha!*

Steve blinked and by the time his eyes were open again there was a brunette, athletic, tan, sitting at the white kitchen table in the simulated apartment. She was smiling warmly, though Steve understood that things like this could never quite be perfected, and an artificial woman will always have a bit of artifice to her smile.

Steve joined her at the table.

Outside the glass walls were digital renderings of sweeping colors, fervent electricity, and easily harnessed storms.

Rob vanished like powder into the winds of a false Jupiter.

"Steve," the woman said, and the flesh surrounding her lips crinkled in a rubbery way, or maybe it was just because Steve knew she was made of rubber.

"Yes?"

"Are you interested in a nap?"

Steve shook his head no.

"Do you want to lay down anyway?"

Steve looked to the walls, to where Rob just sat; now only orange and black clouds.

"Sure," Steve said.

Steve blinked and the woman was now wearing cloth shorts and a tank-top. She was standing beside him, looking down into his eyes, smiling.

"Come on," she said, nodding her head back, toward the bed, as if she was about to fall, smiling, backward. "Let's lay down."

Because Steve had never been on an interstellar thrill-ride before, he imagined certain things being just like they were on Earth. A long line of sweating tourists waiting to board their apartments, the clanking of the chain that would raise the apartment above the planet (that "way up" feeling of dread and excitement banded together), bad music pumped through shitty speakers, a carnival barker describing the exaggerated horrors of the ride and the mettle of those brave enough to try it.

But the launch site at New Jupiter Station 1 was nothing like this.

Steve should have known. This trip was *special*. He hadn't seen another rider (a *Dropper*, Rob said) since boarding the shuttle, though he knew others were on board. Sometimes, at night, he thought he could hear phony turbulence through the walls. Sometimes he even got up and pressed his face to the glass, looking for those people.

But, despite the distant whisper of tinny voices, Steve never saw one. He wondered why. The pamphlet didn't explain the significance, though Steve could guess; if a man could handle a year of semi-isolation, surely he could withstand two months surrounded by the real thing. The view itself ought to occupy him and he probably wouldn't have time to think about silly things like isolation, solitary confinement, and the fact that he couldn't step outside the four glass walls for sixty days.

For the most part, Steve didn't think about other people at all. The virtual women who appeared, suddenly, were so well timed it was as if Downey had a direct line to his brain. The moment Steve dipped below a certain level of happiness, an athletic blonde would appear; small breasts, big eyes, bigger smile; Steve's ideal physical woman, a thing he hadn't really known himself before boarding the shuttle. Steve allowed these mysteries to belong to the men and women who built the ride. Who cared how it all worked? What difference did it make why the apartment wouldn't explode halfway through the planet? Who cared how Disney and Downey knew there was no life on Jupiter and said it would be a mistake to think otherwise?

Who cared?

On the day he arrived at New Jupiter Station 1, Steve thought again of the waitress from the diner near his apartment back on Earth. As the men and women in white helped him out of his simulated apartment and escorted him down a long winding hall, Steve thought of her smiling when he told her he'd registered for the Drop. It excited him, knowing that when he returned home he'd have the story of all stories for women (*real* women!) with smiles like that.

Four agents escorted him, their tight jackets and pants showed off their own athletic builds, and Steve did feel something like a celebrity, a special person, a person of great interest. His own formfitting yellow suit was the only color to stand out in the tunnel and he couldn't help but imagine a daisy, himself as the potent pollen centerpiece, traveling confidently toward the real thing, the actual apartment, all simulations and getting-used-tos accounted for and over with.

"You did *wonderfully* in your training," one agent said, quietly, then gently tugged on his elbow, steering Steve around a bend to a second long hall.

Only this hall wasn't white.

This hall was as transparent as the walls of his apartment would be.

Steve stopped walking.

Below him, he saw it for the first time, horrifyingly massive, the colors and motion much more severe than anything he had been prepared to face.

Jupiter.

"Jesus."

He felt a tinge of embarrassment, as if the Downey men and women would be disappointed to discover their prized Dropper was actually, in the end, scared silly.

He crouched and planted a flat palm against the glass floor and stared down into the abyss he had volunteered to experience.

"Jesus," he said again. And the planet seemed to respond, seemed to swirl into a lifeless, mean grin, before the clouds and gases dispersed, creating new shapes, new illusions.

The agents helped him up.

Ahead he saw the leviathan metallic crane-arm and the empty transparent apartment, so out of place!, gripped in its claws.

"So," Steve said, a tremble in his voice. "So … it just … *falls* from there?"

"*Drops*," one of the Downey men said. The others smiled brightly. "Welcome, Steve, to The Jupiter Drop."

Intense, an almost overwhelming sensation, standing beside the table, taking in the apartment (much nicer than the simulated one), noting the glass door, too, trying not to make eye contact with the men and women operating the crane, the agents standing on the platform, waving goodbye.

Either Jupiter was loud as Hell or the machinations of the crane were bringing Steve to cover his ears. Would the next two months be just like this? Should he say he wanted off?

"All good?" a voice asked, stronger, less tinny in here.

Steve nodded.

He wondered when they were going to strap him in. Did the pamphlet talk about this? He recalled the word "equilibrium," saw it a hundred times on the pages. Homeostasis. Maybe he should've read more, trusted less?

Jupiter's surface moved, constantly, beneath him. Steve tried not to look down. Don't look down. But the pamphlet didn't say not to look down. The whole point of this was to look down.

So Steve looked down.

Shapes below, the size of countries, then colorful webbed fingers gripped the arc of the surface, then reached, spread till they vanished over red horizons; golds and yellows swarmed as one new hue; fresh fingers rose, fresh countries, a sudden and improbable perfect circle, before its circumference melded into the heads of meeting storms.

*I want off.*

The Downey agents were waving goodbye; no barker here, no sale; Jupiter sold itself.

Numbers through the speakers. Decreasing. A countdown?

Steve gripped the edges of the tabletop, sat down in a chair. No seatbelt? No safety?

He thought of Dennis Coleman, nicked by the front bumper of Steve's car. One minute raking leaves, the next falling back, head hitting a tree...

"Hey," Steve said, rising, then sitting back down. "Hey, am I supposed to be strapped in?"

Waves from the staff. As if animatronic. Only the arms move. From the elbow down.

Waving.

Goodbye.

Goodbye, Steve.

The numbers continued to decrease and Steve tried to count down with them but God damn the noise of the crane and the volume of the storming below obscured them. How close was he to falling, to dropping, to spending two months inside *that* madcappery beneath?

"Hey," Steve called again. "Is there a safety harness? A belt? Is there—"

He heard the number seven. All by itself. Not seventeen, not seventy-anything. Seven.

Steve rose.

He yelled.

"HEY! Hey, I want off! HEY! I WANT OFF!"

Waves from the staff, a purple mist rising about them on the enclosed platform, as if the planet below was counting down as well, reaching up to make an exchange, to take the apartment from the crane.

Hadn't seven seconds passed? Absolutely. Must have been seventy then. Steve went to the glass door and pushed, pulled, knowing of course that the thing was locked, coded, from the outside. Nobody ought to be able to open a glass door as they're falling through a planet. But he tried. Tried to open the door.

"Hey, I'm getting off now! Sorry, but I've had second thoughts!"

A tremble in his voice, then a hand upon his shoulder and Steve turned quickly, too quick, and saw the slightly uneven face of an otherwise beaming brunette. The purple mist rising behind him reflected black in her eyes and when she opened her mouth it was as if she were counting down the muffled numbers herself.

"What?" Steve asked. "What did you say?"

She smiled and shook her head no, playfully, get away from the door silly, you can't open it from the inside silly, come sit down with me at the table, wanna lay down?, wanna touch my rubbery belly to take your mind off the planet?

Steve turned back to the door, the glass, the platform, pounding now with both hands.

"*I WANT OFF, DAMMIT!*"

Fingers upon his chin, turning his face toward her, her dark eyes so close to his, her breathless mouth open, relaying numbers, yes, no doubt, the number one, in fact, solitary, not one hundred, not one thousand, not one and one again.

Then—

—the drop.

And Steve screamed as the storms below rose to meet the floor of the apartment.

Immediate thoughts of Dennis Coleman. Thoughts of Amy, too, leaving him, taking the kids, telling him the kids can't watch their father lose his mind over an accident; he was teaching them the wrong things about guilt, the wrong way to get over something; the way he was carrying on the kids were going to think it was okay to spend your whole adult life trying to change one silly moment, history, your own history, move it an inch or two to the left.

The kids were going to think they could move history, Amy said, she actually said.

Steve, standing with both hands against a glass wall, couldn't take his eyes off the scenery, the sights, the planet. The lights framing the apartment made it so no sun was necessary and even inside what should be the darkest, most dense areas of Jupiter, he *saw*.

And yet, he thought about Dennis. About Dennis Coleman never seeing anything so incredible, so absolutely horrifying and invigorating at once. If Steve had seen this before that autumn day on Miller Street, would he have nicked poor Dennis's knee? He didn't think so. He *knew* the answer was no. There was no way a man could be a part of such an infinitesimal oversight had he seen the depth of the cosmos in person. Steve was changing, right now, one day deep, would never be the same, would never see Earth the same way again, would never not notice a man raking leaves into a gutter one house before his own.

Dennis. Dennis Coleman should have got the chance to see this. Had he seen this he would never have raked leaves in the street to begin with. He'd have valued each and every passionate second of life and he would've let the leaves rot rather than stand in a street, a place where a car could come, could come nick a knee.

The view was...

There was no word for what the view was and no word for the darkness beyond the view either, the infinite (no, there are boundaries, an end to this) chasm of black the apartment lights couldn't reach. Steve wanted to do more than tell his ex-wife, write his kids about it, call Dennis Coleman's grave. He wanted to *show* them. Show them the green fingertips that turned orange as they connected with the glass, then spread like something sentient across the ceiling, the floor, until Steve was completely entombed in an orange, then red, box, then seeing clearly again as the gases the mists the webbed fingers released the apartment and allowed it to fall, to drop; the beginning of a two month descent into gorgeous improbabilities.

Eventually, thoughts of Dennis receded, and Steve stepped from the glass, stepped deeper into the apartment, took stock of the options afforded him. The small toilet and shower were sectioned off by a white curtain. The bed, white sheets, white headboard, was flush against a glass wall. No television in here. No computers. Nothing more entertaining than Jupiter itself, and the inside of Jupiter, and if a man or a woman needed something more than *this* ...

Steve stepped to the kitchen nook and poured himself a glass of orange juice. He carried it with him to the bed, sat on the mattress edge, and stared. He watched the blues and blacks and heard the howling of violent winds.

He lay back on the bed.

"I'd like a friend," Steve said, then blinked, and when he opened his eyes he saw a funny, tan blonde seated at the table. He wondered if the Downey knew not to send the brunette from the Drop, the one who had held his hand as the apartment was released by the crane. He was grateful for this woman instead.

"Pretty incredible, huh," Steve said. Because he had to say it to someone, even someone who wasn't alive.

*Alive.*

THERE IS NO LIFE ON JUPITER! IF YOU THINK YOU SEE LIFE ON JUPITER, YOU ARE MISTAKEN!

But Steve was alive. Wide awake alive. Experiencing the apex of human stimulation alive.

And Dennis Coleman was not.

"Come here," Steve said and the blonde got up and Steve saw she wasn't wearing any shorts at all, no underwear, nothing, and he wondered again if the apartment knew, was somehow wired to his brain, his desires, knew he wanted to lay on his back as this blonde climbed upon him, as the walls and ceilings went blue then orange then white beyond her.

The "virtual mom" pitch in the advertisement seemed unnecessary to Steve when he first read it. But a week into the Drop, "Mom" was as welcome as she'd been in childhood.

"Have you noticed you've entered the far north temperate zone, honey? You're still very far from the rings. You might not see them from here, but you know, it's nice to know they're *there*."

*There there.* Mom always used to say "there there."

"No," Steve said, fixing a sandwich at the marble counter. "I mean, yes, but I didn't know that's where we are."

A clucking of a tongue. Mom.

"You should've read the *brochure*, honey. It's all in there."

Steve smiled. Strange relief, so alone out here, to be nagged by Mom again.

"I noticed the clouds," Steve said, knowing this vague statement wouldn't be enough for her.

"Counter-rotating cloud bands, dear."

Steve carried the sandwich to the glass wall, watched the fresh colors curl in and over one another, vibrant snakes in the mist.

"I also noticed the sound has picked up, Mom. It's gotten louder in here."

She sighed.

"It's bad, yes. But you know what? It's the price you pay for the view."

She was right. And she was right-on, too, so exactly like his mother in tone and content that Steve had to wonder how extensive the interview process with her must have been.

"Steve, dear."

"Yes."

"No need to think about that nasty accident out here."

"I wasn't."

"But you were. And that's okay. But this isn't the place for guilt. This is a new journey. An experience all its own."

Steve ate his sandwich and observed Jupiter's colors overlapping; a bright flash of lighting so close to the apartment that Steve recoiled.

Leave it to Mom to make him feel guilty for having felt guilt.

"I know it, Mom. But..."

"But what?"

"Do you think it could have been anybody, Mom? Anybody driving down Miller Street that day? If I hadn't nicked him ... would somebody else have?"

Silence from Mom. Steve wondered absently if she was searching somehow for the right response.

"You're talking about Fate," Mom said.

"Am I?"

"Yes, dear. You're talking about things happening no matter who is there to start or stop them."

Steve ate another bite.

"I guess I am."

"Oh, honey. Don't talk with your mouth full."

"Mom."

"No, I don't think it would've happened had you not been driving down Miller Street that day."

Steve smiled. Sadly. Now this was as close to Mom as possible. She would never have gone for Fate.

But she knew other ways to sooth.

"But is it your fault that microbes are dying in your mouth as you eat? And who's to say we're any more important than them? And aren't you but a microbe here, a week into Jupiter, passing the north temperate zone?"

Steve rose from the table fast and stepped to the glass. He'd seen something outside.

"Mom, did you see that?"

"See what, dear?"

"I thought I saw ... I swear I thought I saw a ..."

"A what, Steve?"

"Nothing."

But he didn't take his eyes from the glass wall. Didn't stop staring into the motley abyss and wouldn't remember to take another bite of his sandwich for another five minutes.

Steve woke to a tapping on the glass.

He opened his eyes in the dark, the outer lights off for the "night," for sleeping. Tomb-like darkness hugged him close, wrapped its own black fingers around his ankles, his wrists, his neck, slunk down his throat as he opened his mouth to say something, then finally did, the one word piercing the black, fracturing the opacity like a different kind of storm.

"Lights!"

And the lights came on and Steve hardly noticed the myriad hues, like stained water, swarming the walls of his apartment. All he noticed was that there was nothing to knock on the glass. Nothing by the walls. Nothing on the ceiling or beneath the bed, either.

Nothing at the glass door.

Two weeks into the Drop and Steve was disinterested in the transmuting bands, the morphing paint, the way the world beyond the apartment constantly shifted, never to repeat its exact self again.

But he wasn't tired of the shapes he saw, the quick flashes, in strobe, a figure here, a configuration there. Sometimes, if you looked for too long, you could see a person out there, arms extended, as if falling, dropping, without an apartment, without the assistance of Downey.

Steve stared. He sat upon the edge of his bed and looked up, through the ceiling, into a wash of chromism, magnificent tincture and dye. Every now and then an eye would look back; not the dreaded red eye of Jupiter, but an eye as small as his own, peering out from the vapor, the greasy luminosity, beseeching; the look of someone forlorn, worried, in need of help.

Shelter.

Steve got up.

"Mom."

"Yes, dear?" Never a sleepy take on her voice. As if Mom never slept.

"I saw something out there. And I believe it was a person."

A slight intake of air. Perhaps the sound of a smile.

"You most certainly did *not*. There is no life on Jupiter. And if you think you saw life on Jupiter? You are mistaken."

Steve mouthed the second half of her statement with her.

"I'm not convinced," he said, feeling emboldened by it, suddenly, as if having Mom to argue with was exactly what he needed in order to believe in what he was saying.

"Well, do. Do be convinced. Fixating on life out here is as silly as fixating on death at home."

But Steve brought his nose to the glass and stared deep into the miasma beyond. He pressed one hand against the wall and, for the first time, wanted to touch Jupiter, wanted to actually feel what the planet felt like, to smell it taste it hear it without the protection of the Glasgow walls.

He thought he could hear Mom breathing, through the speaker, or like she was in the room with him, behind him, so clear that he turned to face her and then after finding nobody no Mom he turned to face the wall again and thought maybe it was the sound of Jupiter breathing, the planet itself, and all this pigmentation, this iridescence, was the effluvium of a single intake held, then released, his apartment riding the living waves of something so large, he couldn't see it.

Mom told him he'd reached the equator but Steve didn't need to hear her say it; it'd been a month in the apartment and the world outside his walls went solid white, solid blue, then colors too deep for his human eye to process. He knew that the core of Jupiter was hot, sun-hot, and he knew too that it was larger than the Earth, much, but the jets had steered him far enough away from the ice and rock to be safe, leaving him momentarily in a sort of interstellar purgatory, a less interesting, less colorful limbo.

And yet...

It was here, level with the center of Jupiter, that Steve saw a form so complete, so perfectly *made*, that there was no way (to him, for him) to credit a random crisscrossing of mists.

It was a man, something like himself anyway, with two legs and two arms, no apartment to speak of, though Steve looked for one, thinking (perhaps crazily) it was a fellow Dropper. He asked that the lights be turned up, brighter, but was informed that they were set at their maximum luminosity, and there was no greater vision to achieve.

That was okay. Steve believed he had seen it; swarmed by piebald worms, flashes of frightening gales, swallowed by a gob squall, an inhuman blizzard at Jupiter's equator.

Or below it now. Steve wasn't sure. As the colors began to resemble the hues he'd seen days prior, still on his way *to* the equator, perhaps he was seeing their mirrored selves *from*.

*If you think you see life on Jupiter...*

A touch on his shoulder, cold fingers, and Steve turned to see an athletic woman, full lips, her belly showing beneath the fabric of a loose fitting half shirt. He glanced once more through the wall, suspicious in that moment that someone was trying to distract him, then faced her again.

"Hello," he said.

"Hello," she said, and Steve kissed her, held her close and tried not to think of Amy driving away from the house, the silhouette of the kids in the backseat, their small heads, Amy driving up Miller, away from him, the same street he'd been driving when he struck (no, *nicked*) that poor man who was kind enough to smile after averting a much worse accident only to discover it hadn't been averted; still falling back, dropping, south of the equator now, toward a tree that would connect just hard enough to kill him.

How could Amy take that street? Of all the streets in the world to drive away on...how could she take *Miller*, the very street that had delivered them all their problems to begin with?

"Hello," the woman said again, her voice a hair too tinny, *just* unreal, justifying perhaps the death-creed of The Jupiter Drop, the "YOU ARE MISTAKEN" that rattled in Steve's mind like loose teeth, extra marbles, rolled for the noise of it, the roll of it, entertainment in place of television, a computer, even the cosmic masterpiece beyond.

Steve got on his back as the woman sat up, he inside her, he *looking at her*, watching the rise and fall of her small breasts, the way her rubber lower lip hung loose when she opened her mouth to moan, watching *her*, no doubt *not* looking past her, not above her, not beyond her, not intentionally, to the ceiling, lit up, but finding himself staring there indeed, because something had moved, yes, something was crouched upon the glass ceiling and was peering into the apartment, into the *life* within.

"Get off me!" Steve cried. He gripped the woman by the waist. His fingers sank into the rubber too far, unnaturally, and he pulled her aside. He rose, standing on the bed, pointing to the ceiling, crying *look! LOOK!* But he wasn't (couldn't be) sure himself, as the colors sifted again, the tendrils of murky fog dispensed then returned in the form of a new shape. No. He couldn't be sure he'd seen anything at all but as the woman spoke and as Steve stepped from the bed to the floor, racing for a different angle, a fresh view of the receding pattern above him, he couldn't shake the image of something crouched, followed by that something sucked up, vacuumed, into Jupiter's cruel sky above.

Steve wondered, is this what it's like, dying and being dead?

Six weeks deep and falling through a planet alone had gotten as lonely as advertised. And yet, Steve *did* have a hobby; the continuous staring through the walls, the ceiling, the floor. Most nights he'd wake, call for the lights, look under his bed, find a cluster of clouds approaching, maroon shapes that might have been larger than the Earth or as small as the mattress that held him. Sometimes he'd cry, from the sheer awesomeness of it all; other times he'd stare, waiting to see something staring in return.

Mom told him they were level with the Great Red Spot, though the apartment was much too far from it to see.

"I'm going to take a shower, Mom."

Up and out of bed, Steve couldn't be sure if it was night or day and these terms didn't mean much to him now. He felt buried, buried alive, and wondered, with alarming regularity, if this was what death felt like; the dark colors, the emptiness that wasn't really an emptiness, the vast and brilliant existence that he couldn't touch.

No more than Dennis Coleman could touch another tree.

"Go ahead, honey. Make sure to wash behind your ears."

Steve crossed the apartment and felt a slight tremor, turbulence, though it was never as bad here in Jupiter as it was in the simulated apartment on the flight through space. He paused, waited for it to pass, and continued to the corner bathroom. There he disrobed and ran the water, able to see the currents swirl down into the drain and leave the apartment immediately, falling into the abyss below, as if Steve were responsible for the tiniest raincloud in all this storm.

He stepped inside and closed the white curtain though there was nobody to see him showering. It was all beginning to be too much for Steve; the onslaught of impossibly gorgeous images, the endless run of brilliance, zenith sights, the apex of human observation. Sometimes it felt good to draw the curtain on that.

Steve lowered his head under the hot water. He closed his eyes and opened them to see the bar of soap was down to a sliver; he'd need to open a new one soon, next shower. He ran shampoo through his hair and hummed a tune. He closed his eyes. He opened them, watched the water rain out through the floor as if there was no floor at all, as if Steve showered without an apartment, just a man standing above it all, falling, cleaning himself on the way.

Steve washed his face, rubbed his eyes, closed them, opened them and saw a shadow, something obscuring the light beyond the white curtain that cocooned him.

"Mom?" It was the first word he thought to call.

Yes, he thought. It looked like the shadow of a person.

Steve held the edge of the curtain. All he had to do was pull it aside, fast, and see what was there, what was pressed to the glass, what blocked the light.

"Yes, dear?"

Mom's voice, Mom talking, asking after him, asking if he was okay.

Steve pulled the curtain aside and was sure, *sure*, that he had seen it move, tear itself from the glass, allowing the atmosphere of Jupiter to reclaim it, to vacuum it back into obscurity.

But Steve saw nothing against the glass. Nothing remained.

"Mom," Steve said. "Did you see something, someone, outside?"

That smiling breath from the speakers.

"There is no life on Jupiter, honey. If you think you saw life on Jupiter, you are mistaken."

Steve turned off the water but did not step out from the shower. Instead, he stared long through the glass, imagining something capable of flying out there, something strong enough to withstand the storms.

And the isolation, too.

Steve knew it was the worst thought he could allow himself to have.

*I wanna go home.*

It was a thought he'd had in Germany, when he and Amy had taken a trip, this before the kids and long before the accident on Miller Street. They'd scheduled three weeks but Steve got the itch, the bug to leave, ten days deep. Almost involuntarily he'd voiced it. A fight ensued.

*I wanna go home.*

Bad thought to have while falling through Jupiter.

Sitting at the table, Steve laughed.

Oh, Amy, he thought, if you could see me now. You thought Germany was a mindscrew?

Taking his glass of orange juice, Steve rose from the table and stepped to the kitchen counter.

On the way he saw a man tapping on the glass wall.

Steve dropped the orange juice. It pooled by his feet, clung to him, as if frightened of the storms below.

The man was alive, yes. Tapping on the glass.

He wore a suit. His hair flapped from the fall. Steve looked to his feet.

He was floating. Yes, nothing to support you out there.

Steve screamed. Like a child, like one of his own children, he screamed and he stepped on a piece of the broken glass and brought his foot up to his hands but did not take his eyes off the man outside his apartment.

"Hi, Steve."

Words? Actual words? Steve heard Mom's voice above, asking if he was alright, telling him no, he must be mistaken, there is no life on Jupiter.

Lightning flashed beyond the reach of the apartment lights and Steve saw the man in full. Thin enough to be skeletal. Like he'd worked hard all his life.

In the flashing lightning, Steve approached the wall.

The man did not fly away.

Another tap on the glass.

Lightning; rash pink clouds; green tendrils beyond the man, mindless disorganized eels in the mist.

A tap. A tapping.

"Stevie, buddy. I'm coming in."

More assured now, and Steve, shaking his head no, no man could survive out there, no, this is mistaken *I* am mistaken no, Steve standing at the glass, his own nose only the width of the wall from the other's, only the glass between them.

Then a flash of lightning, bright enough to expose storms Steve hadn't known he was traveling through, dropping through, and in this new light the man blinked, Steve was sure of it, and his expression silently said,

*Whether or not you want me to, Stevie ol' buddy, I'm coming in.*

"LIGHTS!" Steve shrieked and the lights went off and the world outside the apartment went black and Steve, trembling, inched back from the glass, one hand out behind him, feeling for the bed, finding the bed, then crawling up and onto it, under the covers, where he could hide like his children used to, crying out for their parents in the night, Daddy! Mommy! running down the carpeted hall to knock on his and Amy's bedroom door.

*We're coming in!* They'd cry.

Ready, Stevie, buddy?

"NO!"

Steve screamed it and he screamed it again and Mom came to him, Mom's voice as concerned and wise as the real thing.

"Steve, dear? Do you know we've passed the Great Red Spot? Did you know we're that deep into the planet now? Don't worry, dear. And don't cry. If you cry you'll blur all these beautiful sights and won't see a thing."

And Steve in the dark, on the bed, clutching the bed sheet, shaking his head no as Mom carried on, in beat with the tapping, the tapping of bone thin fingers against the glass wall of the apartment.

The bowels of Jupiter, storms, endless, but only the sounds now, only the music they made.

Steve in the dark. No lights on in the box.

Do you remember when Amy told you that you smelled different? Do you remember thinking it meant she'd fallen out of love with you? You were wrong. It was dying she smelled. You've been dying since you nicked the knee and the head nicked the tree. You've been falling back, dropping, like Dennis fell back, dropped. He was smiling. You remember that? You were smiling, too, when you told the waitress you might try it out, take The Jupiter Drop. You were smiling and she was smiling and Dennis was smiling, saying without words *that was close, thanks for stopping, could have been a lot worse* until his expression changed, involuntary, contact with the tree, a sudden scrunching, the air sucked out of him.

The air has been slowly vacuumed from Dennis Coleman since. Dehydrated flesh. Airless body. Did you see that man, Steve? Did you see that life on Jupiter?

No no! No life on Jupiter.

So is this death?

"Steve, honey?"

Mom.

Mom's voice in the dark. How long had Steve been sitting in the dark? Falling? Dropping without an image beyond the glass walls, nothing to see, nothing seen? He'd eaten in the dark. Pissed and shit, trembling, in the dark. Slept and woke and waited and slept again.

"Yes, Mom?"

"We've reached the far south temperate zone. Not much longer to go. A shame really."

Steve nodded in the dark. Wiped his nose in the dark.

No, this isn't death, he knew.

Right?

This was just the Drop. Surely if he'd read the pamphlet he'd have been warned of mistaking life for death and vice versa.

Maybe there had been no man at the glass. No man in a suit. No man who said hi Steve, I'm coming in Steve, are you Steve?

It was a strange feeling, the *want* to be delusional.

"Mom?" Steve asked, his voice so vivid, physical in the dark.

"Yes, dear?"

"What do you know about cabin fever? About hallucinations?"

Trembling, shaking for days.

"Well if you'd read the brochure you'd know that hallucinations are very common, and they usually come in the form of things that do bother you in your 'real' life."

"What do you mean?"

"Well, honey, a man who is worried about money may hallucinate open suitcases full of dollar bills falling through Jupiter, too. A wife worried about her cheating husband may hallucinate an affair in the clouds out there. Strictly speaking cabin fever, since you asked."

Steve looked up to the ceiling, saw lighting so far away, the quick spread of purple veins in a blue thumb, then gone, swallowed by the enormous blackness again.

"Mom."

"Yes, dear?"

"Let me know when it's the day we land."

"Sure, dear. But why? That's still another week away. You're not planning on sitting in the dark all that time, are you, dear?"

Steve didn't answer. He kept his ear to the walls, to the ceiling, to the floor, where he thought he heard something, a scratching, a different sort of tapping, the sound, perhaps, of cold hard fingertips pressing buttons, attempting to discern the code that unlocks a door.

"Steve, dear." Mom said, with no visible speaker to give the words shape. "We land today."

Still, the dark. Still.

Steve sat up in bed. He'd been teetering on the steeple of sleep.

"Thank you," Steve said anxiously, swinging his legs over the mattress side.

He crossed the apartment fast and felt for the coffee maker then made himself coffee in the dark.

"Thank you for everything." His genuine gratitude for all Mom had done for him these last two months.

He was close, close to the catch pad, New Jupiter Station 2, close to exiting this apartment and boarding the Disney shuttle back to Earth.

He knocked into a cupboard and something fell inside it, a glass perhaps, and the sound startled him. Sounded something like a closed fist on a glass wall.

He packed in the dark. Feeling for his shirts and pants scattered by the side of the bed. Outside the apartment, he could still hear the storms. Mad Jupiter wheezing.

The ride was almost over.

He latched his suitcase closed, sat on the bed, and waited.

And waited.

He fell asleep this way, sitting up, then woke to the sound of a voice.

"This isn't Dropping. Stevie."

Steve leapt from the bed, away from the sound, and crashed against the glass wall.

*Lights,* he thought. *Tell Mom to turn on the lights.*

"Who's there?!" he screamed.

"This isn't Dropping," the voice repeated. (*a man, a thin man in a suit, a man who can survive out there OUT THERE!!*) "Do you wanna Drop for real?"

Steve looked down, but down was the same as up, the same as side-to-side. All dark. The distant veins of red lightning in all directions.

"MOM!"

"Mom can't help you anymore, Stevie."

Only a voice in the dark of the apartment.

"Who—"

"You're a big boy now. All grown up. What can Mom do for you that you can't do for yourself?"

But Steve heard her, in the distance. Mom was talking to him. Telling him he was mistaken.

*Lights*, Steve thought again. But he didn't want to see this man, didn't want to see him seated at the kitchen table, his legs crossed, any expression on his thin face.

"This isn't free-fall," the man said. And his voice the whistling of a cosmic wind over teeth. "If you wanna really Drop, you gotta step outside."

Steve shook his head no in the dark.

"No," he said. "No no no no—"

"Yes. Go on, Stevie. Step outside the apartment. *Free fall.*"

Steve slumped down against the wall. Fell to a fetal position on the glass floor. He looked through it, below, down, into the dark. And deep in there he thought he saw a light. Not the celestial light of another storm, but something more familiar. A bulb, perhaps. A man-made flicker in the abyss.

"How did you get in here?" Steve asked, trembling.

"I know the code."

"How did you survive out there?"

The man laughed.

*Lights*, Steve thought. But no, not yet.

"There's nothing to it," the man said. "They tell you you can't survive out there so that you don't try it."

Lightning flashed close to the apartment and Steve saw him,

the man, not sitting at the table, but crouched upon it.

Darkness again. Complete.

"Wanna get over the anxiety, Stevie? The guilt? Wanna...be free?"

Steve looked down again. Saw that flicker die in a swirl of black sludge.

"Yes," he said.

Mom said something, far away.

Something about being mistaken.

"Go on, then. Step outside the apartment."

"The door is locked from the inside. So that nobody jumps out, so that nobody—"

White lightning again and Steve saw the man was now crouched upon the bed and beyond him the door was open, a crack, just enough for Steve to imagine his own fingers gripping the edge, opening it wider, allowing himself to step outside.

Steve slid along the glass wall, toward the corner of the apartment, away from the bed.

But the man was moving, too.

Motion. In the dark.

Shoes on a glass floor.

Mom talking about no life.

The steps closer.

Mom talking about mistakes.

No life.

Shoes.

Taps on glass.

Shoes.

Mom.

Life.

"LIGHTS!!"

The lights came on inside and outside the apartment and Steve saw no man coming, no man upon the bed, the table, or anywhere.

Wide-eyed, getting up, Steve looked everywhere. Under the bed. Behind the shower curtain. In the cupboards. Outside.

"MOM!"

"Yes, dear?"

The door was still open. Just enough that he could pull it open wider. Could step outside if he wanted to.

He looked down. He thought of Amy and the kids. How Amy must have taught the kids how Dad was a nervous man, a wreck, a shell, ever since nicking Dennis Coleman on Miller Street, ever since Dennis Coleman nicked the tree.

"Yes, dear?"

"What do you know about…getting over things?"

Steve was crossing the apartment, stepping toward the unlocked glass door.

"Getting over things? Well, for starters I'd guess a person needs to face their fears head on. But that's what everybody says, and yet, most people don't get over things, do they. So then that's not the answer, is it?"

Steve was halfway across the apartment. The glass floor was cool against his bare feet and Steve realized, distantly, that he'd spent most of his time in the dark without wearing socks or shoes.

"So I'd think it'd have to be something more like…" Mom was thinking. "Experiencing the thing for yourself, the thing to get over."

"Yes."

"What are you trying to get over, dear?"

"The top of it. The all of it."

"I'm not sure I understand. But yes, I imagine the only way to get over something is to go straight through it."

"Yes."

Steve was at the door. His lips curled into an imitation of the smile Dennis Coleman wore, the expression Steve saw through the windshield, as Coleman fell back toward the tree.

He felt for the edge of the open door. A flash of red lightning helped him find it.

"Now, dear. We'll be landing in less than an hour and I know you'll be happy about *that.* You'll be on the shuttle and headed back to your daily life in no time."

"My daily life," Steve thought.

THERE IS NO LIFE ON JUPITER. IF YOU THINK YOU SEE LIFE ON JUPITER, YOU ARE MISTAKEN!

Steve opened the door.

"Dear?"

But Steve was already stepping outside. As Mom started to tell him to look down, that the lights of New Jupiter Station 2 were visible at last, Steve was already too far away to hear her, her voice sucked up and swallowed by the storms, unseen waves, and the astonishing volume of a planet with no indomitable apartment to hush it.

Free fall.

Steve was falling. Steve was breathing. Steve was seeing, too.

Below him, the propulsion jets on the top of the apartment glowed like distant cigars in the dark, four men playing cards perhaps, gambling, someone's life on the table.

The apartment was far below him, moving faster than him, and beyond it was (*yes*) the catch pad, an enormous pentagon of elastic material (Glasgow, just like the walls of the apartment, all the unbreakable stuff was Glasgow), and standing upon the catwalks and solid bridges were men and women in white, Downey agents, ready to escort Steve

(*Steve's not home anymore, Steve stepped outside*)

to the Disney shuttle that would take him back home.

Home.

It was impossible not to hold your arms out as far as they could go, to spread your fingers, your legs, to keep your eyes open, wide, as you fell. It wasn't just *wind* in your hair, Christ no, it was the *storms of Jupiter* against your clothes, your face, your teeth. Steve felt rains he'd never felt before. Snow? Who knows. At times the current was so thick it felt like arms and legs against his own, at other times so thin as to be mere fingertips, tickling, and Steve smiled and laughed, an honest laughter that felt as free as advertised. The laughter of a man who wisely, calmly knows it's okay to laugh, no matter what comes next in life.

*Life.*

Below him, at what appeared to be the bottom of Jupiter, the planet's very edge, nestled into the impossible, gaseous surface, was something that looked like...

"Amy's hair."

Steve laughed again, but it was clipped now. Not because he was saddened by the correlation, but because the object (objects?) was so out of place as to be shocking, astonishing; a tangle of dark roots, unmoving, still despite the raging winds that shook the glass apartment below.

*Life.*

Steve, still alive, still falling, free falling, recognized the tangle as roots indeed, as though he were coming up from under the ground, as if her were digging rather than falling, rising, up up up, to the surface, and just below that surface were, yes, the roots that nourished Life, that supported the whole song and dance to begin with.

Roots.

Life.

"A tree," Steve said, and blue winds toyed with the syllables, keeping them near, before they were sucked up into the cosmic tempest above.

THERE IS NO LIFE ON JUPITER.

Yes, a tree.

The apartment's jets sputtered, slowed as the glass box came level with the tree and in the apartment's lights Steve saw the bark in great detail, the branches like petrified lightning, the knots and the nicks...

"The nicks..."

Above the tree (Steve could see a crown now upon the tree, the green head in full bloom) New Jupiter Station 2 sat like a second sun, all man-made lights aflame, the pentagon catch pad ready for the coming apartment. Steve understood, then and only then, that gravity ought to be working against him, that there is no top and no bottom of Jupiter, no more than there is to planet Earth.

And yet... falling... still...

(*Wanna get over the anxiety, Stevie? The guilt? Wanna be free?*)

...free falling.

The empty apartment reached the catch pad, the Downey agents waved hello, hello Steve Ringwald, you've been gone two months, you did it, you didn't lose your marbles in isolation, didn't go nuts and try to drown yourself in the sink, try to chop your fingers off with the bagel slicer, no blood, no mess, didn't try to open the door, didn't open the—

The door swung loose. Open.

Steve saw clearly their expressions as the apartment landed, as nobody waved back to them from within, as the glass box was empty, easily seen, all the way through.

A magic trick. The vanishing man.

But the agents knew where to look. The agents looked up. The leviathan ball storming above them, the Dropper Steve Ringwald dropping dangerously close to a tree.

*(up? down? There is no top or bottom to Jupiter...)*

Steve heard Mom, then. Heard her voice as though she were still beside him, as he fell, so close to the tree, no longer using one of the speakers, her tone clear and full, her syllables emerging and slipping back into the thick then thin winds, the blues, the oranges, the browns, the blacks, the—

"The tree," Steve said, as he reached it, as his body careened hard against the roots, as he tumbled up the body of the bark.

Mom spoke.

"THERE IS NO LIFE ON JUPITER. IF YOU THINK YOU SEE LIFE ON JUPITER, YOU ARE MISTAKEN!"

Below, the agents were searching under the bed, in the shower, in the cupboards, too.

Steve crashed hard against a thick branch, fell up to another, to another, thought:

*That wasn't Dennis Coleman.*

But it didn't matter who it was, who had advised him to step outside, to leave the safety of the apartment, to free fall through the center of a thing he couldn't get over.

"They're looking for you, dear," Mom said, her voice Jupiter's thunder, the sound a lifecycle might make. "But they can't find you."

Steve crashed into another branch. Another.

"Where are you, dear? Steve? Where did you go? Are you hiding under the bed? Are you hiding in the shower?"

Steve connected with another branch.

His head this time.

"Are you hiding in the dark, Steve?" Mom's voice echoed through Jupiter. "Are you still there...hiding...in the dark?"

# THE UNIVERSE IS DYING

## PAUL MICHAEL ANDERSON

The world is ending, but you don't know that yet.

You are James McIntyre, 31, and the instant before the smartphone on your nightstand rings is the calm before the storm.

You hear Deanna in the other room on the phone with her agent. You take a final moment to adjust the ends of your tie. You smell the cool saltiness of the Pacific wafting in through the bedroom windows. You think of nothing but what notes the producers gave Marty about the latest draft of the screenplay. This is your life, and it, as far as you can gauge, is perfect. This is your life and it is all calm.

The calm passes when you pick up the phone and hit ACCEPT, when you bring it to your ear, when you say "Hello?"

The storm arrives when the boy's voice at the other end asks, "Where the hell have you been, Jimmy?"

The boy's voice wakes up your brain in a big-bad way, like the biggest hit of coke, but you've done coke a few times and coke is not like this. Great Klieg lights flash on in the center of your head, banishing mental shadows you didn't know existed, showing the shapes of things too big and too numerous to take in at once, showing how little had actually been visible, how little you'd been working with. You can't even be confused yet.

"You need to come home, Jimmy," the boy says and your head is nodding and the Klieg lights begin to fade, and darkness flows in, and you make a strangled noise in your throat. The darkness takes your few memories—coming out to La-La Land, getting the coveted Universal writing internship, signing with Marty, *meeting Deanna—with it, but not before you see how flimsy they are, hurried sketches to a storyboard of a film trapped in pre-production hell. You did not live these times. They are not yours and, as such, you lose them.*

*Deanna calls your name, but you don't hear her. A hum fills your head, rising quickly, becoming a ringing and beginning to swallow you.*

*And you say, as the ringing reaches a deafening level, as the darkness descends over one final glimpse of the Pacific and Deanna's strained face, "I have to go home now."*

*Deanna opens her mouth, but the darkness falls.*

The ringing, like the aftermath of a gun going off next to someone's ear, dragged McIntyre back to consciousness slowly, receding as he became more aware. He looked without seeing through the windshield, at the intersection made surreal by the moving curtain of water on the glass.

And then the intersection flickered like a television with bad reception.

"Gah!" he yelled, dropping his smartphone and jamming the heels of his hands into his eyes. He pressed until neon colors flashed, then warily removed them.

The intersection—the puddles of rain in the street depressions, the drooping, dying trees along the corners, the low one-storey YMCA across the street—did not flicker. He took it all in and a name bubbled up from the back of his mind: Traumen, Ohio.

He was home and his mouth dried. "What the hell?"

He looked around the car—no key in the ignition, a tape-deck in the dash. The interior constricted around him. Heart thudding, he got out, grabbing the smartphone in his lap out of habit. The rain soaked him as he backed away from the car, a nondescript 1990s-era four-door he'd never seen before. It sat in the center of the intersection, paused in the middle of turning left

*(off of petroleum street and onto west front street)*

He shook his head. It felt crammed full of newspaper

*(like we used to put into our snowboots when they were too big)*

He turned the way he presumably had come and faced a girder bridge

*(the petroleum street bridge)*
with a raging gray river beneath.

He looked back at the intersection, but saw nothing there. No other cars in sight, not even parked along the curbs. No other people. The only movement the rain plunking into the street puddles. It was all so still, a movie set waiting for cast and crew to arrive.

A rising panic filled his head with static, closed his airways to a straw, pressed weight against his chest. Never mind Traumen, how he'd gotten here. Figure it out later. Just get away. Get away *now*.

McIntyre did, running from the car, running for the bridge. He'd run right down the center, run right out of town, run—

—right into what *looked like* nothing else, but what *felt* solid.

McIntyre bounced back hard onto his ass. He looked up unbelievingly, the panic momentarily pushed aside. The bridge was there, the grey sludgy water beneath, but this close, it was obviously a matte-painting landscape, something Alfred Whitlock would've done in *The Birds* or the 1982 remake of *The Thing*. This close, McIntyre could see the brush strokes.

"The fuck?" he muttered, approaching. He couldn't see the end of the painting and—Jesus, that was all an effect, anyway, something superimposed over a green-screen shot during post-production. The paintings, in reality, were small; they only *looked* large when the effect was complete.

"Like I'm in a movie," he said.

The rain went *through* what his mind insisted was a matte-painting and it made his eyes cross. He raised his hand, hesitated, then put his fingertips to it. A jolt like static electricity snapped at his hand and a nauscating sense of vertigo swirled through the center of his head, followed by a *ping* of pain, like a sharp jab to a pressure point. For the briefest moment, the sting of hospital cleaner—bleach insufficiently masked with perfume—slapped his nose, the chocolate-y-sweet taste of HoHos flooded his mouth, and he heard the opening piano chords to a song that sounded distressingly familiar.

McIntyre stumbled away, hugging his stomach, holding onto his balance through sheer will alone. The saturated tails of his ties slapped his chest as he retched. Nothing came up but thick spit.

*(of course not when was the last time I ate)*

He straightened, wiping his mouth with the back of his hand like a kid, and turned back to the town.

"How the hell did I get here?" he asked. He realized he still held his smartphone and a brief burst of hope rose—only to deflate when he turned the screen towards him to see it covered by a thin green-plastic stick-on coating, something the effects crews would put on electronics during shots so they could insert the CG

*(like a matte-painting)*

later.

McIntyre peeled the sheet off and tried to turn on the phone.

The screen remained black.

With a sinking feeling, he peeled off the rubber case and opened the battery-housing. Empty, of course.

*(a prop)*

*(like in a movie)*

*(this isn't some fucking movie)*

He threw the phone down and it bounced with a crack off the asphalt. He touched his pockets, but they were empty.

"How the fuck did I *get here?*" he yelled.

*(i'd been getting ready the phone rang and)*

And nothing.

*(where the hell have you been jimmy)*

And he was back in Traumen, Ohio.

*(you have to come home jimmy)*

But, looking through the intersection where

*(petroleum street)*

began its uphill climb, the roofs of post-World War II houses like a giant's shaky staircase, nothing came to him. Just names. Barely factoids. Things he might've pulled off Google Maps and a read-through of his IMDB profile: *James McIntyre, screenwriter to the adaptations of* Paper Towns *and* 13 Reasons Why *was born in Traumen, Ohio, and*—

—but there *was no* "and."

"Oh shit, I don't remember *any* of this." He squeezed his fists to his aching temples, as if pressure could force the memories out.

There was just this moment, this instant. Before now was La-La Land and Deanna and Marty, but even they lacked any depth in his mind. More names. Like half-assed amnesia.

*(hurried storyboards for a film trapped in pre-production hell)*

*(you did not live these times)*

And before that? Just black. More complete amnesia. He might've been created this moment, whole and breathing at the age of 31 with only the roughest sketch of backstory.

"*Fuck.*" McIntyre dropped his hands. The odd certainty stole over him that every end of the intersection was a matte-painting, that he was trapped here. It was ridiculous, but then so was the matte-painting over the Petroleum Street Bridge.

*(or waking up in a town i haven't thought of in years with no memory of getting there)*

Movement flickered out of the corner of his left eye and he turned to look down West Front Street.

A figure stood at the far end, where the street curved to the right.

Or, more accurately, a *boy* stood at the far end, his green shirt and blue pants the brightest thing in this gray area, so small that McIntyre could've blotted him out with his pinky-nail.

*(where the hell have you been jimmy)*

*(you need to come home jimmy)*

He started after the boy before he even knew he was moving. "*Don't you move!*" he yelled. The rain sapped the strength of his words. "*Don't!*"

It was like running in a nightmare, his effort to move faster unmatched by the distance he covered. He winced when he approached the edge of the intersection, his nerves anticipating the crunch of another impact.

But his shoes splashed through puddles and he kept going. He passed brick commercial buildings to the left, a blocky medieval structure that according to the sign was the Traumen Public Library to the right. The idea that this was a set, that this was all fake, persisted. These were all wooden constructions—hollow inside, something the art department and production design teams whipped together.

And then, crossing the intersection of West Front Street and Center Avenue, the world flickered again.

It wasn't like before, but instead like the curtain of the world had been tugged back to reveal...nothing.

Darkness.

McIntyre's foot came down, but his nerves pulling his weight back, certain he was going to plunge into darkness, and he went sprawling. He hit pavement—tumbling and rolling, the world completely solid again, shredding the elbows of his shirt, pain flaring up.

He raised his head, but the boy was gone.

"No he isn't," McIntyre muttered, getting to his feet, and running again, battling the pain in his joints. The boy wasn't gone. The boy had moved out of sight. McIntyre would find him. He had to. He had nothing else at the moment. That boy

*(where the hell have you been jimmy?)*

was the only straw he could cling to.

*(unless you're having a nervous breakdown unless you're strapped to some hospital bed)*

He reached the corner of State Street and West Front and zipped across—the idea of checking for traffic was a joke no one laughed at. He glanced and to his left was the Veteran's Memorial Bridge, wide and slightly curved, with no buildings or trees to hide the view of Traumen's east side and the gray, dead Ohio sky above. The name came to him with no fuss whatsoever, and he recognized the view before him, but none of it held any context beyond a minor tug at the back of his aching mind.

He ran in the opposite direction, up State Street. The boy hadn't gone over the bridge.

*(presuming there is a boy)*

*(there is a boy goddammit)*

*(how do you know and how do you know you're heading for him?)*

He passed a commercial building with a bar-and-grille called the Ven-Bar on the corner and something *ping*-ed in that dull throb in the center of his brain: he'd taken a date here once. They'd had the dining area to themselves, which was good because the girl had had the loudest *laugh*—

"You guys have fun tonight?"

The man's voice was a gunshot next to his ear. McIntyre jumped, bouncing off the wall of a PNC bank—and did he feel the building *give* a little bit?

*(never mind)*

He spun a full-circle, even as he knew he was alone.

*(nervous breakdown sounding any better?*

But he *knew* that voice; he *knew* it.

But he didn't know how; like Traumen, like its streets, it lacked context. Lacked depth. Errant puzzle pieces. How can you remember something, but not remember it at all?

And then, as if his brain was trying to taunt him—

*(i'm glad you're getting out jimmy it's what she would have wanted—)*

He smacked the heel of his hand against his temple, like his head was an old television on the fritz, even as his feet began moving of their own accord, turning him down 2$^{nd}$ Street. "Shut up, shut up, shut up," he said.

His shoe scraped against something metal.

He looked down to see a large tin sign reading BAKER'S MARKET—half-obscured by a faded Coldwell Banker sign. He wasn't terribly surprised at the now-very-loud *ping* of memory it brought.

*(a trail of mental breadcrumbs)*

*(to what?)*

McIntyre looked up at the little building the sign had fallen from. Through the front window, he could see the wooden counter to the right, Ohio Lotto scratch-offs sealed beneath old shellac; the squat ice-cream case catty-corner beyond, as if someone had made an apathetic attempt at removing it; the corkboard back wall, metal display hooks half-torn away; the comics rack lying in the center like a dead dog.

"I remember this," he whispered and the glass shimmered like an old-movie-flashback effect. The interior was now well-lit, the ice-cream case humming, the hooks stocked with single-serving chips and gummy candy, the comics rack standing and flush with an early-1990s run of Marvel Comics: *Uncanny X-Men, Spectacular Spider-Man, What If…?* All as he remembered it.

As he *remembered it.*

He reached out—

—and his fingertips touched not glass but dry, papery skin.

McIntyre screamed and staggered back, holding his hand by the wrist as if he'd burned it. He could *feel* that skin, and that familiar, loathsome—

—nothing.

His hand felt only cold and wet. Rain filled his palm.

Something in his head teetered, close to just falling over with a crash. His thoughts, half-formed, crashed and entangled together.

*(no memory)*

    *(a trail)*

        *(no backstory)*

            *(of mental breadcrumbs)*

                *(to what?)*

*(you're getting out jimmy it's what she would've wanted—)*

His will broke and he bounded down 2nd, his feet working on automatic and turning him up Imperial Avenue. Old Sears & Roebuck catalogue houses marched along the street, guarded by older curbside trees, their root structures upsetting the sidewalk plates.

McIntyre saw none of it. This was white-out time, broken-will time. A yellow stitch unzipped down his side, but he'd run forever, not even after the boy now, just to get away, get away, *get away*—

He stumbled and there was time for a single thought to zip across his head—*It's my day for falling down, all right*—before tired flesh met old cement. Pain bit into his elbows and knees like hot wires.

When he came to a stop, McIntyre opened his eyes and saw a pebble, a loose bit of the sidewalk, an inch from his nose. Extreme close-up.

He lifted his head and saw, diagonally across the street, home— the fact, like all the rest, came unbidden.

305 E. 3rd Street.

What little breath he'd accumulated escaped in a rush. "Shit."

It had been an old home when he'd lived there, stuck onto the corner of Imperial and E. 3rd, and the intervening years since he'd left—

*(when DID i leave?)*

—hadn't been kind. The second-floor windows sagged in their frames like dead eyes. Aluminum siding peeled from the house like flecks dead skin. The front lawn was an almost-neon-yellow.

The air between him and the house shimmered, like quicksilver in the distance, and the knuckle of pain in his head grew more pronounced. McIntyre sat up before it could get worse, before another one of those damned *pings*—

—and saw the boy, *the boy*, barely three feet away, standing beside a fire hydrant and *flickering*—not once, but continuously.

McIntyre recoiled, covering his eyes. The glimpse of the boy had only been for an instant, but it was like trying to look through thick glasses when you had perfect vision.

"Not very pleasant, is it?" the boy said and it was the voice from the phone, the voice that had called him back home.

*(where the hell have you been jimmy?)*

"What are you *doing* to me?" McIntyre yelled, driving his fists deeper into his aching eyes.

"What are you doing to yourself," the boy replied flatly and McIntyre heard something much older buried beneath that I'm-not-yet-in-puberty voice.

He grunted.

"Look at me, James," the boy said and the youthfulness was completely gone, replaced by something akin to gravel grinding together. *"Look at me, James McIntyre."*

Something outrageously hot slammed into the backs of his hands. He screamed, throwing them out, his shoes digging in and shoving him away. His back fetched up against what felt like a stone wall.

*(???what stone wall???)*

He opened his eyes and saw

*(jump cut just like a movie)*

they were no longer on the corner of E. 3rd and Imperial anymore. Old Victorian houses with manicured lawns marched away to their left and right.

*(bissell avenue holy christ i'm on bissell avenue)*

His eyes tracked the houses, the intersection a few yards away, each sight bringing with it another *ping*.

His eyes landed on the flickering boy standing at the curb. What made looking at him hurt wasn't the flickering itself—how many goddamn science fiction films featured a flickering hologram?—was that he *changed*. One flicker, the boy's hands were at his sides. Another, he held a heavy hardcover book with a red-and-white dustjacket. Still a third had the boy grasping a softball of creamy light.

The boy's green tee was long, with an embossing of the Tasmanian Devil. Faded jeans, worn along the back heels. Knock-off Jordans. His hair was a shaggy, dirty blond.

McIntyre locked onto the boy's eyes, recognizing them without any sort of *ping*. Didn't he see those same eyes—cradled in stress-wrinkles, it was true—every morning in the mirror?

James McIntyre was face-to-face with Jimmy McIntyre, eleven years old, still two years away from the growth spurt that would give him his adult height of six-two.

He had called *himself*—brought *himself* back home to Traumen, Ohio—or whatever this place actually was.

He started shaking. "Why are you doing this?" he asked and his voice was a croak.

"Why are you doing this to yourself, James," Jimmy said, his hands ever-changing.

McIntyre bared his teeth. "I'm not doing *anything*."

"You're fighting me," Jimmy said. "That's why it hurts. You *always* fight me."

"I'm not fighting *anything*."

"Oh?" Jimmy said and McIntyre didn't think so much mockery could fit into such a small word. "Why does your head hurt, James? Why do you keep having these *ping*s whenever a memory escapes from that goddamned graveyard you have in your head?"

McIntyre looked up, suddenly numb. "How—"

Jimmy turned so McIntyre could see across the street. "Do you remember waving to the hearse?"

It was another Victorian House, but a cloth canopy extended from the front porch to the sidewalk. An ornate wooden sign with

REINSEL FUNERAL HOME & CREMATORY dominated the extravagantly landscaped yard.

"What—" McIntyre started to say, and—

*(—you're walking past men in black suits who don't want to put their hands in their pockets but don't know what else to do with them. you hear soft and not-so-soft sobbing but you can't respond to it; you feel numb. you turn right, into the first viewing room and start down the row made by the folding chairs, all directing you to the front, where—)*

*(NO NO I CAN'T I WON'T THINK OF THAT)*

*(—you're on the curb, and you're waving at the hearse as it drives past, turning onto Harriot Avenue, but you don't know why and you stop. a man— who?—has a hand on your shoulder, as if you might bolt, but you won't. the only thing you're feeling is your itchy rented suit. the man behind you says, choked up, "christ, jimmy, i don't know if i can go up there, don't know if i can see—")*

—McIntyre's stomach revolted, lurching him onto his hands and knees and expelling bile onto the rain-slick sidewalk. The knot of pain in the center of his head felt like a cluster of diseased teeth.

"I saw what you did there," Jimmy said. "It's what you've *always* done. Whenever you get too close to it, you bolt."

McIntyre rested his feverish forehead against the blessedly cool concrete. "I don't understand. I don't know what any of this *is*."

"Of course you don't," Jimmy said and the contempt turned his words into little knives in McIntyre's ears. "But now we've run out of time. I can't be a ghost forever, any more than you can be a dream forever."

McIntyre raised his head. Oh, his head *ached*.

"I have hope for you," Jimmy said. "But maybe that's because you're our last chance."

He raised his hand and flicked it, like someone working out a kink in his wrist. The world around them *flattened*, became as two-dimensional as a matte-painting seen up close. The rain stopped.

Fissures zig-zagged down, top to bottom, like a child using black marker to draw lightning. The world blew apart in a thousand pieces, revealing a blackness that was the apotheosis of black. No up-down, left-right, north-south-east-west. The kind of black that ate light. It rang, beginning like the hum he'd heard back in California, becoming the ringing that had pulled him conscious here. It was constant and consistent.

Neither McIntyre nor Jimmy plummeted or stumbled, although McIntyre's entire body clenched, nerve-endings anticipating a drop. They stood on nothing McIntyre could feel, but they did not fall.

"This is the core of everything," Jimmy said and he no longer flickered. He held the softball of creamy light, its illumination throwing his face into stark relief, making him appear both ridiculously young and unbelievingly ancient. His voice had given up any pretense of sounding like a boy. "Our universe. I don't know how it is with other people, but this is ours. It was once filled with light, each one a different life, following its own path. Ever hear of quantum physics? Like that."

McIntyre felt warmth in his palms and looked down to see his own softball of creamy light, flashing and dimming, a bulb about to die. He couldn't feel *the object* that made the light, the tangible *thing* he was holding, couldn't let go or collapse his hands.

For the first time, the pain in his head took the backseat. "What happened?"

"What always happens. A car accident. A fire. A mugging gone bloody. A suicide. A heart attack. Sometimes our minds simply can't take what it's been shown and gives itself an embolism, which is so funny, given the circumstances, I want to shriek. The light dies and there's one less version of us."

He hunkered down in front of McIntyre. "It's because our universe is broken. Incorrect. Filled with false versions sparked by a single instance of understandable cowardice."

His eyes locked with McIntyre's. "James, what happened when you were eleven years old?"

A switch might've been thrown and the knot of pain in McIntyre's brain exploded, drenching his head in pure white-hot agony. He shrieked, and fell onto his light, hugging it to his stomach.

Above him, he heard Jimmy: "Stop this! We don't have *time* for this! *Stop fighting this!*"

McIntyre's lips peeled back from his teeth.

"I'm not... fighting... *anything.*"

"*Bullshit!*" Jimmy yelled. "Do you know how many versions I've had to go through to get to this moment, over and over again, just to go rocketing back when you can't take it? It takes me twenty *years* to reach you *each time*—and not just on *any* day during that twentieth year, but a *special day.* Do you remember?"

McIntyre opened his mouth, but—

*(—whiff of hospital cleaner—)*

—he shrieked again.

"We don't have any more chances, James!" Jimmy yelled. "What happens after we're gone, after this last chance is wasted? I don't know. *I've never been able to know.*"

He put a hand on McIntyre's shoulder. "I've run out of lifetimes," Jimmy said. "You're my last shot—*our* last shot—or it *all* ends. I brought you back to Traumen. *I made it like a movie, hoping you'd see how fake it was.* I pulled you off the soundstage and *brought you here*, to the core. I am out of options and out of time. *You need to remember.*"

McIntyre hugged his ball of dying light. "But I don't... remember ... *anything.*"

Jimmy's hand left his shoulder.

"James," he said, softly. "Look at me."

He did, gingerly, and Jimmy's face was inches away. Liquid arcs from their respective lights stretched towards one another.

"You don't have that luxury, anymore," Jimmy said, and shoved his light into McIntyre's.

The world exploded white, swatting the blackness away, and McIntyre—

*—is sitting in that goddamn orange vinyl chair, and you're holding your mother's hand as she lies comatose in the hospital bed.*

*You are Jimmy McIntyre. It is the evening of November 21, 1996, and you have to watch your mother die.*

*(NO NO NO NO YOU CAN'T MAKE ME YOU CAN'T MAKE ME SEE THIS)*

*But you can't shake yourself free. This is what you've hidden from yourself for twenty years, what you've buried, what you've built multiple lifetimes to avoid. The moment that separates you from the boy.*

*Oh god, the weight is crushing. Sitting there, holding your mother's hand, your fingertips over the prominent bones, the papery skin, it hurts to draw a breath. Your throat is narrowed to a straw. Your eyes boil, but you do not cry. You've promised yourself you would not cry. To cry out, to show the grief, would make it true. Your mother is dying.*

*Sitting there, marveling how the woman who was as close to god as a small boy could understand could make such a small impression under the sheets, you hold her hand, and she seems to hold yours back and you think of crossing busy streets. An I-will-protect-you-grip. An I-am-not-letting-go grip.*

*But you want to scream as the doctor pulls the breathing apparatus from her lower face, showing the damage that the hemorrhagic stroke, and the subsequent two-week coma, has wrought. Her skin looks waxy and taut under the fluorescent bar of light above her bed, rendering her eyes deep purple eye sockets. Her hair, already thin, looks like a tangle of old spider webs.*

*Her mouth hangs slightly open and you think—as much as you can think—she would've hated to look slack-jawed like that. The urge to shriek grows, but it doesn't escape. It burns, a hot molten core in your heart.*

*Her eyes half-open, giving her a doped-look, and you straighten. Your grip on her hand tightens. Her eyes are black, but they see you, and, if she's seeing you, that must mean it's all right, right? Turning everything off doesn't mean it's over, right? You've seen episodes of E.R. Sometimes the patient just needs a jumpstart.*

*You swallow and your throat clicks. A hand grips your shoulder, the way it will at the funeral.*

(STOP THIS NOW I CAN'T SEE THIS I WON'T)

*You think her head turns, but it really doesn't—her chest has just stopped moving. She's still looking at you, but her eyes have become the eyes of a taxidermy product, glassy, molded to convey an emotion.*

*But the irrational hope doesn't die; you still have the hand, holding yours, gripping yours, and that means she's still there, right? She still knows you're there, right? It can't be too late if she can still hold you. Right?*

*"She's holding my hand," you say.*

*The owner of the hand on your shoulder squeezes in a way that's supposed to be comforting and isn't. "It's muscle memory, Jimmy," the owner says, his voice thick.* "*Her hand muscles are responding to the pressure of your hand.*"

*The words fall like bell tolls on your ears. Your head burns, your chest flattens, yours eyes bulge and scald and the scream is just behind your lips, dying to be let out, and you bear down mentally:* I will not do this, I will *not*, I *will not*—You can't make this real. *Even now, with the truth in front of you, you can't let out that which makes this* real.

*And then the burning . . . cools. The scream retreats. The weight in your chest lessens. It all . . . dwindles, until you feel almost nothing at all.*

*You're still holding your mother's hand, but the grip is a lie, just like her intense I'm-seeing-you gaze, and the loose skin—the dry skin, the thin skin—is all you can feel.*

"*I'm sorry, Jimmy,*" *the man says and his voice is all snot and closed-throats, full of an emotion that you suddenly can't feel. It is at this moment you and the boy separate, the boy stuck in his hellish frozen instant and you going on with your pale half-lives.*

*And, inside, the you remembering all this screams and screams and screams, until the light comes again, until you're yanked and—*

—he lay on his side, cradling his ball of light, now gray and dim. Jimmy stood in front of him.

"Pain is a bridge," the boy said. "Who you are on one end is not who you are on the other. You experience the pain and you cross and it changes you. But, with us, somehow, it *didn't*. I got stuck on one end and you—you *all* . . . jumped. You didn't feel any pain, but you weren't alive the way you should be."

He knelt beside McIntyre. "You need to accept it, James. You need—"

McIntyre couldn't breathe; his nose was clogged, his lungs filled to capacity. The pain was gone from his head, replaced with a hot buzzing that reminded him of cicadas. All he could see was his mother's dead eyes, all he could hear was the sound of her *not* breathing, all he could feel was the thin skin of her hand—

—and he shrieked.

It boiled up from his core, rolling up and out and into the ringing nothing. Just a great animal bellow of pain and grief, rolled over and over with interest, not just for twenty years, or twenty times twenty years, but for all of them. Every half-life. Every pallid dream, every false continuation of the man known as James McIntyre. His throat shredded. Every muscle, every nerve, every cell, cried out into the darkness, reaching higher and higher, dissembling the pieces until nothing was left.

And then the scream built McIntyre back up again even as it dwindled to a rattle, assembling his form, cell by cell, imbued not with the falseness of his lives, but the passage of the pain—even as he knew it wasn't finished yet. *He* wasn't finished yet.

And then, finally, silence.

And James McIntyre opened his eyes.

McIntyre held his dying ball of light between him and the boy. They watched it ebb and flow, ebb and flow, each fluctuation fainter, until only darkness remained and McIntyre's hands held nothing at all.

He stood and the boy, a silhouette limned with the faintest etching of light, looked up at him.

"The end," he said.

"Not yet," the boy said. "One final step." He saw the boy's silhouette turn his head and McIntyre followed his gaze.

Far away, a single light burned.

The final star was the boy's. The true star, the true core.

"Are you ready?" Jimmy McIntyre, both eleven years old and impossibly ancient, a ghost of an unlived life, asked.

"Yes," James McIntyre, both thirty-one years old and not alive at all, replied.

The boy offered his hand and the false-man took it.

And, together, they walked towards the light.

## Coda:

*The star explodes in rays of creamy light, with the core becoming the horizon.*

*Sound—the distant beep of pagers, the almost syncopated* deet *of many machines doing many jobs, the opening piano chords of a Top 40 hit song.*

*Smell—cafeteria food and Latex and hospital cleaner. The scent of vanilla perfume that the false man will always associate with middle school girls and the boy will have no association for whatsoever.*

*Finally, sight—the rays of light becoming the angles of the hallway, top-bottom-left-right, with color filling in the gaps: speckled white for the tile floor, beige for the walls. Wide doorways swim into existence, wheelchairs standing guard.*

*At the end of the hallway, just before it opens into the wide central area of a nurse's station, a small boy sits in a wheelchair, holding a book.*

*The false-man sees with no surprise whatsoever the boy sitting is the exact twin of the boy whose hand he is holding. They approach. The boy's hunched over his book—*Insomnia *by Stephen King, the false man sees—but isn't reading. He glares at the red-and-white dustjacket.*

*The boy holding his hand lets go and walks over to his twin.*

*"One final step," he says again and the expression on his face is one of weariness. "Are you ready?"*

*"Are you?"*

*Instead of answering, the boy touches the exposed back of his twin's neck. There's a soft flash of creamy-white and his hand sinks into the other boy.*

*He sits down where his twin sits, becoming more intangible with each movement. Before they connect, the boy offers the man a single final look that the man has no problem discerning.*

Don't let us down, *it says.*

*And then the boy is gone with another soft flash of creamy light and it's just this ghost and the boy in the wheelchair. Behind him, the Counting Crows goes into its first chorus of "A Long December."*

*The man reaches out, hesitates, then touches the back of the boy's neck. Immediately, the aftertaste of Ho-Hos fills his mouth. Instantly, weight gets added to his chest.*

*His hand sinks into the boy's neck with more creamy-white light and he feels pulled, drawn in. He almost yanks his hand back, but the boy's last glance at him*—don't let us down—*keeps him going.*

*He turns himself around and sinks into the boy, that pulling sensation intensifying. Memories, twenty years' worth, whistle through the remaining second of his half-life, but, again, they recall nothing for him. They aren't his.*

*Before he full submerges, he looks back one last time, where he and the boy had come from, but sees only darkness, held back by the light.*

*An apt metaphor, he thinks, and disappears.*

Jimmy blinks as disorientation sweeps through him. He has the odd feeling of both sitting down and getting up. The nerves in his legs twinge, confused.

"Stupid," he mutters, rubbing his eyes, but he freezes. To anyone looking, he would be some kid wiping his eyes because he's crying, because he's mourning, because he's about to become a dumb fucking orphan and all he can fucking do about it is cry. They'd see him and be so *full* of sympathy, as if that could do anything about his fucking—

*(don't say it don't say it)*

—dying mother.

He grinds his teeth until his jaw aches and drops his hands. No one would see him cry. He would *not* cry. He would *not* give in.

But, Jesus Christ, who would've thought this would hurt so much? The *weight* he feels on his chest. He's had the air knocked out of him a few times, but this is nothing compared to that; it feels, instead, like he's clamped into one of those table-vices in shop class and some malicious bastard is turning it and turning it.

His vision shimmers as his eyes grow hot.

"Jimmy," a man says from behind him.

He looks up and John is standing there, his tie loosened, the bags under his eyes making the rest of his face paler. He's ten years Jimmy's senior but, right now, he seems twenty or thirty.

"They're turning her off," John says and his voice cracks on the last word. His eyes are cherry-red-rimmed. "You need to say goodbye."

Jimmy nods. It feels like his throat is closing.

He picks up his book and stands on legs made of Silly Putty.

John steps aside, allowing Jimmy to enter first. "Are you going to be okay?"

*HOW CAN YOU EVEN FUCKING ASK THAT?* he wants to scream, shriek, bellow, but he doesn't. He won't. He won't even look at John. It's stupid, but a part of him believes with a childish fierceness that if he doesn't give in, she won't go. She'll have to stay. If he stares at John's face for too long, thought, he won't be able to hold it back. Can't he see the truth on his brother's face?

He steps into the doorway and stops.

The room is dark except for the single shaded fluorescent bar. A trio of machines stand to one side, science-fiction doctors brooding on their failure. The human doctor, so unimportant that Jimmy immediately forgets him, stands back a respectful distance.

Finally, Jimmy looks at his mother.

Something shifts within and the strangest sense of *déjà vu* hits him. He thinks two thoughts, equally nonsensical and impossible, simultaneously: *I've been here before* and *I can't go through this again!*

He reaches out and grasps the doorway, leaning like a drunk. He senses John behind him, but Jimmy sees only their mother, lying there, *dwindling* there. His throat hurts, as if he's already been screaming. That sense of *déjà vu* gets stronger, becoming an odd, horrible form of vertigo.

*I've been here before*, he thinks, but on some level doesn't think it's his voice at all.

*I have to live this again*, he thinks and his throat burns, his chest closes. He blinks and his eyes are wet.

He wants to call out to her, something that would appear dramatic but couldn't match the wrench of emotion twisting in his chest, but he can't, can't even open his mouth. The air is locked in his throat.

Behind him, John says, "Jimmy—"

He puts a hand on Jimmy's shoulder and, this time, it's comforting. He feels something give inside, and the weight...shifts.

Jimmy McIntyre, eleven years old and thirty-one years old and impossibly ancient all at the same time, finally screams, finally lets it out, finally makes it true, and, finally, begins to live.

# FALLEN FACES
# BY THE WAYSIDE

## GARY A. BRAUNBECK

"Thou com'st in such a questionable shape
That I will speak to thee..."
– Shakespeare, *Hamlet*; Act 1, Scene 4

It wasn't the best set he'd ever done, but when Paul Cormier left the stage of *The Funny Bone* that Wednesday (read: Amateur) night, it was to applause that, if not exactly thunderous, was far more than he expected; several members of the audience were still laughing at the closing gag, and a few of them even loudly repeated the punchline as he made his way through the rows of tables toward the bar. He took his usual seat at the end, ordered a rum and Coke, and was about to ask the bartender if there was any fresh popcorn when Jim Woodward, the manager, came up behind him and put a hand on Paul's shoulder.

"Question: how long have I been inviting you to come back here on Amateur Night?"

Paul shrugged. "Every other week for about two years, I guess."

"You guess. Wow. Powers of instant recall that well-honed humble such mere mortals as myself."

"Does everything you say sound like you wrote it down ahead of time and memorized it?"

Woodward signaled the bartender to bring him his usual, and

then took the seat next to Paul. "As a matter of fact, yes, but we're not here to discuss my dreadful personality problems. You got a manger yet?"

"Three guesses."

"What I figured." He took a sip of his drink, then waited a few moments for dramatic effect. "Carmen Borgia is upstairs in my office. He wants to see you."

Paul could barely find his voice. "Y-you mean *now*?"

"You ought to see your expression—Bo-Bo the Dog-Faced Boy looked more intelligent. *Yes*, now. For some reason that puzzles even as resplendent a personality as mine, the Borgia Agency is interested in managing your shaggy WASP ass. You interested?"

"Three guesses."

"My God, the snappy repartee that must crackle throughout your home." He leaned closer and lowered his voice. "Here's the thing: you know I like you, and I like your act, but what's more important, the *audiences* like you, else I wouldn't keep inviting you back. Are you paying attention? This next part's important and there may be a quiz later. There's going to be an announcement tomorrow. Jay Leno's going to be appearing here three weeks from this Friday, it's a charity thing. You know how Leno likes to discover new talent, right? Well, when Carmen set this up, Leno asked to see tapes of six amateur comics from the area. One of the tapes was yours, and Leno was blown away by your impressions—I sent the tape where you started with Nixon singing "If You Could Read My Mind" and closed with Richard Pryor and Jesse Helms doing *In the Heat of the Night* instead of Portier and Steiger. Remember how you killed that night? Leno picked you—I figured he would. Now, the thing is, I can't offer you a paying gig unless you've got management. The owner and the union tend to frown upon doing it otherwise, go fig.

"All you have to do is go up to my office, shake Borgia's hand, and try not to pass gas; your days as home computer service technician will then be numbered."

"Hey, I got your system upgraded in less than a day—by the way, thanks for specifically requesting me. My boss remembers things like that."

"No prob. You know your stuff."

"It pays the bills...*and* I like it."

Woodward took Paul's drink out of his hand and pulled him to his feet. "My office, go. One foot in front of the other, then repeat until you either walk into a wall or are stopped by a small, well-dressed Italian."

Paul was starting to make his way toward the private stairway when Woodward said: "Hey, Paul."

"Yeah?"

"I know you were a little off tonight. Don't worry about it, okay? Tell you the truth, I didn't expect you'd even show, let alone be as good as you were...considering that tomorrow would have been your sister's birthday."

Paul was genuinely touched that Woodward remembered. "Thanks, man."

"Why are you still here?"

"You—"

Woodward dismissed him with a wave of his beefy hand. "Excuses, excuses. I'm surrounded by indifference. No wonder I weep alone nights. Should've been a cesspool cleaner like my mother wanted."

Paul did not so much walk as shamble up to Woodward's off-ice, convinced that this was all some set-up for an immense practical joke. To Paul's mind, the universe was a model of chaos, not nearly as benign as people would have you believe, and even if it were, *he* never had this kind of luck, and so at once began looking over his shoulder for whatever it was that would soon catch up with him and sink its teeth into the soft parts of what little optimism he was still able to affect.

Not the most beneficial state of mind to be in when you were about to meet the biggest talent agent in the Midwest.

He surprised himself by not pausing at the office door; instead, he walked right inside and up to Borgia.

"Five minutes," said Borgia, looking at his watch. "Took you five minutes to get up here. Most comics would've burned skidmarks in the carpeting if they were told that—oh, wait. Did you hear that?"

"Hear what?"

Borgia began pacing. "The sound of my death getting thirty seconds closer. Sit. Stand. Squat. Dance the hoochie-koo for all I care. Mind if I smoke?"

"No."

"Damn. And I quit two years ago. Never mind." Then he grinned. Carmen Borgia was a short, intense, sinewy man with bright hazel eyes and the energy of a dozen five-year-old children who'd fed on nothing but pure sugar since birth. If he hadn't been a talent agent, Paul figured Borgia would have been the actor who had the career Joe Pesci should have had.

"Woodward tell you all about it?"

"Yes, sir."

Borgia stopped his pacing. "Did I just hear the 'S'-word issue from your mouth? Please tell me that I did not. The 'S'-word irks me—and when was the last time you heard someone properly use the word 'irk?'"

Paul blinked. "You know, if I left now it would be like I never came into the room."

"That supposed to be funny?"

"Actually, I was going for a Robert-Ryan-in-*The Wild Bunch*-type of tragic-irony thing."

"Great movie. So-so delivery on your part." Borgia walked up to Paul and held out his hand. "You're very talented, you're very funny, and I would like to represent you. I also have a couple of computers in my home that need tending to, but we can discuss that later. Very hush-hush, under-the-table type irony, since my wife and children think I know everything about everything."

"Great delivery. So-so continuity." He shook Borgia's hand. "I am honored that you want to represent me, and I—"

"Wazzy-wazzy-woo-woo, yeah, great, fine, you're now a client of the Borgia Agency. Here." He pulled a thick envelope from his jacket pocket and slapped it into Paul's hand.

"What's this?"

Borgia sighed. "Do you see how much time you just wasted there? You could've just opened the damn thing and looked inside and we could already be on to a new subject. You think I'm gonna live forever?"

Paul smiled nervously and looked inside the unsealed envelope. "What the—? Oh. My. God."

"Don't bother counting it," said Borgia. "Five thousand, cash. Yours to keep—providing you sign something."

"A representation agreement."

"No. You did that when you shook my hand." Borgia waved Paul over to Woodward's desk. Everything had been cleared from the center except for a dark blue folder; Borgia opened it and removed one sheet of official-looking stationary. "Have you ever heard of Scylla Enterprises, Paul?"

"Um...yes."

"*Really?* You've really heard of them?"

"About six seconds ago, actually."

"Good. You had me worried. The Borgia Agency—and you may repeat this to your wife but to no one else—is a division of Scylla Enterprises. What I have here is a confidentiality agreement. Sign this, and you not only get to keep the five thousand, but that will be your weekly salary until such time as I choose to raise it."

"I don't ... *five thousand?* ... I mean—what about your ... commission and—?"

"I find complete sentences can be of great benefit to entertainers. My commission is taken care of, don't worry that too-big-for-your-body head. By the way, that whole George-Harrison-hair thing's got to go." He offered a pen. "Read it first. If you choose *not* to sign, you keep half of the cash and the agency still represents you—you'll just be assigned to one of my other agents. Sign it, and I handle you personally. You know my rep. I *never* personally handle more than ten clients at the same time, and those I do are either already very big or about to be."

"I know, believe me."

Paul took the pen and began to sign the confidentiality agreement when Borgia gripped his wrist. "*Read* it, Paul. It's short and flensed of any convoluted legalese."

There was a seriousness in Borgia's tone that invited no further questions.

Paul pulled the pen away and read the agreement.

He reached the end of the last paragraph and felt his mouth go dry. "Oh, man."

"It's not nearly as ominous as it sounds."

"What do you mean by 'trial period?'"

"First of all, *I* don't mean anything by it, Scylla Enterprises does; second, the trial lasts exactly six hours, starting the moment you walk into the offices; and third...I honestly can't tell you."

"You don't know?"

"Oh, I know, I just can't tell you. We can talk about it after, but until then I'm Shultz from *Hogan's Heroes*: I know nut-ing."

Paul read the agreement again. "So at the end of the trial period, I'll be offered an official contract with *Scylla*—"

"—and by default, my agency."

"If I choose not to sign it, I'll be given ten thousand dollars for my time and sent on my way, providing I never tell anyone about what happened."

Borgia nodded. "And if you do sign it, you're in Scylla's employ for the rest of your life."

"Oh, man..."

"You said that already. Gotta keep the material fresh."

Paul stared at the agreement and felt a thin line of perspiration form on his upper lip. What a time to get a case of flop-sweat.

"Paul?"

"Yes, sir?"

"There's the 'S'-word again. Irksome, very irksome."

"Sorry."

Borgia leaned against the end of the desk. "Tell me about your sister."

At nine-forty the next morning, Paul drove up to the building which housed the local offices of Scylla Enterprises: even though it was right smack in the middle of downtown, there was a parking space directly in front and the meter had nearly two hours left.

He pulled in with no difficulties, killed the engine but left the radio on, then turned to his wife and said: "I'm doomed, you know that?"

"Of course you are," said Kim. "But keep in mind that your sole purpose in life might be to serve as a warning to others."

He blinked. "Is that supposed to make me feel better?"

Kim shrugged. "No—but I'm guessing that you don't *want* to feel better right now, you prefer to feel anxious, insufficient, foolish, and inept. It's part of your charm." This said with not nearly as much humor as Paul would have preferred.

He looked at the glassy, monolithic building and shook his head. "What the hell do they want with me, anyway?"

"I'm guessing they might drop a couple of hints during the interview, if you ever actually go inside."

He wiped some perspiration from his forehead, then checked his watch.

At that moment, the classic rock station he and Kim had been listening to began to play Mountain's "Theme From An Imaginary Western."

Paul felt his chest grow tight. He reached down and turned up the volume. "God Almighty." He felt the familiar tightness in the back of his throat and the burning behind his eyes.

Kim leaned over and put her hand on the back of his neck. "Hey, c'mon...maybe this is a good sign."

He looked at his wife as the first tears crept toward the corner of his eyes, dangled there for a moment, and dripped down onto the sleeve of his jacket. "I never really liked this song all that much, you know? I mean, I always preferred 'Mississippi Queen' or 'Nantucket Sleighride,' but Beth always liked this one. Anytime Mom or Dad would go off and start pounding one of us, she'd always come to my room later and ask me if I wanted to listen to records, and she always played this one. I asked her why once, and she said: 'it's sad but it makes it sound okay to be sad.' The more I listened to it with her, the more I came to love it. It's genuinely wistful.

"Her favorite line in the song was that one about fallen faces by the wayside looking as if they might have known. She said she sometimes dreamed about fallen faces, that they were happy and resting and not afraid anymore. I always wanted to tell her that the fallen faces were actually the dead bodies of Settlers who didn't make it, who died along the way, and what they might have known was the new world that they never reached, the land and life that was waiting for those Settlers who *did* make it ... but it seemed mean to ruin that for her. She was only six years old and so much had been ruined for her already."

Kim scooted closer to him. "Shh, Paul, c'mon, baby, don't do this to yourself."

"I should've been there, Kim. I mean, I *thought* Mom and Dad had gotten better, that it'd be all right to take that camp counselor job. It was just for a month, but everything seemed to be better."

They did not speak for a moment, only sat listening to the song reach its refrain.

"That's bullshit," Paul whispered. "The truth was, I couldn't look at it anymore, I couldn't stand being in that fucking house with them, walking on eggshells, never knowing when one of them might go off. I figured I might earn enough money to buy a couple of bus or plane tickets so Beth and I could take off, go out to Kansas and stay with Grandma—at least, that's what I always told myself. Especially later, after—"

"Just stop it. Stop it right now."

He pointed at the radio. "In the last twelve hours, two people have said something to me about Beth—and one of them had never met me until last night, and now I'm sitting here with you on what would have been Beth's sixteenth birthday, and I'm waiting to go in there and the radio starts playing *this*, of all songs. *No one* plays this goddamn thing, Kim. No one."

"Then look at it as a sign. Maybe it's Beth's way of telling you that you don't have to keep yourself on the hook anymore, that she doesn't blame you. It's time to just pay the fine and go home."

Paul wiped his eyes and blew his nose. "You picked one helluva time to get mystical on me."

"It's just a song, and their playing it now is just a coincidence, that's all. It's nothing to get freaked about."

The song finished, then the announcer's voice came on: "That one goes out to Elizabeth Cormier on her sixteenth birthday."

Paul looked at Kim, who was staring at the radio.

"Okay, now I'm a little freaked," she said.

"What the hell is going on?"

Before Kim could say anything to him, a uniformed security guard knocked on the driver's side window. Both Paul and Kim jumped. Paul snapped off the radio as if he were squashing a bug, took a deep breath, and rolled down the window. "Is there something wrong?"

"Not at all, Mr. Cormier," said the security guard. "I'm here to escort you up to the offices." The guard leaned down and smiled in at Kim. "Good morning, Mrs. Cormier. Your husband will be here until four this afternoon. If you'll come back then, this same space will be waiting for you."

Kim laughed nervously. "You're kidding?"

"No, ma'am," replied the guard, his smile seemingly frozen in place. "We're to give both Mr. Cormier and yourself the red carpet treatment today. The space'll be here."

Not waiting for a response, he opened the door and stepped back so Paul could get out.

"Good luck, honey," said Kim, and then kissed Paul. "Everything'll be all right. You'll be dazzling."

"Wrong reading," he replied, trying to sound cheerful.

"Okay, then: Don't fuck it up, we could use the money."

"There's my girl." He kissed her, then climbed out of the car and followed the security officer up the stone steps and over to a glass elevator that ran up the outside of the building.

"The Scylla offices aren't accessible to the public from inside, Mr. Cormier."

"Do all Scylla employees have to use this same elevator?"

"No, sir, only escorted visitors. There's a block of private elevators inside, but since I'm Escort Security I don't have clearance to use them."

Paul leaned against the inside railing in the elevator, and as the doors slide closed, it began a surprisingly rapid ascent. "So they're big on security, huh?"

His smile unchanging, the security guard replied, "*Very* big on it." He reached inside one of his pockets and removed a laminated I.D. card attached to a ribbon of thick blue thread which he offered to Paul. "Scylla Enterprises took the liberty of making this temporary I.D. for you, Mr. Cormier. Please hang it around your neck and make sure that your photo is visible at all times."

"Where'd you get my picture?"

"From the DMV's computers." He offered no further information. "Please put it on now, sir, we're almost at the main Scylla floor."

Paul hung the I.D. around his neck, making sure his photo faced forward.

The elevator stopped, the doors opened, and one of the most beautiful women Paul had ever seen was standing right outside waiting, flanked on either side by two other security guards.

"Mr. Cormier," she said, offering her hand. "Welcome to Scylla Enterprises. My name is Cathy Brown, I'm Mr. Smyth's assistant. Would you follow me, please?"

Flanked on either side by Ms. Brown's personal goon squad, Paul followed her through a maze of corridors and offices and two doors which required her to slide not one, not two, but three security cards through a small electronic reading device installed next to each one.

And you couldn't walk three yards without encountering a security camera peering down at you.

Paul, now anxious as hell, let out a small laugh.

Without turning back to look at him, Ms. Brown said, "Something funny, Mr. Cormier?"

"I didn't mean to offend you."

"No offense at all, Paul—may I call you Paul? I was just curious."

Giving a quick glance to each security guard, Paul cleared his throat. "Well, I couldn't help but notice the security measures taken here. When I was in college, I went on a tour of the Pentagon—at least, the areas where the public is allowed. *They* didn't have this much security."

"Ah. Well, actually, the Pentagon does, but they're not quite so overt with most of it. Put enough cameras and enough electronically locked doors in enough fortuitous locations, and people tend to be on their best behavior."

Paul exhaled, but didn't feel relieved. "So you don't have quite as much security as it seems?"

"No. We have much more." They paused at a set of large oak doors with bright brass doorknobs. Ms. Brown turned toward him and smiled. "In fact, Paul, this particular floor has just slightly more security than the inside of the West Wing of the White House."

"You're kidding?"

"This is Scylla Enterprises, Paul. We may joke about a lot of things, but security is not one of them." Her smiled grew wider as she opened one of the great doors. "Come with me."

Paul followed her, but the two security guards remained in the corridor.

As soon as they were inside the next room—what Paul assumed was the reception area—a large, dangerous-looking man with a buzz-cut and hands so big a ten-year-old could comfortably sit in one, came up to Paul and said, "Please raise your arms."

Paul did so. BuzzCut ran over his body with a hand-held metal detector.

"He's clean," said BuzzCut, taking two steps back and folding his hands in front of him.

Paul looked at his watch. "Why didn't…why didn't it go off? I mean, there's my watch, there's the change in my pockets, my belt buckle…I've got a pin in my left hand from where I broke it skiing when I was twenty-one—"

Ms. Brown raised one of her hands, silencing him. "The detector that he used is designed to sound only if it recognizes certain alloys."

"You mean like in a gun?"

"I mean like in a gun, or certain types of detonation devices."

"What if I had one of those all-plastic guns—what're they called, Glocks?"

"Yes, they are. You were x-rayed for any plastic or plastique while you rode up in the elevator." She gestured toward a large, ornate desk—assumedly hers—and the two even larger oak doors beyond it. "Mr. Smyth's background checks are exceptionally thorough. If for some reason, you had a condition which made x-rays detrimental to your well-being, you would have been brought in another way and patted down.

"Before we get too far off the track, Paul, take my word for this: there is absolutely, positively, beyond any doubt *no way* a weapon can be smuggled into these offices ... and we're one of only nine places in this country where that holds true." She walked over to her desk and pressed a button. "He's here, sir."

"Ten A.M. on the nose," replied a voice. "Were we right, did he pull up in front twenty minutes early?"

"That he did, sir."

"Excellent. I'm guessing right now he's got one more question to ask you. Answer it for him and then send him in."

Ms. Brown looked up at him and waited.

Like an actor who'd missed his cue during a run-through, Paul started, blinked, and said, "Oh, yeah, right—how did he know I'd get here twenty minutes early?"

"Because our studies have shown that that's your pattern when you have any sort of an appointment. You'd rather be there forty minutes early than one minute late. Your average time of arrival is twenty minutes prior to your appointments."

"*How do you know that?*"

"Mr. Smyth will answer that for you, Paul." She pressed a button, a buzzer sounded, and the two massive doors swung open.

Paul waited a few more seconds, then shrugged and walked into the office beyond. As soon as he was inside, the buzzer sounded again and the doors closed. He wondered if they were locked.

Several things registered with him simultaneously; the small kitchenette, the large leather sofa, the large desk where two-engine airplanes probably landed on a daily basis, the washroom off to the left, three smaller doors which he assumed led into closets or storage areas, a wet bar, and very plush carpeting. No surprises there.

The surprises came when you looked beyond the expected executive amenities and saw the decor; framed movie posters (the one for *The Wild Bunch*, autographed by all the cast members as well as Sam Peckinpah himself, caused him to actually gasp), a dart board, bookshelves filled with various toys and dolls still in their shrink-wrapped boxes, a lava lamp collection, an expensive stereo system which currently played The Band's "The Weight," and countless knickknacks.

"Paul," came a voice from inside the washroom. "Have a seat. Pour yourself a drink. Wait, scratch that, reverse the order. There's a good fellow."

Paul remained standing.

A few moments later, Mr. Smyth emerged from the washroom.

Paul had frequently heard terms like "presence" and "charisma" applied to various actors, politicians, and performers, and had always thought that they were over- as well as ill-used. He himself had never met anyone who could mesmerize simply by walking into a room ... until now.

Smyth was of average height, a bit on the thin side, and dressed in a surprisingly casual manner for a man who ran such a powerful company; his hair was thick, wavy, fashionably unkempt, and a tad longer than you'd expect to see in the corporate world, and his left eye was covered by a large black patch. These details in themselves weren't enough to take anyone's breath away, least of all Paul's, but Smyth carried himself in such a way, and emanated such confidence and power, that even the most jaded person would stop and stare at him as if his approval were the most important thing in the world.

*Spellbinding*, thought Paul. *That's the word.*

Smyth stopped, looked at Paul, and grinned. "You should see your expression—Bo-Bo the Dog-Faced Boy looked more intelligent."

"Jim Woodward said the exact same thing to me last night."

"I know," replied Smyth. "It's a great line, so I stole it. But don't tell him."

"We're not that close."

"Bullshit—but good delivery."

"Carmen Borgia gave me a bunch of grief on my delivery."

"That a fact?" Smyth moved to his desk and sat down, then picked up a folder and opened it.

*Jesus; even doing that, he's hypnotic.*

"You planning on taking a seat or would you prefer to buy real estate and build?"

Paul took a seat.

Smyth finished looking through the folder, at one point removing the confidentiality agreement Paul had signed and asking him to verify that it was signature, then closed the folder, tossed it onto the desk, sat back, and said: "Ever visit your dad in the slammer?"

Something inside Paul's stomach pulled a knife from its pocket and began whittling away at the tissue. "Wh-what?"

"You heard me."

"How the hell do you know about—"

Smyth sighed impatiently, then said: "Your mom was acquitted of complicity in your sister's death and committed suicide five months later. You were living with one of your aunts by then. Your dad was found guilty of second-degree murder and is currently serving his time in the state pen. Have you ever visited him there?"

Paul swallowed. Once. Very loudly. "No. And I never will. The fucker can rot in there for all I give a shit."

Smyth nodded. "An honest one. Points in your favor."

Paul reached into his jacket pocket and took out a cigarette. He almost never smoked but always kept a pack in his pocket for times when he was either severely anxious or dangerously angry. Right now he was a lot of both. He lit up, inhaled, then released the smoke through his nostrils.

"What if I were to tell you this is a non-smoking building?" said Smyth.

"I'd tell you I don't care."

"You're upset. I can tell. You're breathing fire."

"Very funny."

"Not really, but I try."

"How do you know all of this? I mean, I can see how your background check would turn up all the information about my parents and my sister—"

"—did you enjoy the dedication on the radio? I thought you might like it."

"Yeah. It was a rockin' good time. How could you possibly know that my 'average' arrival time for appointments was twenty minutes early?"

"We've been watching you."

Something cold slid a slow path down Paul's spine. He pulled in another drag. "You've been having me tailed?"

"*Tailed?* Wow. Very forties-tough-guy, very *noir*-ish, very Raymond Chandler. Gave me chills. See my goosebumps? Never mind. Yes. We've been 'tailing' you for almost eighteen months."

Paul stared at him, unblinking. "They're the same," he said, more to himself than Smyth.

Smyth sat up a little straighter, seemingly taken aback but something he hadn't been expecting. "I beg your—"

"Last night when I was talking with Borgia, something about the way he spoke kept ringing bells in my head but I couldn't figure out what it was. Now I know. Jim Woodward, him, and now you. All three of you speak the same way."

Smyth shrugged. "We're businessmen, on-the-go guys. Gotta be quick on our feet, quick in our speech; helps us to look like we're five steps ahead of everyone. In fact—"

"That's not it," snapped Paul. "It's not that your speech shares some similarities—it's almost exactly the same, all three of you. The inflections, the pauses, the cadences and turns of the phrase you employ…it's too precise to be a coincidence."

Smyth stared at him for several moments and then, slowly, a smile spread across his face, revealing absolutely perfect white teeth. "I *knew* you were the right guy for this."

"For what? What's going on?"

"Just a sec." Smyth pressed the intercom. "Cathy?"

"Sir?"

"Two minutes, thirty-one seconds."

"Wow."

"Tell me about it. Make a note about the speech patterns, will you?"

"Done, sir."

Smyth released the button and beamed at Paul. "Do you know how long it would have taken most people to spot that? *Days*, more probably weeks, if ever." He rose from behind his desk and gestured for Paul to follow him to one of the bookshelves, the only one in the office actually containing books.

"You haven't really explained anything to me."

"Patience, Paul, patience ... but I am surprised you haven't asked why there are so few books and so many toys in here."

"Let's say I have."

"Then let's say I tell you that Scylla Enterprises has dozens of subsidiary companies, as well as controlling interests in companies which were not originally part of our organization. We make everything from dolls to guidance systems for airplanes. We are involved in research to find cures for cancer, AIDS, Parkinson's, migraine headaches, and hangnails. We build cars and houses. We make major Hollywood motion pictures. We work to save the environment. We supply the space program with under-the-table funding. We assassinate dictators. We supply weapons for oppressed peoples to stage coups in Third World countries. We fight famine. We own record companies. We—oh, I could go on, but ... let's see—ah! Did you ever see Mel Brooks' *Silent Movie?*"

"Yes."

"Remember the offices of Engulf & Devour, the evil corporation? Remember their slogan on the wall: 'OUR FINGERS ARE IN EVERYTHING'? Well, that's us, in a way. There's not a lot we aren't involved in. But I digress."

"Can I ask who controls Scylla?"

"I do. There is no board of directors, only some folks we keep on hand for show. I'll tell you much more later, but for right now, let's get back to your having spotted the similarities in the speech patterns of myself, Carmen Borgia, and your friend Jim Woodward." Smyth looked over the bookshelf. Paul counted: there were exactly thirty-five books, ranging from a couple of bestsellers to more literary fiction (*The Complete Stories of Kobo Abe*) to older, more obscure novels (*Tryst* by Elswyth Thane and *Trout Fishing in America* by Richard Broughtigan), several textbooks on math, surgery, and home plumbing repair, a handful of children's books, various editions of the Bible, Koran, and Talmud, poetry collections, and other books whose titles gave no hint to Paul as to what they were about.

"Your reading tastes are a bit ... eclectic."

"Oh, yes ... I like to spend my evenings going from Stephen King to dissertation of Heisenberg's Uncertainty Principle, with a bit of *See Spot Run* and *Goodnight Moon* thrown in for good measure." He pulled a thick volume from the lower shelf: *Famous Documents From History*. Paul noticed that only a few pages were marked, and as Smyth opened the books, saw that only one or two passages per page had been highlighted.

Smyth handed the book to Paul. "Please read this aloud, only, read it as Burt Lancaster—you do Lancaster, right?"

"He's one of my favorites."

"Please read the first few lines."

"Can I have a drink of club soda with lime first?"

"Club soda?"

"In my act, I always take a drink of club soda with lime before doing Lancaster. It helps ready my vocal cords."

"Go for it."

Paul went to the bar and fixed his drink, took two shorts sips and one deep swallow (just like in his act), held the last bit of it in his throat for a few seconds, then swallowed. He hummed like Kermit the Frog very quickly, then took the book up again and recited the first six lines of *The Declaration of Independence* in his best Lancaster.

When he was finished, he handed the book back to Smyth, who replaced it on the shelf and said, "That was amazing. You do

Lancaster better than anyone I've ever heard. Quite possibly better than anyone ever has."

"Thank you. I don't think I'm *that* good, but—"

"Do you know much about the science of fingerprinting, Paul?"

"Not really."

Smyth gently took hold of Paul's right hand and held it up. "Each fingerprint pattern on each finger, as I'm sure you know, is unique. Because you have ten fingers, the ten fingerprints are going to differ slightly, but all of them will share certain characteristics, namely the whorl pattern and reference points—by those, I mean the semi-circular patterns of the lines and the various breaks, scratches, and marks that are found along those lines. Are you following me so far?"

"I think so."

Smyth released Paul's hand. "Voice-prints are the same way. Each person has certain patterns to their speech, certain ways of breathing which affect the timbre, certain patterns of inflection, certain base vibrations that make it impossible to *exactly* duplicate their voice by electronic means. But, like fingerprints, there are 'reference points' in the patterns. In fingerprinting, one need only match six reference points for identification; the best impressionists can match up to eight voice-print reference points. Watch this."

He pressed a button on the wall, and a hidden panel slid open to reveal a pair of computer monitors built into the wall. Under each monitor was a keyboard. Smyth pressed a key on each and the monitors flickered to life.

"What this?"

"This, Paul, is a state-of-art, high-tech, one-of-a-kind thingamajig, not to be confused with your run-of-the-mill whatchama-callits used by NASA or the commonplace whoseewhatsits you can pick up at Radio Shack. This, Paul, is a digital speech analyzer. Listen."

He hit a key, and Paul heard himself doing Burt Lancaster reading from the *Declaration*. As he read, a series of jumpy red lines rose from the bottom of the monitor screen and flickered at the top like the tips of flames. Every time a line flickered, a blue dot appeared and remained in that spot on the screen.

"Now, old Burt himself, from *The Devil's Disciple*, I think. One of the costume dramas he did, anyway."

Another key was pressed, and Burt Lancaster himself read from the *Declaration*. Jumpy red lines, leaving hundreds of small blue dots at their flicker-points.

"Notice anything?" said Smyth.

"No...?"

"Nothing up my sleeve." He entered a command. "...presto!"

Both recordings were played simultaneously, two sets of jumpy red lines on the same screen, two sets of small blue dots... only it seemed now to Paul that there weren't as many small blue dots.

Once it was finished, Smyth enhanced the uneven line of blue dots, then entered another command: a blinking green cursor made its way across the screen, stopping at each set of blue dots that overlapped. Once that was finished, the dots which didn't overlap disappeared from the screen.

"Look at that," said Smyth. "Eighteen matching reference points would qualify as a perfect-enough match; you hit twenty-three points in your imitation. The best I've ever seen... heard... you know what I mean—the best I've ever encountered matched sixteen. You, sir Cormier, are the best impressionist I've ever encountered."

"Again, thanks ... but can't you just reproduce their voices digitally?"

"If all I were interested in was movie stars, yes—but even then I'd be limited to the soundtracks of their films and whatever recorded interviews I could lay hands on. But hold the questions, we're not finished yet."

For the next ninety minutes, Smyth had Paul listen to the voices of various celebrities, politicians, and people whose voices he didn't recognize, then imitate them while reading selected passages from a book chosen at random. Each time, Paul hit no fewer than twenty reference points in the voice-prints.

When the last of them had been done, Smyth nodded his head and grinned. "I had you do this so you could see just how good your impressions are. Don't say anything yet. The collection of books on this shelf weren't selected at random, nor were the highlighted passages inside them. If you were to start reading only the highlighted passages in the first book on the top, and repeat the process until you came to the last highlighted passages in the last book, you would have made ninety-seven-point-eight percent of every sound in the English language—more than enough to enable someone with sophisticated enough equipment to accurately reproduce another person's voice—"

"—and program that voice to say whatever you wanted."

Smyth nodded. "I've had language experts working on this for years. Part of your new job, Paul, would be to listen to recordings of other peoples' voices—not celebrities, but everyday individuals whom we have recorded—then learn their voices, imitate them as well as you did old Burt's here, and then—"

"—read the highlighted passages from these fifty books so you can reproduce their voices, making them say whatever you want."

Smyth shook his head. "That's only a part of it—still, don't make it sound so ominous."

"I don't see why—"

Smyth held up his hand, silencing Paul. "We're done here for the time being. Go with Ms. Brown. The next part of your trial period starts now."

"But—"

"No questions. I'll tell you everything you want to know later. For now, go." Smyth pulled a small remote control unit from his pocket and opened the office doors. Ms. Brown and BuzzCut stood there waiting for Paul.

"Mr. Cormier," said BuzzCut. It sounded too much like a command.

Paul stepped back out and the doors closed behind him.

"I take it things went well?" asked Ms. Brown.

"You tell me—I have no *idea* how things went . . . except very quickly."

"Feeling a little confused?"

"That's about the size of it."

BuzzCut nearly smiled. "Wrong reading."

"Huh?"

Ms. Brown laughed once, very softly, then cleared her throat. "Our research has shown that to be a favorite phrase of yours, and I'm afraid the staff has, well ... *borrowed* it from you."

"It's called stealing."

"I know," said Ms. Brown. "But we're far too nice people to do something like that."

"Is everyone here a comedian?"

BuzzCut gently took hold of Paul's hand and guided him back through the maze of doors and corridors until they stood facing a different elevator than the one in which Paul had come up.

"Are you allowed to talk to me?"

BuzzCut shrugged. "Don't see why not."

"Have you been with Scylla for long?"

"About fifteen years."

Paul waited for BuzzCut to elaborate, but the man offered no further comments.

"Ho-kay, then ... can you tell me what's going to happen now?"

"We're going to make a pick-up."

"Uh-huh ...?"

The elevator doors opened. They rode down into a private parking garage located below the Scylla building. There only a few dozen cars parked down here even though the garage could have easily held twenty times as many vehicles. With parking space the rare and priceless commodity it was downtown, Paul knew without asking that this private garage had to set Schlla back a tidy sum each month.

He followed BuzzCut until the other man stopped beside a car that was so incredibly non-descript Paul almost missed seeing it.

He walked over and stood by the passenger door. BuzzCut was grinning. Paul wondered if the man were ill.

"What's so funny?"

"Nothing," replied BuzzCut, unlocking his door. "It's just it never fails to amuse me how new recruits always nearly walk right past this car when they come down here with me. Don't look at me that way, I'm not trying to say you're stupid or nothing; this car was *designed* not to be noticeable."

"Why?"

Both of them climbed inside, put on their seatbelts, and Buzz-Cut started the engine as he continued to explain. "Okay, I might as well explain some things. First off—and whether or not you want to take my word on this is up to you—if you are offered a contract with Scylla, there are going to be times when you'll be asked by Mr. Smyth to do something that on the surface, is gonna look like it maybe ain't so legal. Sometimes it isn't, but you ain't never gonna have to worry about being arrested or nothing like that."

Paul stared at him for a moment. Then something occurred to him. "The plates on the car, they're—"

"—government plates. Federal. You're the first recruit to notice that. Good eye."

"So Scylla is also a branch of the Federal government?"

"Not officially." They had driven up to the exit by now, and BuzzCut turned effortlessly into the pre-lunch-hour traffic. "But if for some reason the police were to stop this car, the officers who did the stopping would be on paid suspension the minute they got off the horn from calling in the plate number."

Paul's earlier anxiety now bordered on outright fear tinged with panic. "How powerful is Scylla?"

"Scylla is Mr. Smyth, Paul, and Mr. Smyth is probably one of the ten most powerful men in the world—not just one of the richest, but the most powerful."

"Where are we going?"

"Remember when I told you that there were going to be times when you'd be asked to—"

"—do something that on the surface doesn't look so legal?"

BuzzCut nodded his head. "We're on our way to do such a thing right now."

"Will it be dangerous?"

"There's always that possibility—that's why the confidentiality agreement, and that's why this is called a 'trial period.'"

Paul felt his hands begin to shake, a sure sign that he was three breaths away from a panic attack. "And this thing, this not-so-legal-looking-on-the-surface thing we're on our way to do, what might it be?"

"It *might* be any one of a million things."

Paul shook his head. "Let me guess: Wrong reading?"

BuzzCut's only response was to smile.

"Fine," said Paul, "then this thing that we're going to do … what *is* it?"

BuzzCut reached over and flipped down the glove compartment door. Inside was the ugliest looking semi-automatic pistol Paul had ever seen. BuzzCut removed it, closed the door, and laid the weapon in Paul's lap.

"I think the technical term for it is 'kidnaping'," said BuzzCut. "I'd pick up that gun and point it at the floor if I was you, unless you like the idea of them shaky hands of yours blowing your pecker off."

As BuzzCut pulled the car up to the curb in a fairly generic-looking middle-class neighborhood, Paul's first instinct was to open the door and run like hell. BuzzCut must have sensed this, because he pressed a button and electronically locked the doors. "Don't bother trying to unlock them, only the driver can do that."

Paul lifted the gun. "I could just shoot out the window."

"I'd like to see you try it. They're bullet-proof."

"Oh."

BuzzCut checked his watch, then removed a pair of small binoculars from a compartment beside the driver's seat and began focusing on a house about a third of the way down the block.

"Hey," whispered Paul.

"Yeah?"

"I don't know your name."

"And if you sign on with Scylla, I'll be happy to tell it to you, but not until then. The fewer names you know now, the better."

"But if—"

"Shh." BuzzCut leaned forward a little, then offered the binoculars to Paul. "See that grey house down there, the one with the chain-link fence?"

"Yes."

BuzzCut checked his watch again. "In about a minute a little girl is going to come out of that house and start walking in our direction. Her name's Jeanne Brooks. She's six years old. Every morning at 11:30 she leaves this house and walks to a small family market two blocks from here. She buys herself a can of Sprite and then stands around looking at the comic books for about forty-five minutes."

"Why every morning?"

"In the last eighteen months, Jeanne's been removed from this house by Childrens' Services three times, and three times she's been sent back after her mother and stepfather have completed the bare-ass minimum amount of couples' therapy required by law."

"What's that got to do with—"

"Watch."

Paul focused on the front door of the house. BuzzCut reached over and pressed a button on the binoculars and with a soft electronic *whirrrrr*, the lenses extended, allowing Paul a crystal-clear view of the front door and porch. The only way he could be any closer was if he were standing in the front yard.

The door opened and Jeanne Brooks came out. Her clothes were old but appeared to be clean. She looked down as she walked, as if she were afraid the earth might open up at any given second and swallow her whole if she dared look anywhere else.

She was halfway down the steps when the front door opened and a man in his early thirties—the stepfather, Paul assumed—kicked open the screen door, stormed out onto the porch, and threw something at Jeanne. It hit her squarely in the back of the head, knocking her to her knees.

"That piece of shit," Paul said through clenched teeth.

Jeanne picked herself up, the expression on her face unchanged, and then retrieved the object her stepfather had thrown at her.

A videocassette of *101 Dalmatians*.

"Her birthday present," said BuzzCut. Even he didn't bother disguising the anger and sadness in his voice. "They didn't buy it for her, mind you, they gave her two dollars so she could rent it. If I were a betting man, I'd put the farm on her never having gotten to watch it."

"God ..." whispered Paul, because now Jeanne had left the

yard and was walking in their direction. Only now—aided by the electronic binoculars—did Paul see why she walked with her face toward the ground.

Scars.

Some were old and greyish-white, others were pink, still healing; all of them were restricted to the left side of her face, but that was enough. In places the scar tissue was so heavy it nearly covered her left eye.

"Grey and pink, right?" asked BuzzCut.

"Huh?"

"The scars."

"...yes..."

"She leaves here at the same time every morning because her mom and stepfather deal crank out of their garage between 11:45 and 12:30. Neither the police nor Children's Services have been able to nail them for it, and suspicion alone isn't enough for permanent action to be taken."

"Did they...did they do that to her?"

"Not that she's ever admitted to anyone. But, yes, they did that to her."

Paul lowered the binoculars. "We're going to take her?"

"In a way," said BuzzCut, opening his door. "You stay right in here, got me? Anyone besides me tries to get in this car, flash the gun and odds are they'll go away. If flashing it doesn't work, then squeeze the trigger and I *guarantee* you they'll go away." He hit a button and unlocked all the doors, then opened the rear driver's-side door just a crack. "Keep an eye on me at all times, right? If anything happens, if for some reason anything goes wrong, you scoot over and drive the hell out of here, understand?"

"Yes." Paul's heart was pounding hard against his chest.

"This'll happen fast, so pay attention." BuzzCut slammed the door and walked across the street at the same time a tan minivan with tinted windows came around the far corner.

Paul swallowed once, then blinked.

Fine, I'm fine. Really.

BuzzCut removed something from his pocket and opened it.

A wallet.

Several bills of various denominations spilled onto the sidewalk.

BuzzCut got down on one knee and began scrambling to pick up the money.

Jeanne saw this and stopped a few feet away, asking something. *She wants to know if he needs any help.*

BuzzCut nodded his head and offered an embarrassed smile.

The van pulled to the curb two yards away from both of them. The side door came open but was not slid down the track.

Jeanne came over and started helping BuzzCut pick up the money. They spoke quietly. At one point Jeanne stopped helping and looked to where BuzzCut was pointing.

At the car.

Jeanne saw Paul and smiled.

Paul offered a small, nervous wave.

The side door of the van began to slowly slide the rest of the way open.

BuzzCut stood. Jeanne offered him the money she'd picked up. BuzzCut shook his head. Two other men dressed exactly like BuzzCut climbed out of the van. Both checked their watches.

BuzzCut pointed to them and Jeanne looked over.

The other two men nodded, then turned back into the van and helped someone else climb out.

Paul's breath caught in his throat.

Because Jeanne Brooks—scars and all—had climbed out of the van. She was dressed exactly like her other self.

BuzzCut took Jeanne's hand, led her across the street, and put her in the back seat of the car.

"Hello," she said to Paul.

"Hi, Jeanne."

"I don't gotta stay there anymore," she said.

"That's good."

"Yeah, it is." There was a combination of glee, wistfulness, and genuine sadness in her voice that broke Paul's heart about ten times over.

One of the men from the van touched something on the other

Jeanne's back and she blinked once, twice, then walked over to pick up the videocassette and go on her original way.

The men climbed back into the van and drove away.

BuzzCut climbed in, released the parking brake, and drove off.

Paul looked at him and started to say something.

"Not now," said BuzzCut. "Later."

Paul turned back to Jeanne.

"Did you...uh...did you get to see the movie for your birthday, Jeanne?"

"No. They had headaches."

"Do you still want to see it?"

Jeanne brightened. "Oh, *yes!* That would be nice."

Paul tapped BuzzCut's shoulder. "There a K-Mart or a Media Play or something like that along the way?"

"Yeah...?"

"We need to stop there."

"We can't, we're supposed to—"

"We're stopping," said Paul. "Please? I think Jeanne deserves a birthday present."

"But they don't rent movies at K-Mart," she said.

"I'm not going to rent it, Jeanne. I'm going to buy it for you."

Her eyes widened. "Buy it? For me?" As if the idea of being given a present was just some myth she'd read about in storybooks.

"Yes, Jeanne, for you. Is that okay?"

"I guess." She was quiet for a moment. Then: "Will I be able to watch it when we get to my new house?"

Paul looked at BuzzCut, who sighed, gave Paul an irritated glance. "We'll make it a Best Buy. Pick up a player, as well."

Paul smiled. "Sounds good to me."

"I get into trouble with Mr. Smyth or Ms. Brown, I'm dragging your butt down with me."

In the back seat, Jeanne giggled. "He said 'butt.'"

Paul looked at her and they both laughed.

Ninety minutes later Paul found himself sitting in Smyth's office once again, only this time Smyth was visibly irritated.

"That was a damned foolish thing you did, taking her into a store to go shopping like that."

"It made her happy. Looked to me like she needed to be made happy."

"Do I look like I'm arguing over that?" snapped Smyth. "The whole point of this was to get her the hell out of there so she can receive therapy and surgery and be placed in a loving, healthy environment."

"Will she?"

"*Of course* she will! From this day on, her life will be safe, and everything will be done to make her happy. It's what we do."

"'Our Fingers Are In Everything,' eh?"

Smyth glared at him. "Don't be so smug, Paul. You broke protocol—admittedly, you've yet to be fully briefed on what protocol is, but that's beside the point. You took a kidnapped child into a public place where any one of a hundred people might have recognized her. These operations are carefully planned weeks, sometimes *months*, in advance, and sticking to the schedule is crucial. *Crucial*, do you understand? The only reason I haven't had security show your skinny WASP ass the door is because you demonstrated a very stubborn resolve to do something kind for that little girl."

"That's not the only reason," Paul said in his best Jack Nicholson.

Smyth shook his head. "Everybody does Nicholson, pal."

"Then I shall endeavor to be more original," replied Paul in his still-in-progress Chief Dan George.

"That's very good. The Chief was one of my favorite actors. Should've gotten an Oscar for what he did in *The Outlaw Josey Wales*."

"Agreed."

Smyth sat down and released a long, slow breath. "Okay, I've chewed you out, I feel better."

"BuzzCut's not going to get in trouble, is he?"

"A mild reprimand, nothing more. Push came to shove, once you were out of the immediate situation, he put the child's happiness first, as well. It's just damned fortunate that no one who knew Jeanne or her mother and stepfather saw you."

"Who was she?"

"Who? Jeanne?"

Paul leaned forward. "The *other* Jeanne. The one who got out of the van."

"She's a robot."

Paul stared at Smyth in silence for a moment. "Say that again."

"She was a robot, Paul. Outwardly—and going beneath the surface of her skin for about an inch—she has all the appearances of being human. She can bleed, eat, excrete waste, cry, whine, and complain just like the rest of us. The difference is, one inch and one centimeter beneath her skin, she becomes a very complex network of alloys and electronic components. When Jeanne's mother and stepfather decide to beat her tonight, they'll be pounding on something that feels no pain but has been programmed to *appear* it's feeling pain. Her voice and all the words she—it—will speak have been prerecorded and pre-programmed into her memory, thanks to another of Borgia's clients—a gifted impressionist, like yourself, who listened to a recording of Jeanne's voice and then read all the selected passages from my books *in* Jeanne's voice, in seven different modes: happy, confused, frightened, excited, sad, terrified, and in shrieking horror—the seven states in which her parents are accustomed to hearing her voice.

"When you start with us, you'll do the same thing. You will perfect your impression of a voice you hear, and then you will read all the selected passages in that voice, in various emotional states. We'll take it from there."

"Is this what you do? Create robots of...of—"

"—of abused and severely at-risk children who, if not removed from their current environments at once, will either die, be killed, or manufactured into monsters. We do what other agencies cannot because of red tape. And for the most part, no one notices."

"You're kidding?"

"No. Isn't that pathetic? The Brooks's will continue to beat and abuse the robot they *think* is Jeanne and never notice that child doesn't bruise any longer. We've performed over fifty switches in this city alone in the last three years, and in all but one instance, the abusers have failed to notice. In the one instance they did notice something was amiss, they simply drove the child outside the state and abandoned it. Good thing we have tracing devices installed."

"So this is the sole purpose behind Scylla having so many diverse business interests?"

"This is an expensive process, Paul. The Jeanne robot you saw today? All in all, she cost about thirty-five million dollars from conception to switch."

Paul sat in silence for several moments, trying to let it all sink it. "Where were you guys ten years ago?"

"Still in Vienna. I moved the main offices to the States only four years ago. But that's one of the reasons why you were selected, Paul—not just because of your talent, but because you would understand better than most potential recruits the importance of what we do, and the reasons why we choose to do it in the way we do."

"I thought that might have something to do with it."

"Listen to me—if we had been in the States ten years ago and had been made aware of the situation with your sister, we would have done the same for her. In a heartbeat. I know there are probably about a thousand questions running through your mind right now, and we'll answer all of them as we go along, but first and foremost I need to know: are you with us?"

Paul stared at the floor for a moment, remembering the smile on Jeanne Brooks' face and wishing he could made his sister smile like that just once.

He shook his head. "Robots."

"Whether you know it or not, Paul, in the last twenty hours you've interacted with at least four robots."

He snapped his head up. "BuzzCut? Was he a robot?"

"No. He acts like it sometimes. He's my cousin, flesh and blood as I."

"Oh."

Smyth stared at him, drumming fingers on desktop. "I need an answer, Paul. If you say no, then everything stays as explained to you; if you say yes, then there's a recording of a ten-year-old boy's voice I need you to listen to right away so we can get started." He leaned forward. "So tell me, Paul: are you with us or not?"

Paul looked at Smyth and grinned. "Wrong reading. Too melodramatic, too much as if you know I'm not going to say yes."

"Is that a Yes?"

Paul grinned. "Three guesses."

# WHAT GOES UP MUST COME DOWN

## JANET HARRIETT

My fatigue is getting worse. When the porter sets our luggage down at my usual compartment door, I can't muster the energy to panic. No one—not the porters, not the space elevator attendants and certainly not Corey standing beside me—knows I have grieved for twenty-six clones in that compartment.

Corey doesn't even know I've been here before. When I tell him that medical researchers need me for a few weeks of tests, I do go to Brazil. I just don't I stay there. In all the ethically questionable things I've done to help cure Nascimento-Pitanga Disorder, I have never once lied to my husband. If he were to ask whether I enable human cloning on an orbital research platform that answers to no Earth laws or codes of ethics, I would say yes.

"Didn't you say you reserved an outside cabin, dear?" Corey asks.

The porter looks at me, at the door number and back at me several times. Corey has to have noticed. "Is the lady not staying in her—"

I clear my throat sharply to cut him off, and trigger one of the violent coughing spasms characteristic of Nascimento-Pitanga. I fold to my knees on the deckplate and fight to breathe as my body fights to rid itself of its own hardened alveoli. I'm the only Nas-Pit patient who has ever won the battle against my body even once. To the bafflement of both Dr. Nascimento and Dr. Pitanga, along with every other medical professional on the planet and a few off it, I've managed to keep from coughing up my own lungs for close to forty years. Corey drops beside me and extracts my inhaler from my pocket. The gasps for air between coughs aren't deep enough to suck the medicine in.

My eyes water with the effort of keeping my body from turning itself inside out, and I can just barely make out Corey waving off the porter. I can't hear if they say anything. I hope not. Everyone here knows things Corey doesn't need to know, at least not yet.

The shooting intercostal pain feels like a rib breaking again. Fifth left, it feels like. I'll check when I can breathe, unless this is the time my lungs finally win. I would laugh at the irony of that if my diaphragm weren't otherwise occupied trying to kill me. The pain from my rib stabs harder with every cough, and I hope it doesn't puncture anything. My inhaler isn't helping, and I give up the effort to hold on to it.

It clatters to the deckplate and slides to an open compartment door, stopping against the toe of a pair of trainers. The woman above the shoes is young, with eyes full of three lifetimes of pain, regret and anger. She's heard this cough before. Recently. From a much smaller set of lungs. I don't need to look for the cherry pin that the parents wear. I know the look they give me. I am the ghost of what they didn't get with their own children.

Corey fishes in my purse for my injector pen, which I suspect works by overriding the cough reflex with the need to scream regardless of what it injects. I hope he's too distracted stabbing a dose of Demerol into my thigh to look at the passport that I use to get to the Earthside space elevator terminal. It is Asa's; mine is in hundreds of pieces under the gladiolas. It should be decomposed before Asa will need to lift the bulbs for winter. I've left her instructions for the gardens.

The coughing subsides, and I puddle into Corey's arms, drained of what energy I had.

"Do you want some help?" Corey asks.

"I think I can make it."

I keep my eyes toward the floor, away from the woman frozen

in the doorway, and try to get my own legs under me again. I know without looking that she's giving me the same look every parent gives me. The look I started sneaking off to Earth-orbit to stop. I don't want to carry the weight of everyone else's lost possibilities. My own twenty-six, born of trying to shake everyone else's thousands, are more than enough to bear.

My legs don't want to push the weight of my torso against Earth-normal gravity. The lower gravity on the station is the only thing I look forward to on this trip. "Maybe I do need a little help getting up. Careful the left side."

Corey scoops me up like a groom carrying his bride across the threshold. The spasms are getting worse, and the heavy unspoken secret between us—one of them, anyway—is that this is the last anniversary we get. Corey doesn't know how much time after our celebration we don't have. I can still feel the woman staring at me as we disappear around the curve of the elevator car corridor.

Twenty years ago, high on the endorphins of young love and outside the reach of Earth's legal system and ethical quandaries, the deal I made with the researchers on the space station seemed like a much better idea. Ten years ago, it still seemed like a fine idea, because I was sure I'd be dead by now.

Corey sets me on the bed in our compartment. I reserved the one with the biggest observation window for both the ascent and descent. Neither Corey nor Asa have seen Earth dropping away or rushing up. I can reach the door from the bed, so I fumble to latch the door behind us. My fingers don't work as well as they once did, and they've never worked as well as a healthy person's. A doctor in Cuba is looking into the possibility that the condition could eventually affect fine motor control, but the doctors think everything is a symptom of advanced stages of Nas-Pit. I think I'm just naturally clumsy. With a cure, Asa can have faults that aren't side effects. I've wondered what that would be like.

Corey slides his hand over mine and closes my fingers around the latch for me.

"I've told you, you should tell the parents what you're doing," Corey whispers, looking out across an expanse of the Pacific. "They should know how hard you're working for them."

"I doubt that talking about it will help." In five days, he will not be nearly so eager for me to tell anyone what I'm doing. I regret that I finally have to tell *him*.

"Even if it doesn't help, it can't hurt."

"I'm tired of being the public face of Nas-Pit research. I'd like to, just for a while, be a wife taking a nice vacation with her husband."

Corey smiles and kisses me. "Deal. We're just a normal couple sharing a new adventure together. You and me."

You and me and twenty-six ghosts. I've never told anyone, not even Asa, of the clones who died before her. Died so that the doctors could discover the exact stage of embryonic development when the disorder became irreversible. Died so that the doctors might figure out how to reverse it before then. The ghosts are too much weight to ask anyone to carry. But I carry them. Someone needs to.

The elevator starts its ascent like an amusement park tower ride that just keeps going up. We watch out our compartment window as the ocean drops away. I've seen the horizon start to curve more times than I care to count—the twenty-six trips up for the clones were in addition to my obligations according to my arrangement with the doctors—so I watch the look of fascination and delight on Corey's face more than the view out the window. I'll miss blue sky, but I'll miss Corey's face more.

We climb into black sky in an hour, then the elevator picks up speed. I have five days left.

"It's a shame to waste part of the trip sleeping," Corey says as we tuck into the bed, careful of my broken rib. We've watched a full sweep of the stars in the black sky through our observation window as the Earth carries us around.

"It's five days up to the spaceside terminal. We have to sleep sometime." I don't want to sleep either, but I'll have what's left of the rest of my life for space. I don't want to waste any of the last four days I have with Corey. Even if he doesn't storm out, I have to leave. That was the deal I made with the station doctors. They get my body when I'm dead, and that day is coming fast.

He's been awake for a day and a half, so Corey's breathing quickly falls into a regular rhythm of light snoring. I lay awake, cuddled under his arm, nursing my broken rib. I'll miss him. He will have no reason to miss me. I made sure of that.

Eighteen years ago, on the twenty-seventh clone, the treatment took. Asa lived, then she kept living. Now that she's old enough, she'll keep living my life, the way it should have been. Corey won't need to mourn me.

The intercom panel chimes and stirs Corey partly awake.

"Go back to sleep. It must be a mistake," I whisper. By now, the instruction to leave me alone is part of the new employee orientation. Elevator attendants don't know why, and if they want to keep their jobs, they don't ask.

"Tem uma chamada de Asa Lowery," the electronic voice announces.

Shit. Someone is getting fired for this.

I tell them to take a message and, ignoring the intercostal pain, slap at the panel until I manage to put it in Do Not Disturb mode. That is supposed to go without saying.

Corey is looking at me, forehead furrowed. "When did you learn Spanish?"

"Portuguese. Go back to sleep, dear."

I pull the blanket up over his chest, and his soft snoring starts up again.

I stare at the stubble on his chin that is just barely starting to show grays. I have four days. Four days to break Asa to Corey. Four days to figure out why she would be calling me.

The click of the compartment door closing wakes me up. The bed is empty. So is the rest of the compartment. The Earth below the elevator car is dark, broken by a thin line of lights along the Brazilian coast. We're on a space elevator, I tell myself. He can't be going far. He has nowhere to go, and three days until he will want to.

Three days for him to love me still.

He has left my inhaler and injector pen on the night table next to my head, right where they are supposed to be, never out of arm's reach when I'm kitted out to be left alone. I close my fist around my inhaler, and the surge of adrenaline subsides.

I fumble with the latch on the compartment door. My fingers, perpetually cold, can't work the latch. I try using my right hand to close my left hand around the latch, and it still slips from my grip.

The door opens, and Corey sets a tray with two plates of soft-boiled eggs and toast points on the night table.

"I got us some breakfast."

"You didn't have to go out. They deliver."

"The cook was surprised you weren't having room service."

I grab the inhaler tight. I can't panic. If I panic, I'll start coughing, and I don't have the strength for another battle with my lungs so soon. "What did you tell him?"

"That he must have you confused with someone else."

I relax my grip and take a sip of tea.

"I arranged for dinner in the lounge. The view is incredible."

"I like our view." That is uncomfortably close to lying.

"You can see the other side."

"I don't want to run into that woman with the Nas-Pit baby."

"Her name is Marna."

"Huh?"

"Marna. I ran into her getting breakfast. She introduced herself and asked me to thank you."

"Thank me?"

"It was even more strange than the cook. She said you were giving her a chance to have her baby back."

"Yeah. Strange."

"And she hoped to see you on Epsilon Station. Do you know what that is about?"

"Some of my doctors are on one of the stations." That is true enough to not be a lie.

"So you've been here before."

I should have three more days to break the news gently about the real reason for taking our last vacation together into space.

"Are you crazy? You know what kind of things they say go on up on the orbital medical stations."

"That's why I work with them. It's not like what you hear." Armchair ethicists and rumor-mongers lack imagination. There's a freedom that comes with being declared the embodiment of society's ills. On the platforms, they cross lines that people on the surface don't even know exist.

"There's a fine line between cutting-edge and morally reprehensible. Gene splicing, human cloning…"

"The human cloning was the easy part." I realize after I hear it that I've said that out loud.

Corey perks up. "So they finally found a cure for you?"

I wish he hadn't put it like that. For as long as we've been together, I've relied on a semantic loophole. They're curing the disorder, but I've never been under a delusion that they were curing me. It's a delusion I've carefully allowed Corey to keep, until now.

"It's more of a prevention."

"So how does that help you?"

"It doesn't, but they can make sure babies don't have the disorder."

Corey looks at me, confused.

"They still can't cure it once you're born, but if they know that a baby is going to get Nas-Pit, they can short-circuit it beforehand."

"So their solution is to…"

"Clone the babies, cure them, and let the babies live out their lives, healthy as little clams."

It only sounds bad until it's a person's last desperate hope.

"And you never thought to tell me?"

"It never seemed like a good time to bring it up."

"Why now, then?"

I launch into my prepared answer. "On Earth, it's take, take, take. They take blood. They take cerebrospinal fluid. They take bone marrow. They take brain scans—"

"Brain scans? What would they need brain scans for with a lung disorder?"

"Some doctor in Cleveland had some crazy idea that the disease mechanism would also affect higher reasoning capability. Isn't that just the craziest thing you've heard?"

Corey says nothing and stares at me.

I pick up the rehearsed speech where I left off. "I get the feeling he would have taken the brain if they could. I'm not sure how much lung I have left, but I swear they've taken at least a full lobe's worth of tissue samples, not like I need it or anything. A person can only stare down so many biopsy needles before thinking maybe there should be some give with the take."

"You're compensated."

True enough. Except for the chronic pain and having to take time away from Corey for doctors, not dying has turned out to be an easy way to make a decent living, after I got used to the needles.

"When the doctors on the platform contacted me about a possible treatment, they offered to give me something in return. Something more than money."

"Like?"

"A future. Not exactly for me, but you two can have the future we should have had."

"I would have taken a present with you, you know. Twenty years could have been a nice run if you'd been there."

I kiss his lips, and feel nothing back.

I would take the ghosts that every one of those mothers carried, rather than this. The parents never look at me like I'm personally responsible for the lost possibilities. To them, I'm a ghost, not a thief.

I was supposed to have three more days.

# GUMI-BEAR

## ERINN L. KEMPER

The refrigerator kicked on with a pulsing hum. Mary blinked and tried to remember why she was there, in her nighty, shivering in front of the sparse offerings of half-eaten takeout, wilted lettuce and moss-green bread-ends.

Milk. That was it.

Something to help her sleep. Even if she didn't have the desire to drink it, just the act of stirring the milk as it heated on the stove might help focus her whirling thoughts. It was impossible to sleep with Dan away, and since he was always away now she passed through the days and nights in a fog of baby-worry, and wondering when her husband would call.

A chilled, mushy hand patted Mary's leg. She looked down and the Gumi-Bear, its gel-filled body pale blue, beckoned her to follow. She closed the fridge, sending the room into darkness. The bear switched on its night-light setting, the fiber-optic wires bright enough to keep her from tripping as she followed it—pudgy, toddler-high—down the hall.

"He has a fever again?" she asked.

The fact that the Gumi-Bear was set to cool-down, instead of cozy-blanket temperature made the question redundant, but she couldn't help asking. She nodded when the Gumi-Bear made a fist and bobbed it up and down in the sign for 'yes.'

The baby was too young to use sign language, but Mary disliked the Gumi-Bears with their cheery puppet-voice program, so she kept this one set to sign-speak.

In the darkened nursery, the bear gripped the bars of the crib with its hands and feet and climbed up and over. Stumpy legs sticking out in front, it settled on the mattress near the baby, and placed hand to forehead. The temperature popped up on the wall-monitor. 101. Not too hot.

"Wake me if it goes up."

The Gumi-Bear signed 'ok' and lay down next to the baby. It placed a cooling hand gently on the back of the baby's neck and sagged into monitor-mode. She stood for a moment, looking from baby to bear, then around the nursery. Shelves stacked with all the new toys, rocking chair with its special pillow and blanket, mobiles, and cartoon animals painted on the walls. Dan made sure they had everything.

Mary returned to her room and sat in bed, waiting for the bear to come and wake her in the morning.

"I can't believe he's left you alone with a sick baby, Sis." Samantha, on the other end of the video-call at her own sun-streaked kitchen table, picked at her teeth with a fork. Behind her, the twins raced back and forth, bonking each other on the heads with long foam tubes while the TV screen flashed primary-colored cartoons.

"He's got work to do." Mary kept her voice flat, hands pressing into the table top, out of her sister's view. "It's not like his being here would make any difference. The baby would still be sick. Besides, he got us the bear."

Mary resisted the impulse to look behind her. No way the Gumi-Bear was listening. It would be in the nursery with the baby, like it always was.

"That thing? Have they even finished testing them? Does he really think it could prevent what happened last time? Besides, isn't it creepy—a little robot zipping around changing diapers and what-not?" Samantha studied the tines of the fork, then resumed her tooth-picking.

Mary shrugged. She didn't want to admit to her sister that when the Gumi-Bear first moved in she'd shuddered at the sound of its feet slip-padding across the tile floor. She would stare for hours at the opaque sack that hung in its stomach, a balloon organ hiding the mystery of its inner workings. And the bear had stared back, it's blank, half-formed features seemed set in judgement.

"It doesn't change diapers. It's not big enough for that. Besides, the experts say changing diapers is an essential component to the forming of the mother-child bond."

"Yeah, right. Gagging at the stench of their shit? Getting pissed on by a free willy? Which experts? The dads who don't want to do the changing, that's who."

Mary shrugged again. "It's not that bad."

Samantha set down the fork and smirked, her nostrils dark tunnels that flared as she leaned close to the camera. "So, still bottle-feeding? Or did the baby finally figure out what a boob is for?"

"Oh, we've been at breast feeding for a week now." Mary didn't know why she lied, but her sister nodded and settled back in her chair. Mary knew she'd played this better than the diaper comment—avoided yet another lecture on the importance of breast feeding and imprinting and all that natural-mother baby guilt.

The truth was, she didn't like breast feeding. The way the baby opened its mouth like a leech blindly straining towards the call of warm blood. The way her skin stretched and gathered around the baby's mouth. The tugging on her nipple. Those small, damp hands, fingers flexing and clenching, the milk flooding in slow contractions down into the gurgling stomach.

"It's such a beautiful thing." Mary said.

Samantha's expression softened and her gaze grew distant. "Ah, it was so much easier then. When they were babies."

Mary considered asking her sister how she had dealt with the constant crying. With never, no matter how hard she tried, being able to do the right thing to make it stop.

One of the twins ran into the kitchen and whacked her mother with the foam tube, then beat on the table, a hollow smack that sent the monitor jiggling.

"Hey, go to your room with that. I'd better get these monsters fed before they start melting down." Samantha reached out and the screen went blank.

The sudden quiet overwhelmed Mary. Her chair screeched as it skidded back across the tile. Sliding her hand along the cool white walls, she went to the starkly furnished living room. When they'd first moved in she'd loved this house with its clean simplicity. White walls, big windows, stainless kitchen and tile floors reflecting sunlight. She didn't know she'd be spending so much time alone here. And with all the hard surfaces and sharp corners, it didn't feel like a good place to raise a child.

Mary clicked on the TV. It was set to the Weather Channel, and she left it there. There was no judgement in the weather, nothing she could improve or control. She turned the volume up and the weatherman's confident banter echoed loudly down the empty hallway to the laundry room where she went to wash the clothes. If she wasn't going to eat or sleep, at least she could get some chores done.

If the baby needed something, the Gumi-Bear would come and tell her.

User Name: *Mary Wheeler*
Date: *June 18th, 2019*
Product name: *Gumi-Bear*
Consumer Feedback: *The Gumi-Bear monitors the baby's temperature, sleeping and eating habits and informs me when the diaper needs changing. The Gumi-Bear does not require any supervision or maintenance, so it doesn't add to my workload. Makes it easier to complete chores as I don't need to constantly check on the baby. I took a shower today without worrying about being unable to hear the baby crying.*

Dan's company wanted daily reports of her experiences with the Gumi-Bear. It seemed pointless to Mary. The bear's behavior was consistent—she had chosen settings that suited her needs, and that's pretty much what the bear did.

Should she have added to the report that while she stood, eyes closed, under the hot jets of the shower, water trickling into her ears with a tidal hiss, she had forgotten about the baby for just a moment, forgotten about Dan and his job and colic and fevers, SIDS and feeding schedules, her mind filling with nothing but the static of falling water. How when she'd opened her eyes and looked out through the steam-fogged glass, the Gumi-Bear had been standing in the bathroom doorway, glowing cozy-blanket pink, just standing there. Watching.

"Hey hun, how're you holding up?" Dan's voice came through the phone muffled and clipped. "Just running to another meeting. Looks like the fever's going down?"

Both his and Mary's phones received real-time data from the Gumi-Bear on the baby's status, so Mary didn't have to update her husband.

"I'm fine. Good. Got a lot done today."

"You're still sending out for groceries, though. Why don't you get someone to stay with the little guy for a few hours and get out of the house?"

"Well, you know, Samantha doesn't want the twins exposed to…"

"Not your sister. How about Bill's wife? He told me she offered, but you said you had enough help. The bear doesn't count, you know. It doesn't allow you to get a proper break." Dan dropped his voice to just above a whisper. "You sound so tired."

"I'm fine. I'll be better when you get home. When are you coming?"

"Shit. I've got to go. I'll send you my updated calendar. Love you, hun." The line disconnected before Mary could reply.

2:40 A.M. Mary sat in bed reading. The words kept slipping away, sucked back into the paper, sliding past comprehension. She turned the page. Blinked to focus her eyes against a gritty dryness, a dull ache that turned the lamp-light watery.

She looked up across the rumpled covers and saw the Gumi-Bear, standing in the doorway, its fiber-optic wiring bright as a lightning bolt in its clear-gel body.

Mary closed her book, the pages slid over one another with an insect-scraping. She crossed her arms over her chest, still the bear didn't move. The monitor next to her bed flashed from the time to an update, the baby's temperature was normal. When she looked back at the doorway, the bear was gone.

Then a movement at the foot of her bed. The covers gathered and stretched. First one transparent hand reached up onto the mattress, then the other. The Gumi-Bear's head came into view as it climbed onto the bed, features flat, placid.

Mary's heart thrummed, and she jerked reflexively when it placed a hand on her foot. She tensed, then relaxed as the bear slid its fingers over her toes and onto her ankle. Through the covers she could feel the strength of its grip.

Slowly the Gumi-Bear pulled the covers down, and the cool air stirred goose-bumps. Mary's nipples tingled as they hardened. The bear's face never turned from her gaze. Its hands resumed their firm grip on her legs as it slipped closer. Mary allowed her legs to separate, just enough for the bear to climb up between.

Smooth-as-glass fingers stroked and kneaded her thighs, slipped around to grip her hips, her buttocks, pulling at her flesh hard enough to spread her. She held her breath. The wet sound of her as she spread open the only sound in the room.

The bear lowered his face...

A warm pressure on her shoulder and Mary opened her eyes. The clock read 2:40 A.M.; the bear glowed pink in the dark near her bed. Mary rubbed her eyes.

"What is it?"

The bear signed 'hungry' and turned, his feet sponging softly across the floor.

Mary rolled over and sat up—cringed at the slippery-warmth between her legs. The Gumi-Bear stopped in the doorway to wait, glowing pink, pulsing for her.

The baby screamed from in the stroller. Its face siren-red, its fleece of hair pasted wet to its scalp. Lines of spittle barred its open mouth.

Mary put her hands over her ears, trying to mute the sound, trying to think. Her heart pounded, pounded, pounded under the press of her palms.

Hungry? Wet diaper? Another fever? The updates on her phone said no. She looked at the bear. He stood a few feet away, arms at his sides.

She imagined opening the front door and pushing the stroller out into the sunshine and birdsong with the baby bawling, fists in knots, eyes scrunched and leaking tears of rage. She couldn't do it.

With a snap she unclipped the stroller's seatbelt, lifted the rigid, sweat-slick body and carried it back to the nursery. A fog of milk-gone-sour smell emanated from the baby's hot flesh. Gumi-Bear followed, climbed up into the crib, and she touched his smooth head before she left the room and closed them both in.

Numb, exhausted, Mary leaned on the door, the baby's cries muffled now, grateful they'd moved to the suburbs where her neighbors wouldn't be disturbed.

Finally the baby slept. Mary stood in the front yard, unable to remember why she'd gone out. The sky had clouded over a steely grey. A dog barked a few blocks away. Just one sharp bark, then silence. A delivery truck cruised slowly down the street, the driver, scanning the mailboxes, didn't notice her.

She turned to look back at her house. The big bay window reflecting the darkened sky. Gumi-Bear stood, looking out at her, one hand flat against the glass. Mary smiled and went inside.

"Sorry I couldn't call earlier." Dan's voice was low, a bit muffled. "We're at a delicate stage with the buyers. Field-test data keeps coming in on the units, and they aren't totally convinced by what they're seeing. Trying to deal with their concerns."

Mary pictured her husband sitting in the back of a conference room, hunched around his phone, hand cupped in front of his mouth so his voice could be heard only by her.

"It's okay. Everything's fine."

"Are you going to go out? You should take him to the dog park, I miss little buddy's silly grin when he spots a puppy. You've been getting plenty of sunshine out there for a nice walk."

Mary wasn't surprised the bear's updates to Dan included the weather. He was a stickler for details.

"Yes. We went out a little while ago. But he stayed home."

"You went out without the baby?"

"No, the bear. It stayed home."

The ocean sound of Dan putting a palm over the phone, and muted voices spoke in a quick tempo.

The hand came away. "Hey, hun..."

"Oh, sorry, Dan. I hear the baby. I'd better go."

Mary hung up.

On the floor in front of her, Gumi-Bear sat, looking up, his gaze neutral, unconcerned about her small deceptions, glowing a soft-pink that warmed her feet. She took a deep breath and settled back into the chair. Only the quiet. His eyes. The warm glow. The quiet.

The baby's mouth opened as she offered the nipple of the bottle, jaw already chugging up and down as though drinking. She slipped the nipple in and looked up at the monitor. No sign of the fever. Gumi-Bear climbed into the crib next to the baby.

"You do it." Mary took the bear's hand and placed it on the bottle, his fingers tightened, holding her a moment, before she slipped her hand away. "I'm going to order some dinner."

Mary left the door open, and went to the living room to turn off the weather report. She'd had it on with the volume muted, but the endlessly shifting picture created too much clutter. She sat in the dark and breathed slowly into the silence.

The bear's schedule suggested a bath. Mary dismissed the prompt. When she changed the baby's diapers she used wet-wipes. A good scrub with those would do for now. The baby squirmed at the cool cloth-on-flesh, but didn't cry. All creamed and powdered, she set the baby back in the crib. The bear followed her into the kitchen.

Mary put some leftover Chinese in the microwave to heat. She pulled the plate of steaming chow mein out seconds before the timer ran down and the microwave beeped. Vinegar-sweetness curdled in her nostrils. At the table she sat and stared at the mass of glistening noodles, turned the fork prongs-up, prongs-down, then stared at her phone as it blinked with a message from Dan.

*"Hope little buddy enjoys his bath. Give his chubby bottom a pinch for me."*

She'd turned off all the phone's alert options. Every time the ringers and beeps pierced the quiet her heart raced. The bear would keep her posted on urgent matters. He waited beside her now, ready.

Mary stood, then looked at the bear.

"What was I going to do?" Her stomach churned, her skin flushed hot, as she searched her mind for the thing that had prompted her to stand.

The bear's face remained calm.

"We'll take a nap, too, I guess."

The bear waited.

The baby was crying again. Mary lay in bed, in the dark, listening. The bear had been in her room. She should go to him.

Gumi-Bear sat in the crib, glowing white so she could see. He placed a hand on the baby's head. The monitor updated: No fever. Dry diaper. No feeding.

The baby cried, fists waving, toes curling and spreading, head rocking side to side, filling the room, the house, with undulating wails.

Mary walked over to stand beside the crib. She looked down at the baby, then at the bear. His half-moulded features calmed her. Mary took a deep breath, the cool white of the bear's filaments seemed to flicker with her exhale.

Still the baby cried.

She reached into the crib to arrange the blankets without taking her gaze from the bear. The crying continued. A hiccupping screech that made her skull ache, her skin stretched thin and vibrated with it.

She brought the nursing pillow over from the rocking chair and pushed it down. Held it down.

The crying stopped.

Silence.

The bear flickered white light. Then the light caught fire, turned swirling, pulsing red, washed the room in a crimson haze.

The bear stood in the corner of the nursery with its hands at its sides. Its body clear again, the wires inside extinguished.

Two paramedics strapped Mary to a stretcher with hard words

and quick hands. They had already taken the baby away in a small bag.

"What do we do with that thing?" the one with the mustache nodded toward the Gumi-Bear.

"Back to the manufacturer, I'm guessing." The one with the paper-white teeth kicked the brake on the stretcher and started pushing. "Husband works for the company. He's on his way. That thing alerted him the moment it happened. Said to leave it here so he could see the full report."

They rolled Mary from the room, and the Gumi-Bear disappeared from her sight. Her heart ached for it, despite the bitterness that soured her stomach. How long would he have to wait, alone? Outside the night air swept across her face, cooling her tear-stung cheeks.

# THE FOURTH LAW
## OR
# THE CHILDREN'S POUND

## MARGE SIMON

*Dear Mama,*

*I guess you know she left me. I haven't felt up to writing about it. I hope you are feeling well and the allergies are under control.*

*Today I took the children to the pound. You know it was not an easy decision, but I am acting in their best interests in accord with the laws. I assure you it was necessary. I just don't have time to raise them.*

*The pound provides comfortable cages for them and three meals a day. They will be given lots of chances for exercise. The domain behind the building is wide and there are trees and flowers to remind them of home.*

*Why isn't there a Fourth Law, Mama? What about children? Shouldn't it be against the Laws for a mother to leave her kids?*

He crumpled the letter up and tossed it into the bin.

• • •

He had been sitting in the kitchen a long time. It should have been long enough. When the envelope from the Shelter came, he didn't open it immediately, but sat watching two lines of sugar ants form a spiral around the teapot. A helix in flux.

And it all came back in a bright glare not of sunlight but of memory.

Her face behind a parted curtain. The smell of rose petals in a chipped bowl. Paella and fresh bread on the cedar table he'd made from scratch. The scent of their union.

And what came of it later. Her belly swollen and depleted twice. For each one, a decision too late now to regret.

The children were a novelty for her. She took full charge, enjoying the attention of her women friends. They came daily to fuss, bringing gifts and precious cocoa, even real teas from far away lands. He was left out of it. At first, he didn't mind. His job took him away from home. Away from their bedroom. Weekends were spent there with her. He rarely had time alone with the children.

"I have to get out of here," his wife said. You understand, don't you? People I know, they want me back in the City Dominion. It was my life…" her voice trailed off. She fingered the button at the top of her blouse. "Will you keep the little ones?"

Seeing his face, she added, "There's always the pound."

He closed his eyes. "I'll take care of it." She smiled and lifted her hand to touch his face. He watched her leave and she was walking as if she were alone. So he'd done what a man is allowed to do when his mate leaves. It was not illegal, but certainly unusual to have offspring in these times, with the world population at total max and heavily rationed.

At the pound, he paid the processing fees and promised to return when times improved. But times would not improve. She was never coming back. That night, he got quietly and thoroughly drunk.

A middle aged couple strolled along the cages. The woman stopped, tapping the bars with her umbrella.

"These two are new. See there? One is looking our way. Smile at it. Toss it some of that candy you brought."

The man whistled and clapped his hands. When the child didn't respond, they moved to another cage.

A thin man seated himself at the desk. His body appeared youthful, but his face was pinched and lined with purple veins. He nodded while the clerk was speaking.

"They've all their shots. You'll have to bring them back in five years for neutering. That'll be an extra charge," she licked her lips. "I presume you have read the terms of the contract? Yes? Then sign here."

He took his time opening the post. It was a copy of the contract. Natural parents had no further claim. The children's whereabouts and new identity would never be disclosed.

When she came back, it was an explosion. So much remorse for such a small woman. So many tears. Until finally, she stopped sobbing and asked where they were. He turned to the mirror in the hall, his fingertips on her reflection in the cold glass.

# ABOUT THE HUMANS

**PAUL MICHAEL ANDERSON** ("The Universe is Dying") is the author of the short-story collection *Bones Are Made to Be Broken*, out in the fall of 2016 by Written Backwards/Dark Regions Press. An editor, teacher, and sometime-journalist, he lives with his wife and daughter in Northern Virginia, which is much quieter than he expected (or, sometimes, wanted). His most recent piece is "How I Became a Cryptid Straight Out of a 1980s Horror Movie" in *Space & Time* magazine.

**LAURA LEE BAHR** ("The Cause") is a multi-award winning writer, performer and director. She is the author of two novels, *Haunt*, and *Long-form Religious Porn* (Fungasm Press). *Haunt* is available on audiobook and recently was translated into Spanish under the title *Fantasma* by Orciny Press. Her debut feature as writer/ director, *Boned*, is distributed through Gravitas Ventures (available everywhere). A collection of her short stories, *Angel Meat*, will be published in 2017 by Fungasm Press.

**MICHAEL BAILEY** (Editor) is the multi-award-winning author of *Palindrome Hannah*, *Phoenix Rose* and *Psychotropic Dragon* (novels), *Scales and Petals* and *Inkblots and Blood Spots* (short story & poetry collections), and editor of *Pellucid Lunacy*, *Qualia Nous* (nominated for a Bram Stoker Award; winner of the Benjamin Franklin Award), *The Library of the Dead* (winner of the Bram Stoker Award), *You Human*, and the *Chiral Mad* anthologies. He is also the founder of Written Backwards and the Managing Editor of Science Fiction for Dark Regions Press. His most recent story, "Time is a Face on the Water," can be found in *Borderlands 6*.

**HAL BODNER** ("Keepsakes") is a Bram Stoker Award nominated author whose freshman vampire novel, *Bite Club*, made him one of the top-selling GLBT authors in the country. The royalties continue to keep him in "cigarettes and nylons"—even though he quit smoking and never did drag. He also wrote several paranormal romances, most notably *In Flesh and Stone*. His upcoming thrillers paint classic "noir" with a lavender glaze. Hal is married to a wonderful man, half his age, who never knew that Liza Minnelli was Judy Garland's daughter.

**GARY A. BRAUNBECK** ("Fallen Faces by the Wayside") is a 7-time Bram Stoker Award-winning writer who has published over 200 short stories, and whose novels include *In Silent Graves*, *Keepers*, *Mr. Hands*, and the forthcoming *A Cracked and Broken Path*. His Stoker-winning nonfiction book, *To Each Their Darkness*, is now being used in several creative writing programs. Two of his stories have been adapted into short films, the most recent being "He Didn't Even Leave a Note." Follow him at facebook.com/groups/4988614289.

**JASON V BROCK** ("The Unity of Affect") is an award-winning writer, editor, filmmaker, and artist whose work has been widely published in a variety of media (*Weird Fiction Review* print edition, S. T. Joshi's *Black Wings* series, *Fangoria*, and others). He describes his work as Dark Magical Realism. He is also the founder of a website and digest called *[NameL3ss]*; his books include *A Darke Phantastique*, *Disorders of Magnitude*, and *Simulacrum and Other Possible Realities*. His filmic efforts are *Charles Beaumont: The Life of Twilight Zone's Magic Man*, *The AckerMonster Chronicles!*, and *Image, Reflection, Shadow: Artists of the Fantastic*. Popular as a speaker and panelist, he has been a special guest at numerous film fests, conventions, and educational events, and was the 2015 Editor Guest of Honor for Orycon 37. A health nut/gadget freak, he lives in the Vancouver,

WA area, and loves his wife Sunni, their family of herptiles, running their technology consulting business, and practicing vegan/ vegetarianism.

**MORT CASTLE** ("Robot") has won three Bram Stoker Awards, two Black Quills, a Golden Bot, and has been nominated for an Audie, the International Horror Guild Award, the Shirley Jackson Award, and the Pushcart Prize. He's edited or authored 17 books, more than 500 shorter works, and many comic books. Recent titles: *Annotated Classics: Dracula; Shadow Show* (the graphic novel); and the Leapfrog Fiction contest winner *Knowing When to Die*, a short story collection. He's been married for 45 years (to Jane) and a publishing writer for almost 50.

**RICHARD CHIZMAR** ("Ditch Treasures") is the founder/ publisher of *Cemetery Dance* magazine and the Cemetery Dance Publications book imprint. He has edited more than 30 anthologies and his fiction has appeared in dozens of publications, including *Ellery Queen's Mystery Magazine* and *The Year's 25 Finest Crime and Mystery Stories*. He has won two World Fantasy awards, four International Horror Guild awards, and the HWA's Board of Trustee's award. Chizmar (in collaboration with Johnathon Schaech) has also written screenplays and teleplays for United Artists, Sony Screen Gems, Lions Gate, Showtime, NBC, and many other companies.

**AUTUMN CHRISTIAN** ("Pink Crane Girls") is the author of two novels (*The Crooked God Machine, We Are Wormwood*) and a short story collection (*Ecstatic Inferno*). She's currently working on a sci-fi novel about an Edgar Allan Poe video game. She is waiting for the day when she hits her head on the cabinet searching for the popcorn bowl and all consensus reality dissolves.

**GEORGE C. COTRONIS** (Cover artwork) lives in the wilderness of Northern Sweden. He makes a living designing book covers. He sometimes writes. His stories have appeared in *XIII* and *Lost Signals*.

**SCOTT EDELMAN** ("101 Things to Do When You're Downloaded") has published more than 85 short stories in such magazines and anthologies as *The Twilight Zone*, *Dark Discoveries*, *MetaHorror*, *The Mammoth Book of Monsters*, and many others. His collection of zombie fiction, *What Will Come After*, released in 2010, was a finalist for both the Bram Stoker Award and the Shirley Jackson Memorial Award. His science fiction short fiction has been collected in *What We Still Talk About*. He has been a Bram Stoker Award finalist six times. Additionally, Edelman worked for the Syfy Channel for more than thirteen years as editor of *Science Fiction Weekly*, *SCI FI Wire*, and *Blastr*. He was the founding editor of *Science Fiction Age*, which he edited during its entire eight-year run. He has been a four-time Hugo Award finalist for Best Editor.

**CODY GOODFELLOW** ("Key to the City") has written five novels, and co-wrote three more with New York Times bestselling author John Skipp. His first two collections, *Silent Weapons for Quiet Wars*, and *All-Monster Action*, each received the Wonderland Book Award. He wrote, co-produced and scored the short Lovecraftian hygiene film *Stay At Home Dad*, which can be viewed on YouTube. He is also a director of the H.P. Lovecraft Film Festival – San Pedro, and cofounder of Perilous Press, an occasional micropublisher of modern cosmic horror. He lives in Burbank, California, and is currently working on building a perfect bowling team.

**JANET HARRIETT** ("What Goes Up Must Come Down") is a writer and freelance editor. Her stories have been published in *Not Our Kind: Tales of (Not) Belonging* and *Weirdbook*, and she made a nonfiction guest appearance in *For Exposure: The Life and Times of a Small Press Publisher* discussing her experiences as Apex Publications' senior editor. Find her online at janetharriett.com.

**ERIK T. JOHNSON** ("The Immigrants") is the first Written Backwards DARWA Voice Award-winner whose fiction pops up in cool places, such as *Space & Time Magazine*, *Tales of the*

*Unanticipated, Qualia Nous*, and all three volumes of the *Chiral Mad* series. He has published three novellas, most recently in *I Can Taste the Blood* (along with Josh Malerman, Joe Schwartz, J. Daniel Stone, and John F.D. Taff). He's definitely going to have a book of short stories published in the near future and he's working on a novel and in a coal mine, going down down down. Kick Out the Jams, do other stuff when it suits you, yeah alright.

**ERINN L. KEMPER** ("Gumi-Bear") lives in a small town in Costa Rica on the Caribbean Sea where she operates a vacation rental, runs with her dog on the beach, watches the howler monkeys at happy hour, and plans to write her second novel from her hammock. Erinn has sold stories to *Cemetery Dance Magazine, Black Static, Dark Discoveries* and *[NameL3ss]* and appears in anthologies including, *The Library of the Dead, A Darke Phantasique,* and *Shadows Over Main Street 2.* Visit her website at erinnkemper.com for updates and sloth sightings.

**STEPHEN KING** ("I Am the Doorway") is an author of more than 50 novels of contemporary horror, supernatural fiction, suspense, science fiction, and fantasy, which have sold more than 350 million copies worldwide. King is the recipient of the Bram Stoker Award, World Fantasy Award, British Fantasy Society Award, the O. Henry Award, the Edgar Award, and nominated for the Nebula Award, among others. The National Book Foundation awarded him the Medal for Distinguished Contribution to American Letters in 2013. He is also the recipient of the World Fantasy Award for Lifetime Achievement, the Canadian Booksellers Association Lifetime Achievement Award, the Grand Master Award from the Mystery Writers of America, and the Lifetime Achievement Award from the Horror Writers Association.

**MARC LEVINTHAL** ("The Pretty Puppets") is a writer and musician from Pasadena, California. He is the author of the novel *Other Music* (forthcoming from Dark Regions Press, and the co-author of *The Emerald Burrito of Oz* (with John Skipp). His short fiction has appeared in *Aboriginal Science Fiction, The Magazine of Bizarro Fiction*, and anthologies such as *Mondo Zombie, Amazing Stories of the Flying Spaghetti Monster*, and *Thirteen: Stories of Transformation*.

**JOHN R. LITTLE** ("The Goldilocks Zone") is the author of 16 books. He has been nominated for the Bram Stoker Award four times and has won once, for the novella *Miranda*. One of his books, *Ursa Major*, is currently in pre-production to become a major motion picture. He has been publishing dark fiction for more than 30 years and has enjoyed his fans' reception to each one. John's story in this anthology is one of his own personal favorites. He encourages you to connect with him on Facebook or visit his website at johnrlittle.com

**JOSH MALERMAN** ("The Jupiter Drop") is the author of the novels *Bird Box* (ECCO/HarperCollins, 2014) and *Black Mad Wheel* (ECCO/HarperCollins, 2017) as well as the novella *Ghastle and Yule* and a score of short stories such as "The Bigger Bedroom" (*Chiral Mad 3*), "Danny" (*Scary Out There*), and "I Can Taste the Blood" (*I Can Taste the Blood*.) He's also the guitarist/songwriter for the rock band The High Strung, whose song "The Luck You Got" is the theme song for Showtime's hit series *Shameless*.

**TOM MONTELEONE** ("The Star-Filled Sea is Smooth Tonight") has published more than 100 short stories and 40+ books. He is a 4-time winner of the Bram Stoker Award in four different categories—novel, collection, anthology, and nonfiction—and he's pretty sure no one else has ever done that. Many of his novels have been optioned for films; he's written scripts for stage, screen, and TV. He also wrote the bestselling *The Complete Idiot's Guide to Writing a Novel* (now in a 2nd edition). *Submerged* is his latest novel. With his wife, Elizabeth, he lives in Maryland. Despite losing much of his hair, he still believes he is dashingly handsome—humor him.

**B.E. SCULLY** ("Dog at the Look") lives in a crooked red house that lacks a foundation in the misty woods of Oregon with a variety of human and animal companions. Scully is the author of numerous novels, short stories, poems, and articles. Published work, interviews, and odd scribblings can be found at bescully. com.

**MARGE SIMON** ("The Fourth Law" and the poetry within this anthology) lives in Ocala, Florida and is married to Bruce Boston. Her stories have appeared in *Daily Science Fiction, The Pedestal Magazine, Morpheus Tales*, and more. She has won the Strange Horizons Readers Choice Award, the Bram Stoker Award for Poetry, the Rhysling Award, and the Grand Master Award from the SF Poetry Association. She has work in anthologies such as *Chiral Mad 3* and *Scary Out There*. More information at margesimon. com.

**JOHN SKIPP** ("Hopium Den") is a Rondo Award-winning filmmaker (*Tales of Halloween*), Bram Stoker Award-winning anthologist (*Demons, Mondo Zombie*), and New York Times bestselling author (*The Light At The End, The Scream*) whose books have sold millions of copies in a dozen languages worldwide. His first anthology, *Book Of The Dead*, laid the foundation in 1989 for modern zombie literature. He's also editor-in-chief of Fungasm Press, championing genre-melting authors like Laura Lee Bahr, Violet LeVoit, Autumn Christian, Danger Slater, Cody Goodfellow, and Devora Gray. From splatterpunk founding father to bizarro elder statesman, Skipp has influenced a generation of horror and counter-culture artists around the world. His latest book is *The Art Of Horrible People*.

**LUCY A. SNYDER** ("Executive Functions") is the five-time Bram Stoker Award-winning author of 10 books and over 80 published short stories (some of which are collected in *While the Black Stars Burn*). Her writing has appeared in *Apex Magazine, Nightmare Magazine, Pseudopod, Strange Horizons, The Library of the Dead*, and *Best Horror of the Year, Vol. 5*. She is faculty in Seton Hill University's MFA program in Writing Popular Fiction and holds an MFA from Goddard College. Learn more at lucysnyder.com or follow her on Twitter at @LucyASnyder.

**DARREN SPEEGLE** ("The Cosmic Fair") is the author of five short story collections, the latest of which, *A Haunting in Germany and Other Stories*, was released in February by PS Publishing. His short fiction has appeared in various venues, including *Subterranean, Postscripts, Clarkesworld, Crimewave, The Third Alternative, Dark Discoveries, Cemetery Dance*, and *Subterranean: Tales of Dark Fantasy*. His horror novel, *The Third Twin*, will be a 2017 Crystal Lake Publishing title. Also look for Darren's human evolution themed anthology, *Adam's Ladder*, in 2017 from PS.

**L.A. SPOONER** (Fiction artwork) currently lives and works in the South of England. Having graduated from the University of Portsmouth with a first class degree he is now a full time illustrator working under two aliases; 'Carrion House' for his darker work and 'Hoodwink House' for his work aimed at a younger audience. He believes that the job of putting someone else's words into a visual form, to accompany and support their text, is a massive responsibility as well as being something he truly treasures.

**DYER WILK** ("It Can Walk and Talk, and You'll Never Have to Worry About Housework Again") is an author, illustrator, and poet living in Northern California. His short fiction has been anthologized in *Lost Signals, Trouble In The Heartland: Crime Fiction Based on the Songs of Bruce Springsteen*, and the forthcoming *Semi-Colonic Irrigation*. He is currently at work on a novel.

**F. PAUL WILSON** (Introduction) is the genre-hopping and New York Times Bestselling author of the Repairman Jack series, The Adversary Cycle, LaNague Federation, and young adult novels featuring Repairman Jack. He is the author of more than sixty books spanning science fiction, horror, medical thrillers, and some that defy genre, including *The Tomb, The Keep, Harbringers, Nightworld, Black Wind, Virgin*, and most recently, *Panacea*. Most of Paul's short stories are collected in *Soft & Others*, *The Barrens & Others*, and *Aftershock & Others*. He is the recipient of the Promethus Award, the Porgie Award, the Bram Stoker Award, the Inkpot Award, the Pioneer Award, the Grandmaster Award, and the Horror Writers Association's Lifetime Achievement Award, among others.

**ORION ZANGARA** (Poetry artwork) is an illustrator and comic-book artist who lives in Sterling, Virginia. He is a graduate of The Kubert School, an art trade school with a concentration in sequential art, founded by his grandfather, Joe Kubert. Currently he is illustrating a trilogy graphic novel called *The Stone Man Mysteries* written by Jane Yolen and Adam Stemple for the Lerner Publishing Group. And he finds it very strange describing himself in the third person! You may find him at orionzangara.com.

www.ingramcontent.com/pod-product-compliance
Lightning Source LLC
Chambersburg PA
CBHW030647120726
47905CB00001B/92